The Sisters of
THETA PHI KAPPA

The *Sisters* of THETA PHI KAPPA

Kayla Perrin

ST. MARTIN'S PRESS ■ NEW YORK

www.stmartins.com

ISBN 0-312-28290-7

First Edition: October 2001

10 9 8 7 6 5 4 3 2 1

DEDICATION

For Jennifer Enderlin, my editor:
Thank you for two things—your unending belief in me
and your infinite patience while I completed this
project. Your enthusiasm made me believe I could
do anything.

And for Helen Breitwieser, my agent:
Your faith and confidence in me mean the world.
From the beginning, you shared my vision and my
dream. Thank you for believing that I could reach for
the stars. Without you, I couldn't have grabbed one.

ACKNOWLEDGMENTS

First and foremost, the credit for this book goes to my amazing editor, Jennifer Enderlin. Thank you, Jen, for offering me the opportunity to explore the wonderful world of sorority sisterhood in fiction!

While the Theta Phi Kappa sorority is a fictional black sorority, it is inspired by the four black sororities that exist—the Delta Sigma Theta sorority, the Alpha Kappa Alpha sorority, the Zeta Phi Beta sorority, and the Sigma Gamma Rho sorority. In this story, I have tried to convey the same principles of educating, giving back, and dedication to one's communities that the above-mentioned sororities pride themselves on. Thank you, sorority sisters everywhere, for your desire to make the world a better place.

I had many questions while writing this book, and those who graciously allowed me to pick their brains deserve acknowledgment. I wish to thank Dawn Hawkins, a proud Delta, for answering my incessant queries! I'd like to thank fellow author and friend Cecelia Dowdy for her endless help as well. And much thanks to my good friends and fabulous brainstorming divas, authors Brenda Mott and Cindy Carroll.

Of course, I would be remiss if I didn't thank my agent, Helen Breitwieser, for constantly keeping me on track when I veered off the path! So, thank you. You're a true gem.

Girlfriends are a blessing, and I thank the Lord for all the wonderful ones in my life. Much love to Allette Brown, Diane Kurtz, and Melinda McGowan for being constant pillars of emotional support while I was writing this book, 'cause I sho'nuff needed it! You laugh with me when I'm happy and you pick me up when I'm down. Where would I be without you?

Finally, to every sorority out there—thank you for giving women the opportunity to make lasting friendships. May the spirit of sisterhood live on!

The Sisters of
THETA PHI KAPPA

Chapter One

IT CREEPS LIKE A PREDATOR in the night, lurking in the shadows, waiting.

It deceives like a con artist, making you believe it's dead and buried, when it's really alive, watching your every move.

It bides its time like your opponent, deftly calculating its strategy, waiting for the best time to strike.

The Past.

It struck Jessica Bedford on a cool but bright day in early February, a day that held the promise of spring. There was nothing different about the day it returned with a vengeance, not a different feel in her bones, a different scent in the air, a different energy around her. Nothing at all that would have prepared her for its arrival.

So when the couriered letter arrived, the one marked PERSONAL AND CONFIDENTIAL in big, bold letters on both sides, Jessica had no reason to suspect that she was about to open a bomb.

"What's this?" she asked Julie, the blond-haired production assistant who'd handed her the package.

"I don't know."

Jessica flipped it over and reached for the tab.

"But," Julie interjected quickly, and Jessica's hand stilled. "It will still be here at the end of the day. Right now, we need to get you to hair and makeup ASAP."

Jessica's hand lingered over the tab, but she finally pulled it back. "All right. Just let me get rid of my stuff, grab a coffee, and I'll head straight to Redmond after that."

"Oh, I can take your coat for you," Julie offered. "Even bring you a coffee."

Her smile was sweet and she sounded genuine, but that was her job—to get Jessica ready for the show as quickly as possible. But Jessica wasn't about to be pressured out of the few minutes of solitude she so cherished each morning. "That's okay. I do like seeing my dressing room on occasion."

Julie flicked her wrist forward and looked at her watch. "Okay. But please hurry. We're on a tight schedule."

When weren't they? Life at the network was always hectic. "I will."

The letter was too big to stuff into her purse, so Jessica slipped it beneath her arm as she continued down the brightly lit hallway. She hoped it wasn't another bizarre letter from some loser declaring his undying love for her.

"For crying out loud!" That was Redmond's desperate bellow. "Where's the coffee?"

Damn, there was no coffee. And she needed some badly, like an addict needing an injection of heroin. Her morning jog had failed to give her the daily boost it usually did. She was just plain exhausted this morning, but at least she was smiling. Douglas, her husband of eighteen months and a producer at the network, had kept her up most of the night with the hottest sex they'd had in weeks. She hadn't minded, but had known she would pay the price in the morning.

"Hey, sweetie," Jessica said to Redmond as she rounded the corner and peered into the small kitchen. He was dressed in all black, except for his beret, which was a myriad of colors. Despite his dark complexion, he could wear black well.

At the sight of her, his scowl turned into a smile. "Hey, baby." He opened his arms to her, and she walked into his embrace. He squeezed her hard, as he did every morning, then pulled away. "Mmm. Do you ever smell good. But that head of yours, we have to do something about it."

"I know." Suddenly self-conscious, Jessica ran a hand through her thick, tightly curled hair. It was always frizzy after she washed it. "You think you can do me something soft and nice, maybe some drop curls? It looked so flat yesterday."

"Girl, you know I can do anything." The scowl returned. "As long as I have me some coffee. I'm gonna try the newsroom kitchen. Give me ten minutes to wake up, then come see me so I can fix that hair."

"Sure."

Jessica headed to her dressing room, where she'd dump her purse and coat. Then she'd do like Redmond and make her way to the newsroom kitchen for a strong cappuccino.

"Ms. Bedford!" she heard before she even had a chance to flip the light switch in her dressing room. She cringed. Couldn't she even get her coat off before everyone expected her to be someplace, do something?

She hit the lights, then dropped the letter and her purse on the love seat. Before she could completely slip out of her long cashmere coat, Denise was in the doorway. The poor girl was out of breath, like she'd just run a marathon. "Morning, Denise."

"Morning, Ms. Bedford."

"*Jessica,*" Jessica corrected, as she did every morning, wondering when Denise would ever call her by the name her mama gave her. Probably around the time Denise stopped acting like a nervous wreck. And Jessica didn't see that happening any time soon, not while the intern continued to work for Phillip, who no doubt gave her endless grief.

"Jessica." Denise seemed to say her name with difficulty. "This is for you." She handed Jessica a clipboard with a stack of papers, on top of which was a copy of a book. "Phillip wanted you to see the new notes as soon as possible, considering the change in plans."

"I know." Without even glancing at the material, Jessica placed the pile on the love seat with her purse and coat. "He faxed them to me before I left this morning."

"He did?"

"Yes. Bright and early." She hadn't bothered to read the notes then, preferring to do so once she was in the studio.

"Oh." Denise's expression said that if Phillip had faxed her the changes, she couldn't understand why he'd sent her to deliver them.

"That's Phillip. Always making sure he has every avenue covered."

"I guess so."

"Look, I need a coffee."

Taking the hint, the young black woman moved past her to the corridor, and Jessica followed her out, closing the door behind them. She headed in the direction of the newsroom.

"Uh, Phillip wanted to make sure you understand everything."

"Mmm-hmm," she replied, not breaking her stride as she marched down the hallway.

Denise scrambled to keep up with her. "So, do you?" Her voice was soft and tentative. "Understand everything?"

"There's not a lot to understand. The guy I was supposed to interview was in a car accident, so I have to interview this other person."

"LaTonya Green."

"Right." Jessica brushed her hair off her face, but when the unruly curls fell back over her forehead, she pushed her sunglasses upward and into her hair to act as a hair band. "And her book is called?"

"*Mama Says: 101 Ways to Heal Your Battered Soul.* It's a self-help book geared for African-American women."

Stopping, Jessica faced Denise. "Is Ms. Green here yet?"

"Yes. She's in the green room."

"All right." She'd have to fake her way through this interview, but it wasn't like she hadn't done that before. And she had no doubt it would go smoothly. All the authors she'd ever interviewed couldn't say enough about their books. If LaTonya was anything like the others, she'd barely have to say a word. "I'll look over the notes as soon as I'm settled." When Denise opened her mouth in protest, Jessica added, "I've done this before. Tell Phillip everything will be fine."

"Yes, Ms. Bedford."

Jessica knew her words wouldn't comfort Phillip. In fact, he was probably popping antacids as they spoke. The man lived for crises, yet when they happened, he acted like he didn't know how he'd survive them. You'd think he hadn't weathered a million storms, that every crisis was the first one he'd had to deal with.

It wouldn't be long before he sought her out, just to make sure she'd really gotten the information. She'd never known a man so wound up before. Truly, Phillip needed to relax. He'd already had one ulcer this year, and with his constant worrying was bound to have another one.

She couldn't deal with Phillip, not before she got some caffeine into her system.

She turned down yet another hallway; this one led to another hallway that led to the large kitchen outside the newsroom. The smell of coffee filled the air, and Jessica breathed in the rich aroma, feeling as though she'd died and gone to heaven. She reached for a paper cup.

"Jessica."

The stack of cups went flying as Jessica's hand knocked it over. Damn, didn't Phillip know that he shouldn't sneak up on people?

She bent to retrieve the cups.

"Jessica, the shit's hit the fan here."

She glanced up at him then, a little peeved that he wasn't crouched beside her, helping to pick up the strewn paper cups. "Good morning to you, too, Phillip."

"Morning," he grunted, the firm set of his lips clearly telling her that it wasn't a good morning. He had just turned forty-seven, yet he looked like he was going on sixty. If only he'd smile more, he might actually be attractive. "Look, we've got major problems."

"I know. I got your message."

"Yeah, well, we won't have much of an interview since the main player is in a coma."

"How awful. I pray he'll be all right." She hoped what she hadn't said, that it was lousy of Phillip to be concerned only with the show when a man's life was at stake, wasn't lost on him.

"So do I." He paused. "But in the meantime, I have a show to run."

"This author sounds interesting." Scooping up the last of the cups, Jessica stood, then dropped them into the garbage.

"You haven't had a chance to read the book, figure out the questions you want to ask." He blew out a breath that sounded like a pitiful moan.

"It's not like I haven't been in this situation before."

"I know you're good at what you do. That's not what I'm saying. It's just that . . . what if this woman is the type to clam up when the cameras are rolling?"

"Then I'll ask her questions."

"When you haven't read the book?"

Realizing that nothing would appease Phillip, Jessica reached for a clean paper cup. She stuck it beneath the cappuccino machine, hit a button, then listened as the machine whirred. "I'm sure this woman will be just great."

"Yeah, well, she better be. One bad interview and people will turn to another network."

Did he really believe that, or did he just say that because he was a perpetual worrier? If he was anything like this at home, it was no wonder his wife had walked out on him.

She placed a hand on his arm and gave it a squeeze. You'd think he was the one about to risk making a fool of himself by asking an author questions about a book he hadn't read.

Jessica turned back to the cappuccino machine, lifted the cup, then took a quick sip. It tasted divine, and she sure hoped it would do the trick. "I'm going to go see the author now, get a feel for what the book is about."

"Good idea."

While she had the opportunity, she stepped past him and into the hallway. "Don't worry," she added as she walked away. "Things will work out—as they always do."

Phillip muttered something behind her, but she didn't hear what he said. She didn't want to hear. She just wanted to get back to her dressing room, sink into the sofa, and drink her coffee.

Before the real chaos began.

"Fascinating," Jessica said, animated as she spoke before the camera. "So you find that the daily affirmations into the mirror really work?"

"Absolutely." LaTonya Green sat opposite her on a love seat, one leg crossed over the other. "If you can't look yourself in the eye and tell your image that you believe in you, who else will?"

"Good point." Jessica chuckled.

"And if you do it often enough, you'll believe it. But like I said earlier, I think it's also important to surround yourself with images of your dreams, your goals. That's why I like collages. That's something I encourage my young daughters to do. If you visualize your dreams in a very real way as children, I see no reason why you can't achieve them as adults."

LaTonya was an attractive woman in her late thirties. She sounded confident, and as a result, believable. Her book was a combination of tips passed down the generations to her, as well as some she'd created on her own to pass on to her daughters.

"Now," Jessica began, taking the interview in another direction, "a lot of this book deals with relationships, how women can find and be happy with a man."

"Mmm-hmm."

Jessica opened the book to a page that had been marked with a yellow sticky note. "You've got a chapter here called 'The Fidelity Test: How to Figure Out If Your Man Will Cheat on You.' How does that work, exactly?"

"Actually, it's really simple. Now, we all know that looks can be deceiving, that you might meet a man who seems too good to be true. Maybe he is, maybe he isn't. But don't you want to find out for sure before you invest months or even years with him?"

"Definitely."

"Well, what my mama always told me, and what I found worked for me and my sisters, is to give your man a three-part test. Of course, you don't let him know you're testing him. That would defeat the purpose," she added, and both women laughed.

"Now, the first part of the test is really simple. Offer to take him to a movie, but you choose it. Make sure you see something that deals with relationships. You can learn a lot about a man by watching how he responds to such a movie. For example, if the story involves a man who's cheated on his wife, and he shows sympathy for that man, then kick him to the curb and don't look back."

"Just like that?" Jessica asked, snapping her fingers.

"Just like that," LaTonya replied. "Trust me, he's a man who will give you grief later."

"Okay," Jessica conceded, not entirely sure she believed that such a reaction to a movie should make or break a relationship. "And the second part of the test?"

"Invite your boyfriend to dinner at a your place. Now, make sure you have your sister there, or your best friend—a woman you can trust. And when your man arrives, tell him that you need to pick something up but invite him to stay with your friend. Disappear for a while. Long enough to give him time to get comfortable with your girl friend. Later, get the lowdown from your friend. Did he hit on her? Did she feel comfortable around him? Did he ask about you? If he made the moves on her or even flirted too much, then you know you've got a dog and you need to kick him to the curb."

That sounded very much like entrapment, but Jessica was sure it wasn't against the law. "Now, aren't you assuming the worst when you do this—that your boyfriend is going to fail the test?"

LaTonya shrugged. "Maybe, but the truth is, women can't trust most men these days. It's a scary world out there for the single woman."

In her peripheral vision, Jessica saw Julie give her the two-minute warning. "True," she said, suddenly wondering if this test would have worked for her all those years ago. Just as quickly, she dismissed that thought. "And what's the third thing?"

"Ask questions. Men love to talk, and they love it when women listen, so ask questions about his family—his mother, his sisters. By asking a lot of questions, you'll see how he views the significant women in his life, and you can learn what kind of man he is. If he loves his mama to death and would do anything for her, then you can be pretty sure that this is the kind of man who will treat you right."

"Isn't this a lot of common sense?"

"Maybe, but how many women do you know who use their common sense these days?" She paused and gave Jessica a wry smile. "We tend to get caught up in the emotions of falling in love, and too late realize we made a big mistake. You have to look at finding a mate the same way you'd look at any other investment . . . check out all your options carefully before you jump right into a relationship."

"And it's worked for you?"

"I've been happily married for seven years."

For her sake, Jessica hoped she truly knew her husband. "Thank you so much, LaTonya. It's been a pleasure talking with you."

"Likewise."

Jessica faced the camera, lifting the book as she did. "The book is called *Mama Says: 101 Ways to Heal Your Battered Soul* and is available everywhere books are sold. Until next time, that's *The Scoop*."

"Thank you," Jessica said when the cameras had stopped rolling, leaning forward to shake LaTonya's hand. "The book sounds great."

"You can have that copy."

"Oh, excellent. Will you autograph it for me?"

"Sure."

Minutes later, her book was signed, LaTonya was on her way, and

Phillip was back to breathing normally. "Not bad," he said. "At least women will enjoy it."

"It's a good thing more women watch this show than men."

"True."

"I told you it'd be fine." Though she knew the interview would go smoothly, Jessica was proud of how well she'd pulled it off.

"I have a few new show ideas I'd like to run by you. Valentine's Day is approaching."

"In a bit," she replied. "I'm gonna die if I don't eat something first."

"No problem. I'll be in my office."

"I'll be there soon." After she got something to eat and had a quick nap. The interview had drained her.

She snagged a turkey sandwich along the way to her dressing room, and when she stepped inside, she headed straight for the sofa. She sank into the plush cushions, letting out a little sigh as she did.

And then, for some reason, her eyes moved to the love seat and she caught sight of the couriered envelope beneath her coat. The letter.

Rising, she stretched, then walked the short distance from the sofa to the love seat. Moving aside her coat, she reached for the package.

As the host of *The Scoop*, she received a lot of letters, but very few came via courier. She examined the waybill. It told her that a John Doherty, who lived on Jane Street in Washington, had sent the package. The name wasn't familiar, and for a moment Jessica was tempted to toss the letter aside. But on the off chance that it was actually important, she decided to open the package and see what it was about. Maybe it was from her Theta Phi Kappa alumnae sorority; the date for the annual Black History Month event was nearing.

She flipped the large envelope over and pulled the tab open with one swift tug. When she reached inside, she found a manila envelope that simply had her name on it.

She opened that, withdrew a piece of floral stationery, then started to read.

And felt the room start to spin.

The words jumped at her with malicious force, their impact as devastating as if she'd opened a letter bomb. She was instantly shaking, both hot from adrenaline and cold from fear at the same time. Her head pounded and her eyesight blurred, but she could still see the words.

You'll always ring my bell.

That was all it said, but those five words said everything. Everything she wanted to forget.

Who had sent this?

She grabbed the envelope she'd discarded, looking for some clue, some sign she'd missed. But she found none. John Doherty. Oh, shit. John Doherty who lived on Jane Street. What a joke.

But she wasn't laughing. She was trembling. And she suddenly felt so weak and light-headed that she thought she might pass out.

She sought the sofa and dropped onto it.

You'll always ring my bell.

She'd only said those words to one person, and he back to her, but he was dead.

Andrew Bell was dead.

Oh, God. Did someone know her secret?

Her mind scrambled to find an answer. How could anyone know? Beside her, only three other people knew it—her three best friends and fellow sorority sisters from Howard—and they'd sworn on their lives never to breathe a word of it. Ellie, Shereen, and Yolanda had her back all those years ago, from the time the nightmare had started until it had ended. There was no way they would ever do this to her.

No, this had to be some strange coincidence. She didn't have a monopoly on the English language. Anyone could use those same words. Maybe it was some guy who liked the old Anita Ward song "Ring My Bell," and he was telling her in a bizarre way that he wanted her.

Still . . .

Jessica crumpled the note into a ball, then uncrumpled it and shredded it instead, all the while unable to forget the words, unable to forget their significance.

But she had to forget. She'd worked so hard to put it behind her.

She stood and paced, thinking, thinking, then finally went to the phone. Picking up the receiver, she punched in the digits to Shereen's home, then, realizing that it was the middle of the workday, hung up and punched in her office number.

Shereen's voice mail picked up. "Hey, Shereen," Jessica said, hoping her voice didn't sound as shaky as her body felt. "It's Jessica. I was hoping to reach you, but, well, it's not important. In fact, don't worry about it. I'll just talk to you later. Okay."

She hung up the phone, frustrated and flustered, wondering if she should call Ellie. But what would Ellie say? What would any of them say?

Turning slowly, she looked for proof that this was really a nightmare or that she'd imagined the whole thing. But she hadn't. The shredded note was still on the sofa. It was real, but God help her, what did it mean?

She couldn't do this. *Wouldn't* do this. It was behind her. Over. It had to be.

Before she gave the note another thought, she grabbed the loose pieces and marched to the garbage. She dropped them, watching the pieces flutter like flakes of snow, covering the tin bottom with flecks of mauve. And all the while she told herself that it was a coincidence. Meaningless. Someone with a stupid sense of humor had sent her a stupid joke.

That's all it was.

It couldn't be anything else.

Chapter Two

MAYBE SHE WAS JADED, but standing on a street corner in the dead of winter wearing a skirt that barely covered her ass was not Ellie Grant's idea of a decent way to make a buck. Her wide feet were stuffed into too-narrow shoes because there hadn't been anything else, and her toes were now so numb that she didn't know if she'd be able to stand much longer. If she heard one more person say what a beautiful day it was for February, she was going to scream. Yeah, the sun was shining, but it certainly wasn't keeping her warm. And the tights beneath the ridiculous fishnet stockings weren't doing a damn thing to protect her legs from the wind that seemed to get colder by the minute.

"This is bullshit," she said, speaking to anyone who would listen. "How long are they gonna keep us out here?"

"Wish I knew," came the reply from an older man beside her. He jiggled around on the spot, trying to stay warm. "It was nice when we first came out, but the sun keeps dipping behind the clouds and it's getting really cold now." He glanced at her legs. "Must be tough for you."

No shit, Bozo, she wanted to say. At times like this she envied men—they didn't have to worry about skirts and dresses and high heels and all the other sacrifices women had to make in the name of fashion. Bozo probably had several layers beneath his pants right now. She, on the other hand, was standing there dressed like a hooker who'd hit hard times, literally freezing her butt off. Why didn't movie people film movies set in the spring or summer in the spring or summer? Or was that concept too logical for this crazy business?

She needed the money, or she would have walked off the set a long time ago. But she certainly didn't appreciate the fact that the director, who was wearing a thick parka with the hood bunched around his face, kept yelling at the extras for shivering.

"Just picture yourself on a beach in Hawaii," the director had said.

Yeah, right, she'd thought, picturing instead her four-inch heel connecting with a certain part of the director's anatomy.

She wanted to get out of there. The few dollars she would make were certainly not worth the torture.

She was just about to head back to the building and Extras Holding, not caring if they sent her home without any money, when she saw the tall, dark-skinned man approaching. She paused, and when she saw that he was indeed heading for her, a thick coat over his arm and a smile to die for on his lips, she was instantly smitten. She'd have been smitten by anyone offering to save her from the cold then, but it helped that he was gorgeous as sin.

Her eyes took in the length of him. He wasn't her usual type—hell, she didn't have a type other than Richard, the married man she'd been seeing for months. At least she didn't see a ring on this guy's finger. And his smile could melt ice cream even in this weather.

"You must be cold."

Brilliant deduction. But she grinned up at him. How had she not noticed him before? She'd seen him, but hadn't really *seen* him. "Do I still have legs? If so, I can't feel them anymore."

It was the way he looked her over, like he wanted to eat her up bit by bit, that made her feel the warmth spread through her body once again. "Oh, they're there, all right." He placed the long down-filled coat around her shoulders. "Here, take this. I knew you had to be freezing so I asked Wardrobe for it."

"Oh, there is a God!" She burrowed into the coat. "Thanks."

There was that look again, that slant of the eyes, that upward curve of the lips. It was a look that said he definitely wanted to get to know her, and to Ellie's surprise, she wanted to get to know him. It wasn't too often a man as fine as him paid her any attention. Not that she wasn't an attractive woman, but so many men went for that Barbie-thin type, which she certainly was not. Maybe it was the boobs. She'd seen how he'd looked at them, like they were some sort of prize. Men got real stupid when they saw a woman with a healthy chest.

The wind hit her face then, and she remembered where she was. She frowned. "Look, do you know when we'll be out of here?" She didn't care about being seen in the movie, not when it was this cold. "I can't handle much more of this."

"I wish I did, baby. But I'm just a low man on the totem pole. They don't tell me much."

Baby. She loved the way he said that. Or maybe she just loved the way the word made her feel warm when she so desperately needed warmth.

"You're kinda cute, you know that?"

Kinda? Well, she supposed it was better than not being cute at all.

Static crackled over his walkie-talkie, and he spoke into it. "Go ahead. Yeah. Okay, background. First positions." To her, he said, "Sorry. I've gotta take the coat."

"Oh, God. I'm gonna die."

He glanced over his shoulder, then back at her. "Tell you what," he said softly, leaning close to her. "Since we didn't get this shot yet, if you disappear now—say, to use the bathroom—I won't notice."

Her eyes lit up. "For real?"

He nodded. "Better yet, if they ask for you, I'll tell them you're not feeling well."

"Which isn't a lie."

"Go inside and stay warm."

He gave her another one of those looks, and she felt like she was betraying Richard when she felt her skin tingle. She matched the look with her most seductive smile. "Thank you."

"Wait." He wrapped his fingers around her wrist before she could walk away. "Before I let you go, promise me you'll stick around later . . . so that you can give me a way to reach you."

She'd give him more than that, she was so grateful to get out of the cold! But she didn't want to seem too anxious. Shrugging, she said, "Sure."

"What's your name?"

"Ellie."

"I'm Shelton. Remember, don't leave until we've had a chance to talk."

"I won't."

And then he let her go, slowly, as though he didn't want to, and he watched her as she retreated into the building. She waved at him once from behind the glass doors, and he winked in response, then went back to work.

She let out a little howl. Was this for real? She'd been praying she'd find a date to accompany her to the Theta Phi Kappa Black History Month celebration, and she just knew that Shelton was the answer to her prayers. She couldn't go with Richard because he was married. And wasn't it time she found a man to help her get over Richard? She glanced back outside, watching as Shelton directed the extras. Yeah, maybe he could be that guy.

She disappeared and stayed hidden in the Extras Holding area for the better part of two hours. Just until she could feel her toes again. By the time she'd had her fill of coffee and chips and was ready to head back outside, the other extras piled into the room, shivering, rushing for tea and coffee and to gather their belongings, rejoicing in the fact that they were wrapped.

Wrapped. Hallelujah. She could go home.

"Where'd you disappear to?" a woman asked her. She'd played cards with the woman earlier but didn't know her name.

"Uh, I wasn't feeling well. The A.D. let me come back in."

"Lucky you." The woman rubbed her hands together as if hoping they would spontaneously combust. "It's a friggin' icebox out there. Girl, I don't know why I do this shit. I'm an actress. I've worked on Broadway. I don't have to degrade myself this way just to make a lousy buck."

Then why do you? Ellie wanted to ask, but didn't. She'd heard this song and dance from so many people on sets before, that they were really successful actors who just did extra work to pass the time. Yeah, right. But she said, "I hear you," pretending she could relate. Why say anything else? The last thing she needed was a tired story about why this woman was too good for the business.

She changed into her street clothes and joined the line to get signed out. Shelton, who sat at a table paying the extras, saw her and smiled. She smiled back. As she moved forward in the line, he kept making eye contact with her, making her feel like she was some eighteen-year-old knockout rather than a thirty-year-old woman who was too soft where she should be firm. And when it was her turn to collect her cash from him, she made sure to unfold her arms from her chest. It was the one asset she had; she might as well use it to her advantage.

He drew his bottom lip between his teeth and looked up at her slowly, making it clear to her that he liked what he saw. Then, as he handed her the money, he also handed her a slip of paper.

"See you later." From anyone else, it would be the standard parting line, but from Shelton, Ellie knew it was a promise.

"Later." She held his gaze a moment longer, then stepped aside to let him deal with the next extra. A smile spreading on her face, she opened the note discreetly. It read: "Call me. Let's get together soon. 555-0956."

She gave him one last look as she stuffed the note into her jacket pocket. He was, as she'd known he would be, looking at her.

Oh, she'd call him. And she could just hear Jessica and Shereen singing the praises that he was gorgeous *and* single.

That he wasn't Richard.

When the phone rang just after six A.M. the next morning, Ellie was instantly jarred from sleep. There was only one person who called her this early in the morning, and as she reached for the receiver, she couldn't stop a stupid smile from creeping onto her face. "Hello?"

"You're finally home."

Richard. She closed her eyes and sighed, like her very existence depended on this man. "Hey, you."

"You don't know how worried I was, sweetheart."

God, she was so pathetic. The mere sound of his voice turned her on. "You were?"

"Yeah. I had no idea if you were dead or alive. I almost went looking for you."

"Did you?" She didn't believe a word of it, but just hearing the words made her feel special.

"Mmm-hmm. I called several times . . ."

"I'm sorry, Richard. I was working."

"All day?"

He might as well have asked, *Are you sure you weren't in someone else's bed?* Ellie had come to realize that his "concern" and questions when he wasn't able to reach her were his way of checking up on her. And while he certainly had no right to be possessive or even jealous—he went home to his wife every evening—Ellie couldn't deny his possessiveness made her feel appreciated in some perverse sort of way. Like he cared enough about her that he didn't want to share her. Crazy, yeah, but no one had ever accused Eleanor Grant of being sane.

"No," Ellie answered. "I didn't work all day. But when I came home I was exhausted and I crashed."

"You couldn't call?"

"I didn't want to risk it."

She'd made her point, and shut him up in the process. She didn't want to give him *that* much control over her life.

"What are you doing now?" he asked.

"Now?" she asked, sounding surprised. But she'd known it was only a matter of time before he asked that question and her body was already throbbing in anticipation.

"Yeah. Now."

No need to sound too eager. "Well, I *was* sleeping—"

"I'll be there in half an hour," Richard said urgently, cutting her off.

For a moment, Ellie wanted to tell him that she would appreciate his asking her if he could come over, even though she knew their relationship was about sex. Just because he was ready didn't mean she necessarily was. But she knew she'd be lying if she spoke those words. She wanted to see Richard, and considering she could only have stolen moments with him at best, it was a small price to pay that she be available when he called.

Even if it was barely after six in the morning.

"I'll see you soon," she said, but the dial tone sounded in her ear. Richard had already hung up. Ellie replaced the receiver and headed for the shower.

"I have to go."

"No," Ellie protested, tightening her arms around Richard's back. He lay on top of her, still deep inside her, and Ellie wasn't quite ready to let him leave. Though she knew it was wrong, being with him like this felt so right.

"I have to." Richard gave Ellie a quick peck on the forehead, then rolled off her, ignoring her moan of protest. He hopped off the bed and bent to retrieve his pants.

The more they were together, the harder it got to watch him leave. But if Ellie wasn't mistaken, as she watched his back, it didn't seem that hard for him.

"Richard," Ellie called softly.

He faced her. "Yeah, sweetheart?"

Her heavy breasts jiggled as she sat up. "Come here for a minute."

Richard glanced at the bedside clock, then back at her.

"It's only seven-fifteen."

"You know I have to be in the office by eight."

What Ellie knew was that Richard was the owner of his own computer software firm. As the boss, he didn't have to punch in.

"Please, Richard." For the first time, Ellie realized that before sex, Richard begged; afterward, she did.

He glanced at the clock again, but after a moment, lowered himself onto the bed.

Ellie pressed one breast against his arm and ran a hand over his abdomen, then lower.

He placed a hand on hers, stopping it. "Ellie . . ."

"Come on," she purred into his ear. She trailed her other hand down his spine. "We haven't been together in two weeks. That was just the appetizer. I'm ready for a meal now."

He angled his face so that his lips met hers, but the contact was all too brief. "You know I would if I could."

Bullshit, Ellie thought. Her hand stilled on his back. "I don't know why you bother, Richard."

"Bother what?"

She dropped back onto the bed, pulling the thin sheet over her body. "Why you bother coming over at all."

"Come on, Ellie. You're not being fair."

"*I'm* not being fair? Oh, that's priceless."

He stretched out beside her. "Ellie, you know I'd spend all morning with you if I could. But I can't."

"You used to at least take me out for dinner once in a while. Now, all you do is come here for a booty call."

"Is that what you really think?"

She eyed him, pouted. "Yeah."

He placed a hand on her belly, softly stroking her. God help her, her body reacted to his touch at once. Still, she frowned.

"I'm sorry," he whispered. "I know this is hard for you. But this past month, things have been really stressful at work—at home."

"If things are so stressful at home, why are you still there?"

He paused a brief second, and in that moment, Ellie wondered if he was about to lie to her. Instead, he said, "Because."

Ellie stared at his face. He was dark-complected and had smooth, flawless skin. But his nose was too wide for his narrow face, his eyes a little too large. He wasn't the most attractive man she'd ever been with, but still, there was something about him. For the most part, he was sweet and kind, treated her well. And unlike the few pretty boys she'd been with, he knew how to please her in bed.

She could hear Shereen now: "There's more to life than sex. Why are you staying with this guy?"

"Richard, you told me things would be different in the New Year." While he hadn't actually said he would leave his wife, he'd hinted at it often enough. Hell, he had to know that's why she was hanging on.

"They will be. I just have to get some stuff together."

She'd heard this reply so often that hearing it now made her nape tingle with doubt. She remembered Shereen's reaction the last time she'd told her Richard had said that. Shereen had rolled her eyes, then asked, "Girl, when are you gonna learn?" Ellie had defended Richard, saying that she understood how hard it was for him to walk away from his family. But now, looking up at him, she wondered if she was indeed a fool.

The last thing she'd expected when she'd walked into Richard's firm six months ago was to get involved with anyone. But almost instantly, she'd sensed his attraction to her. The way he'd looked at her a little too long. The way he'd do things like bring her a coffee in the morning, when he was the boss. The way he simply made excuses to be around her. Ellie had recently been dumped by a pretty boy she was crazy about and knew she was vulnerable, so she should have been cautious. Instead, she appreciated Richard's attention. He wore his ring, so she knew he was married, but for some reason that hadn't bothered her like it did when other married men blatantly checked her out or came on to her. That made her life less complicated. After all, she wasn't looking for a relationship. But what normal woman didn't appreciate a man constantly checking her out, making her feel like she was the most beautiful woman in the world?

As the weeks passed, her clothes had gotten a little tighter, more provocative. Richard had definitely noticed. And weeks later, when Richard had invited her to discuss her performance over lunch in his office, Ellie had known exactly what the main course would be.

In hindsight, she should have stayed away. But she and Richard had been like two trains traveling toward each other on the same track— destined to collide.

After that first time, they couldn't get enough of each other. They made love every lunch hour—sometimes even after work. And when it became obvious to everyone in the office that they were having an affair, he'd told her it was best she find another job. He'd given her a sizable check, assured her that he loved her and couldn't live without her, and said that it wouldn't be long before they could be together openly. He just needed to get some "stuff" together.

Now, looking up at him, Ellie asked, "What stuff?"

He shrugged. "Just stuff. It's hard to explain."

"I'm listening."

"What do you want me to say?"

"The truth," she answered. "I've been patient, Richard, and now I want to know what it's really going to take for you to leave your wife."

"Can we discuss this later? When I'm not running late for work?"

"You're full of shit," Ellie snapped, and rolled over.

"Ellie."

"Get out, Richard." Part of her knew she shouldn't be angry. She had known what she was getting into when she got involved with a married man. It had been an affair, plain and simple, with no strings attached. His marriage had been a bonus, meaning things wouldn't get complicated. So for the life of her, Ellie couldn't understand why she was acting like she wanted something more.

"Look at me, Ellie."

"No."

"Ellie . . ."

Huffing, she rolled over, but didn't meet his eyes. "Save it, Richard.

I may have been naive when we first got together. I may have been naive last week. But I'm not so stupid, naive, and desperate that I don't know when I'm being played. You're never going to leave your wife. Don't even waste your breath telling me that you are."

"That's not true."

"Just go."

Instead of getting up and getting the hell out of her place, Richard pulled the sheet down from her breasts and lowered his head, taking a thick, brown nipple into his mouth. Softly, he suckled, then reached for her other breast with his free hand.

Ellie tried to fight it, she really did, because she knew this wasn't the answer to anything. But Richard always did know how to turn her on. So instead of pushing him off her, she closed her eyes, arched her back, and moaned.

"You know I love you," Richard said, positioning himself between her legs.

"I know," Ellie replied softly, wrapping her legs around his thighs, urging him closer.

"I don't want to lose you."

At that moment, as he covered her lips with his, Ellie knew that Richard was worth the wait.

She just had to be more patient.

Chapter Three

IT WAS ONE OF THOSE days, the kind where you start off with piss in your cornflakes—and it doesn't get any better.

"Oh, God. Shoot me now," Shereen Anderson said, wondering if the day could get any worse. If she'd paid attention to her horoscope that morning, she would have stayed in bed. Not only was Mercury in retrograde, but the approaching full moon was void of course in her opposite sign, Cancer—a definite indication of disaster for any Capricorn today.

Wincing, Shereen hobbled over to the floor-to-ceiling windows and glanced outside. The sky was still ominously black, though the freezing rain had turned to a light drizzle. Earlier, sleet had caused chaos on Washington's streets, making the morning rush hour drive horrendous. There had been several traffic accidents and personal injuries. Other than running late, Shereen had driven from her Maryland home to her Washington office without incident, only to slip on the building's icy front steps. As she fell, she'd twisted her leg at an odd angle, landing hard on both hands, then on a knee. Even now, hours later, the pain pulsated from her knee through her entire leg, causing her to walk with a limp.

Inside her M&A Graphics office, there had been crisis after crisis since she'd walked through the door. One of the company's large clients had defaulted on a payment. Another had called to complain that the peppers in their brochure were an odd shade of green and they wouldn't pay for the job until it was redone. Then, Shereen had learned that Charlie, their trusted plant manager for the past eleven years, had been claiming excess overtime hours he hadn't worked. She'd had to explain to a not-so-happy Charlie that his pay would be significantly docked.

And now this?

"I figured you'd want to know," Rudy said.

Given the day, Shereen really shouldn't have expected good news when Rudy, her administrative assistant, had entered her office and closed the door behind her only moments ago.

"Since everyone's been talking," Rudy added ruefully.

This was exactly the type of office bullshit Shereen didn't need. Wearily, she turned from the window and stared at Rudy. "*Aaron* dumped *me*?"

"So the story goes. Something to the effect of you two having an affair, then you becoming obsessed with him. He says that's why he's leaving. Because he doesn't feel comfortable here anymore."

"He's leaving because his contract is up!" Aaron Carter, a fresh-out-of-college pretty boy, had been hired as a designer on a six-month contract. Why was he lying? Angry, Shereen hustled back to her desk and plopped down on the swivel chair. But she landed on it too hard, and the chair tipped, swaying precariously on its back wheels. Desperately, she reached for the edge of her desk, but her fingers barely grazed it as the chair flipped backward, taking her with it.

Her head hit the hardwood floor while her legs flew in the air. "Gaawd!"

Instantly, Rudy was above her, extending her a hand. "Oh, my God. Ms. Anderson, are you okay?"

Shereen waved her off as she rolled out of the chair and got to her feet on her own. She wasn't so much hurt as she was completely embarrassed. "Yes, I'm okay." She brushed her hands over her pantsuit, trying to regain her composure. Damn, maybe she should call it a day. At this rate, she was destined for an early grave before the clock struck midnight.

"Mr. Carter's contract is up," she repeated as she righted the chair, though she certainly didn't owe her administrative assistant any explanations. "That's why he's leaving, Rudy."

"I'm just telling you what I heard."

Her copy of the *Black Networking News* had fallen to the floor as she'd fallen. Shereen scooped it up and tossed it in the trash. She didn't feel much like reading anything right now.

"I hope he's not planning anything funky—like trying to sue us for wrongful dismissal." Luckily for Shereen and for M&A Graphics, she'd kept all Aaron's cards and notes. If he tried to claim sexual harassment, she'd be ready for him.

Rudy shrugged. "Sounds bitter to me, that's all."

Shereen groaned as she sank into her chair—carefully this time. "How many people have heard this?"

"About you and Aaron?"

"Yes," Shereen replied urgently.

"You really want to know?"

"That bad?"

"Let's just say, I heard it from Marla."

"God, that's exactly what I need." If Marla had heard this sordid tale, then everyone knew it. Goodness, was her private sex life not her own personal business? Her life was not a soap opera meant to entertain the employees at M&A Graphics.

"I don't know if it's true or not. Either way, it's not my business. But I know that if it were me, I would not appreciate him spreading that story. So, now that you know, maybe you can talk to him."

"Thanks, Rudy."

Rudy offered her a sympathetic smile, then walked out of the office. As soon as her administrative assistant was gone, Shereen shot to her feet, but pain seared through her knee and leg. Grimacing, she limped to the door and locked it.

She sagged against the closed door, thinking that this was a nightmare come true. Why oh why had she been dumb enough, desperate enough, to break her one cardinal rule? Never, ever get involved with a colleague. And Aaron Carter wasn't even a colleague; he was an employee. Much, much worse.

She'd been desperate for a little action since she hadn't had any in a long, long time. That desperation had clouded her judgment.

Shereen's eyes narrowed on the vase of long-stemmed red roses on the corner of her mahogany desk. She staggered to her desk as quickly as she could, grabbed the three-day-old flowers, and dumped them into the nearby trash.

Aaron Carter had some nerve. Not only had he relentlessly pursued her in the weeks since the Christmas party, he'd done so up until a few days ago. She should have dumped the flowers when he'd delivered them, but she hadn't wanted to hurt his feelings. Besides, they'd been too beautiful to simply throw away.

Now, Shereen wondered if she'd in some way led Aaron on.

No, that was ludicrous. One night of sex, and he expected a commitment?

Men. She couldn't understand them.

Exhausted from the effort to stand and walk on her injured leg, Shereen sat on the edge of her broad desk and closed her eyes. Why was it that with some men, a woman could beg and beg until she was six feet under and they'd never commit, while the men women didn't want were the ones they couldn't get rid of?

Hell, if she knew the answer to that, she'd be a millionaire.

This was her own stupid fault. She'd slept with Aaron—once. Once, but the man had fallen harder than a sack of potatoes off the Washington Monument. She hadn't returned his affections, and now he was acting worse than a woman.

Jesus.

With difficulty, Shereen made her way around the desk and back to her large Italian swivel chair. Slowly, she sank into its softness. But not even the comfort of the chair could assuage her troubled spirit.

She wished she could turn back the clock, but knew how pointless such a thought was. She couldn't change the fact that she'd had a little too much to drink at the office Christmas party, and had flirted like a woman who hadn't been laid in a while. Aaron had been attractive, available, and most important, had responded to her flirtatiousness. Somehow—and the hell of it was, she didn't know how—she'd ended up back at his place.

She didn't even remember if he was good in bed.

So much for a titillating one-night stand.

Her three best friends in the world—Jessica, Ellie, and Yolanda— would get a good chuckle out of this story. They all thought she was dying without a man.

Which she wasn't.

She'd never had good luck with men, which is why she was thirty and single. But she didn't care—anymore. There was a time when she had cared, back in college, but that was because she'd been head-over-heels in love. However, she'd gotten over Terrence Simms and had moved on with her life. Though Jessica would disagree, she hadn't been interested in any of the men she'd dated after Terrence, not because she was still hung up on him but because the men simply hadn't been right for her.

And now, Shereen was happy with her life. She had a challenging job at her father's graphic design company as the VP of Finance. She owned a home. She enjoyed her independence, independence that threatened most of the men she dated.

So, who needed men? They weren't worth the hassle.

She had wonderful girl friends—Ellie, Jessica, and Yolanda. And in this world where men dogged you, harassed you, and made your life more complicated than it should be, having girl friends you could count on was all that really mattered.

When, hours later, yet another man was giving her grief, this time her twenty-four-hour-charity-case-live-in-brother, Shereen reached for the receiver. She needed a break, needed to hear the friendly voice of one of her sorors, whom she knew would brighten her day. So she punched in the number to the WGRZ television studio in Washington.

"Jessica Bedford," she said when the receptionist answered.

"Who's calling?"

"Shereen Anderson."

"One moment."

Three tries later, the receptionist finally connected Shereen to the right extension. Either the woman was a ditz or this extra frustration was part of Shereen's projected bad day.

"What's up with that receptionist?" Shereen asked when Jessica answered the phone.

"Oh. Claudia. I don't think she likes me very much."

"She's annoying." Finally hearing her friend's voice made Shereen feel one hundred times better. "You all need to fire her incompetent ass."

"I just ignore her. So, Shereen. What's up?"

"Other than having one of the worst days of my life?"

"Uh-oh. Wanna talk about it?"

"Not really. But what's up with you? I got that cryptic message of yours a few days ago and called you back, but you weren't around. You didn't get back to me."

"Oh, that. It was nothing. You know how it is over here. Crazy as hell. Especially with Valentine's Day approaching. I just wanted to hear a friendly voice."

"I hear you. What are you doing later?"

"I was planning on heading home."

"Forget that. Meet me for dinner."

"Are you paying?"

"Girl, please. You're the famous TV personality." Shereen chuckled. "I'll meet you at the studio in an hour. We can go to that great little Italian place around the corner."

"All right, sweetie."

"No, wait," Shereen said before Jessica could hang up. "You'd better pick me up."

"And come all the way back to the Hill for dinner?"

"I don't care where we eat. I just don't feel like getting behind the wheel of a car right now."

"It's been that kind of day?"

"Hell, yeah. And it ain't over yet."

"What happened to your leg?" Jessica asked as she and Shereen made their way from the parking lot of Viscotti's to the restaurant's front door. The rain had stopped, thank the Lord, but a cold wind wrapped around them like frigid arms, chilling them.

Shereen had been waiting at the curb when Jessica pulled up in front of her office, so Jessica hadn't noticed her limp until now. "Oh, I fell this morning," Shereen replied. "Thought I split open my knee at first."

"Ouch. Sounds painful."

"That's an understatement."

"Did you put ice on it?"

"Oh, yeah. The ice all over the office steps." Shereen grinned wryly.

"I'm serious. You need to elevate your leg and put ice on it. So it doesn't swell."

"Like I have time for that."

"Shereen . . ." Of the four of them, Jessica was definitely the most nurturing, the most momlike.

"Well, if I wake up tomorrow and my knee is the size of a coconut, I guess I'll just have to stay in bed."

They were at the restaurant's front door now. Jessica reached for it and held it open, letting Shereen pass her, then followed her inside. The warmth of the nearby fire enveloped them as they stepped into the restaurant's foyer.

"Table for two," Shereen told the hostess.

The hostess led them to the back of the restaurant and placed their menus on a small two-seater near the entrance to the kitchen.

Shereen and Jessica exchanged a brief look before Jessica said, "Can we sit over there, please?" She pointed to a booth across from one of the restaurant's fireplaces.

"Sure," the hostess replied, but her tone was clipped, and Shereen had to wonder what the big deal was. Though the restaurant was busy, a few booths were open.

"Thank you," Jessica said when they reached their new table. The hostess didn't respond, merely dropped the menus on the table and walked away. Jessica scowled at the young woman's back. "Sheesh, I wonder what her problem is."

Shereen shrugged. "Maybe she's a Capricorn. We're having a bad day."

"I don't care what her sign is. That attitude is completely unprofessional." Pause. "You know what Yolanda would say if she were here, don't you?"

"Oh, yeah," Shereen replied, smiling at the mention of Yolanda. If their feisty friend were here, she'd have a thing or two to say about the hostess's less-than-cordial attitude, not to mention her trying to seat them near the kitchen. Yolanda was undoubtedly the guts of the group. She had certainly gone into the perfect career: law.

"I miss her," Shereen said. Surprising them all, the levelheaded Yolanda had eloped five years ago and moved to Philadelphia with her husband. He'd gotten a job with a law firm there, and Yolanda, who hadn't yet finished law school, had had to transfer from Howard to the law school at Temple University. Shereen, Jessica, and Ellie had seen her every so often, but it just hadn't been the same as when the sorority sisters had all been undergrads.

"I miss her, too," Jessica said. "I can't wait to see her."

"You say that like she's coming to town."

"You haven't talked to her?"

"No." While they were all as close as sisters, Yolanda was closest to Jessica. "Have you?"

Jessica nodded. "She called me a few days ago. Said she's definitely going to be there."

"At the Black History Month event?" Shereen asked for clarification, though with it being early February, Jessica could only be referring to that.

"Mmm-hmm. And—are you ready for this? She's bringing that new man of hers."

Shereen opened her mouth in surprise, but before she could speak, someone else did. She looked up.

"Hello, ladies." The waiter, an attractive young black man, smiled down at them. "What can I get you to drink?"

He was probably a student at one of the nearby universities, Shereen guessed as her eyes roamed over his handsome face and physique. But that thought made her think of Aaron and she quickly looked away.

"I'll have a glass of zinfandel," Jessica told him. "Shereen?"

Shereen made like she was studying the menu. "Sure. I'll have one, too."

"Would you like a bottle?" he asked.

"Shereen?"

"Uh, do you?"

"I've got to drive."

"So do I."

Jessica faced the waiter while Shereen acted like he wasn't there. "Just the two glasses, please." When the waiter disappeared, Jessica eyed her curiously. "What was that about?"

"What?"

"I saw that look you gave him, then the way you avoided him altogether. Almost like you've slept with him."

"What?" Shereen exclaimed, shocked. But what surprised her more was that Jessica had even come close to guessing the nature of her look.

"You haven't been scoping the campuses for hot young men, have you?"

"I can't believe you just said that." At her friend's skeptical look, Shereen added, "No. Goodness, no. It's just that he reminds me of someone."

"Someone you've slept with."

"Jessica!"

"Hey, that would be a good thing. How long has it been?"

"You sound like Ellie."

"Maybe I do. But I can't help but be curious."

Right then, she decided not to tell Jessica about the Aaron fiasco. Not yet anyway. She didn't want to admit she'd been as desperate as her friends believed she was. "Get your mind out of the gutter. Now, you were saying?"

Jessica smirked like she knew Shereen wasn't telling her something. "I was talking about Yolanda. Looks like we're finally going to get to meet this mystery man of hers."

"Wonders never cease. I thought she'd keep him in the closet forever."

"I think she was just being cautious. Especially after James."

"Has she told you his name?"

"She hasn't told me a thing."

"That's beyond cautious. That's neurotic."

Jessica shrugged. "The way she's been so quiet about him, this must be serious."

"Hmm." The times Shereen and Yolanda had spoken in the past months, she'd merely said she was dating. If the relationship had gotten more serious, why hadn't she told any of them?

"Well, whoever he is, he's gotta be pussy-whipped. After her marriage, Yolanda definitely won't let herself get burned again."

"No doubt."

"If she hasn't told you anything, I guess she hasn't said anything to Ellie."

"Other than warn her to stay ten feet away from him at all times?" Jessica chuckled.

"She better make it fifty. Oh, God," Shereen said, a giggle escaping her. "That's awful. I didn't mean that." Her laughter died as the waiter appeared.

"Your wine," he said, placing the glasses on the table. His eyes lingered a little too long on Shereen. "Ready to order?"

"We haven't even looked at the menus," Shereen confessed.

"I don't need to see the menu," Jessica announced. "I'm gonna have the Fettuccine Chicken Florentine."

"Sounds good. I'll have that, too." Shereen gathered the menus and passed them to the waiter.

"No appetizer?" he asked, staring into Shereen's eyes. His look said he'd offer himself up for her pleasure anytime she wanted.

Oooh, he really was flirting with her. And he *was* cute. But she wasn't interested. "No, thanks. The wine will do."

He drew his bottom lip between his teeth. "Well, if you need anything else, let me know."

"We will," Shereen assured him, then shook her head in disbelief as he backed up one step, two steps, then turned and disappeared.

"You *have* slept with him."

"No!" Shereen protested in a loud whisper, leaning across the table to squeeze Jessica's hand.

"Then what was that exchange about?"

"Hell if I know."

"I guess I shouldn't be surprised," Jessica added with a shrug. "Men always go a little gaga when they see you."

Shereen sat up straight. "Yeah, right."

"Shereen, why are you even trying to lie? You know you were the knockout of the group, *Sweet Thang*. Still are. The rest of us are all duly humbled when in your presence." Jessica made a bowing gesture.

"Shut up." Shereen reached for her wine and took a sip. But the mention of her sorority nickname had her smiling. She, Jessica, Ellie, and Yolanda had called themselves the Fabulous Four. She was Sweet Thang. Jessica, Quiet Tongue. Ellie, Wild Thang. Yolanda, Ice Queen. How long had it been since they'd all been together? Not since last summer, seven months ago. And while they kept in touch via the phone, it just wasn't the same as actually getting together.

After they'd graduated from Howard, they'd made sure to get together every Sunday. After a while, once a week had turned into whenever they could, which, as they'd gotten older and more involved in their professional lives, had naturally been less and less. Still, they hadn't gone more than a month without seeing each other as a group. Then Yolanda had married James and moved to Philadelphia, and the amount of times they got together as a group dwindled to maybe two or three times a year.

Still, they had all vowed to not let their friendship slowly but surely die the way so many friendships did when people were out of sight and out of mind. "We have to water our friendship," Ellie had once said. "Stay in touch, make plans to get together, hang out and just get silly. Or like a plant without water, our friendship can wither up and die before we realize what's happening."

"I'm only getting married," Yolanda had responded. "Not moving to the moon."

"I know, but . . . I'm serious. I can't tell you how many people I was close with in high school, but I have no clue where they are now."

"That won't happen to us," Jessica had said.

"You never know." Ellie's voice had broken and she'd reached for her wineglass. For a moment they'd all been silent as they sat in Yolanda's living room, because Ellie rarely cried. And in that moment, as Shereen had looked from Jessica to Yolanda, she could see in their eyes that they were wondering if Ellie was right, if what she'd said could actually happen to them after years of being so close.

"Then let's make a promise right now." Shereen glanced at all her friends in turn. "Promise that we'll always remain friends. No matter what."

"Promise."

"I promise."

"I promise."

So far, they'd kept that promise, even if they only saw each other a few times a year. But no matter what was going on in their lives, the one event they never missed was the Theta Phi Kappa Black History Month celebration.

Like most of the black sororities and fraternities, the Theta Phi Kappa Sorority, Incorporated was founded on the campus of Howard University. The Thetas' Black History Month celebration was the most important event their alumnae sorority held each year. Not only did the Thetas celebrate their black heritage, they recognized and celebrated the contributions made to society by other Thetas. February was also the month they celebrated the chapter's anniversary.

And since they'd all become friends through the Theta Phi Kappa

sorority, it only made sense that the annual Black History Month celebration had come to represent the celebration of their friendship as well.
At least that's what Yolanda had said the year she'd moved to Philadelphia, and they'd all agreed.

Eleven years ago, Shereen, Yolanda, Jessica, and Ellie had all met in
their sophomore year at Howard at a Theta Phi Kappa rush, an infor-
mational gathering for those interested in that particular sorority. Shereen had always wanted to join a sorority, and having heard about the
Thetas' dedication to community and their efforts with mentoring inner-
city children, Shereen had known this was the sorority for her. Jessica
had become a Theta because her older sister had been one years before
her. Ellie—well, Ellie had heard that the Thetas not only worked hard
but partied hard, and she'd been hooked. Yolanda, who had come from
the projects, had been personally influenced by the Thetas who'd come
to her school to mentor underprivileged children. Many times she said
that those sisters had helped instill in her the belief that she could
become anything she wanted. Inspired by their caring nature, Yolanda
had vowed to become a Theta herself one day.

It's funny how life can put you in the path of people you otherwise
never would have met, giving you a chance to get to know them because
you have a similar interest, which allows you to become friends when
in other circumstances you would have shared nothing more than a
pleasant hi and bye. That's the way it had been for Shereen, Ellie, Jessica,
and Yolanda. They were all so very different—Jessica, the shy, private
one; Ellie, the party girl who lived for dating and a good time; Yolanda,
the strong one who didn't take crap from nobody; and Shereen, sexy
and sociable, considered by many as some type of goddess.

But there was so much more to them than what they'd originally
thought of each other. Shereen had learned that Jessica had a heart of
gold and could open up once she felt close to you. Ellie, while she
presented the confident air of a party girl, was really vulnerable and
simply wanted to find Mr. Right. Yolanda, while tough on the outside,
was sweet and loving on the inside. And what they'd all learned about
Shereen was that while she was sexy and sociable, she was also smart
and levelheaded, and didn't cop an attitude about her looks at all.

The Theta Phi Kappa sorority was the path that put them all together.
They'd been on line at the same time and had crossed the burning sands

into sorority sisterhood together. But with a total of thirty-six women on line that year, they hadn't sought each other out as friends. However, they'd really gotten to know each other during the pledge process, when one of the big sisters had hand-picked the four people she thought most unlikely to get along and forced them to work together to get one of their fraternity brothers' prized jerseys. True to the ideology of sisterhood, they had found a way to work together to get the task done despite their differences—but it was an ensuing crisis that night that had brought them together in a way that none of them could have ever imagined.

THE PAST

"THIS IS STUPID," YOLANDA QUIPPED.

"Do you have a better idea?" Ellie snapped. She, Yolanda, Jessica, and Shereen stood behind the bushes at the foot of the stairs leading to the Gamma Theta Psi frat house. "How else can we get close enough to Jordan to get his jersey?"

"I don't really give a damn about his stupid jersey," Yolanda retorted.

"It doesn't matter what you give a damn about." Ellie glared at her. "That's the reason we're here."

"Guys," Shereen said, exasperated. She looked from Ellie to Yolanda, wondering if the two could put aside their animosity and work together. "It's not that big of a deal. We go in there for a few minutes, one or two of us distract him, and then one of us will head to his room and grab his jersey."

"Four women with bunny ears and tight shorts?" Yolanda gave the rest of the group a wry look. "We'll be lucky if we get out of there without getting mauled."

"Guys are visual." Ellie's tone said she didn't want to explain this again. It had been her idea to dress up in tank tops, tight shorts, and bunny ears. "This makes sense. Tonight is a guys-only fraternity bonding thing, so they're not about to let us into the party. But what man can resist sex? Hence, the outfits." Ellie sighed when her argument seemed to fall on deaf ears. "Look, I don't want to do this any more than you do, but we all want to be part of the Theta Phi Kappas, don't we? If we fail at this task, forget passing over into sisterhood."

"The music's loud," Shereen said. "No doubt they've been drinking—"

"Oh, great." Yolanda frowned.

"In other words," Shereen continued, giving Yolanda a pointed look, "if they're drunk, this should be easy."

"Or big trouble," Yolanda muttered.

"There's no point standing around arguing." Shocked eyes flew to Jessica. Clearly, they were surprised that she'd spoken. Hell, they'd probably forgotten she was even there. Not that she could blame them. She'd barely said two words to them since they'd been put together to do this job.

She hadn't known what to say. She wasn't like the opinionated Yolanda; the confident, sexy Shereen; or the outgoing, feisty Ellie. She was plain, shy Jessica, who right now wished she were back in her dorm room, researching her upcoming sociology paper.

Instead, she was outside a frat house hiding in the darkness, preparing to do the most outrageous thing she'd ever done.

It had taken all her courage to dress up like a moronic sex kitten, and now she just wanted to get this job over with. She didn't particularly care about joining this sorority or any other one, but her sister had been a Theta nine years before her and had specifically said, "I know how shy you are, but for God's sake don't go to Howard and hide in a closet." She'd convinced Jessica that joining a sorority would help build her social skills, as well as her confidence.

Now, Jessica wasn't so sure.

"Jessica's right," Shereen said. "Let's go in there and get this over with."

Jessica had heard that the pledging process could be brutal, and now that she was a few weeks into it, she knew it to be true. Thus far, the women on line had been subjected to a variety of humiliating initiation rituals, like cleaning the dorm steps with a red-and-gold toothbrush and acting as maids for the older sisters. Supposedly it was all in good fun, and once they were full-fledged sisters, they'd have the privilege of doing unto others next year what had been done unto them this year. But that thought didn't give Jessica any comfort right now.

Still, she hated her shyness, and if joining a sorority could help her get over that, she'd do it. And she knew that as crazy as this task was, there was a point to it. If she and the others could find a way to get this job done, it would prove that they could work together despite their differences—a necessary quality for anyone entering into sisterhood.

The front door of the dorm opened, jarring Jessica from her thoughts. Two guys stumbled down the steps.

"Come on," Ellie said when they were gone. "Let's go."

Ellie dropped her cigarette onto the grass and squeezed between the edge of the bushes and the red-brick building. Shereen, Jessica, and Yolanda followed her. Seconds later, they were all inside the door, where a muscular Gamma—no doubt a linebacker—gave them all a curious but appreciative look.

"No women allowed tonight," he told them as Ellie tried to walk past him.

"Not even the entertainment?" Ellie flashed a sexy smile.

Turning, Yolanda faced Shereen and Jessica and rolled her eyes. Shereen merely shrugged, not sure there was a better solution. At least Ellie was good at thinking on her feet, which was exactly what they needed to get into this party.

Muscle Man paused a moment at Ellie's comment, then looked her over from head to toe. "If you're the entertainment, how come I haven't heard about you before now?"

"Because . . ." Ellie began, scrambling for something to say that would make sense. "Jordan wanted us to be a surprise. Come on." She gave him another smile as she jutted out her breasts. "Don't you think we'll add a little life to the party?"

Muscle Man's mouth practically watered. "What the hell. This is gonna be fun."

When they had all walked past Muscle Man and into the corridor, Yolanda said, "Brilliant, Ellie. Just brilliant."

"It got us in, didn't it?"

"Maybe, but I'm not about to *entertain* anyone."

"Neither am I," Ellie told her. "Which means we have to be quick and smart."

"Hey, sweetheart." An attractive brother strolled by Jessica and took her hand in his. She yanked it back. He pouted but kept walking.

"Can we do this?" Jessica crossed both arms over her chest in a protective gesture. "Today?"

"What's Jordan's room number?" Ellie asked.

"I *think* it's room two-fourteen," Shereen replied.

Jessica glanced around warily. "Then let's go upstairs."

Again, Ellie led the way. If she was scared or nervous, no one could tell. She looked entirely in her element, smiling when guys gave catcalls, meeting their eyes head-on as though she'd invented the art of flirting.

The music was deafening when they reached the second floor. Most of the Gamma Theta Psis were congregated in the living room area, laughing and talking boisterously. Drinking. A few of them hung in the hallway and immediately noticed when the four scantily clad women stepped onto their floor.

So much for hoping to sneak past a roomful of drunks. Shereen knew the time to act was now or never. "All right, we've been spotted. Two of us should go to the right and two to the—"

A shriek stopped her short. Whirling around, Shereen saw that Muscle Man, who'd come up the stairs behind them, had scooped Yolanda into his arms. "Yo, guys! We've got us some Playboy bunnies!"

Yolanda kicked and flailed her arms trying to free herself, as Muscle Man carried her into the living room. But he was much bigger and stronger than she was and her efforts were useless.

"Oh, my God," Ellie said. "She's gonna kill us."

"*You,*" Shereen clarified. "This was your idea."

"Don't you start on me."

"God, what can we do?" Jessica asked. She looked completely petrified.

"I don't know," Shereen said. "Should one of us go for the jersey?"

Ellie shook her head. "Not yet. We can't just leave her there."

There was a round of hooting and hollering as Muscle Man deposited Yolanda on a table.

"Fuck," Ellie said. "I need a drink."

Ellie was startled when someone passed her a can of beer. A drunken frat brother, she realized in the next instant. But before she had a chance to take a sip of it, he grabbed her hand and all but dragged her to the living room area. Yolanda, who stood with her hands on her hips on top of the table, saw her coming and sent a lethal look her way.

Ellie downed the beer in three large swallows, then got onto the table beside her. More applause and whistles. God help her. God help them all. Maybe this hadn't been such a good idea.

"Hi, guys," Ellie announced, proud of her confident tone. "How y'all doing tonight?"

Exuberant cheers filled the room.

"Get us out of this," Yolanda said in a loud whisper.

"Uh . . . I guess I should tell you that we really only came here to have a good time. You know, to party with the Gammas, since we hear you throw great parties." A few guys howled their agreement. "But if you want us to dance for y'all, that's cool." Yolanda gave her another deadly look. "However, we don't do anything freaky—like take off our clothes. And absolutely no touching allowed."

"We're part of your sister sorority, the Thetas," Yolanda explained, her tone practical but urgent. "Actually, we're going through the pledge process now. And that's why we're here, because it's part of our initiation. So—"

"Shut up and dance!" a guy shouted from the crowd.

Ellie couldn't help it—she cracked up at Yolanda's indignant look. She could have told Yolanda that trying to reason with a roomful of drunken jocks would get her nowhere. After a moment, Yolanda cracked up, too.

"God, Ellie, this is crazy."

"I know." But at least they were laughing about it now as opposed to six months from now.

Shereen and Jessica were suddenly at the foot of the table. Two burly men helped them up. A second later, the music, an LL Cool J tune, went up several decibels.

"One dance," Yolanda shouted above the music. "Then we work our way to Jordan's room." And once they got Jordan's prized football jersey, they could get the hell out of there.

But one dance turned to two, after which they were suddenly dancing with all the brothers in the room. And drinking. And drinking some more. Might as well, since they were there. But they'd gotten no closer to getting to Jordan's room. At least that's what Yolanda thought until Ellie pinched her arm and said, "I got it. Let's go."

"Got what?"

"Jordan's jersey. Come on."

"Wait a minute. How'd you get it?" Yolanda was aware that this was a question she could ask later, but she was actually enjoying the party. More to the point, she was enjoying getting to know Corey Lipton, a tall, dark, and fine basketball player. She'd heard that the Gamma Theta Psi fraternity was comprised of mostly jocks, but not until tonight did she realize just how true that was. How had she not noticed these fine brothers before?

"I'll tell you later. Get Shereen and Jessica. I'm gonna head downstairs before someone realizes I've got it."

"*Right* right now?"

"Yes," Ellie answered, then spun on her heel and hurried toward the stairs.

Yolanda tried, she really did, to say good-bye to Corey right then, but he insisted on one more dance, and his arms felt so good around her that she couldn't find it in her heart to deny him. But she finally did pull herself away when she spotted Shereen, promising Corey that she'd call him tomorrow. If the number he'd written on her arm didn't fade by then.

"Hey, Shereen. Ellie got it."

"Great. Where is she?"

"Downstairs."

"Okay." Shereen took her hand. "Let's go."

Yolanda giggled and waved to a tall, gorgeous brother who had to be a basketball player. Then she blew him a kiss.

"I see you enjoyed yourself."

"Yeah. This was fun!"

Shereen chuckled softly, then placed a hand across Yolanda's shoulder. No doubt she was drunk.

She was at the top of the stairs when Yolanda asked, "Where's that other girl—Jessica?"

"I told her to meet us downstairs in five minutes."

Downstairs, Shereen and Yolanda found Ellie sitting in a corner, her knees pulled to her chest. No doubt she sat like that to hide the jersey. When she saw them, she jumped to her feet. "Come on."

"Wait," Shereen said. "Jessica's not here."

"She just went outside."

"By herself?" Why wouldn't she wait with Ellie?

"No. She was with a guy."

"*Jessica?*" Shereen was truly shocked. Their fellow pledge hardly seemed like the type. "Are you sure?"

"Yes, I'm sure. I told her not to go too far, so let's find her and get out of here."

"Do we have to leave?" Yolanda protested, looking over her shoulder at the stairs.

"Yes," Shereen told her firmly.

Ellie hurried to the front door while Shereen lagged behind with Yolanda. Who would have thought Miss I-Don't-Want-to-Be-Here wouldn't want to leave?

"I don't see her," Ellie said as Shereen and Yolanda stepped outside.

The early October air was cool and thankfully sobering. Shereen looked around. "She's gotta be here somewhere."

Just then, a squeal sounded in the night and all three women looked toward the street in time to see Jessica being forced into a car several feet to the left.

"Hey!" Ellie yelled, charging down the steps. But before she could reach the sidewalk, a man had jumped behind the wheel of the car and started off.

"Oh, my God. Oh, my God," Shereen repeated.

Even Yolanda seemed to snap awake with the seriousness of the situation. "Holy shit! We have to do something."

All three ran to the road, but the dark car disappeared around a corner. Ellie waved her hands frantically at the next car that approached. It stopped, and a middle-aged black man stepped out of a late-model Volvo. "What's the matter?"

"Someone abducted our friend!" Ellie's voice sounded hysterical.

"It was a navy blue Honda," Shereen explained. "It turned left at the corner."

Ellie whimpered. "We have to get to her."

"Hop in," the man said, and they all did.

He burned rubber speeding on the campus road and didn't even pause at the stop sign as he made the left-hand turn.

"Who are you?" Yolanda asked belatedly, her tone wary.

"I'm a drama professor here at Howard. Professor Bell."

There was a collective sigh of relief. At least they were in good hands.

"There it is!" Shereen cried, spotting the back of the Honda in a dark archway between two buildings.

"Son of a bitch!" Ellie exclaimed.

Professor Bell backed up, killed his headlights, then turned down the cobblestone path behind the car. Almost before his own car was in park, he, Shereen, Ellie, and Yolanda were out of the car, storming toward the Honda. Professor Bell went for the driver's side, yanked the door open, and pulled out the young man. Ellie opened the passenger-side door and reached for Jessica.

Jessica was crying when she stumbled into Ellie's arms. "Oh, my God, Jessica. Did he hurt you?"

Jessica shook her head.

Ellie stormed around the car, Shereen on her heels. "You fuckin' son 'a bitch! What the hell is wrong with you?"

"I'm sorry, I'm sorry," was all he would say.

"You stay right here," Professor Bell told him, shoving him into the backseat of the car. Then he headed for Jessica. "Hey, there. I'm Professor Bell. Are you okay?"

Jessica nodded as she wiped her tears.

"Did he hurt you?"

"No. Not yet, anyway."

"I'm gonna call the campus police. Do you—"

"No," Jessica said. "We were both drinking, and I don't know . . . maybe I led him on."

"Jessica," Yolanda said. "For God's sake, don't make excuses for him."

"I just want to go back to my room."

Professor Bell went back to the student and said something to him they couldn't hear. Ellie, Shereen, and Yolanda huddled around Jessica, offering her comfort, assuring her that what had happened wasn't her fault.

Jessica managed a weak smile. "I'm just glad you got here when you did."

"You need to press charges," Yolanda told her.

Again, Jessica shook her head. "I don't want my parents to know about this. I don't want anybody to know."

"Jessica—"

"I'm serious. What if word gets back to Dean Big Sister Sharlene? We can kiss our chances of crossing over good-bye."

Yolanda sighed, frustrated. "You're probably right. God, I can't believe he'll get away with this."

Professor Bell returned. "I've talked to him. He swears he wasn't going to hurt you, that he thought you wanted to go somewhere private."

"Is that so?" Yolanda asked, starting for the driver's side.

Jessica grabbed her arm. "Forget it." Then she faced Professor Bell. "Please take me back to my dorm."

Everyone piled into the professor's Volvo, Ellie in the front seat, Yolanda, Shereen, and Jessica in the back. Jessica laid her head on Shereen's shoulder as the car moved off. Shereen softly stroked her back.

"So what if Dean Big Sister Sharlene gets pissed with us. I still think that asshole—"

"Not now, Yolanda," Shereen told her.

Professor Bell insisted on walking them all from his car to their dorm. Once inside, he told Jessica he needed to speak with her. Yolanda seemed wary even of the professor, but Jessica assured her and the others that she was all right, said a quick good-night to the group, then went to the common area with the professor. He might be a professor, but after tonight's incident, she wasn't about to allow him into her room.

She curled up on the armchair, and he sat opposite her on the sofa. "I'm sorry you had to go through that."

"It's not your fault."

"No," he said softly. "I guess not. You sure you're okay?"

"Uh-huh."

"You think you'll want to talk to someone about this?"

"You mean like a counselor?" When he nodded, Jessica said, "No. Honestly, he didn't hurt me. I'm fine. Just a little shaken up."

Silence. Then, "Look, I think you should report this incident. In fact, as a professor, I'm obligated—"

"Please," Jessica begged, and with that one word, she saw his face change. While it had been stern and professional a moment ago, it was now gentle and sensitive.

"Jessica, right?"

"Yeah." For the first time, Jessica noticed how attractive he was. Not in a drop-dead-gorgeous kind of way, but in a gentle, sincere sort of way. In his early-to-mid-forties, he was over six feet tall, with a well-toned physique. His narrow face was a rich chocolate brown. He had full, thick lips and deep-set eyes. Jessica's gaze lingered on his lips. . . .

"Jessica?"

"Huh?" Her eyes flew to his. She hoped he hadn't caught her staring.

"I think you should reconsider your decision. I don't feel good about letting this go."

"Please," she said again. "Believe me, I've learned my lesson. I won't ever get myself into that situation again. Just please . . . please promise me you won't say anything."

"All right," the professor said after a moment, and Jessica knew he would honor his word. "But if you ever need to talk, my name is Andrew Bell, and I'm in the drama department."

"Okay."

"In fact, why not call me on Monday? Let me know you're okay."

"I will be."

"Call me anyway."

Jessica smiled softly. She appreciated his concern, his persistence. Everyone had rallied around her tonight to protect her, and she was grateful to them all. "All right."

The professor stood, preparing to leave. "It's late. Get some rest."

"I will." Jessica stood to meet him as he turned. "And Professor Bell?"

He spun around, spoke quickly. "Call me Andrew."

"Oh, okay." Pause. "Andrew—thanks."

"Sure."

He stared at her, didn't say a word, just stared. Didn't move to leave. It was an awkward moment, and Jessica found she didn't know what to say. What could she say when her heart was suddenly beating faster than made sense? God, there was a spark between them, an instant attraction she couldn't explain. And it wasn't simply because he had helped save her tonight.

She wondered if he felt it, too.

She finally found a voice. "I'm glad you were there tonight."

"I'm glad I was working late." He smiled softly. "Call me Monday."

And then he turned, slowly, like he didn't want to go, and Jessica wondered if he'd stay all night and talk to her if she asked. Somehow, she knew he would.

But she didn't ask. It was better this way. Proper. So she watched him walk away, the most pleasant of sensations surging through her body.

Then he was gone.

But she'd call him. Oh, yes, she definitely would.

Chapter Four

AS IT HAD BEEN on the third Saturday night of every February for the past two decades, the banquet hall on the campus of Howard University was packed for the Theta Phi Kappa Black History Month celebration. The large room was elaborately decorated in the sorority's official colors, red and gold. Round tables were covered with red tablecloths, the chair backs tied with gold bows. A gold candle glowed from the center of every table and gold serviettes shaped to resemble flowers stemmed from every wineglass. The grand stage along one side of the hall had a red awning at its base with a trim of gold organza. And in the middle of the room hung a large red banner on which gold letters proclaimed: THETA PHI KAPPA: BLACK HISTORY IN THE MAKING.

Jessica stared around the dimly lit room in wonder. It looked even more stunning than it had last year. But perhaps she was biased. Because while the annual celebration was always special for her, tonight it would be even more so. For tonight, she was one of the few chosen to receive the distinguished Emily Bretton award, the highest honor a Theta Phi Kappa could receive for her work in the black community. Emily Bretton, one of the founding Thetas at Howard University in 1926, had exemplified the true ideal of the Theta Phi Kappa sorority by spending countless hours giving back to the black community in a selfless effort to give every underprivileged child a chance at a future.

Their arms linked, Jessica and her husband of the past year and a half, Douglas, strolled into the large room. Jessica was so high on excitement, she practically floated. Looking left and right, she scanned the room for her dearest friends. And then she spotted Shereen. Apparently, Shereen had seen her enter, because she now was scooting toward her.

Shereen, as usual, looked dynamite in a formfitting black velvet gown. Her shoulder-length hair was upswept and drop curls framed her delicate face. Jessica knew that the diva look came easily for Shereen, while she had to spend hours straightening her hair before she could even manage to get it into a decent style. Tonight, she couldn't be bothered with all that effort and had settled on wearing it in its natural kinky state, having gelled it to hold it down and give it a wet look.

"Hey, Q.T.," Shereen said, addressing Jessica by her sorority nickname. "Q.T." was short for Quiet Tongue, though some of the sisters had interpreted it to mean "cutie."

"Schlo Ho to the always lovely Sweet Thang," Jessica replied, greeting Shereen with their sorority's call, then wrapped her in a hug.

"Hello, Shereen." Douglas kissed her on the cheek when she pulled away from Jessica.

"I see you got your wife here in one piece."

"One beautiful piece," Douglas added, smiling down at Jessica. All his love for her was evident in that smile, reminding Jessica for the millionth time since she'd met him just how lucky she was.

"How are you holding up?" Shereen asked her.

She faced her friend once again. "Nervous."

"Don't be. You look gorgeous. Radiant. Just remember, this is your night."

"Thanks."

"Where are we sitting?" Douglas asked.

"Right up at the front by the stage, on the left side." Shereen pointed in that direction.

"Great. Now, if you ladies will excuse me, I'm going to powder my nose."

"You hush." Jessica playfully swatted Douglas's rump as he walked away. Then she sighed, content. He was such a wonderful man. She couldn't imagine her life without him. He filled her days and nights with laughter and sunshine.

"You two are so sweet."

Turning, Jessica beamed at Shereen. "I know. I'm so lucky." She linked arms with her friend. "Where's Ellie?"

"At the table. And you'll never believe this. She's with one of the finest-lookin' brothers I've seen in a long time."

"You mean she's not with Richard?" Jessica's syrupy tone conveyed her sarcasm.

Shereen smirked. "Guess he couldn't make it."

"Really? What a surprise. What about Yolanda?"

Shereen began walking, leading them toward their table. "No sign of her yet. She did say she was coming for sure, right?"

"Yep."

Shereen shrugged. "Well, you know Yolanda. She probably wants to make a statement."

"There is no fashion to her lateness. She just can't get her ass on the road in time."

Chuckling, Shereen pressed her face against Jessica's. "No doubt. In the meantime, let's meet Shelton."

"*That's* him?" Jessica asked as they neared the table where Ellie and her date sat, unable to believe her eyes. The dark-skinned brother was gorgeous as sin.

"What did I tell you?"

"Well," Jessica said succinctly. "Ellie brought a mystery man. Yolanda is bringing one. Looks like tonight is going to be full of surprises."

"Good evening, everyone." Antoinette Warren, president of the D.C. area Theta Phi Kappa alumnae sorority, spoke into the microphone at the stage's podium. The room quieted as everyone turned their attention to her. "Schlo Ho to the beautiful and talented ladies of the Theta Phi Kappa sorority." There was a chorus of "Schlo Ho" greetings in reply. "Welcome to our annual Black History Month celebration. Tonight, as you know, is about celebrating our heritage. But it's about more than that. It's about celebrating our history in the making. Because everything we do today affects tomorrow.

"Tonight, as well as celebrating our heritage, we will recognize some very special women who do good today for a better tomorrow. I know I speak for everyone when I say that we're proud of the achievements these sorors have made. These distinguished Theta Phi Kappas whole-heartedly believe in and demonstrate our sorority's motto: Each One Teach One. They have continued to work in their communities for the betterment of our people, in the areas of literacy, arts, and sciences. And like the extraordinary women who founded this sorority right here at Howard in 1926, the women we will celebrate tonight exemplify the true spirit and ideology of the Theta Phi Kappas."

An exuberant round of applause erupted across the hall. Douglas reached for Jessica's hand and gave it a squeeze.

"This year, four smart, beautiful and caring women have been chosen to receive the Emily Bretton award: Hilary Alton, Jessica Bedford, Arlene Moore, and Sheneska Williams. There are so many sorors who selflessly give to help others, but these four women are exemplary. And you know what's interesting? When I called them to tell them they were this year's award recipients, they were all surprised. No, I'm serious. They all said they thought others were more deserving. They didn't think their efforts were necessarily extraordinary. You know why? Because they're doing what they love. They don't work in their communities for the recognition they hope to receive or because they have to, but because they want to. And that, fellow sorors, ladies and gentlemen, is the true heart of the Theta Phi Kappas."

There was more applause. Jessica smiled—then blushed—when Shereen's and Ellie's loud cheers sounded above the rest of the crowd's. She really couldn't ask for better friends. Which made her wonder about Yolanda. She still hadn't arrived.

Shereen must have read her mind, for she leaned in close to her and whispered, "I don't know, Jess. Even this is a little late for Yolanda."

"Maybe she's stuck in traffic."

"God, I hope that's all it is."

"I'm sure. Remember, she's coming in from Philly, and if she's her classic late self, this is still early for her."

There was another round of applause, and both Jessica and Shereen clapped, though neither heard what the mistress of ceremonies had just said.

"I can't wait to see her," Shereen whispered. "And her new man, of course."

". . . it was Emily Bretton who envisioned a sorority of caring sisters, dedicated to making their communities better places to live. She believed that every child, no matter his or her circumstances, has the potential for greatness. She spent many hours in inner-city schools, mentoring children even the teachers had given up on. Years later, doctors, teachers, engineers, and many other successful blacks gave credit specifically to Emily Bretton for helping them realize that they could reach for the stars."

Another round of applause filled the room.

"Look who just walked through the door." Jessica and Shereen both stopped clapping and glanced at Ellie, then turned their heads in the direction she was looking. Though the entrance of the hall was at least fifty feet away, they could clearly see that Yolanda had arrived.

"Finally," Jessica said.

"Who is that?" Ellie asked. "He kinda looks familiar."

"I can't tell," Jessica replied. Not only was the hall's lighting dim, but Yolanda's mystery man had his back turned to them as he checked their coats.

Jessica turned back to the table, knowing she would see Yolanda's man soon enough. But the shocked look on Shereen's face, like she'd just seen a ghost, had her whipping back around to look at the couple once more.

"No." Shereen's voice was a horrified whisper. "Tell me she didn't."

"Oh, God." Ellie's eyes widened in disbelief. "She did."

"What?" Was Jessica the only one who didn't recognize him? She looked at Shereen again, but knew in an instant that her friend wasn't about to give her an answer. Her face had tensed into a hard expression as she stared at Yolanda and her date.

"I don't believe this," Shereen muttered between clenched teeth.

"Who is it?" Jessica asked, clapping out of habit when everyone else began to clap.

It was the way Shereen looked past her, like the only thing she could see was Yolanda and her date, that made her realize for the first time that something was really wrong.

Jessica turned around again. And suddenly she understood.

Yolanda had definitely made an entrance. Not only had she arrived late, she'd come to the event with Terrence Simms, Shereen's ex-boyfriend from college.

The one and only man Shereen had truly loved. And the one man who'd broken her heart without an explanation.

❖ ❖ ❖

Try as she might, Shereen didn't hear another word the mistress of ceremonies said. She didn't even hear what Jessica said when she went onstage to accept the Emily Bretton award for her dedication and work in the black community.

She couldn't.

All she could hear was the sound of the blood as it rushed in her ears, almost like the sound of an out-of-control train speeding toward an ultimate collision.

Terrence Simms. Lord have mercy.

He barely looked at her, which pissed her off even more than the fact that Yolanda had had the nerve to bring him. After everything they'd once meant to each other, she would have thought he'd at least give her a weak smile. Though why she was surprised, she had no clue. He'd dumped her without an explanation over nine years ago. She'd tried to talk to him then, had begged him to tell her what had gone wrong, but he had ignored her. Avoided her.

Of course he would do the same now.

Yet she couldn't stop sneaking glances at him. His golden brown skin was still smooth and flawless, his lips still full and sexy. In college, he had been clean-shaven, but now he wore a neatly trimmed goatee that framed that sexy mouth of his, almost imploring women to gaze at his lips. Even in the room's dim lighting, his eyes were still mesmerizing. He had the most striking eyes she'd ever seen, an odd mix of hazel and auburn, sprinkled with flecks of gold.

She caught herself looking for at least the hundredth time and tore her eyes away. Yeah, he looked good. Yeah, she doubted the suit he wore would look even half as good on anybody else. But so what? He was her past. Way, way past. She was over him.

Yet if that was the case, if she was truly over him, then why did it bother her that he was here with Yolanda? That Yolanda had secretly been dating him for the past several months?

Because Yolanda was her friend. How could a friend keep something like this from her?

Yolanda chuckled loudly enough for everyone at the table to hear, and Shereen couldn't help glancing her way. Terrence's sexy lips hovered near her ear as he told her something. And strong, no-nonsense Yolanda giggled like a smitten schoolgirl.

Shereen wanted to puke.

Instead, she reached for the bottle of Chardonnay. Finding it empty, she reached for the red—and she never drank red after drinking white.

She filled her glass almost to the rim, then took a long sip of the acrid liquid. As it trickled down to her stomach, she wished she had something stronger. Something that would make this whole night seem like a bad dream instead of reality.

Telling herself that it didn't matter, that she didn't care, she slumped back in her chair, folded her arms over her chest, and tried to concentrate on the soror who was now speaking at the podium.

But she could only hear the sound of steam as the locomotive in her blood continued to speed out of control.

"Shit," Ellie muttered when she saw Shereen heading toward her and Shelton on the dance floor. She'd just settled her head against Shelton's strong chest and was enjoying the feel of his arms wrapped around her.

"What is it, baby?"

"Shereen. God, she's drunk. And she's pissed."

Ellie stepped out of Shelton's arms but not before Shereen reached them. "You knew, didn't you?"

"No," Ellie replied, appalled. "Of course I didn't know. If I knew, don't you think I would have told you?"

"Nobody tells me anything. It's like everyone gets a kick out of sucker punching me." Shereen wobbled and Ellie reached for her.

"Shelton, give me a minute, will you?"

"Sure."

Ellie took Shereen's arm and led her through the crowd of dancing couples back to the table. Once there, Shereen reached for a bottle of wine, then another, and another. "Shit!" she exclaimed, finding them all empty.

"Sit down." Ellie forced her into a chair.

Shereen's eyes lit up as Ellie passed her a glass, but when she took a sip, she frowned. It was water.

"Drink it," Ellie told her.

Instead, Shereen rested her face in both palms. "It wouldn't have been so bad if I had known. At least I would have been prepared."

"I swear to you, Shereen. I had no clue. But I have to agree with you. I about spit out my salad when I saw her come in with Terrence."

"Why would she do this, Ellie? Why?"

"I don't know."

"I don't care," Shereen suddenly announced, but it was clear to Ellie that Shereen *did* care. It had been clear from the moment Yolanda had walked into the room with her former flame.

Shereen had sulked and drank half the wine at the table through the entire award presentations. Ellie doubted she'd heard a word anyone had said, not even Jessica. But she couldn't blame her friend. This was a low blow, especially from Yolanda. Yolanda, the one who had always told Ellie she should find her own man instead of a married one. Well, it seemed to Ellie that there were a lot of brothers in the sea. The last one Yolanda needed to get involved with was one of her best friend's exes.

"Where are they?" Shereen asked.

"Shereen—"

"Where?"

Ellie shrugged. "I don't know. Probably the dance floor."

"I'm going to be sick."

"Drink more water."

"No," Shereen said, turning away from the goblet Ellie extended to her. "God, no." Her head pounded at the same time her stomach lurched. She wanted to get out of there. Out of the crowd, the noise. "I'm going to the bathroom."

Ellie walked with her, an arm wrapped around her waist, and Shereen was glad for her comfort. It was nice to know she had a friend to hold her up when someone had just pulled the rug out from under her.

The stark white walls and bright lights were an assault on her eyes when Shereen entered the doorway of the bathroom. But it was also like a jolt of energy, zapping her back to life. She didn't feel quite so out of it as she had a moment ago.

". . . you're happy?"

Shereen stopped, listened. The haze in her mind cleared enough for her to realize the voice she'd just heard sounded like Jessica's.

"*Very,*" came the reply from a voice that sounded like Yolanda's.

"This bathroom is full," Ellie said lamely. She turned Shereen around. "Let's go to another one."

All doubts Shereen had over whether or not Jessica and Yolanda were around the corner vanished. She spun around. Ellie gripped her arm. But Ellie wasn't strong enough to stop her, wasn't strong enough to stop what had been set in motion from the moment Yolanda had entered the banquet hall. Shereen shook off Ellie's arm and stormed around the corner.

"We'll probably get married in the fa . . ." Yolanda's voice trailed off as she saw Shereen.

Married? Shereen stopped, wobbled. Felt bile rise in her throat. She wanted to throw up, and it wasn't because she'd had too much to drink.

Surprise flashed in Yolanda's eyes as they met Shereen's. The bright smile on her face faded, and for a moment, Shereen felt victorious. That's exactly what she wanted—to wipe that silly smile off her backstabbing friend's face.

But the smile returned as quickly as it had disappeared. "Shereen," Yolanda crooned, walking toward her, her arms widespread.

"*Married?*" Shereen asked, desperately wishing that she'd heard wrong, that it didn't matter. "You and Terrence are *engaged?*"

Yolanda looked dumbfounded, and for the first time in the years Shereen had known her, the opinionated, tough girl was seemingly at a loss for words. "Shereen, I didn't mean for—"

"Yes, you did." Her body shaking, Shereen took a step toward her. And before she could even think, she drew her hand back, much like a tennis player getting ready to strike a ball, then sprang it forth with all the strength she could muster, slapping Yolanda's face so hard it was like she wanted to knock her head off.

Which, at that moment, was exactly what she wanted to do.

The sound of the slap reverberated on the bathroom walls. Yolanda cried out as she went flying, her head spinning around so fast that Shereen could hardly believe what she'd done.

"Oh, my God!" Jessica exclaimed, reaching for Yolanda as she fell. But she couldn't catch her before she landed flat on her butt.

Feeling energized and powerful, Shereen took another step toward Yolanda. Immediately, Ellie was at her side, throwing her arms around her, holding her back.

"Shereen!" Ellie screamed. "Stop."

There were two other women in the bathroom's vanity area. They looked at Shereen with a mixture of fear and fascination before scrambling from the room.

Yolanda's chest rose and fell quickly with each angry breath. Her eyes shot fire at Shereen, but Shereen returned the look with one just as deadly. Yolanda didn't intimidate her. Not while she was the one sprawled on her back, nursing a busted lip.

Jessica shot Ellie a frantic look. "Get her out of here. Oh, God. I can't believe this."

There were a thousand things Shereen wanted to say as she and Yolanda stared each other down, a thousand questions she wanted answered, but she didn't say a thing. Instead, she turned on her heel and stalked out of the bathroom.

The slap had said all she'd wanted to say better than any words ever could have.

"My God, Yolanda. What happened?" Terrence stood when Yolanda returned to the table, his eyes instantly taking in her disheveled hair and swollen lip.

"Nothing."

He knew it was more than nothing. Minutes earlier, Shereen had stormed to the table, grabbed her purse, then hurried off before he'd had a chance to finally say hi. Given her sour expression, he'd guessed she and Yolanda might have had some type of confrontation. But this?

"Yolanda—"

"I said I'm fine, Terrence." Her tone said she didn't want to discuss this any further.

Shaking his head, Terrence pulled out Yolanda's chair for her. She slumped onto it. He was glad that everyone who'd been at their table had either left or was on the dance floor, because he intended to find out what had happened. "Did Shereen do this to you?"

Yolanda huffed. "Terrence, I already—"

"This is because of me."

"You are not responsible for Shereen's actions."

"Damn."

With her thumb, Yolanda twisted the engagement ring around and around her finger. Maybe if Shereen hadn't overheard the bit about her and Terrence being engaged . . . "How were any of us to know she'd act like an irrational fool?"

"Look at me." She did, and he gingerly fingered her cheek. "Damn, baby."

"It's no big deal." Having grown up in the projects, Yolanda had had her fair share of fights. Of course, that was a long time ago . . . and this fight was entirely different.

Terrence groaned loudly. His eyes flitted to the hall's entrance, then back to Yolanda.

"Is she gone?"

He nodded. "Do you know if she's driving?"

Yolanda shrugged.

"I'll be right back." Terrence stood and headed for the front doors.

"Shereen's a big girl," Yolanda said to his back, but he didn't hear her. Thank God, she realized a moment later. The last thing she wanted was to sound petty and jealous. Just because Shereen had slapped the crap out of her didn't mean she wished her harm.

Yolanda blew out a hurried breath, then glanced down at the stunning marquise-shaped diamond engagement ring on her left hand. Every time she saw it, it gave her a little pause. Like she couldn't quite believe it was actually hers. Even in the low lighting of this room, it was breathtaking. Just the kind of ring she'd always wanted.

But now, seeing it made her feel a twinge of guilt.

She dropped her hands to her lap. So what if Terrence was Shereen's ex? They'd dated eons ago. Surely, Shereen had to be over him by now.

The coppery taste of blood filled her mouth, and Yolanda brought a hand to her face, gently touching her swollen lip. She felt the beginnings of a welt on her cheek.

"What were you thinking?"

Yolanda's head snapped up. Above her, Ellie stood with both hands planted on her hips, her head moving from side to side in obvious disapproval. "Not now, Ellie."

"I can't believe you did this to her. After the way you always get on my case about Richard . . ."

Yolanda reached for her water glass. "I said, not now."

When Ellie didn't reply, Yolanda was surprised. Ellie wasn't one to back down from a confrontation with her. But when she glanced up at Ellie once more, she saw that her friend—or ex-friend; who knew right now—was staring at something behind her. Yolanda turned. And smiled. Terrence.

"She's gone," he announced.

Yolanda's smile faded. There was something about the way he said that that unnerved her. And she didn't like the frown that marred his handsome features. She stared at him, trying to figure him out, but he was staring at the table. Great, now he was avoiding her.

"Shereen's a smart woman," she told him. "I'm sure she wouldn't drive in her condition."

He looked at her then, reached for her face. Delicately, he fingered her swollen lip. His touch, his gentleness, almost made the injury worth it. Which was a pathetic thought for someone who prided herself on not needing a man to be happy.

"This looks painful."

"I'll be fine."

"*Excuse* me," Ellie said pointedly, then turned and walked away. Yolanda watched her go. Well, obviously Ellie had taken Shereen's side.

This wasn't about sides. This was about life. Shereen needed to get one and get over living in the past.

"You want to leave?" Terrence asked her.

"Why?"

He gave her an isn't-it-obvious look.

She ran a hand down the length of his chest. "Baby, this party is just beginning." To prove her point, she jumped up and grabbed his hand. "Let's dance."

"You want to dance?"

"Why not?"

"If you're sure."

"I'm sure."

But even as she led Terrence to the dance floor, moving her hips to a funky old-school beat, she couldn't escape the feeling of guilt that wrapped around her heart.

Chapter Five

"I HAD NO CLUE," Jessica told Ellie later that evening as they stood in the bathroom once again—this time, minus Shereen and Yolanda.

"Talk about a fuckin' surprise." Ellie took a long drag off her cigarette, then dropped her hand to her side, keeping the cigarette low so it wouldn't bother Jessica. "I swear she did this shit on purpose."

"Why?" Jessica reached into her small black purse and withdrew her lipstick.

"Gimme a break. You know exactly why she did this. To hurt Shereen." Ellie inhaled another puff off the cigarette, then blew the smoke out of both her nose and mouth. "This smells like payback to me."

"For that whole stupid incident back in school?"

"You know Yolanda never did forgive Shereen for that."

"I don't know." Leaning into the mirror, Jessica applied fresh burgundy lipstick to her mouth, then pressed her lips together. "This is all too juvenile for me."

"Tell me about it." Ellie recalled the night's events, feeling as though the whole sordid scenario was some bizarre dream. "I hate the way she did this. It was so sneaky. So . . . deliberate. She didn't say a thing to you, nor to me. Why would she keep the fact that she was seeing Terrence a secret when we all knew him? It's like she was planning to drop the bomb in person, just to see how Shereen would react."

"She says she's happy."

Ellie scowled. "I'm sure she is. Did you see her on the dance floor? You'd think nothing happened."

"I don't know." Jessica dropped her lipstick back into her purse, then faced Ellie. "God, I hope Yolanda knows what she's doing."

"So do I." Ellie took a final drag off the cigarette, then ground it out in the ashtray. Turning, she faced her image in the mirror. And frowned. "God, I've gotta lose some weight."

"Looks like you've lost a lot already."

"Yeah. I've cut back on the junk food." She didn't add, *Because of Shelton,* because she didn't have to. Everyone knew she always cut down on junk food when her love life was content. She turned to get a side view of her body, then held up an arm and pinched the flab. After a moment, Ellie dropped her arm to her side. "You think Shereen's okay?"

"I hope so."

"She took off before I could stop her." Ellie sighed. "I hope she didn't drive. She was way too drunk for that."

"I should call her."

"She and Yolanda need to work this out."

"I thought they had."

"So did I. I still don't know what Yolanda was thinking. And not telling any of us?"

"They'll get through this," Jessica assured her. "The Fabulous Four always do."

"I guess so." But Ellie's voice relayed doubt.

"How many disagreements have we had over the years?"

"Too many to count."

"Exactly. We're different. We don't always agree. But like sisters, we still love each other. Sure we fight, but we get over it."

"I hope you're right." Ellie didn't point out that this situation was quite different from past ones, that even she wasn't sure Shereen should forgive Yolanda for what could only be construed as a deliberate and calculated plan to hurt her. But that was Jessica, always looking at the positive side. If Yolanda had done this to her, one apology and Jessica would forgive her in a heartbeat. Jessica was sweet to the core and didn't hold grudges. Ellie would have probably done a lot more than smack Yolanda if she'd been in Shereen's shoes. And Shereen—well, she'd fight when push came to shove, but she hated confrontation and was probably already feeling guilty for what she'd done.

"Well, I've gotta go. Douglas is waiting for me."

"Gonna get your groove on." Ellie made a winding motion with her hips.

"You know it." Jessica laughed. "Give me a hug."

Ellie wrapped her arms around her friend. "Congratulations again, Ms. Distinguished Soror of the Year. You deserve it."

"Thanks."

"And have fun tonight." Ellie giggled. "I know I will."

Jessica threw Ellie a sideways glance as they strolled toward the bathroom's exit. "We'll have to talk about Mr. Tall, Dark and Sinfully Gorgeous later."

"Of course." Ellie slowed, stopped. "Oh, Jess. I really hope he's the one. So far, he's been nothing but sweet. I still can't believe he likes me."

"Why wouldn't he like you?"

Ellie shrugged. "I don't know."

"Ellie . . ." Jessica shook her head slowly, clearly disapproving of Ellie's unspoken insecurity. "You're beautiful. You're fun."

"Spoken like a biased friend."

"You are. Shelton clearly has great taste."

"You like him?"

"What's not to like? He's charming. Gorgeous. And best of all, he's not Richard."

"I know." Ellie resumed walking. Her instant attraction to Shelton had surprised her, considering how hung up she'd been on Richard for the past months. But she and Richard didn't have a future. It was time she got over him. "I'm making progress, aren't I?"

"You've made progress before."

"Yeah, well, this time I'm serious." Ellie moved aside to make way for three women entering the bathroom, then continued walking. "Richard knows it's over."

"Let's hope so."

"You watch." They stepped into the darkened banquet hall. "I'm gonna prove to everyone that I can exist without him."

"I know you can." Jessica gave her a peck on the cheek. "Gotta go, hon. Call me tomorrow."

"Okay." Ellie hugged her torso as she watched Jessica disappear into the crowd of mingling guests, then jumped when she felt two strong hands encircle her waist.

Shelton. He'd been waiting for her outside the bathroom.

God, he really was sweet.

"Hey, baby," he said, bending to whisper in her ear. "You ready to get out of this place?"

Shereen was gone. Jessica was leaving. She didn't see Yolanda around, and quite frankly, wasn't in the mood to talk to her anyway.

Turning in Shelton's arms, she snaked her arms around his neck. "What did you have in mind?"

He ran his fingers down her back, cupping her butt. "You know what I have in mind, baby."

Ellie's eyes fluttered shut at the way the word *baby* reverberated in her ear, like a call of passion her body couldn't ignore. "I'm ready when you are."

"Let's go."

Shereen bolted upright, instantly startled awake. The quick tempo of her breathing matched the pounding in her head, making her wonder if she'd had a bad dream—or if something else had jarred her from sleep. A feeling of unease gripped her heart, like something was wrong, like she shouldn't be here. She tried to focus her eyes in the dark room, but instead felt disoriented, like the room was spinning and she was falling. Oh, God. Where was she? What was wrong?

She squeezed her eyes shut, counted to three, reopened them. She saw her dresser, her chaise. Her bedroom, she realized, her shoulders sagging with relief. She was home.

Home. Yet why didn't that realization ease her mind?

She glanced down. Saw that she was on top of her bedspread. Wearing an evening gown.

The party.

Oh, shit. The party.

Groaning, she slowly lay back, snippets of the night gone by zapping in and out of her mind too quickly for her to truly grasp anything. What had happened? How had she made it home? She didn't remember driving. Had she taken a cab? Had someone driven her?

Hell if she knew, which was a scary thought. She never got so drunk that she completely lost her mind. Well, that wasn't exactly true; there had been that night with Aaron—which she totally regretted. And okay, maybe there was one time in college. Two, max. All times she'd been particularly stressed. All times she'd promised herself the morning after that she'd never drink so much again. Other than those times that she could count on one hand, getting totally wasted really wasn't her style. So why had she done it tonight? Gently, she squeezed her forehead as if that could help her remember.

Instead, she felt woozy again, so once again she closed her eyes. Whatever had happened, she'd have to think about it later. Because right now, all she could think about was the fact that her head throbbed and her mouth tasted like bile. And Lord help her, her stomach was so nauseated, she knew that if she moved even an inch, she could retch any second.

She needed water, but she couldn't get it without moving. She contemplated calling her brother, Shaun, into her bedroom, but dismissed that thought a moment later. The last thing she needed was for him to use this against her. And he would. She could picture it now—when she got on his case for drinking, he'd bring up this night. "Oh, I can't have a few beers, but you can get pissed out of your mind?" No, she was on her own.

So she lay still, hoping the nausea and headache would quickly subside. Images floated into her mind—of Terrence dancing with Yolanda, of her slapping Yolanda upside the head. God, had she really slapped Yolanda? It was all so hazy right now, she couldn't be sure if what she recalled was actual memory or a dream.

She had a gut feeling it had happened. Or maybe that was simply her gut heaving, she realized as she felt the first spasm. She jumped from the bed and scrambled to the bathroom.

"What's the matter?" Yolanda asked. "You've been quiet ever since we left the party."

Terrence looked up at her from where he sat hunched forward on the edge of the hotel bed. "I'm just tired."

Yolanda was about to counter that his "fatigue" seemed to have started practically from the moment Shereen had run from the party, but thought better of it. She didn't want to ruin the evening. Instead, she loosened the belt on her silk robe, letting the folds fall apart to reveal a sexy white negligee.

Terrence's eyes widened with appreciation, and Yolanda smiled. Whoever said that the way to a man's heart was through his stomach was wrong—sex was the way to his heart. Yolanda strutted toward him. She wrapped her arms around his neck as she sat on his lap, positioning her body so that his face rested in her bosom.

"I hope you're not *too* tired," she whispered, then lowered her lips to his.

The kiss was soft and slow at first, but quickly grew more intense. Placing her hands on his chest, Yolanda urged Terrence backward on the bed, then lay on top of him. She reached for his thigh, wanting more of him, needing more, until she realized that while her mouth moved hungrily over his, his lips had gone still. Damn, she might as well be kissing a blow-up doll. She opened her eyes and looked down at him. He sighed.

"What's the matter?"

"I don't know." His eyes roaming over her face, he stroked her swollen cheek. "It's been a long night." He eased her off him, sat up. "I'm sorry, sweetheart."

For a moment, Yolanda was speechless. Then, she said, "You think I should have told her."

He faced her, his expression suddenly serious. "Yeah, I do. But I told you that already. You wouldn't listen."

"And just why do you care?" Yolanda couldn't help asking, knowing she sounded lame. "They're *my* friends."

"God, Yolanda." Terrence shot up from the bed. "Forget it. Forget I brought it up."

Yolanda watched helplessly, angrily, as he stalked across the carpet and disappeared into the bathroom. What the hell was that about?

Frustrated, she slipped beneath the covers on the far edge of the bed and rolled onto her side so her back would be to him.

To tell the truth, she wasn't in the mood for sex, either. She had hoped that sex would help her forget the night's events, but in truth it would only delay her thinking about them. Now, as she lay quietly on the bed, listening to the sound of Terrence brushing his teeth in the bathroom, the reality of everything that had happened came crashing down on her.

She'd never seen Shereen so angry. So . . . hurt.

Her hand went to her cheek. It was still tender. At first she'd been furious with Shereen for hitting her. Now she just felt sad.

Maybe Terrence was right. Maybe she'd handled things the wrong way. She probably should have told Shereen that she'd met Terrence months ago, that they'd started dating. She'd kept it a secret because she hadn't been sure how Shereen would react to the news, but surprising her the way she had tonight by bringing him to the party without any warning—it's no wonder Shereen had been livid. Why hadn't Yolanda simply told her?

It wasn't like she'd pursued Terrence in a deliberate attempt to hurt her friend. In fact, she hadn't planned on dating him when they'd met, much less getting engaged to him within six months. It had just happened.

But deep in her heart, hadn't she known that getting involved with Terrence would be trouble? Yet she'd done it anyway when she should have put a stop to it. To be honest, there was a side of herself Yolanda didn't quite understand—a side she didn't necessarily like. Hell, Shereen had every right to be angry with her. Right now, she was even angry with herself.

When the bathroom door opened, Yolanda lay still, feigning sleep. Disappointment tickled her stomach when Terrence climbed into the bed beside her and didn't get close. She didn't have to look to know he'd turned his back to her.

As she'd done to him. What did she expect?

He switched off the lamp, shrouding the room in darkness. Yolanda should turn to him and apologize, end the tension. But it was Shereen she was thinking about now. It was the pain in her friend's eyes that she couldn't forget. She suddenly felt like she was sleeping with the enemy. Shereen was her girl. They went too far back to let another man come between them.

God, what had she done? She'd have to call Shereen tomorrow. They'd have to work this out.

"Come here."

In the darkness of their bedroom, Jessica reached for and accepted

Douglas's extended hand. He pulled her toward him, wrapped her in his arms, and planted a soft kiss on her forehead.

"Congrats again, sweetheart."

"Mmm." A little sigh escaped her. "Thank you."

He dropped his head, running his lips along her jawbone, then lower, to the base of her neck. "God, you're so beautiful."

Jessica closed her eyes as Douglas tilted her head back. She tried to block out all the negative thoughts of the evening and savor the feel of his mouth on her neck, his lips on her lips. But like a movie playing in her mind, all she could see was the horrible moment when Shereen had slapped Yolanda, then Yolanda flying backward. As much as they'd argued in the past, none of them had ever hit one of the others. Maybe she'd been premature in her hopes that Shereen and Yolanda could resolve this.

"You're not into this," Douglas said after a moment.

"I'm sorry."

He ran his hands down both her arms, taking her hands in his. "They'll be fine."

Her lips curling in a faint smile, Jessica looked up at her husband. Though the room was dark, the moon provided dim lighting, enough to see his handsome features and the gentle expression he always wore. Now, that expression offered assurance, assurance she desperately craved.

"I hope so," she said softly.

"Hey, it wouldn't be normal if you never fought."

"I know. And it's not like we haven't fought before. But this . . . this is different." She'd told Douglas about the slap, but he hadn't made any judgment. He'd simply been a sounding board for her disappointment. "It's been so long since we've all been together. This was the last thing that should have happened."

"Mmm-hmm."

"On one hand, I don't blame Shereen. I mean, I was stunned when I saw Yolanda walk in with her old flame. But then I think she *slapped* Yolanda. Actually slapped her. God."

"Sweetheart?"

"Hmm?"

Douglas pressed his forehead against hers.

"Oh, God. I'm spoiling the mood, aren't I?"

"Maybe just a little." But there was a smile in his voice.

She chuckled softly. "I'm sorry. You should have stopped me."

"Hey, I tried to shut you up."

More laughter. "I guess you did."

"Mmm-hmm." With a thumb, he gently lifted her chin so that her eyes met his. And then he smiled at her, his brown eyes crinkling in that special way that always made her feel so loved.

And never failed to turn her on.

So this time when he kissed her, slowly and passionately, and her arms encircled the wide expanse of his chest, she forgot all about Shereen and Yolanda and the party and even her award. This time, she simply concentrated on Douglas, the man she loved.

It was one of life's greatest tragedies: a gorgeous black man with a tall, lean frame, a killer body, and a beautiful smile—but one incredibly small penis.

Still, Ellie tried to smile when he moved toward her, suppressing the urge to ask, "Is that all you've got?"

Size doesn't matter, she told herself. *It's not the size of the boat but the motion of the ocean.* And with a body like his, certainly he would know how to use it.

Closing her eyes, she concentrated on those thoughts and let Shelton kiss her. Let him touch her where she wanted to be touched. Let him make her hot.

Then she let him make love to her. And she was pleasantly surprised, because the sex was good—*very* good—despite his small penis. So as he continued to love her, Ellie couldn't help hoping—praying—that he was the one.

Chapter Six

THERE ARE SOME DAYS when you just want to ask God to turn back the clock and give you a chance to start the day again. Forget the day. Today, Shereen wanted to ask God for the chance to start her life over.

If she could have that wish, she would erase from history the day she'd met Aaron Carter. The man was determined to make her life a living hell. She'd also make sure she was an only child. She loved her brother, but right now he was getting on her last nerve. If Shaun's antics didn't kill her, Shereen might just end up killing him.

This morning, she'd nearly had heart failure when Aaron Carter's lawyer had called and hinted at a wrongful dismissal suit. Once she'd caught her breath, she'd *hinted* right back that she'd see Aaron in court for sexual harassment if he went forward with his bogus claim, and assured Mr. Speropoulos that unlike his client, she had the proof. When Aaron called her barely an hour later and asked if she'd give their relationship another chance—and promised he wasn't serious about that "court stuff"—she should have been surprised, but she wasn't. With a full moon, anything was possible. Besides, her horoscope had predicted the first few months of the new year would be crazy at best. "You're deranged," she'd told Aaron. "If you so much as breathe my name aloud, I'll see you in court. And if you ever call me again, show up here, or try to contact me in any way, I'll slap you with a restraining order." After she hung up, she'd said a silent prayer that that would be the end of him.

Other than that, the day at the office had been going fairly well. Until she'd learned of Shaun's latest stunt—and her body temperature had shot through the roof. Not even the cold March air had cooled her down as it stung her face through her open car window. She'd tried to contain her anger as she drove home, but because it was the evening rush hour, she'd had nothing but time to think about Shaun and what he'd done—and the closer she'd gotten to her neighborhood, the more livid she'd become.

So when she entered her town house that evening and found Shaun stretched out on the living room sofa, his size-thirteen feet hanging over the armrests, she marched straight toward him and knocked his feet onto the floor.

"Hey!" Shaun protested.

"What the hell were you thinking?"

"What?" Shaun gave her a confused look as he sat up.

She shoved her latest invoice from American Express into his face. "This."

"What's that?"

"Don't you dare." She dropped the invoice onto his lap. "Jamaica? You told me you went to Baltimore to look for a job. Instead you were soaking up the sun at a resort in Montego Bay. On *my* tab. Who do I look like, Ed McMahon?"

As if he had no idea what she was talking about, he studied the bill. "Damn."

"Damn?" She snatched the bill from his fingers. "You put two thousand dollars on my credit card and all you have to say is damn?"

"I'm gonna pay you back."

"You're gonna pay me back," she repeated dryly. "How, Shaun? You don't even have a job!"

"I'm working on one."

"What?"

"I've got a couple of interviews lined up."

She knew he was lying. He didn't need to work, not when he had a sister to sponge off of. "And just how were you able to charge my card? Surely travel agencies need to verify the signature like every other place of business."

Shaun shrugged. "I booked it over the Internet. I didn't really think it would go through, but they didn't ask for a signature or anything. I used only my first initial, and because both our names start with *S*, I suppose that made it easy."

"Easy." Shereen huffed.

"I don't mean it like that. Look, Shereen—"

"What you did was wrong, Shaun. You didn't ask me, you just used my credit card. That's fraud."

She stormed into the kitchen, and he was instantly behind her, his six-foot-eight-frame looming over her. "You're not gonna do anything stupid, are you?"

"Like have your butt thrown in jail?"

"C'mon, Shereen. I'm sorry."

"Oh," she said slowly, dramatically. "Now you're sorry."

"I'm gonna pay you back."

"You better believe you're gonna pay me back." Though in truth, Shereen wasn't about to hold her breath.

She opened the fridge and grabbed the container of orange juice. Then scowled at her brother when she found it had less than a few spoonfuls left. Cancer men—God, were they ever annoying. She'd bet Aaron was a Cancer like her brother. She chucked the container into the trash.

"Sorry," Shaun said. "I didn't have time to go shopping."

"Whatever." For a man who didn't have a job, Shaun certainly didn't have time to do anything. His breakfast dishes were still piled in the sink. He hadn't put up the pictures she'd asked him to hang over a month ago. No doubt the laundry still needed to be done.

Shereen reached for the bottle of distilled water and filled a glass. She couldn't live like this anymore. Down on his luck, her brother had moved in with her *temporarily* eleven months ago. Just until he found another job, he'd promised. For eleven months, he hadn't been able to find and keep a job because the wages were too low, the bosses were racist, the bosses were jerks, the hours weren't right. You name it, Shaun had thought of the excuse. Now, Shereen knew the real reason why he couldn't find and keep a job: her brother was lazy. She'd seen his lazy ass stretched across the sofa one time too many to deny that fact.

What angered her was the fact that her brother hadn't always been lazy. In college, he'd been a tremendous athlete, heading for a career in the NBA. But a night of partying after a college game win had turned tragic, with her brother getting into a car accident. He'd survived but busted his knee, killing any dreams he'd had of superstardom as an athlete.

Now, he was bitter. She sympathized with him, but it had been eight years since the accident, and it was time for him to take control of his life again.

"Shaun, you know I love you, but I can't keep living like this. If you don't have a job by the end of the week, I want you gone."

"Gone?" He stared at her like she had lost her mind. "Where am I supposed to go?"

"I don't know." She wasn't about to tell him that she really wouldn't kick him out. This tactic would be pointless if he knew she was bluffing.

"Man, you're not being fair."

"I haven't had a vacation in years, yet you went to Jamaica for some fun-filled raunchy holiday and you don't have a job. *That's* not fair, Shaun. I may be your sister, but I'm not going to be a sucker for the rest of my life. You want to be someone's dependent, you go back to Mom and Dad's."

"Like I can do that."

"Exactly. So you shouldn't be able to do it with me, either."

"Why are you being like this? I'm family. You know if the shoe was on the other foot, I'd be there for you. Damn, you know I was gonna take care of all of you. Give you everything. If it wasn't for the accident . . ."

"You heard what I said," Shereen told him.

"Oh, man," Shaun muttered.

Shereen downed the water, placed the glass in the sink, then left Shaun to his thoughts. She didn't want to hear all his excuses as to why he couldn't get a job that quickly, why she should feel sorry for him.

She was almost at her bedroom door when she heard Shaun's voice. "Shereen?"

"What, Shaun?" She couldn't hide her frustration.

"I forgot to tell you. Someone called for you."

Descending the stairs, she retraced her steps until she was back in the living room. "Who?"

"Some friend. What's her name again?"

Home all day and he couldn't even take a message. He needed to stop wasting his brain on trashy television talk shows.

"Yolanda," he said, snapping his fingers.

Shereen's stomach fluttered at her friend's name. "Yolanda? You're sure?"

"Yeah."

"Did she say what she wanted?"

"Naw. Only that she'd call back."

Shereen hadn't spoken to Yolanda since the fiasco at the Black History Month event two weeks ago. Yolanda had called twice and left messages saying she was sorry for all that had happened, that she wanted to talk to her and would Shereen please call her back, but Shereen hadn't. She'd been too angry.

And too stubborn.

Maybe it was irrational, but Shereen figured Yolanda shouldn't have left an apology about something so sensitive on her answering machine. Not only that, but every time Yolanda had called, Shereen had been at the office. Coincidence? Hardly. Shereen couldn't help wondering if Yolanda didn't actually want to talk to her—or if she simply didn't have the guts to call when she'd be home. And if it was a matter of not having the guts, why should Shereen make it easier for her by being the one to call her back so *she* could apologize?

Besides, talking to Yolanda meant hearing about her relationship with Terrence, and those intimate details Shereen could live without.

Still, she wasn't happy with the way things were. Despite her anger over what had happened, she wanted to resolve this situation with Yolanda. She hated the tension between them. She hated the fact that the last time she'd spoken with Jessica, Jessica had started to talk about Yolanda, then quickly bitten her tongue. She hated the uneasy feeling in her stomach right now, all because Shaun had said Yolanda had called. It never used to be like this, and it wasn't right. They'd been friends.

They *were* friends . . . weren't they?

God, Shereen didn't even know.

All she knew was that every time she thought of that night, she felt horrible. Yes, she'd been angry—and rightfully so—but she was embarrassed by the way she'd behaved. Slapping Yolanda had been so . . . immature. She'd been drinking more than normal, but she couldn't completely blame her actions on the alcohol. Quite frankly, Shereen hadn't believed Yolanda's interest in Terrence was genuine. Engagement ring or no engagement ring. Despite the fact that they'd been friends for years, after that incident with Lawrence back in college where Yolanda thought she'd wanted her man, Yolanda had always seen her as some sort of rival. Shereen had figured Terrence was merely a pawn in Yolanda's game of payback.

It had taken Shereen the last two weeks to realize that she didn't care. Years had passed since Terrence had walked out on her without an explanation, so why should it matter to her whom he dated now? If Yolanda wanted him—even if her motives weren't completely noble— by all means, she could have him.

"Did she say whether or not she was in town?" Shereen asked Shaun.

Shaun shook his head. "Only that she'd call you back."

Shereen drew in a deep breath and blew it out in a rush. Butterflies still danced in her stomach. Maybe they always would until this situation was resolved.

Still, she wasn't quite ready to call Yolanda. Not tonight, anyway. She'd had too rough of a day. But if Yolanda called her again—and she found herself hoping she would—Shereen would be ready to talk to her.

And set this situation right once and for all.

Chapter Seven

PALE MOONLIGHT. A WHISPER of wind. Like lovers in the night, they meet in the large oak tree outside the bedroom window, Moonlight caressing the bare branches, Wind fondling them. Their love, tangible and real, flows through the tree's limbs, making them quiver with delight, creating a pattern of dancing shadows and light across the bed.

For a long while, Jessica lay still and awake, unable to sleep. She watched the shadows and light as they moved in a sensual rhythm across Douglas's bare chest. How many times had she and Douglas made love with the moonlit branches of the oak dancing across their naked bodies?

There was something magical about making love under the moon-light, a oneness with not just each other but with nature. Yet tonight had been different. While Douglas had given her all of himself, even more so than he'd done in the past, Jessica had held back. Douglas hadn't noticed—thank God—yet she still felt awful.

Because she'd lied to him. And now she didn't know what to do.

As her hand lay flat on Douglas's chest, she could feel the steady beat of his heart. He was sleeping, she was sure, but she watched the rise and fall of his chest and listened to the heavy sounds of his breathing a little longer, to be doubly sure.

Slowly, she lifted her hand. He didn't budge. Satisfied that she wouldn't wake him, Jessica quietly slipped out of his embrace and off the bed. Her feet sank into the plush carpeting as she stood. Feeling like a thief in the night, she stole a glance at him over her shoulder, and her heart nearly split in two.

But that didn't stop her. In the darkness, she made her way across the bedroom. She slipped soundlessly into the en suite bathroom and locked the door behind her. She stood for a moment in the pitch-black room, giving herself the chance to change her mind. But then she flicked on the light, opened one of the sink's drawers, and reached way back to find her packet of birth control pills. She popped a pill into her palm and stared at it for a good five seconds before throwing her head back and dropping it into her mouth. Though it tasted bitter, she swallowed it without water so she wouldn't make any noise.

Then felt guilty as hell.

Tonight, before they'd made love, Douglas had told her he was ready for a baby. Shock washing over her, Jessica's mouth had fallen open, but she hadn't been able to form any words.

"Hmm? What do you think?" Douglas had asked.

"A baby?"

"Yeah," he'd said, then stroked her cheek. "A little you or a little me running around."

Jessica hadn't been able to look him in the eye. *God, a baby?*

"What do you say?" he asked.

"I don't know." Her career had only just begun. In television especially, a pregnant woman was practically a no-no. "There's the show to consider."

"You won't lose your job, if that's what you're worried about."

Douglas was a longtime producer at the station, and in truth, Jessica owed her job as host of *The Scoop* to him. With her limited on-camera experience, the station might not have hired her if she hadn't been Douglas's wife.

"No, I guess not . . ."

"That's assuming you want to work once you have the baby."

Once you have the baby . . . He was speaking as if she were already pregnant.

"I can give you everything you want and need, so you certainly won't have to work. But that's up to you."

They had a gorgeous house in the elite Gold Coast section of Washington. Between them, they had three luxury cars. No, she wouldn't want for anything if she gave up her job, and it meant the world to her that Douglas wanted to give her everything, to take care of her.

She knew Douglas would make a good father. It was one of the qualities that had attracted her to him. That and the fact that he'd shown so much love and respect for his mother. The two were very close, and Jessica knew he wanted to finally give her a grandchild.

"You're really ready?"

"I'm not getting any younger."

No, he wasn't. Douglas was forty-four, fourteen years her senior. She'd known when she married him eighteen months ago that he'd be ready for children before she was because of his age, and she'd been okay with that. Mostly because the idea of children had seemed so far away.

Now . . .

"I can't tell you how happy it would make me."

And Douglas had already made her so happy, given her so much. So, in that moment, she'd smiled up at him and said, "Yes, Douglas. I want to have your baby. Our baby."

And now she was in the bathroom taking her birth control pill.

She replaced the pills in the back corner of the drawer. Douglas never went through her toiletries, but there was no point in taking chances.

Minutes later, she was back in their bed, back beside her husband, listening to the comforting sound of his breathing as he slept.

He was a good man, and she truly wanted to make him happy, give back to him because he had given her so much, but she couldn't do this. The moment he'd started kissing her she had realized she was far from ready to get pregnant. The very thought of having a baby brought back memories of the last time. A last time Douglas knew nothing about.

And if he did, God only knew if he'd want anything to do with her.

"*This* Saturday?" Jessica asked Phillip. They sat on opposite sides of the desk in his office. "As in two days from now?"

"Yeah," Phillip replied. "Will that work for you?"

Jessica considered the information. It was short notice, but she had most of the day clear. "What time?"

"Around noon."

"Hmm. Noon's not a good time."

"That's the time Mitchell Wright said he's available."

Since she'd received the Emily Bretton award just over two weeks ago, two newspapers and one radio station had interviewed her. Now, Mitchell Wright, a staff reporter with the *Washingtonian* magazine, wanted to do a feature on her. She was flattered by the attention, but also overwhelmed. None of the three other award recipients were getting any media attention. But she was Jessica Bedford, host of WGRZ's morning entertainment show, suddenly important because she was a television personality.

"If that's the only time he's available, then I can't do it."

Surprise flashed in Phillip's eyes, as though he thought she was crazy for turning down this kind of exposure. "I already told them you would."

"Phillip." Jessica looked at him long and hard, then sighed. "You just asked if Saturday was good for me, now you say you've confirmed the interview?" She'd never understand this man.

"He wanted an answer right away. This is the *Washingtonian*, Jessica. I didn't think you'd say no."

"It's not that I'm saying no." Rising, Jessica walked to the side window and peered through the glass. Phillip's corner office overlooked the studio's courtyard. In the spring and summer, the view was stunning, with lots of colorful flowers and greenery; now it was lifeless, gray and bleak. While February had held the promise of spring, thus far March promised more winter. It would be weeks before flowers bloomed and anyone ate lunch outside. "I'm sure you meant well," she said, turning to face him. "But I wish you would have asked me. I'm busy every Saturday from eleven till one, helping children learn how to read. I thought you knew that."

Phillip didn't answer. Instead, he said, "Maybe they can interview you there."

"No," Jessica said without hesitation. Obviously, Phillip *had* remembered her Saturday commitment. He'd probably suggested noon to the reporter. He'd do anything for ratings. "I don't want to turn the school into some media sideshow."

"Think about it. You received an award for your work in the community. What better place to be interviewed than where you actually volunteer?"

It wasn't a bad idea. And perhaps more of D.C.'s movers and shakers, the type of people who read the *Washingtonian*, would follow her example, mentor a child or two. "I don't know."

"That's the kind of thing they're going to want, anyway. Pictures of you in action to accompany the article."

"Maybe," Jessica conceded, returning to the chair. "If they show up near the end of my day. That way I won't lose time with the children. I can do the interview after one o'clock, and they can still get the pictures they need."

"You really care about them, don't you?"

"The children?"

He nodded.

The question wouldn't have surprised her if it had come from a white person. But because it came from a black man who knew the plight of Washington's inner-city children, she was disappointed.

"Of course I care. Somebody's gotta give back, Phillip. Somebody's gotta care about the future of our people."

He pressed his lips together tightly. Her comment had hit its mark.

Jessica stood. "I've got to get back to my notes for tomorrow's show. Let me know about the interview."

Phillip stood, too. "I'll call Mitchell back, tell him what you suggest."

"All right."

On the way back to her dressing room, Jessica popped into Douglas's office. His secretary, Lorna, frowned when she saw her. The woman's dislike for her was blatant, and if Jessica was a different kind of person, she'd give her a piece of her mind. Instead, she said, "Is Douglas around?"

"Checking up on him?" Lorna's laugh didn't meet her eyes.

"Tell him I came by to see him," Jessica replied, ignoring Lorna's rude remark. "No, forget it. I'll see him at *home*."

In her dressing room, she checked her voice mail before going over her notes and was shocked to find a message from Yolanda. Yolanda never called her at the studio. Even more surprising was Yolanda's message—she was considering a move back to D.C.

Why? Jessica wondered. If Yolanda was moving back to D.C., did that mean things were sour with Terrence? Or were things sour at the firm?

She had the receiver in her hand, ready to call Yolanda, when there was a knock on the door. Replacing the receiver, she crossed the room to the door and opened it.

It was Denise, Phillip's intern. "Hi, Denise."

"Uh, Miss Bedford?" As usual, Denise looked and sounded nervous. One too many of the assistants here treated Jessica like she was some all-important diva—or like they feared she'd throw a temper tantrum because they dared insult her with their presence.

"Jessica . . ."

"Jessica."

"What urgent business is Phillip sending you on now?"

For a moment, Denise looked surprised. "Oh," she said, recovering. "Nothing. I mean, well . . . someone brought this letter to Phillip's office, so I'm bringing it to you."

Jessica looked down at the large manila envelope. "This is for me?"

"Yeah."

"You said someone brought it to Phillip's office?"

"Uh-huh. I don't know why."

Denise passed her the envelope, then hurried off before Jessica even had a chance to say thanks. Oh, well. Absently, Jessica closed the door, her eyes searching the envelope for some sign of where it came from.

There was none. Not even a return address.

She walked to the sofa and sat, placing the envelope on her lap. It was heavy, like it contained a contract or a small newspaper. Perhaps it held copies of the *Washington Post* or *Capital Spotlight* feature stories on her—a few fans had already clipped and sent the articles to her. She lifted the flap and withdrew the envelope's contents.

There was a stack of typing paper. Blank typing paper. Jessica frowned. That didn't make sense. She lifted the first blank page, then the second. On the third sheet, she found a handwritten letter.

And the writing . . .

God, no. It couldn't be.

Jessica, my love . . .

As if she'd been scorched, Jessica dropped the stack. The papers fell to the ground, landing with a thud. Either by some weird power or by strange coincidence, the letter dangled in the air, then floated away from the rest of the blank pages, landing face-up near her left foot.

Jessica, my love . . . God, this couldn't be happening. Only one person had ever started letters to her that way. If it was just the words, *maybe* she could ignore this. But the handwriting . . . Was he haunting her from the grave?

She wanted to run, to scream, but instead her eyes took in the letter, read its words, tried to understand.

Jessica, my love,

When I awake in the morning, I think of you. When I go to sleep at night, you are the last thing in my thoughts. I dream of you constantly.

I miss you. When I can't hold you, touch you, kiss you, simply be near you, I go crazy.

I'm going crazy now. It's been too long, Jessica. Let's get together again.

Soon.

"No . . ." The word escaped on an anguished breath. It couldn't be. How could it be? This didn't make sense.

Leaning forward, she reached for the letter. But as if it had a life of its own, it fluttered away. She dropped onto her knees, chasing the paper, chasing the ghost. All the while she could barely breathe.

"Jessica."

"No!" She tried to block out the voice as her hand landed on the paper.

"Jessica." Firm, real.

Her head whipped up. The voice wasn't from the past, but the present. Douglas stood in the doorway of her dressing room, a confused look on his face. "Jessica, what's wrong?"

Oh, God. Did he know? Had he seen the letter before she'd gotten it? Had someone sent him a copy? "D-Douglas. Wh-what are you doing here?"

"What am I doing here?" His eyes narrowed. "Lorna said you were looking for me."

"Yes, of course." She attempted a lighthearted laugh, but it sounded more like a strangled cry. She was so flustered, her hands trembled and she could barely speak.

When he stepped into the room and closed the door, Jessica quickly lifted the letter, then reached for the pile of strewn papers. She hid the letter in the stack as she gathered the pile. "You startled me, and I . . . I dropped these papers."

"Let me help you."

"No," Jessica said—though perhaps too harshly, if the perplexed look on Douglas's face was any indication. She grabbed the last of the papers and stood, then faced her husband with what she hoped could pass for a genuine smile. "I've got it."

"What's wrong?"

She placed the loose pages on the sofa behind her, double-checking to make sure the letter wasn't visible. Then she faced Douglas. "Nothing's wrong."

"Are you sure?"

"Well, maybe today's show has me a little on edge." She'd interviewed a local rap artist, but it had been like pulling teeth to get him to talk. So she'd embellished the little she knew about him to the camera to avoid major lulls in the interview. "I always am after a taping like that, wondering if the viewers will know I'm full of crap." The lie sounded credible to her own ears.

Douglas slipped his arms around her waist. "I can make you feel better."

"Can you?"

"Mmm-hmm." He kissed her cheek. "I know just the cure for tense talk show hosts."

"Douglas," Jessica protested when he brought his mouth to her ear. She knew where this was leading, to a spontaneous coupling right there, and if this were any other time she might have been in the mood. But she kept seeing the letter . . .

"Something *is* wrong." He stared at her with concern. "What, sweetheart?"

"Douglas, I'm sorry. It's just that . . . Julie—you know Julie—she's coming here any minute to go over tomorrow's schedule."

"Oh."

"I'm sorry."

"That's okay." He pecked her forehead. "I really just came by to see your lovely face."

Or to check up on her? Lord, why had that thought popped into her mind? *She'd* been the one looking for *him*. It was the stupid letter. It was making her go crazy.

She wished she could ignore the letter, but how could she? She'd passed the first one off as coincidence, and after not receiving another one for weeks, she'd been convinced that that's what it was. Some bizarre coincidence that meant nothing. But this letter—this one made it clear that the first one had been no accident.

Someone knew her secret.

Oh, God.

Who?

Douglas's lips on hers pulled her back to the here and now. "I'll take that as my cue to leave," he said.

"I'm sorry—what did you say?"

"It's all right." He walked to the door. "I'm gonna be here late this evening. So I'll see you at home later."

"Okay. See you at home."

She watched him disappear, feeling a sense of hopelessness. Why was this happening to her? Why now? And what did this person want? To hurt her? To hurt Douglas?

The phone rang, and Jessica jumped. Damn if the letter didn't have her on edge.

She hurried to the phone, happy for the diversion from her thoughts. But as she brought the receiver to her ear, a chill ran down her spine. "Who is this?"

"An obsessed stalker," came the reply, then a giggle. "Jessica, what kind of greeting is that?"

At the sound of Ellie's voice, a relieved breath whooshed out of Jessica's throat. She sank into the chair opposite the phone. "Sorry, Ellie. It's been a long day. What's up?"

"Did you hear from Yolanda?"

Yolanda. She'd completely forgotten about her. "Yeah, actually. She left me a message but I haven't called her back yet. Did you talk to her?"

"I just got off the phone with her. She said she gave notice at her firm and might be moving back to D.C."

"You're kidding."

"Nope. She said she was tired of the mostly male team. You know Yolanda."

"This probably has as much to do with her mother as anything else." Her mother's health wasn't the best, and Yolanda hated being so far away.

"Probably."

"So, she might actually be coming back? Wow. After all this time."

"That depends on who hires her. She's applied to some firms in D.C., but also to some in Philly. I told her she should go out on her own, but she's not ready for that."

"Has she talked to Shereen?"

"I didn't ask. *But* she did say she'd be in town this weekend and wants to get together."

"All of us?"

"So she said."

Why, at that moment, Jessica's eyes went to the stack of papers, she didn't know. Except that she couldn't get the letter out of her mind. Damn, who was doing this to her? Only Shereen, Ellie, and Yolanda knew the truth about her affair with Professor Bell—and the truth about everything that had happened afterward.

"Jessica?"

"Huh?"

"Are you free Saturday night?"

"Uh, Saturday?"

"Yeah. Around eight?"

"I, uh . . ." She didn't realize she'd been walking toward the sofa until she found herself there. She searched for the letter in the pile, retrieved it. *Jessica, my love . . .* She crushed the paper into a ball. "Uh, did you say eight?"

"Are you okay?"

"Why?"

"Why? Because I'm getting a weird vibe from you and I want to know if you're all right."

"Yeah. I'm fine."

"I know you're worried about what's going to happen. So am I, to tell the truth. But I don't think it'll be a repeat of . . . well, you know."

With the crumpled letter contained in her palm, Jessica felt slightly better. "All I know is that if Yolanda wants Shereen there, she's gonna have to ask her herself."

"No doubt."

"I hope she does. Getting together will do us all some good."

"I agree," Ellie said. Then, "Look, I gotta run. I'm working on a movie set this evening. Shelton called me directly, which is nice. I won't have to pay commission to my agent."

"He's still around." Jessica forced an upbeat tone in her voice.

"Yeah."

"I'm glad."

"So am I. I'll talk to you later. But for now, keep Saturday night open, okay?"

"Okay."

"Later."

Ellie hung up, and the dial tone blared. Yet Jessica clutched the receiver to her ear, not wanting to let go. She suddenly felt very alone. And very frightened.

Then she realized how pathetic she must seem, standing in her dressing room, holding the receiver like it was a lifeline. So she hung up the phone. Next, she uncrumpled the letter and did with it what she'd done with the last—shredded it and threw the pieces into the garbage.

But while she could destroy the letter, she couldn't destroy the unknown threat.

THE PAST

"WHAT DO YOU THINK, GUYS?" Jessica stopped her strut along the dorm room floor, then whirled around for her friends to see her entire outfit. She wore a simple black dress that hugged her slim figure, black tights, a red blazer, and low-heeled boots.

"What I think," Yolanda began slowly, eyeing Jessica up and down, "is that you've surprised us all."

"What?" Anxious, Jessica smoothed her hands over her thighs. "You think this is too sexy? I think it's conserv—"

"That's not what I mean," Yolanda answered. She glanced at Ellie and Shereen, who sat beside her on the bed, before looking back at Jessica. "I think I speak for all of us when I say I'm surprised things have gone this far with the professor."

"Oh." Turning, Jessica walked the few steps to the mirror to check out her reflection.

"No offense, Jess," Ellie said. "It's just that . . . well, isn't he kind of old?"

Jessica shrugged as she fluffed her curly hair. "He's in his forties, I guess."

"At least twice your age," Ellie responded.

Jessica didn't reply. Yes, he was definitely older than her, but that only made him more mature. And she appreciated mature. From what she'd seen and experienced, all the guys on campus were after only one thing: a meaningless roll in the hay with as many women as possible. Andrew was different.

"Age aside," Shereen began, "my concern is that you don't know him that well."

Jessica whirled around and faced Shereen with a firm stare. "I know that he was there for me when I needed him."

"We all were," Shereen commented.

"I know that." Jessica's expression softened. "That's one of the reasons I feel so close to you all."

"And now you've developed a savior complex where Andrew is concerned—"

"That's not true, Yolanda." How could she make her friends understand? What she felt for Andrew was special, real. She would have felt it even if she'd met him under different circumstances. "Look, it's just dinner."

"Again," Ellie chimed.

"So? I already told you, since I joined his drama class late, I have a lot to catch up on." Jessica shrugged again, wondering why she had to explain herself. "And is it a crime that I find him fascinating?"

Ellie lit a cigarette. "Just be careful."

"Yeah," Shereen agreed. "You're . . ." Her voice trailed off.

"What?" Jessica replied defensively. "Naive?"

"I was going to say nice. Hey, all I'm saying is that I don't want to see anyone take advantage of you."

"You all know who I'll be out with. We're going for dinner. I'll be gone for a few hours, max. If I'm not home by midnight, call out the National Guard."

Yolanda hopped off the bed, strolled over to Jessica, then put her arm around her. "All right, girl. We hear ya. You didn't make it to Howard being an idiot. So—" Yolanda looked at Ellie and Shereen. "Have a good time."

Jessica exhaled a nervous breath. "I will. And I'll see you as soon as I get back."

Then she left, butterflies dancing in her stomach even as she smiled at the thought of spending more time with Andrew.

"Where are we going?" Jessica asked. She sat in the passenger's seat of Andrew's car. They'd left the restaurant five minutes ago, but Andrew had just missed the turn that would take them back to her dorm.

"I want to show you some of those costumes I talked about."

"Oh." Over dinner, Andrew had told her about the play he was considering for the spring, a period piece set in the antebellum South.

"You don't mind, do you?"

Jessica grinned softly as she faced him. Maybe she should mind, but she didn't. Like Andrew, she wasn't quite ready to say good-night.

"No, I don't mind. But aren't the costumes at Howard?"

"Actually, the pieces I'm talking about are at my cabin in Virginia. It's not a far drive."

At his cabin. Jessica's heart jumped. She wasn't born yesterday; after all their heated glances over dinner, she knew where this was leading. So why not stop it now? Tell him to turn around and go back to her dorm before they went too far?

Andrew reached across the seat and took her hand in his. "If you don't feel comfortable . . ."

His hand was warm and moist; he was nervous, just as she was. But had she ever wanted anything more? No. So why fight it? They were both adults. "No, I'm okay."

"I haven't done this before," he added softly, gently squeezing her hand.

She knew he wasn't talking about showing a student costumes.

"I mean—"

"I know what you mean," Jessica said, cutting him off. She turned her hand in his and linked their fingers.

"I don't want you thinking that I routinely bring women back to my cabin. In fact, I never do. But you're different."

Jessica's heart fluttered, as did her stomach.

"Do you believe me?"

"Yes," she replied without hesitation.

Andrew smiled, his eyes crinkling. God, he was so attractive! He could have his pick of women, no doubt, but he wanted her. How had she gotten so lucky?

Silence fell over them as Andrew continued to drive through the darkened streets, still holding Jessica's hand.

"I am so very attracted to you," Andrew said after a while.

"Oh, Andrew, you don't know how attracted I am to you." Realizing how eager she'd sounded, Jessica looked to the right and blushed.

"Hey, no need to be embarrassed. Believe me, I'm happy to know you feel as strongly about me as I do about you. I was beginning to wonder if it was one-sided."

Jessica whirled around to face him. Was he kidding? She was certain her emotions were written all over her face.

"I just mean . . . I really care about you, Jessica. Really. And if wanting you is wrong, then, baby, I don't want to be right."

He said the last words in a playful voice, and Jessica giggled at Andrew's corniness.

And then she felt hot.

She couldn't wait to get to his cabin.

*

Chapter Eight

"YEAH, I'M COOL," SHEREEN ASSURED Ellie as she drove along Sixteenth Street toward Q Street. They were heading to Trumpets, a jazz club near Dupont Circle, where they would meet Jessica and Yolanda for dinner and a girl's night out. "How many times do I have to tell you I'm cool before you start believing me?"

"Hey, I just want to be sure."

"If I wasn't cool with this, I wouldn't be going."

"Okay."

Ellie didn't sound convinced, and Shereen frowned. Yes, her stomach had butterflies, but she was actually looking forward to seeing Yolanda again. They'd spoken only briefly when Yolanda had called to say she'd like to see her with the group Saturday night, but that had been fine with Shereen. An apology in person was a much better option. So was forgiveness.

"Though, knowing Yolanda," Shereen continued, "typical controlling Aries that she is, she wants to meet in a public place because she thinks I'll be less likely to cause a scene there."

"That didn't stop you— *Shit!*"

As Ellie gripped the door handle with one hand and the edge of her seat with the other, Shereen's eyes went back to the road. Instantly, she clenched the steering wheel and hit the brakes, cursing loudly as she did. The tires squealed in protest, and both her and Ellie's bodies jerked forward—saved from possible injury by their seat belts.

Damn, some fool had just cut in front of her, driving at least ten miles per hour slower than she was! She could see the short gray hair of an older man. Thankfully, she'd been able to avoid rear-ending him, but damn, drivers these days pissed her off. Her headlights illuminated the bumper sticker on his car that read: DO IT SOBER.

"Fine, do it sober, buddy," Shereen said, quickly changing lanes. "But do it today."

Ellie cracked up.

When she didn't stop laughing, Shereen glanced at her friend, then back at the road. "What?"

"You know what I'm thinking," Ellie managed between chuckles.

Shereen turned onto Q Street. "I have no clue."

Ellie's laughter grew louder, and Shereen couldn't help it—she started laughing, too. "What?"

Ellie forced in several deep breaths, then spoke. "You remember that time . . . senior year. After the basketball game when we were heading back from Baltimore."

"Oh, God," Shereen said. "The time when Yolanda was driving, and Thomas was in the front seat—"

"Mmm-hmm. Oooh, remember that fight? She was driving and giving him a piece of her mind at the same time. How many cars did she run off the road as Thomas tried to grope her?"

Shereen laughed, remembering the incident. "About nine."

"Oh, man. Poor Thomas. 'I don't care if you are the team's star player,'" Ellie said, mimicking Yolanda's stern voice. "'I don't care if you're drunk. Get your filthy hands off me before I sue your ass for sexual assault.'"

"Then she stopped the car on the Beltway and tried to shove him out, but he threw up right there in the front seat of her new Sunbird."

"She was livid."

"So much for a first date."

"That's right," Ellie said. "That was their first date."

"Poor Thomas."

"And Jessica missed it all."

"Oh, yeah. She was back in the dorm, studying for some exam or writing some paper."

"Didn't Yolanda try to go to the dean with a complaint?"

"She wanted to. But we convinced her that Thomas didn't intentionally ruin her new car. Then she wanted to make his life hell, but we assured her she'd done enough of that that night."

"She was mad for what, three months?" Ellie asked.

"Three months? How much you want to bet if you mention his name tonight, she sees red?"

Ellie sighed wistfully. "There Yolanda was, being Miss Prude, while I was in the backseat with . . . God, what was his name?"

"Exactly." Shereen gave Ellie a pointed look before pulling into a parking lot near the club.

"We were crazy back then."

"We? Yolanda was crazy. *You* were definitely crazy. Me—I was always sane."

"Yeah, right."

Shereen pulled into a parking space and killed the engine. She faced Ellie, who gave her a look that said she knew better.

Who was she kidding? Jessica had been the only sane one.

Moments after Shereen and Ellie walked downstairs into the club, Jessica jumped up from a nearby table and waved them over.

"I see our friends," Ellie said to the host, then led the way toward them.

Though only minutes ago Shereen had been laughing about old times, the memory of the last time she'd seen Yolanda replaced those happy memories. She felt wary, uncertain. Maybe things had forever changed between her and Yolanda and their relationship would never be the same.

Realizing that Shereen was no longer walking behind her, Ellie stopped and turned. She retraced her steps and took Shereen by the hand. "Come on."

Shereen didn't budge. "I don't know."

"Girl, you and Yolanda have had worse fights before."

That wasn't exactly true. Shereen had never hit her before.

Ellie tugged on her hand.

"You're right," Shereen said, placing one foot in front of the other, once again walking behind Ellie. *I can do this.* Seconds later, they were at the table.

"Hey, you two," Ellie said, kissing first Jessica on the cheek, then Yolanda.

Yolanda didn't even look at Shereen as she greeted Ellie. Damn.

But then Yolanda was on her feet, throwing her arms around Shereen's neck. Shereen closed her eyes as she hugged her back, feeling some of the anxiety ebb from her body.

"Hi, Shereen."

"Hey."

Yolanda released her and sat back down. Ellie quickly dropped into the spot beside Jessica, leaving Shereen no choice but to sit beside Yolanda. But she wasn't miffed. She was touched. Clearly, Ellie and Jessica wanted her and Yolanda to work things out as badly as she did.

"You missed the first set," Jessica announced. "Best jazz I've heard in a while."

Good, safe topic, Shereen thought, settling into her chair.

"And when was the last time you were out?" Ellie challenged.

"Yeah," Shereen chimed, wanting to keep the mood light. "We all know you and Douglas hardly come up for air."

"Shut up."

"Am I lying?" Shereen looked from one friend to another.

"Come on, Jess," Yolanda said. "I don't have to be in D.C. to know you and the hubby are still honeymooning."

"Whatever." Reddish hues tinged Jessica's fair skin. "How did we get onto my sex life?"

"Hmm, let me see. Jazz, saxophones, sex." Ellie held up a finger for each item she'd mentioned. "Seems like a logical conclusion."

"Spoken by the queen of—"

"Hey." Ellie cut off Jessica before she could finish her statement. When Shereen laughed, Ellie turned to her. "At least I'm getting some."

There was a collective "Oooh" at the table.

"I'll get you for that, Ellie. You wait."

Jessica lifted her menu, fanned herself, then asked, "Anyone hungry?"

"Starved," Ellie replied. Then, "Forget the puns, Shereen."

Shereen chuckled. "Yeah, I'm hungry."

"Oh, Shereen," Jessica said. "You'll like the waiter."

"Why?" Ellie asked.

"Don't listen to her," Shereen warned, immediately catching her friend's meaning.

"What am I missing?" Yolanda asked them.

"You know our Sweet Thang," Jessica replied, as if that said it all.

"Ah. I get it." That came from Ellie.

"Get what? There's nothing to get."

"The waiter's young and fine. Oh, and did I mention young?" Jessica raised an eyebrow. "Ring any bells?"

"Ahh . . ." Yolanda crooned.

"Wait a minute. Since when do I like them young? I don't like them young. Jessica is talking about—"

But no one was listening. They were laughing.

And after a moment, Shereen started laughing, too.

It felt like old times.

The audience erupted in applause as the saxophonist dazzled the crowd with one long blast of music in varying notes that seemed to travel on one breath.

"Oh, yeah!" Ellie exclaimed, raising her hands high as she clapped.

Yolanda stuck two fingers in her mouth and whistled.

When the applause settled, Jessica leaned across the table and said, "Don't look now, but the guy on the drums is checking you out big time, Shereen."

"He is not."

"Yes, he is," Jessica insisted.

Yolanda looked over Shereen's shoulder to the stage. "Yep. He is. Wait, I think he's coming over."

"Bathroom break," Shereen announced, then jumped up.

"Wait." Yolanda stood to meet Shereen. "I'll go with you."

Shereen felt a tingling at the back of her neck. Nerves. She'd hoped that their heart-to-heart would come later, but Yolanda had clearly decided otherwise.

It was just as well.

Shereen maneuvered her way through the thick crowd. Since they'd arrived a few hours ago, the place had filled up. People now stood in almost every square inch of the place.

There were several "Hey, baby"s and the usual appreciative stares from men as they walked by. Shereen ignored them all; she wasn't interested.

"Hey, sweetness," one man said, stepping in front of her, blocking her path. Shereen tried to stride past him, but he moved with her as though they were dancing. Exasperated, she met his eyes. He took her hand.

She yanked it back. "*Excuse* me?" Even in nice clubs like this one, there were bound to be some loser brothers.

"Come on, sweetness. Don't be like that."

Yolanda shoved herself between the man and Shereen. "She's with me."

"Ouch," he said, as Yolanda linked arms with Shereen and led her away. Then, "Hey, that'll work."

"Not!" Shereen giggled as she shook her head. "I swear, where have all the good men gone?"

"They're still out there. You just have to look really hard."

Shereen gave her a doubtful look.

"I'm serious. And if *I* can say that, you know it's true."

In other words, Terrence had made Yolanda believe in love again. Shereen felt the familiar queasiness return to her stomach. Damn, when would that go away?

Maybe once she and Yolanda had cleared the air.

When they got to the rest room there was a major line, so Yolanda asked, "How badly you gotta pee?"

"I can wait a bit."

"Then let's go outside. I need some air."

And some privacy. Which was fine with her. If they were going to have their chat now, Shereen didn't want to do it in a crowded rest room, either.

They made their way up the stairs while others made their way down. When they stepped outside, the cold air immediately embraced them, but it was sobering.

Yolanda faced her. "I'm sorry, Shereen."

Shereen merely nodded.

"I know I shouldn't have shown up at the dinner with Terrence like that, without giving you any warning. I just—"

"Is this about Lawrence?" Shereen had to know.

"*Lawrence?*" Yolanda asked, as if the suggestion was totally implausible. "Is that what you think?"

"N—" Who was she kidding? Deep in her heart, Shereen had never been sure that Yolanda had forgiven her over the whole Lawrence incident, even though it hadn't been her fault. "Yes. Maybe this was your big chance for payback, and you took it."

"Over Lawrence?" Yolanda shook her head. "Absolutely not. God, he certainly wouldn't be worth our friendship."

Shereen just watched her, not sure what to think. Lawrence had been Yolanda's boyfriend early in junior year. Unfortunately, he hadn't understood the concept of fidelity. From the beginning, Shereen had sensed the sneaky Libra was slime, and after Lawrence had hit on her, she'd told Yolanda. But Yolanda hadn't reacted the way Shereen had expected. She'd gotten pissed with her, not with Lawrence, telling Shereen that she must have come on to him, that she'd always known Shereen had wanted her man. She'd gone on to say that Shereen had been attracted to *all* her boyfriends. Shereen had been stunned because that was so far from the truth. Then anger had taken over and she'd said something stupid about having had more boyfriends than Yolanda, which she totally regretted later because she'd realized that Yolanda was insecure and perhaps a bit jealous of her. Still, Yolanda didn't take back her hurtful accusation, so Shereen didn't apologize for what she'd said. The two hadn't spoken for weeks.

Until Yolanda had found out through someone else just how many women Lawrence had been seeing behind her back. Contrite, she'd finally apologized to Shereen and Shereen had apologized to her. After that, they had sworn never to let another man come between them again.

"I guess I can't blame you for asking. Part of me always thought you'd think that, and that's why I didn't know how to tell you. I know that's a lousy excuse . . ."

"No, I understand." She did—sort of. And while the thought that Yolanda and Terrence were dating still bothered her, it didn't make sense that Yolanda had planned this type of payback for over nine years.

"Do you?"

"Mmm-hmm. But I don't want to talk about Lawrence."

"Neither do I."

They fell into silence. Then Shereen said, "How did you meet him?"

"Terrence?" Yolanda seemed momentarily shocked by the question. "Oh, we met by chance at a hotel in Philly. In the lounge area. He was there with a client. I was waiting for one. I looked across the room and saw him, and he saw me, and we remembered each other. So he came over and said hi. That's how it started."

"He's a lawyer?"

"No. He's a sports agent."

"Really?" He'd always been passionate about football, so to learn he had made a career in sports wasn't surprising. "Football?"

"Yeah."

"And you're engaged?"

"Yeah." Yolanda tentatively held out her hand for Shereen's inspection.

Shereen forced a smile as she checked out the huge diamond on Yolanda's ring finger. Smiled as though it didn't matter, yet deep down in her soul it hurt. Of all the men in the world, why Terrence? Yolanda hadn't been in love with Lawrence the way Shereen had been with Terrence.

It doesn't matter, she quickly told herself. Her breakup with Terrence had nothing to do with Yolanda. So what if Yolanda had met him years later and they'd fallen in love?

Terrence was her past.

He was Yolanda's future.

"What's James saying?" Shereen asked.

"James." Yolanda said his name with such contempt, you'd never believe the man had once been her husband. One of those tragic facts of life when people split.

"How does he feel about you getting married again?"

"Girl, I don't talk to James."

"Never?"

"Why should I?"

Looking at Yolanda's sour expression, it was hard to believe she'd ever been head-over-heels in love with James McNab.

So much for talking about her ex. Shereen hugged her torso. "I'm getting cold. You ready to go back inside?"

Yolanda looked at her, her eyes filled with remorse. "I swear, Shereen, if I'd known you would be upset about it, I never would have pursued anything with Terrence."

"Mmm-hmm."

"Do you believe me? That I didn't mean to hurt you?"

Shereen glanced away, then met Yolanda's eyes. "If you say you didn't, then I believe you."

"Thanks." Yolanda embraced her.

"Thank *you* for not being angry with me." In the past, Yolanda could hold a grudge with the best of them; she could easily still be angry with Shereen now. "I really am sorry for hitting you."

Yolanda released her and gave her a smile. "And I thought I was the tough one."

"Guess I learned a thing or two from you."

"Guess you did," Yolanda agreed, then linked arms with Shereen and led her back inside.

Chapter Nine

WHEN IT HAPPENED, ELLIE was lying flat on her back with her legs spread wide and Shelton's face buried between her thighs. Shelton's, yet she cried out, "Oh, God, Richard. Oh . . ."

Shelton stopped. Ellie went cold.

"What did you say?"

Oh, shit. She'd called him Richard. Shit, shit, shit. Still, Ellie played dumb. "I don't know." She closed her eyes and gyrated her hips. "Come on, baby."

"You called me Richard."

"Richard?" Ellie repeated feebly, knowing she sounded lame.

Shelton sat up. "Who's Richard?"

Damn. Why now, why *now*? She'd been so close. "No one."

"No one?" He looked at her with disbelief. "I've got my face between your legs and you call another man's name?"

Ellie groaned, reached for the sheet to cover herself. What could she say? "Richard . . . he's an ex."

"We've been together for almost two months and you've never called his name. Why now?"

"I don't know, Shelton." So much for sex. Frustrated, she rolled onto her side. "It was a mistake. A slip of the tongue. No big deal."

"Then why can't you look at me?"

"Of course I can look at you." She did—then glanced away.

"You still want him."

"No." Yes. Oh, God, yes. And what a way to find out. How could Richard sneak back into her heart at a moment like this?

"Damn, I don't believe this."

Six weeks invested in this relationship and with one wrong name she'd blown it. Like flicking a switch from on to off, it was over.

In retrospect, she should have known it was only a matter of time. Should have known that no matter how attractive the replacement, she couldn't fool her heart.

It was like trying to get over nicotine by smoking those god-awful herbal cigarettes. She simply couldn't do it.

Shelton had lasted longer than anyone else. Any of the Richard replacements, that is. Other men she'd dated had lasted a few days, even a week, before she ended up right back where she'd started.

Wanting Richard.

Pathetic, yeah, but old habits die hard.

Ellie watched as Shelton sprang from the bed, watched him scoop his pants from the floor. "You're leaving?"

"Can you tell me why I should stay?"

Ellie paused. Couldn't think of a damn thing.

"That's what I thought."

She crawled to the edge of the bed, reached for his arm. Damn, but he was fine. Tall and lean and muscular. Why couldn't she love him? "C'mon, Shelton. You're overreacting."

He slipped his T-shirt over his head. "Am I?"

"I can't believe you're doing this. As if you're perfect."

"Sweetheart, I would never call another woman's name while making love to you."

"No," Ellie quipped, not sure why she was being so testy when *she'd* done the unthinkable. "You just check them out whenever we're together."

"What?"

"That last set we were on. Last week. You kept flirting with that woman with the braids. The thin, *gorgeous* woman."

"In case you haven't noticed, I'm not interested in waifs. Is that what this is about? You don't think I find you attractive?"

"Maybe." No, she knew he found her attractive. Yes, she'd caught him looking at other women, but hell, what man didn't? Bottom line, he never failed to make her feel sexy—even when the mirror told her otherwise. Yet she said, "I'm just pointing out that you haven't always made me feel totally secure. . . ."

Shelton gave her a pitiful look. "You're making excuses to justify what you did. You feel guilty, but you can't deal with the guilt, so you're trying to find blame with me when what you need to deal with is the fact that you still have feelings for this guy."

"God, you sound like a shrink."

"I know, I'm a lowly A.D., right? But I did go to college. I was a psych major."

"I wasn't trying to say— Oh, Shelton, please don't go."

"I'm in love with you, Ellie."

Her mouth fell open.

"I know. You're surprised. So was I when I realized it."

"You . . . you love me?"

He buckled his belt. "Hey, it's okay. I know you don't love me. But I can't keep seeing you if you're in love with someone else."

She gave a soft whimper. What was wrong with her? Here was a gorgeous man—not particularly well-endowed, but certainly satisfying in bed—who loved her. And she was in love with someone else.

A man she couldn't have.

She wished she could turn off her feelings for Richard and turn them on for Shelton. But she couldn't. She'd certainly tried. Over the past weeks, she'd told Richard to leave her alone, that she was involved with someone else. He'd stayed away until a couple of weeks ago, when he'd suddenly started calling again, telling her how much he missed her, needed her.

And her resolve had weakened. Damn him.

Surprising her, Shelton leaned over her and softly kissed her lips. With a moan of frustration, he pulled away.

"Do you have to go?" Ellie asked softly.

"I don't want to." He stroked her chin. God, it hurt more that he was being so nice. "Look, I'm a phone call away. If you get over this Richard guy . . ." He let his statement hang in the air.

And then he turned and walked out of her bedroom, leaving Ellie feeling a mix of disbelief and disappointment.

Shit.

She plopped backward on the bed. When she heard the apartment door close, she reached for the pack of cigarettes on her night table. Her fingers trembled as she withdrew an extra-light, slim DuMaurier.

Lord help her, she was certifiable. There was no way she could tell her friends about this. If they knew she'd let a gorgeous, single man who loved her walk through the door because of Richard, they'd have her sent to a loony bin faster than she could say "Orgasm."

Ellie lit the cigarette and inhaled deeply. She had hoped for more with Shelton, had prayed for more, because she wanted this to work. But how could it, when the only man in her heart was Richard?

"Richard," she said wistfully.

Yeah, she was certifiable, all right.

Two days later, Shelton hadn't called. And Ellie hadn't called him. Richard, however, hadn't stopped calling, even after Ellie had told him to stop.

"Come on, Ellie," Richard had said last night. "Why are you being like this?"

"Go away," she'd told him, and slammed down the phone.

It rang again, and again, and she ignored it until it finally stopped.

Thus far, Richard hadn't bothered her today. But the Caller ID had shown one call from Shelton while she'd been in the shower. She'd immediately called him back but he wasn't home. So when the doorbell rang shortly after noon, Ellie hurried to answer it, hoping to find him. She still felt horrible about what had happened between them, and if he gave her another chance, she would try her best to love him.

Shelton wasn't at the door, but something better was. Ellie went weak in the knees when she saw the extravagant flower arrangement. It wasn't every day a man sent her flowers.

She tipped the deliveryman, then brought the gorgeous arrangement into her apartment. It brightened her small kitchen instantly. She opened the card, knowing it was from Shelton.

I need to see you. Tonight. Six o'clock at Tsung's. I miss you.
Richard

Richard. God, she hated herself, but a smile actually broke out on her face. A smile, when just moments before she'd been hoping to see Shelton. Oh, why deny it any longer? She wanted to see Richard as much as he wanted to see her. The fact that he hadn't given up on her in all these weeks meant he truly loved her and didn't want to lose her.

Hours later, Ellie walked into Tsung's, a quaint Chinese restaurant on H Street in Georgetown. While she and Richard went to several restaurants, this was their favorite spot.

As always, Richard sat at the bar waiting for her.

Seeing his back, she smiled. Then forced the smile off her face. She wouldn't make this easy for him. As much as she loved him, she didn't want to go back to him if he was still with his wife. Being with Shelton had proved that at least someone else could love her, so why waste another moment with a man if he couldn't commit?

He seemed to sense her, for he turned as she made her way to the bar. Seeing her, an ear-to-ear smile spread across his face.

"Hey, baby." He stood to meet her, wrapped her in his arms. "God, I've missed you."

Somehow, Ellie played it cool. She stepped out of his embrace. "What do you want, Richard?"

His face grew serious. "We need to talk."

"About what?"

"Our relationship. I have something to tell you."

Nerves tickled Ellie's stomach. Richard seemed different somehow, and she couldn't help thinking that maybe this was it. Maybe he had finally done what he'd promised to do for so long. "What do you want to tell me?"

"Not here. Let's get a table."

Minutes later, a hostess led them to a back corner booth. The moment Richard was seated, he spoke. "I told her."

Ellie's heart raced, but she spoke coolly. "Who is *her*?"

"My wife."

God, this was it. "Told her what?"

"That I'm leaving."

Instantly, Ellie's guard dropped, replaced by excitement. "Richard—did you really?"

He reached across the table and took her hand. "Baby, I was going crazy without you."

Ellie practically melted. "You were?"

"When you told me you were seeing someone else, I could hardly sleep."

"I had to get on with my life."

"I know. But that made me realize you were right. That I wasn't being fair to you. Nor fair to my wife. And the bottom line is . . ." He took a deep breath. "I want to be with you. Only you. You're the one who makes me happy."

"Oh, Richard." Ellie's eyes misted. She'd waited so long for this. "So what happens now? Are you moving out?"

"Soon. But for now I've moved into a different bedroom. I have to see about getting a place. And I wondered . . ." The waitress arrived, but he shooed her away. "How would you feel about moving in with me?"

"Move in with you?" Her delighted squeal attracted the attention of some nearby patrons but she didn't care. "Of course I'll move in with you. Oh, Richard, of course."

Richard stretched his body across the table, framed her face, and kissed her. Then they both giggled, giddy with happiness.

But as he settled back in his seat, a moment of reality marred Ellie's bliss. And a moment of guilt. She suddenly wondered if this was the right thing. Never in her wildest dreams would she have imagined getting involved with a married man, but for some reason, Richard was different. If she truly believed he was happy at home, she would have ended their relationship before it started. But Richard told her over and over again just how unhappy he was, how he'd been unhappy almost from the beginning, how he and his wife had stayed together for the children. And he constantly told her how she'd changed his life forever that day she'd walked into his office—changed it for the better. Ellie, the girl guys seemed to get a kick out of hurting, the girl they wanted for sex but not much else. She'd never meant that much to any guy before—ever—so was it wrong to want to be with Richard? Yes, he was married, but clearly he wasn't getting the happiness he deserved at home. Why should he stay in a loveless marriage?

The waitress arrived with green tea. She seemed wary, but Richard nodded and she placed the tea and cups on the table.

"Richard, are you *sure*?"

"Yes. I'm definitely sure."

"My apartment is too small for both of us," Ellie began, "so we'd have to move somewhere else. I haven't been there a year yet. They'll charge me to break the lease."

"We don't have to rush into this. Just work toward it."

Ellie squeezed his hand. "I just want to be with you so badly, Richard." When had she become this person? Pathetic, weak, needing him so much.

"At least now I'll be able to spend more time with you," he told her. "Stay the night. Stay several."

No more sneaking around. "Does she know about me?"

He shook his head. "I didn't want to hurt her—more than was necessary. This situation is tough enough. The important thing is that she knows our marriage is finally over."

"Richard." Ellie looked away, then into his eyes. "This isn't because of me, is it? Because I was seeing someone else and you felt pressured into making a decision? I know this is going to sound hypocritical, but I really believe that marriage is sacred. I don't want to be responsible—"

"My wife is my problem, not yours."

"You always say that, Richard, and I never argued that point because . . . well, because it meant I didn't have to be accountable for my actions. But this suddenly seems so real, so serious. So if a part of you still loves your wife, then you shouldn't do this. You should stay and work things out."

"I already told you, Ellie. It was over for me and my wife almost from the time it began. We were never truly in love. We've just hung around for the children."

Ellie wanted to say she was sorry, for there was a part of her that was. Despite her behavior, she believed in marriage. She believed in fidelity. Her parents were still together after thirty-two years. If she ever got married, she wanted it to last for life.

But she also believed that two people shouldn't stay together simply for the sake of their children.

The waitress arrived, but again Richard waved her away. "Can I spend the night?"

All thoughts of sadness and guilt fled her mind. "You know you can."

"And maybe next week, we can start looking for a place. Where do you want to live? Georgetown? Foggy Bottom?"

"Oh, Richard." A tear fell down her cheek. A tear of joy.

At last Ellie had found Mr. Right.

Chapter Ten

THERE'S SOMETHING SPECIAL ABOUT the rain. Something comforting in the sound of its steady, unfailing rhythm. Something mesmerizing—calming, even—in the way it looks as it falls. And there's definitely something refreshing about the way the world smells after a good, long shower.

Yolanda loved the rain. Walking in it. Driving in it. Watching it fall from a bedroom window. A light shower or a major storm—she didn't care. She loved the scent of it, the feel of it, the sound of it. She loved its power—the power to cleanse, the power to give life.

April showers especially. They washed away the last of dreary winter and promised the beauty of spring.

A new season. A new start.

Yolanda listened to the light pitter-pattering of drops on her roof as she drove south along I-95 toward Washington. The rain was a good sign, a sign that she was doing the right thing. It was something she should have done a year ago after her divorce was final, and she would have, had it not been for work. Her Range Rover was crammed with the things she couldn't live without—her clothes, her books, her computer. The other items, like her bed and furniture, she'd sold. Items she'd fought to keep during the divorce, remnants of James she shouldn't have wanted anyway, and now they were gone.

She was going home. Starting fresh.

And Terrence, bless his heart, supported her move. Because he was an independent sports agent he could live pretty much anywhere and would soon join her in D.C.

She fiddled with the radio dials, found WJZE-FM, a Washington station that played jazz, and smiled. Funny, she'd spent five years in

Philadelphia, yet hearing a familiar D.C. radio station made her feel warm and fuzzy inside. Like returning home after a long vacation. She liked Philadelphia, but it just wasn't the same as Washington, the place she'd spent her formative years.

It wasn't home.

She was looking forward to spending more time with her best friends, participating in more alumnae sorority functions. She was looking forward to her new job. In a week, she'd be starting with a new law firm, one where she actually had a hope of making partner. When her firm in Philadelphia had once again passed her over for partner and given it to yet another man—and she had deserved it—that had been the last straw.

But most important, she was looking forward to spending more time with her mother. While Philadelphia was only a three-hour drive away, she hadn't been able to see her as often as she would have liked. And her father was too busy with his new family to check up on his ex-wife. Her mother was lonely, Yolanda knew, and she wanted to be there for her.

Several weeks ago, her mother had fallen down the icy front steps of her apartment building and broken a hip. Since then, she'd been sedentary but was slowly trying to get back to her regular routine. However, even doing small things like making the bed was a major effort, and the last time Yolanda had seen her mother, her place had been a mess. Yolanda had tried to convince her mother to sue the building, but Edna didn't want to. Still, Yolanda had talked to the management on her mother's behalf, and they'd offered to take care of her rent and medical bills until her mother was back on her feet.

Before returning to Philadelphia the last time, Yolanda had called her father and said, "After everything, you owe it to Mom to help her out. She has no one."

Her father had replied, "Your mother isn't my problem anymore, but I'll drive by her place, see if she's okay."

Yolanda had hung up then, unable to bear the sound of his voice a second longer. If ever there was a man who had no conscience, it was Collin Burke. She loved him, he was her father, but sometimes she was ashamed that his blood flowed through her veins.

Men were just different from women, she realized. They could end a relationship and start over without ever looking back. Yolanda had been fourteen when her father had walked out on her mother. At the time, he'd assured her that he would always love her, even though he and her mother would no longer be together. Yolanda hadn't understood that then and she still didn't understand it now. How could a man love his child yet have absolutely no regard for the woman who'd given that child life?

Edna had been crushed. She had literally withdrawn into a shell for months after Collin left her. Those months had been precarious at best, with Yolanda acting as mother and Edna acting as helpless child. Yolanda had taken care of her the best she could, all the while fearing that her mother would wither away and she would lose her, too. Eventually, her mother had gotten over the dark depression, but she had never been the same. To this day, she had never loved anyone beside Collin Burke.

After witnessing her sometimes aloof but otherwise strong mother become nothing more than a weak shell of a person when she lost the man she loved, Yolanda vowed to never suffer the same fate. She wouldn't let a man devastate her life the way her father had devastated her mother's. She had almost given James that power, having fallen hard for him the moment she met him at Howard's School of Law. She'd followed him to Philadelphia when he'd been offered a job with a firm there, and they'd eloped shortly afterward. Three years into their marriage, he broke her heart: she found him in their bed with another woman. And just like that, their marriage was over. James had apologized, promised her this was a one-time thing that would never happen again, then begged for her forgiveness. Yolanda had kicked his ass out and filed for divorce a week later.

Yes, it had hurt, but it would have been worse to stay and wonder if she could trust him, wonder where his hands had been before they were caressing her, where his lips had been. She had trusted James, but he had forfeited that trust. It was as simple as that. Yolanda had given herself no alternative but to ignore his pleas for forgiveness and move on.

She hadn't been looking for love when she met Terrence. In fact, when she'd met him again at a hotel bar and they'd shared a friendly drink, she'd expected that would be it. But at the end of the night,

Terrence had asked for her number. He'd called her days later, and they'd gone out the following weekend. Then again. And again.

And one thing had led to another.

Her feelings were different for Terrence than they had been for James, but different in a good way. She didn't feel that heart-stopping, all-consuming passion, but that kind of passion was dangerous. Instead, what she felt for Terrence was admiration and respect—and love, of course, but a mature kind of love. One she could control instead of it controlling her. She and Terrence would be a team, equal partners in every way, and that's exactly the way she wanted it. James had always had the upper hand in their marriage—he'd supported her through her last year of law school, supported her while she looked for work. It hadn't been an equal relationship, and ultimately, James had broken her heart.

Now she was a different person. Smarter. Self-sufficient. In control of her emotions. She wouldn't let anyone break her heart. Not again.

Life is for the living. If you have it, be grateful. Grasp it with full force and enjoy all it has to offer. Never waste a moment, because life is short, oh so short.

Why can't you do that, Mama? Why can't you grasp life?

As Yolanda stared at her mother, watched her rock back and forth in a chair by the window, sadness clenched her heart. She wasn't one to live by sayings, to spout them at every appropriate moment like some people did. But right now, she wished she could convey to her mother the simple truth that life was too short to waste. For the past sixteen years Edna had simply existed, not really lived. And since her fall, she had retreated even more into a dark void. Seeing her mother alive yet virtually dead pained Yolanda deep in her soul.

"How are you feeling, Mama?"

Back and forth Edna rocked, her hands gently stroking the quilt draped over her lap. She watched the rain fall, seemingly mesmerized by the drops that splashed against the windowpane.

"Mama?"

Weary sigh. "I'm fine. Still breathin'."

But waiting to die. "How's your hip?"

The rocking chair squeaked, but Edna didn't respond.

Yolanda hadn't expected her mother to rise and greet her when she arrived, for she still moved with difficulty, but she'd expected *something*. A gleam in her eyes. An attempt at a smile. Something that showed she was happy to see her. But her mother seemed incapable of giving even that much, as if it was too much of an effort.

Yolanda fought the tears. Her mother was wasting away. Before her injury, Edna's life had consisted of work and sleep, nothing else. She never dated. She never went to a movie. Now, she no doubt spent her life in this rocking chair, looking out at life but not truly living. She was thinner than normal, like she hadn't been eating properly. Yolanda felt helpless. She had no clue how to put the spark back in her mother's eyes.

Swallowing her sadness, Yolanda strolled toward her mother, kissed her on the cheek. Her mother stroked Yolanda's face, but still she didn't smile. It was a tender caress, almost like she was reaching out for life, yet couldn't quite grasp it.

Yolanda crouched before her. "You should see the new house, Mama. It's beautiful. It's got a huge backyard. It even has a porch swing. I think you'd like that. And it's got four bedrooms. You can come anytime."

"Sounds nice."

"It is. It's very nice. In fact, there's no reason for you to stay here alone." Her mother's apartment was small and cramped and in a less-than-desirable part of town. "There's more than enough room for you at the house. And with your hip . . . you wouldn't have to climb any stairs or wait for an elevator all the time. There's an office on the first floor, but I can convert that to a bedroom . . ."

"Oh, that's all right, sweetheart." Edna patted Yolanda's hand. "I'm fine here."

But not happy. Conversations with her mother were increasingly like this—less and less. Yolanda had no clue how to relate to her anymore.

Which made her even angrier with her father. He had done this to her mother. For that, she would never forgive him.

"You don't have to decide right away. I still have to get settled. The furniture's been delivered, but it'll take a while to get it fixed up. So in the meantime, think about it."

Silence.

"Promise me, Mama. Promise you'll think about it."

In response, Edna ran a hand over Yolanda's hair, then turned back to the window.

"Mama?"

"Oh, sweetheart. I love you for caring. But you're young. About to get married again. You're just starting your life. You don't need me around."

"Of course I need you." She gripped her mother's hand. "I'll always need you."

Her mother's eyes fluttered shut. "I'm tired."

"Let me help you to your bed."

"No, I'm fine here."

"Here? You sure?"

"Mmm. I like it here."

"That can't be good for your hip."

"Oh, stop fussing. I'm fine."

"Okay." But Yolanda didn't feel good about this. Still, she lifted the quilt around her mother's shoulders. She couldn't resist stroking the soft, aged skin of her mother's face.

A faint sound, almost like a contented sigh, escaped Edna's throat. "Thank you."

"You're welcome, Mama."

Then Yolanda sat on the nearby sofa. She watched her mother, still rocking, get comfortable in the chair. Seconds later, the rocking stopped and the sounds of her heavy breathing filled the small room.

At least sleep had come easily. At least in sleep, she'd have peace.

It was a quaint single-family house with a large wraparound porch, a popular style on this quiet, tree-lined, Cleveland Park street. It was an old house, but wonderfully maintained. The wood frame was painted a pale yellow while white trimmed the large windows. Foliage surrounded the house, giving it a country feel. It was the kind of house that said, "Welcome. Come on in and stay a while."

The inside of the house was a stark contrast to the outside. While the outside was quaint and charming, the interior was the ultimate in modern style, with sparkling hardwood floors, bright white walls, and lavish cornice moldings. The large living room had a real fireplace. Aside from the dining room and kitchen, there was a small room on the main floor that Yolanda would use as a home office if her mother didn't come live with her. The house was based on an open concept, which gave it the appearance of being larger than it was.

"I still can't believe how beautiful this is." Ellie set a box on the counter. The kitchen had been completely redone. It boasted a modern center island, a ceramic backsplash, and a skylight. Bleached oak cupboards and beige Italian tiles added color to offset the white walls. "I love it."

"Thanks." Yolanda smiled as she took a seat at the kitchen table. The major furniture items had already been delivered and set up, so she and her friends were now unloading the boxes of glassware, housewares, and other trinkets she'd had shipped. Considering all the stuff she had—how did people collect so much stuff?—she knew it would take a while before the interior of the house looked the way she wanted it to look, but she was proud. This was her first foray into home ownership. Yes, she and James had owned a home, but this was different. This was strictly hers.

At least until she married Terrence. Even then, she wasn't sure if they'd live here or buy a place somewhere else.

"I agree with Ellie. It's gorgeous." Jessica bent to place a box marked FRAGILE on the floor, then proceeded to open it.

"Girl, take a break."

"All right." Seeming more than happy to hear those words, Jessica moved to the table and sat beside Yolanda.

"I can't get over the price you paid." Shereen stood with her hip resting against the counter. "What a steal for this part of town."

"It was a gamble, but it paid off." Yolanda had explained to them how she'd made an offer on the house based on some photos her real estate agent had couriered to her. The agent had called it "the deal of a lifetime" and said Yolanda would be crazy to pass it up—despite the fact that she hadn't seen it. In the end, the agent had been right, and Yolanda was glad she'd followed her advice.

"Estate sales are great," Jessica agreed. "When you can find them."

"What's your agent's name?" Ellie asked.

"Why? You looking to buy?"

"Maybe . . ."

"You need a steady job first," Yolanda told her, then chuckled.

"Or a record deal." Shereen raised an inquisitive eyebrow. "What's happening with that, Ellie? Didn't you say you were gonna try and make a demo?"

"Oh." Ellie waved a hand dismissively. "Not enough money. Not enough time."

"Ellie . . ." Jessica wagged a finger at her.

"I'm still writing songs when I have the time. Who knows? One day."

Shereen strolled to the back door and peered outside. "Gosh, the backyard is so big. I love a house with a big backyard."

"Perfect for a family," Ellie pointed out. "Which I guess is the next step, right? A couple of little—"

Ellie suddenly stopped talking, and silence fell over the room. Apparently everyone was thinking the same thing, for all eyes went to Shereen.

Sensing their stares, Shereen turned and faced them. The quick lift of her lips didn't hide the flash of pain in her eyes. Damn. Until Ellie had said it, Yolanda hadn't given any thought to a family. Shereen's startled expression said she hadn't considered the possibility, either.

"Yeah. I guess it is." Shereen turned, looked back outside.

Her voice didn't betray any negative emotion, but Yolanda still felt the need to do damage control. "Terrence and I haven't even talked about a family. God, can you picture me as a mother?" She laughed, but it was stilted. "We haven't even set a wedding date."

"How's your mother?" Ellie asked.

Lame, but Yolanda was thankful for the change in subject. "She's pretty much the—"

"Excuse me." Shereen turned and started down the hallway toward the living room.

Again, silence. Moments later, when a door closed, Ellie ran her hands over her face. "I'm sorry. God, I'm such an idiot sometimes."

Jessica glanced in the direction Shereen had disappeared. "She went to the bathroom. You think I should go see if she's all right?"

"No." Ellie shook her head. "It's best you don't say anything."

Yolanda frowned. "Maybe I should talk to her."

"What if she's just gotta pee?"

"I doubt that," Yolanda said, punctuating the statement with a soft moan.

Ellie looked down the hallway, then back at Yolanda. "You two have already talked about this, right?"

"Yeah."

"And she's all right with the situation?"

"So she says."

"Then let her be. Besides, Shereen isn't going to want us treating her like she's some kind of emotional cripple."

"I guess not." But Yolanda wasn't convinced. Should she seek out her friend and say something? Assure her it was okay to tell her what was on her mind?

"No," Jessica agreed. "Ellie's definitely right."

More silence. Then the toilet flushed.

Ellie gave a quick shrug of her shoulders, then started talking. Something about center islands, but Yolanda tuned her and Jessica out. Despite what Ellie had said, she couldn't forget the surprised look in Shereen's eyes at the idea of her and Terrence having children. Would it always be like this when one of them mentioned Terrence? Or would Shereen soon get used to the fact that he and Yolanda were a couple?

Yolanda hoped it was the latter.

She hoped Shereen wasn't still in love with Terrence Simms.

Much later, when the doorbell rang, Yolanda jumped up from her spot on the living room floor and hurried to answer it.

"Here," Jessica said, waving a twenty-dollar bill at her.

"No, I got it."

She opened the door, retrieved the large pizza from the delivery guy, tipped him, then went back to the living room and placed the pizza box on the coffee table.

"Sorry, Jessica. No anchovies."

"You said you'd put them on half," Jessica whined.

Yolanda flashed her a skeptical look. "And you were gonna eat a whole six slices by yourself?"

"What a way to ruin a pizza." Shereen shuddered.

"Tell me about it," Ellie agreed.

"You all don't know what you're missing."

Yolanda lifted the bottle of red wine and emptied the dregs into her glass. Thanks to her friends, almost all the boxes were unpacked, and for the past hour, they'd been taking a break to chat and drink some of the wine they'd brought to christen the house. "Anyone want more wine?"

"Please," Ellie said, as though her life depended on it.

"Don't wait for me. Dig in." Yolanda stepped over Shereen's legs as she made her way out of the living room. In the kitchen, she grabbed a roll of paper towels and another bottle of wine, then headed back to the living room. She returned to her spot on the floor, crossing her legs.

Ellie had two slices of pizza folded together, sandwich-style. "Forget my diet. This is a special occasion."

"Damn straight," Jessica agreed. She'd had her share of wine and was clearly feeling happy. "Our girl is back in town."

"To us," Shereen said. "To being back together again."

"We already drank to that," Ellie said, but still she raised her glass.

"Who the hell cares? We can drink to that again, and again." Shereen faced Yolanda. "We're just glad to have you back."

Yolanda raised her glass to Shereen's. Her concerns over Shereen's feelings for Terrence had dissipated when Shereen had returned from the bathroom, happy as a peach. "Thanks."

"I don't know about anybody else." Jessica looked at them each in turn. "But after Yolanda ran off to Philadelphia with *James*, I thought she'd never come back."

"Shut up, girl." They still liked to bug her about how hard she'd fallen for James. Having been dubbed the Ice Queen, she was the last one they'd expected to go goo-goo gaga over a man, much less pick up and move with him for *his* career. Hell, she'd surprised herself.

Ellie laughed. "I didn't expect to see her ass back here, either."

"Goes to show we can all have moments of temporary insanity."

"Speak for yourself." Shereen poured more wine into everyone's glasses.

"Speaking of James," Ellie said. "How is he?"

Yolanda made a face.

"Oh. It's like that."

"Girl, James is my past. Terrence is my future."

Shereen tipped her head back and downed a liberal sip of her wine. When she realized everyone was looking at her, she said, "Will you guys stop? Yolanda is engaged to Terrence so I'm gonna hear his name. We're gonna talk about him. And I'm not gonna fall apart."

"Of course you won't." Ellie reached across the coffee table to squeeze Shereen's hand. Shereen gave her a smile.

"I want to make a toast." Yolanda lifted her glass.

"Here we go." Ellie rolled her eyes.

"You hush, Ellie." She wasn't *that* long-winded—well, except when she was drunk. "Just for that, I'm gonna give you a speech." Yolanda cleared her throat, then began. "When I became a Theta, I figured I was joining a group of caring sisters who were concerned about their communities and wanted to give back. And that was fine. That's all I wanted. To give back because the Thetas had helped encourage me as a child. But I *received*. And that's why this sorority is so special to me—because it gave me such great friends. You've always been there for me, even though I can be overbearing—"

"Temperamental."

"Controlling."

"Moody."

"Well, damn. And I thought you all loved me." Yolanda feigned a crushed tone.

"You know we do," Shereen assured her. "God only knows why, but we do."

"*Anyway* . . ."

Shereen mimed pulling a zipper closed along her lips.

Yolanda went back to being serious. "All I really want to say is that you're the best friends a girl could ever ask for. I love you all."

There was a hum of ohs, aws, and we-love-you-toos, then everyone clinked glasses and drank to that. Both Shereen and Jessica dabbed at their eyes.

After a moment, Yolanda slapped her hand on the coffee table. "Oh, I forgot to tell you this. I met a woman in Philly—she was a client. She's sitting in my office, we're talking about her case. Then she sees my red-and-gold tote bag, so she asks if I'm a Theta. Of course I say yes. Well, turns out she's also a Theta, went to Temple. Anyway, we get to talking and when I tell her I pledged at Howard, you'll never believe what she asked me."

"What?" Shereen queried.

"She asked if the legend of the *Playboy bunnies* was true."

"The *legend*?" Ellie gaped at her.

"I swear to God." Yolanda held a hand over her heart.

Shereen stifled a laugh. "Get out."

"I'm serious. I about fell out of my chair. We're a friggin' legend, and I had no clue."

"Maybe she was talking about something else."

"You'd like to think that, *Wild Thang*—considering the Playboy bunny getup was your bright idea. But she knew the whole story. How the women were out to get some guy's jersey. I don't need to go on. Anyway, it's amazing how stories can spread. Can you believe it?"

Ellie continued to gape. "What did you tell her?"

"That it was bullshit."

Everyone cracked up. Everyone except Jessica.

Yolanda looked at her from across the coffee table, but her friend's head was lowered and she looked a million miles away. "Jessica?"

Her head whipped up. "Can I ask you something?" Her voice was nervous, high-pitched.

Shereen placed her wineglass on the table. "What is it?"

"Did one of you—" She stopped abruptly, shook her head. "Forget it."

"Forget what?" Yolanda asked.

"Nothing."

Yolanda frowned. "It had to be something if you brought it up."

"Well . . ." Again, she shook her head. "No, it's nothing."

"Jessica . . ." Ellie stared at her with concern.

"It was just one of those stupid life questions, but I can't even re-member now what it was. Whoa, I'm drunk." She reached for her wine-glass as if to emphasize her point.

Yolanda stared at her a moment longer, not sure what to think. But that look of urgency was gone. "Well, if you *do* want to ask us some-thing, you know you can."

"Thank you, Counselor." Jessica giggled. "Come on. You know me and alcohol."

"Ain't that the truth," Shereen agreed.

"Speaking of alcohol . . ." Yolanda reached for the wine bottle and shook it, wondering where it had all gone so fast. "If we're gonna get drunk, we may as well do it right."

"As long as you don't mind us all crashing on the living room floor," Shereen said.

"Like that's an issue."

"Then get some more wine, girl," Ellie told her. " 'Cause I've got this buzz right now and I don't want it to fade."

Yolanda stood, smiling. When was the last time she'd gotten plastered with her friends?

Not since—not since forever.

Yeah, tonight they'd get stupid. Just like they used to before they'd set out to conquer the world.

THE PAST

"TURN THAT SHIT UP, GIRL!"

Shereen danced her way across her dorm room to the ghetto blaster on her desk and pumped up the volume on the TLC tune.

"Ain't too proud to beg . . ."

"Sing it, Wild Thang!" Yolanda snapped her fingers and bumped a hip against Ellie's. Ellie gyrated her hips as she continued to sing, then giggled as Shereen got in front of her and mimicked her sexy motions.

Jessica, who lay on her stomach on Shereen's bed, laughed at the sight of her friends getting stupid.

"What's so funny?" Shereen asked, placing her hands on her hips as she stared at Jessica.

"You all make me laugh," Jessica replied.

"Get your butt up here," Yolanda told her. Yolanda danced over to the bed and reached for her. Jessica let her grab her hands and help her to the floor.

They all danced their hearts out until the song was over. Then the tempo changed as Peabo Bryson's and Roberta Flack's voices filled the airwaves, singing, "Tonight, I celebrate my love . . ."

"Put in a tape or something," Ellie said, catching her breath.

"No," Jessica quickly interjected. "I love this song." As the song played, she hugged her torso and swayed her body back and forth. She closed her eyes, remembering the last time Andrew's hands had been on her body. They'd made love with this song playing in the background more than once.

"What's up with Jessica?" Shereen asked in a playful tone.

Ellie said, "I don't know, girl. She's acting all strange."

Jessica opened her eyes to find her friends staring at her with curious expressions. "What?"

"You're off in friggin' la-la land, that's what," Ellie replied. "Something you want to tell us?"

"I love this song,"Jessica answered simply.

"Uh-huh," Ellie said. "Girl, I know that look. Don't tell me you've gone and fallen in love."

Jessica couldn't contain her smile. "I think I have," she responded, her voice dreamy.

"With the professor?" Shereen asked, even though it couldn't be anyone else.

"With *Andrew*," Jessica clarified.

"Girl," Yolanda began, "when did this get so serious?"

Jessica shrugged. She didn't know why her friends were so surprised. She'd been seeing Andrew for over two months. It was obvious her feelings for him had grown during that time.

"I don't know," Jessica answered. "I only know that this is the best feeling in the world." She suddenly pivoted on her heel, turning for the door. "I have to go."

"Hey, where are you going?" Shereen asked.

"I need to see Andrew." She had something very important to tell him, something she hoped he'd be as happy about as she was. "He's getting back into town tonight . . ."

Shereen looked at the clock. It was shortly after nine P.M. "Can't you see him in the morning?"

"Nope." Any other day, she might wait until the morning, but Andrew had been out of town for a week. She missed him and she couldn't wait to tell him her good news.

"Oh, so you're just gonna diss your girls for a man," Yolanda said in a mock-hurt tone.

"You all know I love you."

Ellie made a sour face, even as a smile shone in her eyes. "Mmm-hmm."

"Of course I do." After the night they'd met Andrew, Jessica, Shereen, Yolanda, and Ellie had all grown very close. She loved them like they were her *real* sisters. "But . . . well, you understand."

"Not really," Yolanda quipped playfully.

"Well *I* do." Ellie giggled. "And if I had to choose between a man and y'all, I'd be out that door so fast . . ."

"Thanks," Shereen said wryly.

"Like you wouldn't," Ellie answered.

"You're just a sex-crazy Scorpio," Shereen told her.

"Hey, sex makes the world go 'round."

"*Love* makes the world go round," Yolanda said.

"Who told you that shit?" Ellie countered. "You can't count on love, but sex—"

"Y'all are crazy." Jessica giggled.

"I know." Shereen traipsed over to Jessica and hugged her. "Go have fun."

"Thanks, Mom." As Jessica pulled away from Shereen, she felt a warmth in her heart. She could share anything with these three women, she knew that.

But not this news, not yet. Not until she told Andrew first.

The wind howled, low and seductive, like a lover's moan.

Appropriate, considering where Jessica was and whom she was meeting.

She killed the engine of the Chevette, the car she'd borrowed from Ellie for the trip, but didn't get out. Instead, she stared out the windshield, looking at the cabin. There was a trail of white Christmas lights along the porch's railing that hadn't been there the last time. A smile touched her lips. It seemed fitting that this place should be filled with Christmas cheer tonight.

Because tonight was different.

She opened the car door and stepped out, her boots crunching on the gravel driveway. The cold wind bit at her skin immediately, and she huddled into her jacket, bracing against the chill. She hoped Andrew had a fire burning. She loved a fire on a cold winter night.

She hustled to the porch, but instead of knocking or trying the door, she peered through the window. It was cold enough for frost to have formed on the panes. Somehow, it seemed more romantic that way. That while outside was cold, inside would be filled with warmth and love.

The only light inside the cabin came from the blazing fire and a few candles placed around the living room. A comforter and two pillows lay on the floor before the fireplace.

She knew Andrew wouldn't disappoint her. He was passionate and romantic, and this night would be incredibly special.

But where was he?

She saw him then, entering the living room from the kitchen at the back of the cabin. He was carrying two snifters with brandy. Such a simple thing, but her heart filled with joy. She watched him a moment longer, for she loved to simply watch his sexy, masculine movements. God, she loved him so much!

Then she knocked on the window, and waved when Andrew looked in her direction. Immediately, his face lit up with one of his sweet smiles, like the mere sight of her made his whole day worthwhile.

He placed the drinks on the table and hurried to the door. "My sweet love," he said, opening the door for her. "Come in out of the cold."

Jessica stepped into the cabin, warmth wrapping around her like a velvet blanket, though she didn't know if it was the warmth from the fire or the warmth from Andrew.

Probably a bit of both.

No, of course it was Andrew. Always Andrew.

He kissed her lips softly, the way he always greeted her, then took her coat. She watched as he placed it on the coat tree, captivated by every move he made. Was it normal to find such simple things erotic?

"How was the drive?" he asked when he turned back to her.

"It wasn't bad." He took her hands as she spoke, pulling her toward him. Toward the fire. "Just cold."

"Don't worry, my love. I'll keep you warm."

Though he was considerably older than her, Jessica hadn't found another man more attractive than him. Certainly not one of the fraternity brothers, not even the ones all the girls lost their heads over. No, Andrew was sexy, right from the inside out, in a way that the young guys couldn't compete with.

Maybe it was his maturity. Maybe it was the way his eyes crinkled when he smiled at her.

God, she didn't know. She only knew that she loved everything about him.

"Oh, Andrew. I missed you so much."

"I know." He kissed her forehead, yet she felt it way down in her toes.

"I don't want us to be apart like that again, Andrew."

He brushed his lips over hers. "My love, the last thing I want is to be away from you for a minute, let alone an hour. But I think our time apart was a good thing. We've been spending so much time together, people are starting to get suspicious. And despite how we feel about each other, we can't let anyone know."

She sighed. He always said that, but it wasn't like she was a child. So what if he was her professor?

"Not until the semester is over," she clarified. She knew she sounded needy, but she did need him. She needed to know they could be together. Before she told him her news.

"Of course. Once exams are over and the final marks are in." He smiled. "Don't worry."

She relaxed against him, resting her head against his chest. His words made her feel better. She didn't know why she was so antsy these days. Maybe the hormones.

"Are you hungry?"

"I ate before I got here." *Now all I want is you.* She giggled at her thought. Though they'd made love several times, she was still shy about telling him things like that.

"What's so funny?"

She snaked her arms around his waist. "Nothing."

"You want dessert, don't you?" He raised an eyebrow. She giggled. "Don't be shy. You can tell me what you want."

She merely shrugged.

"I know I want you. To taste your skin." He kissed her neck. "To feel your heart beating against mine." He crushed her breasts to his chest.

Her eyes fluttered shut. "Oh, Andrew."

He kissed her hard, holding her to him like he wanted to meld their bodies. She surrendered to him instantly, wholly, like she always did.

She wanted to tell him now, but she could hardly think of anything other than the love she felt for him and how much she wanted to be in his bed.

Then he began to disrobe her, and she thought, *I'll tell him later.*

Chapter Eleven

"I DON'T KNOW WHY I'm doing this." Shereen frowned at Jessica, who was driving. They were en route to meet Douglas and one of his friends (that is, a prospective future mate for Shereen) at a restaurant in Georgetown. This was the third time in as many weeks that Jessica or Ellie had tried to set her up with someone, but the first time Shereen had agreed to meet the guy. She'd finally given in because Jessica hadn't stopped pressuring her. "Jonathon's a sweetie, I'm telling you. You have to meet him." Though neither Jessica nor Ellie would say it, they were still concerned about how she was dealing with Yolanda's engagement to Terrence, the only man she'd ever loved.

"Shereen." Jessica's tone was frank. "What can it hurt to meet him? We're not talking life commitment here. Just dinner. And if you really, really don't like him, I won't hold it against you if you leave before dinner."

"I hope you don't mind if I borrow your car."

"Why do you have to be so negative?" Jessica faced her briefly before turning her attention back to the road. "What if you actually like him? What if *he* wants to drive you back to the office to get your car? What if *you* want him to?"

"Jessica, please." Against her better judgment, Shereen had agreed to drive in Jessica's car because her friend wouldn't take no for an answer. But if worse came to worst and the night was a total bust, she could always catch a cab back to the office. "I don't know why you all think I'm dying without a man, anyway. I'm not."

"There's nothing wrong with meeting new people. That's all this is."

"What's his sign?"

"I don't know."

Shereen folded her arms over her chest. "I hope he's not a Gemini."

"Dinner, not marriage. Remember that."

Minutes later, Jessica and Shereen strolled into the Caribbean restaurant. It was packed with an after-work crowd. Shereen glanced around and quickly spotted Douglas among the group of professionals at the nearby bar. He was tall, handsome, and easily stood out. But it was the man with whom Douglas chatted who got Shereen's attention. Well over six feet, he was sharply dressed in a double-breasted navy suit. Though Shereen could see only a partial view of his face, it was obvious he was very attractive.

"Close your mouth, dear," Jessica said, a smile in her voice.

"What did you say he does?"

"Publicity for the network."

"And where have you been hiding him?"

Jessica's smile was victorious. "I take it you approve?"

Shereen looped her arm through her friend's, then started toward the bar.

"Hi, sweetheart." Jessica gave Douglas a quick hug. "Jonathon, this is my friend Shereen. Shereen, this is Jonathon."

He turned, fully facing her, a sexy smile gracing his beautiful mouth. Shereen's heart did a little flip-flop. Mmm-mmm-mmm, he was fine. Even better, his eyes lit up as he stared at her, making it clear he liked what he saw.

"Nice to meet you, Jonathon."

He took her hand in his, brought it to his mouth, and gently kissed it. "The pleasure is all mine."

"Hello, Shereen."

Shereen's cheeks flamed at the sound of Douglas's voice. Seeing Jonathon, she'd all but forgotten that Douglas and Jessica were there. "Hey, Douglas."

"Let's get a table," Douglas suggested.

They sat at a booth in the no-smoking section. A definite plus. Jonathon didn't smoke.

"Shereen, Douglas tells me you're the VP of Finance at M&A Graphics."

Shereen's name sounded as smooth as warm chocolate on Jonathon's lips. God, she could get used to that voice. "Yes, I am. My father started the company fifteen years ago, and it's grown to be one of the largest graphics firms in the Northeast."

"Impressive." But his eyes roamed over her face, and Shereen wasn't sure if he was referring to the business or to her.

"What about you? How did you get involved in publicity at the station?"

"It was the first job I got out of college. I worked at an affiliate station in New York until two years ago, when I was transferred here."

"You like Washington?"

"I love it. And I have a feeling I'm going to love it even more now."

Jessica kicked Shereen beneath the table. When Shereen looked at her, Jessica discreetly raised an eyebrow.

"Let me look at this menu," Shereen said, needing to escape Jonathon's gaze. Not that she didn't enjoy looking at him, but she had a feeling she could lose herself in his face, in the sexy angles and grooves. And in his smile. He had the most mesmerizing smile

"Red or white wine?" Douglas asked.

"Red," Jessica replied.

"Sweetheart, you're not having wine, are you?"

"Oh. Oh, no. Of course not."

Shereen's eyes shot to Jessica, but she didn't meet her gaze. What was *that* about?

Jonathon's voice pulled her back to the here and now. "Shereen, red or white?"

"Whatever you like. I'm not fussy."

"Then how about a Chardonnay?" Jonathon suggested.

Good choice, Shereen thought, giving him a warm smile.

Though Shereen hadn't been able to imagine it at the beginning of the evening, she was now glad that Jessica had driven her to the restaurant.

Because now Jonathon could drive her back to her office, where she'd left her car. Which, she realized as she got into his late-model Mercedes, she really wanted him to do. She liked him and wanted to spend more time with him.

There were no lulls in the conversation as he drove to her downtown office. Strangely, they talked with the comfort level of two people who had known each other all their lives. Feeling an immediate connection with a man was something that rarely happened for Shereen, and she couldn't help thinking that it was about time.

"Oh, that's it. Wait. You just passed it." Shereen giggled. "Sorry. I wasn't paying attention."

"Neither was I."

Shereen watched Jonathon's strong hands as he negotiated the steering wheel for a U-turn. He drove a short distance in the opposite direction, then made another U-turn until he was in front of the red-brick building that housed M&A Graphics.

And with that, the trip was over. Much too soon.

"So," he said, turning to face her.

"So."

Pause. Then Jonathon chuckled softly, and so did she.

There was another pause, after which he said, "I like you."

"Do you?"

"Yeah, I do. You're not seeing anyone, are you?"

"No. You?"

"Uh-uh. I haven't been involved with anyone since my divorce two years ago."

So he was divorced. No big deal. Enough time had passed that he wouldn't be on the rebound.

"I'd like to see you again."

"I'd like that, too." He was attractive, charming, had a great career. And best of all, he was available.

"What are you doing this weekend?"

"I don't have any plans."

"Then we should do something."

"Like?" To Shereen's surprise, she sounded sexy, playful.

"You can show me some of the Washington sites."

"I'm sure you've seen them already."

"Maybe, but they'll be much more interesting if I see them with you."

Shereen actually blushed.

"Give me your number and I'll call you."

Shereen searched for a pen and a scrap of paper in her purse, wrote down her number, then passed it to him. She didn't ask for his. She'd let him make the first move.

He looked at the number. "Maryland?"

"Yeah. Prince George's County."

Jonathon stuffed the paper into his interior jacket pocket, then turned back to Shereen. Suddenly she had no clue what to say. But she didn't want to leave, she knew that much, and it was obvious by his silence that he didn't want her to leave, either. It was as if they both thought that by staying silent the inevitable good-bye would never come.

"Can I ask you a question?" Shereen suddenly asked.

"Sure."

"What sign are you?"

He thought a moment. "Virgo."

An earth sign, like her. *Thank you, God.*

"Is that good?"

"Oh, yeah. Virgo is good."

As she stared at him, he drew his bottom lip between his teeth. A subtle yet powerful gesture that let her know how much he wanted her.

Lord, was this gorgeous, sexy *Virgo* truly available? The stars were definitely lining up in her favor. "I'd better go."

"I guess so."

She reached for the door handle at the same moment he leaned forward and kissed her, catching her completely by surprise. The kiss wasn't too short, which would mean he wasn't interested, nor was it too long, which would make him too forward.

Damn, it was just right.

And as Shereen settled behind the wheel of her car, her heart pumping with excitement, she felt for the first time in ages that perhaps she'd been lying to herself.

Maybe she did need a man in her life.

She just needed the right one.

Chapter Twelve

"THE SUN HAS FINALLY made an appearance. Beautiful, you have brightened my day."

"Morning, Red." Jessica leaned forward and pecked him on the cheek.

Placing both hands on his hips, Redmond angled his head and gawked at her. "Now I know I didn't do anything to offend you, so why you gonna do me like that? Where's my hug?"

"Sorry." Jessica wrapped her arms around him. "You know I'm happy to see you, Red."

He gave her a good long squeeze with much more enthusiasm than she had given him, then released her. "Girl, you're as stiff as a board. What's got you in this funky mood?"

"I'm tired." She yawned for emphasis.

"I may only do your hair, but I see you every morning and I know when you're cool and when you're not. Is it Claudia again? 'Cuz if it is, you just tell me and I'll—"

"No, it's not Claudia." Claudia, one of the network's receptionists, was still giving her grief. She continued to do things like forward Jessica's calls to the wrong extension—she'd gotten lots of complaints about that from her friends—childish things that were more annoying than aggravating. For the most part, Claudia wasn't particularly rude, but she wasn't particularly friendly, either. But last week, she'd brazenly assaulted Jessica. She'd bumped into Jessica on her way out of the kitchen—deliberately, Jessica was sure—spilling coffee over the sleeve of Jessica's silk jacket. Claudia had muttered an insincere apology as Jessica scrambled to get paper towels. She didn't stay and try to help clean the jacket, didn't offer to have it dry-cleaned. Rightly pissed, Jessica had told Redmond about the incident while he'd styled her hair.

For some reason, Claudia hated Jessica. Jessica suspected she had a crush on Douglas, but had no real proof.

"Then what, baby? Is it Douglas?"

Redmond had a knack for pulling things out of her she'd normally keep to herself. Like her concerns over whether or not people at the network thought she'd married Douglas for his money, or for what he could do for her career. When she'd first gotten the job as host of *The Scoop*, she'd heard grumblings to that effect. She'd also heard grumblings that she wasn't qualified. She'd soon proven herself and the griping had died down, but still, she felt a degree of insecurity. She'd confessed that to Redmond as well.

The negative comments hurt her. The naysayers would never know how hard she'd once worked to get over her shyness, that this job meant so much not because of the public spotlight but because she'd proven to herself she could succeed, face her demons and win. She'd once been so shy she'd given up a track scholarship, afraid to be in the spotlight, afraid of success. Afterward, she'd hated herself for blowing a chance at the one thing she was passionate about: running. She had vowed to get over her crippling shyness, which was why she'd joined a sorority, then taken a drama course. She'd discovered a new love in performing. But after graduation, two years in New York had proven to her that she didn't have what it took to be an actress. However, she had a good on-screen presence and a great speaking voice, so her agent had told her, and subsequently he'd sent her for host auditions. She'd landed the first such audition and had hosted an infomercial for a car company. After that, she'd hosted twelve episodes of a children's show on a specialty channel. But she'd always dreamed of a career in network television. It was a dream that had come true.

No doubt because of Douglas, but that didn't mean she wasn't qualified.

Still, Jessica sometimes expressed doubts, and when she did, Redmond always assured her she was talented, beautiful, and more than qualified. And in his charming, not-so-tactful way, he told her not to give a rat's ass if people spoke ill of her. "They're just jealous," he'd tell her, never missing a beat as he styled her hair. Jessica always left his chair with a smile, feeling very much like she'd had a therapy session.

"No," she said in response to his question. "Douglas is great." It was a white lie, but her personal life with Douglas was strictly off-limits.

"Well, whatever it is, child, you know you can talk to me."

"I'm fine. Really. But thanks for caring."

"Baby, you know I care. Now sit." He patted the stylist's chair.

Aside from having an exciting career at the network, Redmond was one of the people who made coming to the studio each day a treat. Some days she was certain he was straight—he'd look her up and down like he wanted to eat her with some melted butter. Other days she wasn't sure if he was gay, but still in the closet.

Right now, she wondered if he was gay. Which wasn't really fair, she knew, to assume he was gay just because she could talk to him like she could talk to one of her girl friends.

"How can I please you today?"

Jessica couldn't help smiling at Redmond's double entendre. No, he was straight. No question.

She pulled her hair back tightly from her face. "This is my problem, Red. My hair. I swear, I'm ready to cut it all off."

"Oh, no. No, baby. All you need to do is give it some tender loving care." He fluffed her hair around her shoulders. "That's why I'm here."

Sometimes he was a little too effeminate, like now, as he fluffed her hair. No, he had to be gay. "I don't know, Red."

"Trust me. When I finish with it, you won't even recognize yourself."

Sighing, Jessica closed her eyes and let Redmond do his job. Though her hair wasn't really the problem. Her life was.

Last night, Douglas had brought up baby names. *Baby names*—only minutes after she'd secretly taken the pill. As they'd lain in bed, his arm protectively draped over her waist, he'd asked what she wanted to name their child. He'd said he liked Douglas Jr. if it was a boy and was that okay with her? Jessica's head had started to spin. Even now, she didn't know what she'd said in reply, only that she had tried to sound enthusiastic. She felt guilty as hell for lying to him, but she was already weaving her web of deception. How could she get out of it? And she was scared. Douglas was bound to start asking questions soon—questions about why she wasn't yet pregnant.

"Girl, something *is* wrong. I can feel it in your shoulders. You're so tense."

"I'm fine."

"Okay. You want to be secretive. I guess everyone's gotta have at least one secret, hmm baby?"

"*Excuse* me?"

"Baby, we all have secrets. I have a closet full. I wonder what someone as sweet as you has buried in yours."

What was Redmond talking about? Jessica looked at him in the mirror. He had a silly smirk on his face.

Seemingly harmless—but was it?

Oh, God, did he know? And if so, how? Had he seen one of her letters?

Jessica chuckled nervously. "Why are you asking this, Red?"

"It's okay, baby. You don't have to tell me."

Redmond continued doing her hair, and the tension Jessica had felt moments before ebbed away. Like she always did, she completely relaxed as Redmond worked on her hair.

All too quickly, Redmond finished with her. When she looked at her reflection in the mirror, his words rang true: she barely recognized herself.

"Wow." She brought a hand to her hair, pulling on one of the ringlet curls. "I *love* this."

"Of course, baby. When do I not satisfy you?" He did a little head rotation, full of attitude. "Now, you couldn't do this if you cut off all your hair. Whatever it is going on in your life, please don't take it out on your hair. Okay?"

She gave him a weak smile as she stood. "Okay."

"Love you, girl."

"Love you, too." She leaned forward to kiss his cheek, but he turned his face and her lips caught his mouth.

He's not gay, she thought, her spirits lifting. No, Redmond was definitely straight.

She used to love receiving mail. A letter, a bill—it didn't matter. There was something depressing about opening a mailbox to find it empty, something wonderful about finding a mailbox full. Almost as if the presence of mail validated your very existence.

Now, every time she received a letter at the studio, she felt a moment of anxiety. Because every new letter could be from the person who apparently knew her secret.

"Wow." Jessica stared down at the bag of mail Julie had just handed her. "This weighs a ton."

"You're getting more and more popular." Julie smiled, clearly pleased with that fact.

"I guess so." Jessica's voice was shaky. Her whole body was. She didn't want to open this bag. What if it held a letter that could further shatter her life?

Until that bombshell two months ago, the worst letter she'd received was from a viewer who thought she looked horrid in beige. That, and a few letters from oddballs, but never anything threatening.

Last week, she'd received a letter that had simply said, "I'm watching you." It had come by regular mail, unlike the two couriered letters about Andrew Bell, and Jessica couldn't be sure if it was from the same person.

"I'll see you later," Julie said.

"Yeah. Later."

As Julie disappeared down the hallway, Jessica forced a deep breath in and out of her lungs. She dropped the bag onto the floor, then lay down on the sofa. She was afraid to go through the letters. Afraid, like a piece of paper could hurt her.

The paper couldn't, but the person sending it could.

After the troubling "I'm watching you" note, Jessica had given the situation some serious thought. Andrew was dead. She'd stood at the back of the church during his funeral, had watched from afar as his casket was lowered into the ground. Sure, strange things happened, but the idea that he was actually alive was simply too absurd. Yes, in some rare instances people wrote suicide notes, then faked their deaths, but why would Andrew do that? And if he had, why come back now, nine years after his supposed death? Just to drive her crazy?

No, he was dead. Even the truck driver whose rig he'd driven into had been at the funeral, weeping from guilt beside her in the back row. There was no way Andrew could have written her any letter. But maybe—though she didn't know how this could have happened— someone had found one of Andrew's old letters and forwarded it to her.

Where? Where would someone just happen upon such a letter so many years after his death? No, that didn't make sense. Groaning, Jessica closed her eyes.

Maybe it was one of her sorors. She opened her eyes, that idea seeming to fit this crazy puzzle. Yes, that made sense. Maybe Elizabeth Vodden. Because Jessica had always been quiet, Elizabeth had considered her snooty. She also thought Jessica was trying to get into the Theta Phi Kappa sorority on the back of her sister's reputation. For that reason, Elizabeth had singled her out for the worst tasks during the pledging process. Sleep deprivation, scrubbing toilets—anything to make Jessica suffer.

And while Elizabeth hadn't been able to prove it, she was certain that Jessica was the one behind the prank that had ruined her car. In truth, Jessica was, but Elizabeth had been begging for some type of payback. And it was Ellie, wonderful Ellie, who'd suggested getting some of the frat brothers to lift Elizabeth's small Chevette into one of the school's fountains. Elizabeth had been livid and had immediately pointed the finger at Jessica, but none of the big sisters believed the always quiet, always demure Jessica had anything to do with it, and she hadn't been reprimanded.

God, it really could be Elizabeth, Jessica decided. While Elizabeth, like most of the sorors, had learned of her involvement with Andrew Bell, she hadn't known everything. But what if she'd done a little digging? She could have hit pay dirt, found the one secret Jessica never wanted anyone to learn.

It was a long shot, but one that made sense.

She glanced at the bag of letters. Then jumped to her feet. She couldn't live this way. Constantly being afraid. If there was another letter about her secret in that bag, ignoring it would do no good. She had to know the truth.

She spent the next thirty minutes going through every piece of mail, briefly glancing, then tossing aside. So far, everything had been harmless.

When she lifted the last envelope, she held it in her hands for several seconds, simply checking it out. It had no return address. Just like the others. Her stomach lurched. *Please, God, no. Don't let this be another one.*

She tore open the envelope, withdrew the letter, then started to read.

Ms. Bedford,
    Congratulations on your feature in the Washingtonian!

A letter from another viewer. Harmless, like the rest. Nothing about Andrew.

Jessica's shoulders drooped as relief swept over her.

And then she started laughing. The sound was hollow at first, tentative, but grew more boisterous as each second passed. Louder, harder, until she threw her head back and gripped her stomach, unable to stop the laughter even as tears fell from her eyes.

THE PAST

LATER, AFTER THEIR LOVEMAKING, Jessica lay in the crook of Andrew's arm, content. Behind them, the embers danced on the firewood as the flames smoldered, nearly burning out.

Jessica lifted her head, balancing her chin on his chest. "Do you love me?"

Andrew met her eyes. "Of course I love you. You know that."

Her lips curled in a grin. She did know, but she just liked to hear him say it. "I love you, too."

He patted her rump. "Get some sleep."

She laid her head back down, ready to do just that, but then she lifted it again. Why was she afraid to tell him? He loved her. And he deserved to know.

"Andrew," she said slowly, and he opened his eyes. "There's something I have to tell you."

He tightened his arm around her waist. "What is it?"

Something held her back. The fear of what people would think, what they would say? *How silly. It only matters what Andrew thinks, how he feels. That he loves you.*

"I'm pregnant, Andrew."

Andrew grew very still, so still that Jessica wondered if he had suddenly become a block of stone. Behind them, the last of the embers did a final two-step, then died.

It seemed like an eternity before he spoke. "What did you say?"

"I'm pregnant."

"Are you sure?"

Something was wrong. This wasn't the way she'd imagined he'd respond. "I didn't go to the doctor, if that's what you mean. But I feel it,

Andrew." She placed a hand on her belly. "Here." Then she placed a hand on her heart. "And right here."

"You need to go to the doctor. Find out for sure."

Something was definitely wrong. "I will. But I wanted to tell you first."

He sat up. "Damn."

"You . . . you're not happy?" Her heart dropped to her stomach.

He didn't respond.

"Andrew, you said you love me."

"I do." He didn't sound the same. He sounded curt. Unhappy.

"Then what's wrong?"

"A baby?" He laughed mirthlessly.

"I know . . . Oh, Andrew. Is it because we're not married? Because if it is, well, this isn't the way I planned it, either, but what can we do? It happened."

A look of horror—and something else, Jessica wasn't sure what—passed over his face. "You said you're not sure."

She half nodded, half shrugged. "No . . ."

"Good. Then before we discuss this anymore, I want you to go to the doctor."

"Okay." But what did that mean? Go to the doctor to find out so he would know whether or not to be happy, or find out so he could tell her to have an abortion?

She shuddered at the last option.

Andrew stood, taking with him his warmth. "I need to use the bathroom."

He disappeared without another word, leaving Jessica confused and frustrated. Her mind worked overtime, trying to come up with some reason for his attitude. What was it? Didn't he want to have children? Or was he concerned with what the university's staff would say?

That had to be it. He'd been overly concerned that the faculty might find out about their relationship, but a baby would be definite proof of their affair.

But still, he'd told her only hours ago that they could be open about their relationship after the semester.

Maybe it was his old-fashioned sensibilities. But this was the nineties. There were certainly worse things than being pregnant out of wedlock.

She'd switch schools to be with him if she had to, if that would make it easier. God, she'd do anything. As long as he didn't shut her out.

As long as he wanted the baby.

Because Jessica didn't need a doctor to tell her she was pregnant. She knew it in her heart. . . .

Chapter Thirteen

"SHEREEN." YOLANDA'S EYES WIDENED with surprise when she opened her front door. "What are you doing here?"

"Hey, girl," Shereen said cheerfully. "I didn't see you at the school today so I thought I'd come by and check on you. You okay?" Shereen was proud that she didn't smirk as she asked the question. She, Ellie, and Jessica had all deliberately "forgotten" Yolanda's birthday, which was yesterday. They'd all come up with reasons why they were too busy to get together this weekend, and Yolanda's no-show at the school's literacy program was an indication that she was peeved.

"I'm okay," Yolanda replied halfheartedly.

"Mind if I come in?" When Yolanda didn't respond immediately, Shereen added, "You're not busy, are you?"

"Why would I be busy?" Yolanda's voice held a hint of sarcasm, as did her grin. "Sure. Come in."

Shereen stepped into the house and looked around. In the last few weeks, the house had become a home. The place looked beautiful. In the living room were an expensive leather sofa and matching love seat. A colorful silk rug adorned the bleached oak floor, on top of which sat a bleached oak coffee table. African-themed paintings hung throughout the living room and the rest of the house. Yolanda had shutters, not blinds. Every piece of furniture, every ornament, spoke of taste and money. Which didn't surprise Shereen. Yolanda, who'd grown up without, was always determined to prove she had escaped that past.

"Oh, wait," Shereen said suddenly. "I left my purse in the car. My cell is in there."

"You can use my phone."

"I'm expecting a call."

A frown marred Yolanda's face. "O-kay."

Seconds later, Shereen was back at the car. As she opened the door she said, "She's pissed."

Ellie finished lighting the candles on the cake. "Did she say anything about her birthday?"

"Uh-uh."

"That's Yo," Ellie said. "Too proud for her own good. Here." Ellie handed the cake to Shereen, then got out of the car. Jessica exited on the other side.

Jessica said, "You lead the way, Shereen."

Shereen gave the cake back to Ellie, then led the way to Yolanda's front door. She gestured for Ellie and Jessica to stay hidden as she opened the door without knocking. Yolanda sat on the sofa with her head back and her eyes closed.

Turning to Ellie and Jessica, Shereen silently beckoned them forward. As soon as they were all in the doorway, she mouthed, *One, two, three.*

"Happy birthday to you!" Yolanda's eyes flew open, registering shock, then a smile erupted on her face at the sight of her friends. "Happy birthday to you! Happy birthday, Yolanda—"

"—You miserable little thing, you," Ellie sang as she approached Yolanda with the cake.

"Happy birthday to you!"

While Yolanda smiled her face off, Jessica and Shereen cheered. Ellie placed the cake on the coffee table.

"You guys . . ." Yolanda's voice trailed off.

"I know." Jessica plopped down beside her and gave her a sloppy kiss on the cheek. "You thought we forgot."

"Yeah, I did."

Ellie tsked. "You know we could never forget your birthday. Hell, you'd never speak to us again if we did."

Yolanda wiped at a stray tear.

Shereen sat on the opposite side of her. "Why are you crying?"

Yolanda shook her head. "I should have known better."

"Yeah, you should have. But at least we surprised your ass." Shereen grinned her pride. "For once."

Leaning forward, Yolanda checked out the cake. "God, what's with all the candles?"

"You ain't getting any younger."

"Go ahead. Make a wish."

"Blow them out."

"Shush! I'm trying to think." Yolanda closed her eyes tightly as she thought of a wish. Then with one gust of air, she blew out all the candles.

"Wow," Shereen said. "That's pretty good for someone your age."

"Shut up."

"I'll get a knife and some plates." Jessica scooted off to the kitchen. Ellie took the spot Jessica had vacated.

"I hate you guys," Yolanda said, looking from Ellie to Shereen.

"I'll forgive you for that," Shereen said. "Because you're an Aries, and I know how much Aries hate not being in control."

"Oh, no." Yolanda covered her ears. "Don't start that astrology crap."

"It is not crap. I keep telling you, you need to have your chart done. Believe me, it will amaze you."

"What if it tells me I need new friends?"

Ellie guffawed. "Like you could ever live without us."

"Or do better."

Yolanda took both their hands. "No," she said softly. "I don't think I could."

Much later, after their fill of cake and wine, everyone was gathered in the living room. Ellie was speaking when Shereen tuned back in to the group. "So, what do you think?"

Yolanda shook her head. "Don't do it. Any kind of pyramid thing, run, don't walk, the other way."

"But this one sounds good. I went to one of their meetings, where people who've worked for the company tell you how they managed to become successful. You should see all the blacks who have made something of themselves through this company."

"Please," Yolanda scoffed.

"Communications is the way of the future," Jessica pointed out.

"That may be true, but do you see AT&T or Sprint out there recruiting people to help *those people* make millions? I don't think so."

"It's just a different way to do business. I'm telling you, you can really be successful at it."

"I don't know," Shereen said. "There are a few sorors involved in businesses like that, where they get a percentage of everyone's phone bill or light bill or whatever. I don't see them driving Jags or Porsches."

Ellie said, "It takes time."

"Ellie"—Yolanda spoke matter-of-factly—"what do you really want to do?"

"I want a career. I want to finally make my mark in the world."

"Then why don't you get a demo tape made, go to New York or L.A., and pursue your singing once and for all."

If Jessica had said those words, no one would have been surprised. The fact that the words came from Yolanda, practical Yolanda, shocked everyone—but from the look on Ellie's face, it surprised her most of all. "You—you really think I could?"

"Girl, I've heard you sing. Even when you all sang happy birthday to me, your voice stood out."

"Thanks." Shereen smiled wryly.

"Seriously," Yolanda told Ellie. "You dabble in the movie business. You do a bit of this, a bit of that. It's been eight years since we graduated, yet you haven't found a career. Why do you think that is? Because you're not ready to settle down and get a 'real job.' And you know why? Because what you really want to do is sing."

"Damn." Shereen was impressed. Out of all of them, Yolanda was the type who normally scoffed at artsy careers. "What's gotten into you?"

Yolanda sat back. "It's obvious that no matter how much any of us tell her to get a real job, she's not going to. She may as well go after what she really wants."

"I don't know." Jessica, normally always supportive, was now a voice of dissent. "A career in the spotlight isn't what it's cracked up to be."

"I wouldn't be doing it for the attention."

Jessica shrugged, but didn't meet anyone's eyes. Shereen stared at her, then at Ellie and Yolanda, but they didn't seem to notice anything wrong with Jessica, so Shereen let it go.

"I don't know," Ellie continued. "All my life I've had this dream of being a singer. That one day I'd get a record deal, make an album, and finally live my dream. Be famous." She smiled softly. "My parents never believed in me, and maybe—maybe they're right. Maybe all I'll ever have is the dream. I mean, who am I? Aretha Franklin?" She made a goofy face to make light of her comment, but it was apparent to all that it wasn't a joke. In all the years Shereen had known her, Ellie hadn't taken herself seriously. "No, I have to find something serious to do. A real career. At least so my father will get off my case for not going into medicine."

"You could be Aretha Franklin and your father would still think you should be a doctor."

"I know, Shereen. Still . . . We'll see."

Yolanda reached for the wine bottle. "Jessica, you ready for a glass yet? There's not much left."

"I'll pass on the wine tonight," Jessica replied.

Shereen gave Jessica a curious look. "You didn't have anything to drink that night we went out. You're not drinking today. Is there something you're not telling us?"

Ellie's face lit up. "Girl, are you pregnant?"

"Pregnant?" Jessica asked, mortified. "God no." And then her face crumbled. Everyone watched her, not sure what to say, what to do. "Oh, God. I don't know what to do. Douglas wants to pick out colors for the baby's room, do all this baby stuff, like I'm already pregnant. And I keep saying yes, 'cause I don't know what else to say. But I don't want this. God, I feel so awful."

No one said anything. They didn't have to. They had a kind of friendship radar and were often zapped with the exact same thought at the exact same moment. Right now, Ellie knew what Shereen and Yolanda were thinking because it was the same thing she was thinking: Jessica wasn't ready for children because it made her remember the first time she'd been pregnant. And Ellie also knew that none of them would dare voice their thoughts. Not now that it was all behind them.

So instead Ellie said, "Well, hell, you've just started your career. I can understand why you're not ready."

"Yes. Yes, exactly." Jessica sounded thankful for Ellie's spin on the situation. "Maybe in a year or two . . ."

Yolanda stretched an arm over Jessica's shoulder. "Hey. Hey, sweetie. Don't beat yourself up. You don't have to feel guilty for not being ready."

"But I'm lying to Douglas. I told him I'm off the pill, but . . . I'm still taking it."

"Jess, it's okay." From her spot on the floor, Ellie rubbed Jessica's knee.

"It's gotten to the point where I don't even want to make love to him anymore. Because he's soon gonna start asking why I'm not pregnant yet, and knowing Douglas, he'll want to do all sorts of tests. And . . . God, I can't deal with this."

"Why don't you just tell him you're not ready?" Yolanda asked. "Tell him you want to concentrate on your career. Give it another year or two."

"I would. I just don't want to disappoint him. He's done so much for me . . ."

"Just like you've done for him," Yolanda said pointedly. "Don't ever forget that. Women never give themselves enough credit."

Jessica shrugged. "I don't know. Forget it. I'll deal with this."

Everyone regarded Jessica cautiously for another moment, but she waved off their stares and said, "Honest. I can't believe I fell apart like that. I'm fine. I'm being stupid."

Shereen wanted to tell Jessica that if she was this upset about it, then she wasn't being stupid at all. She wanted to suggest that she get counseling, but Jessica would probably deny her fears had anything to do with the last time. Instead, she changed the subject and asked, "Any of you going to the sorority's Mother's Day bash? They've been calling me steady for the past two weeks."

Jessica guffawed. "Definitely not."

"I was trying to get my mother to come to town for the event," Ellie said. "But she's not, so I'm gonna pass." She frowned. "Actually, I'm kinda worried about her."

"Why?" Shereen asked.

"I don't know. Every time I talk to her she sounds . . . preoccupied. Like something's going on with her that she's not telling me." Ellie shrugged. "Maybe I'm just feeling guilty for not going home in ages. What about you, Yo? Are you going with your mother?"

"I'd go if she were up to it, but she's not up to much these days. Because of her hip."

Shereen had been hoping to go with her friends simply to get out again. And perhaps to salvage her reputation. People were still wondering what had gotten into her at the Black History Month event, and she wanted to prove to everyone that she was very much sane.

"I guess I'll send a check, too," Shereen finally said.

The energy among the group was suddenly different. Something was lacking, but Shereen couldn't quite put her finger on it. Everyone was off in her own different world, despite the fact that they were here for Yolanda's birthday. "Yolanda, pass me the wine." Then, because she wanted to change the mood, she said, "Oh, I never did tell you. I'm seeing someone."

"You?" Ellie's eyes bulged as she stared at Shereen.

"Yes, me," Shereen said, a tad defensive. Just because she'd been without a significant other in her life for ages didn't mean she would die a spinster. "Jessica introduced me to him. His name is Jonathon, and he works at WGRZ as a publicist. And let me tell you, he is *fine*."

Jessica managed a halfhearted grin.

"I like him. It's too soon to tell yet if he's The One, but things are hopeful."

"Great, great." Yolanda smiled. "That's wonderful."

"So far so good."

"Speaking of *fine* men," Yolanda began. "What about that gorgeous guy you were dating, Ellie? You haven't mentioned him in a while."

Shereen added, "Shelton, right? And didn't you say he was in the film business? Maybe he has a few contacts in the music industry."

Ellie shrugged. "He might, but I'm not about to ask him."

Yolanda's eyebrows shot up. "Why not?"

"Because we're not seeing each other anymore."

"It's over?" Shereen asked in disbelief. "It barely began."

Ellie shrugged. "He wasn't my type."

"Why not?" Yolanda challenged. "Or can't you deal with guys who are attractive *and* single?"

"I wasn't feeling it," Ellie replied simply.

Yolanda shook her head. "Some things never change."

"Hey, remember Marlin?" Shereen asked. "The Gamma?" Ellie shook her head. "The muscular guy who let us into that party." When Ellie continued to give her a blank stare, Shereen added, "The quest-for-Jordan's-jersey party. Come on. You remember him. He had his eye on you ever since he saw you in that Playboy bunny outfit."

"Oh. Him."

"Yeah, him. I ran into him at a mall a few weeks back, and you'll never believe this. He asked about you. I told him you were seeing someone, but he was still interested. And he's *single*. I think he said he was a doctor."

"Great. My parents would love him."

"Anyway, I didn't mention it because of Shelton, but he gave me his number to pass along to you."

"Please." Ellie rolled her eyes. "I don't think so."

"What's wrong with Marlin?" Shereen was taken aback by Ellie's instant rebuttal.

"Girl, I don't want no red man." She chuckled. "With a red man, you turn on the lights and it's like a rainbow . . . they've got so many different skin tones."

"Ellie, have you looked in a mirror lately?" Yolanda asked.

"Yes, I have. That's exactly why I don't want a red man. We can't both be red. I like my man's skin the color of dark chocolate."

They all laughed.

Shereen said, "It's not about color, or having the right skin tone. It's about who you love."

"Exactly." Ellie stressed the word.

Shereen's stomach dropped. "I'm not sure I like the sound of that."

"You said it," Ellie pointed out. "It's about love. And . . . I know you won't want to hear this, but I'm in love with Richard."

"God, Ellie." Shereen shook her head. "I thought it was just a fling."

"Things have changed. You'll like this," Ellie assured them when Shereen covered her face. "Richard and I—we're moving in together."

"*What?*" Yolanda shot her an incredulous look.

"He's leaving his wife."

Silence fell over the room.

"Oh, Ellie," Shereen finally said. She gave her credit—she didn't gloat.

"What do you mean, 'Oh, Ellie'? This has been in the making for a while."

"How long has that man been stringing you along?" Shereen asked.

"He hasn't been *stringing* me along. I told you before, he's with her for the children. They haven't been happy in years."

"You really think his wife has a clue that he's planning to leave her?" As Yolanda said the last words, she used her fingers to signal quotation marks.

"We're looking for a house."

"My God."

"Look, I know you all didn't like me seeing him because he's married. This is hardly ideal, I know, but I . . . I didn't plan this. And I never would have gotten involved with him if he was happy at home. But he's finally told his wife it's over and he means it. We're seeing more of each other. He was at my place for an entire week after he told her the news. He's *never* done that before."

"Do you have any idea how pathetic you sound?"

"Don't start, Yolanda."

"Just because he spent a week at your place doesn't mean he's really leaving his wife! For all you know, his wife was away on vacation. Or maybe she kicked him out because she was mad at him. But I can guarantee you, the moment she's back, he'll be back in her bed."

Ellie's eyes widened for the briefest of moments. Clearly, she hadn't considered those alternatives, and judging by the look on her face, she now was—and she wasn't quite as confident anymore. After a moment, she said, "Listen, Yolanda, you barely got back into town. You don't even know Richard."

"But I know pigs like him."

A nerve flinched in Ellie's jaw. "You have no right—"

"Yes, I have a right, because I happen to have been there." Yolanda's voice was slightly raised. "I was the one on the other side of the coin— the wife. And I don't know what James told his bimbo secretary, but he never once told me he was unhappy."

"Yolanda," Shereen said. "This is your birthday."

"So I'm supposed to ignore this bullshit?"

"I've been there, too," Ellie countered. "Practically every guy I've dated has fucked around on me. So don't tell me that I don't understand. Like I said, I didn't plan this, and maybe I was stupid, but at first it was just eas- ier. I didn't want to get my heart broken. It was wrong, but I thought Richard was safe. I didn't plan to fall in love with him."

There was silence again.

Looking at her friend, Shereen couldn't help feeling sorry for her. She put up a front like she was confident and in control, but she was really insecure. Once, she had dropped about thirty pounds in a month when she'd fallen hard for some guy in college—Shereen forgot his name. Ellie had looked great, but Shereen had wondered if she'd become bulimic. When what's-his-name hadn't returned Ellie's affections, she'd quickly packed the pounds back on.

Yes, Shereen understood her frustration with men, but the way she saw it, Ellie was setting herself up for another big fall.

"If I were you," Shereen said, breaking the silence, "I'd make sure and see the divorce papers before moving in with him."

"Forget I said anything." Ellie sank into the armchair, sulking.

"Honestly," Yolanda continued, not willing to let the matter drop. "You've got to use your head. Hell, you graduated from Howard."

Ellie shot to her feet again. "Shut up, Yolanda. Don't you dare preach to me about using my head. I'm not the one who got engaged to Terrence just to piss Shereen off."

"I can't deal with this." At the sound of Jessica's voice, everyone looked to her, startled. Until now, they hadn't realized that she hadn't spoken on the subject. She quickly stood. "I've got to go."

"Me, too." Ellie grabbed her purse from the floor.

Jessica didn't glance back as she went to the doorway and gathered her leather jacket. Shereen looked at Yolanda, shrugged, then stood.

Shereen met Jessica and Ellie in the doorway. "Jessica, what's the matter?"

"I'm not in the mood for this tonight." She hugged Shereen. "See you later. 'Bye, Yolanda."

Ellie kissed Shereen, then shot a glare at Yolanda before stepping outside with Jessica.

"Well," Shereen said, walking back into the living room and sitting across from Yolanda. "That was weird."

"Something's up with Jessica."

"Maybe she just didn't agree with you."

"Jessica?" Yolanda flashed her a look that said "Gimme a break." "Jessica is just as anti-Richard as the rest of us. No, it's something else. Has she talked to you?"

"No. Other than what she said tonight about Douglas, she hasn't said anything. I don't know."

They fell into silence, awkward and heavy. Shereen folded her hands in her lap and looked at a spot on the hardwood floor. When she glanced back at Yolanda, Yolanda was staring at a painting on the wall, clearly as uncomfortable with her as she was.

Ellie's comment about Terrence had caused tension between them. Shereen sighed. This was stupid. Either they were gonna be friends or they were gonna be enemies. She didn't want any in betweens.

"So, how's the job?" Shereen finally asked. "Are you liking it?"

"It's great. I've always wanted to deal with women's issues, so now I have the chance. And Terrence thinks . . ." Yolanda's voice trailed off. She ran both hands over her face. "I can't believe it. Everyone thinks I deliberately set out to hurt you."

"Ellie didn't mean that. She knows it's not true. *I* know it's not true."

Yolanda didn't answer. Shereen finally said, "So . . . Terrence thinks?"

Deep breath. "Terrence thinks the job is good for me. He says I seem happier. But I think the truth is that I'm just happy to be home. I didn't realize how much I missed Washington until I got back here."

"You just missed us," Shereen told her, smiling.

"That too." Yolanda returned her smile. But the smile quickly faded. "Look, there's something you should know. Terrence—he's moving to Washington."

Shereen's heart jolted, and the strangest tingling spread through her body. Terrence was moving to Washington. Why did the news seem like a bombshell? What had she expected? That Yolanda had bought this house with no plans to share it with her husband? That she and Terrence would remain engaged forever? "He is?"

"Yeah. He's representing a couple of the big players on the Redskins and wants to be closer to them. Besides, he can pretty much work anywhere. So, it just made sense."

"I see."

"You're upset."

"No." Shereen wasn't sure exactly what she felt, but for the sake of their friendship, she was going to keep her promise. She would not let Terrence come between them. "You're engaged, right? You gotta live somewhere."

"Honestly, are you okay with this? Me and Terrence?"

Shereen hesitated. She wanted to say yes, that she was okay. She wanted to ask, Why Terrence? But instead she asked, "Did he ever tell you why?"

"Why?" Was that discomfort Shereen saw in Yolanda's eyes? "Why what?"

"Why he dumped me." Shereen fiddled with her hands in her lap. "Maybe it's silly, wanting to know. It was so long ago. But . . . he never said anything to me. He just cut me off, didn't return my calls . . ."

For a moment, Yolanda considered telling Shereen the truth. But only for a moment. What good would it do for Shereen to hear about the lie she'd inadvertently told Terrence years ago? Yolanda had been drunk at a frat party and had pointed out to Terrence how much of a flirt Shereen was—implying that maybe she was involved with Brad, a jock who'd been hanging all over her when Terrence had stepped into the party. Yolanda couldn't pay for male attention that night, while Shereen had been fighting off man after man. When Terrence had entered the party, Yolanda had seen the startled look on his face, then had watched him wait for Shereen to notice he'd arrived. But she'd been dancing with Brad and she hadn't noticed.

Yolanda had approached Terrence. "Hey, Terrence."

"Hey," he'd replied in a clipped tone.

Yolanda looked toward Brad and Shereen, who were chatting and laughing as they danced to a slow tune. "They look pretty comfortable, don't they?"

"Hmm."

"Must be hard," Yolanda said in a sympathetic tone. "How do you deal with so many men wanting her?" When Terrence didn't respond, Yolanda continued. "Brad . . . he's been her shadow all night. He definitely wants her. She obviously likes him, but of course, she's seeing you." Yolanda looked into Terrence's eyes. "But you trust her, right?"

The expression on Terrence's face was lethal. Yolanda noticed that he'd clenched his hands into fists.

"I'm outta here."

"Hey, where are you going?"

Terrence disappeared without another word.

Later, Shereen had asked Yolanda if she'd seen Terrence.

"Naw, I haven't seen him."

As Shereen had frowned, Yolanda had contemplated telling her that she was kidding, that yes Terrence had been at the party but he'd left angry. But she didn't.

Just as she couldn't tell her the truth now. Telling Shereen the truth at this point in her life would only hurt her further, and she'd already done enough of that. Besides, Shereen wouldn't understand.

"No," Yolanda finally said. She shook her head for emphasis. "He didn't tell me a thing."

Shereen shrugged. "Oh, well. It doesn't really matter." Then she reached for her wine and took a good, long sip.

Chapter Fourteen

WHY IS IT THAT JUST when your life seems right on track, something happens that you totally aren't prepared for? Something so unexpected that the impact makes you feel like you've been sucker punched, literally leaving you breathless from shock?

The afternoon that Shereen stepped into her office and found Terrence sitting behind her desk, she was so stunned that she made a total fool of herself. She screamed bloody murder and dropped her bowl of chicken soup to the floor.

"Jesus!"

He was the last person she expected to see, the last person she wanted to see.

Terrence Michael Simms.

Lord have mercy.

"I'm sorry," he said, hurrying to her side, crouching with her on the carpet and taking the Styrofoam bowl from her hands. "I didn't mean to scare you."

Her chest rose and fell quickly with each frightened breath. Still startled, she watched him scoop the chunks of chicken back into the bowl.

"You have paper towels in here?"

"O-outside." She found the strength to stand and exit her office. Rudy stared at her above her eyeglasses, but Shereen ignored her. She didn't know what Terrence had said to her administrative assistant, but somehow he'd convinced her to let him into her office.

Less than a minute later, Shereen returned with a roll of paper towels from the bathroom. "Here."

"Thanks."

Terrence cleaned up the mess the best he could, then walked to the garbage with the wet paper towels. Absently, Shereen pressed a wad of paper towels onto the carpet, not paying much attention as moisture seeped into it. She was caught up in watching Terrence's strong back as he bent over her garbage.

He turned.

Shereen dropped her eyes to the floor.

With two long strides, he was beside her. "That's probably the best you can do for now," he told her, as if he stopped by her office every day, as if they were friends. He took the trash from her hands. "Please, send me the bill."

As he went to the garbage once more, Shereen rose to her feet, though her legs were wobbly.

He smiled casually as he strolled back toward her. "Shereen."

"How did you get in here?"

"Your secretary."

"She shouldn't have done that. She shouldn't have . . . Why are you here?"

He stepped closer. "I wanted to see you."

Her heart was beating so fast, she wondered if she might drop dead any second. God, this reaction to seeing him was embarrassing. "Why?"

"We never got to say hi back at that party." He shrugged. "I wanted to say hi."

He wanted to say hi. This was crazy. Shereen walked toward one of the large windowpanes behind her desk, staring out at the bright blue sky.

When she turned, Terrence was approaching her. His movements were slow, confident, utterly sexy. It didn't make sense, but he looked even better now than he had that night in February. No doubt about it, he was a stunning specimen of male beauty.

"How are you?" he asked.

"How am I?" Shereen asked incredulously. "I'm fine."

"You went to work for your father after all." He spread his hands wide, gesturing to the office. "I always knew you would."

"You know nothing about me, Terrence. Nothing."

"I know more than you think," he said softly.

"Cut the bull, will you?" She was being harsh, but that's the way she had to be. She didn't understand why Terrence was here, and truth be told, she didn't want to understand. She just wanted to go back to her life before she had stepped into her office and found him sitting behind her desk like he owned the place.

"I'm sorry."

"Don't do that. Don't apologize."

"You don't want to see me."

She should have agreed with him and sent him on his merry way. But she was tongue-tied.

"I'm sorry," she said after a moment. "I'm . . . you just scared me. I didn't expect to see you." She paused. "Why aren't you with Yolanda?"

"I'll see her later. Right now, I wanted to see you."

"Well, you've seen me."

"You look great."

"God, Terrence. Don't."

"I can't give you a compliment?"

She swallowed hard. "No, you can't. Why would you want to?"

Terrence didn't reply, merely met her confused gaze with an intense look. Shereen turned away from him, for she didn't want him to see how much his visit was affecting her. She squeezed her eyes shut, wishing this was all a dream, then opened them and turned.

He was still there.

Shereen sat down. It was safer than standing. "So, you and Yolanda." She sucked in a deep breath. "I never did get to congratulate you, so congrats. That's wonderful."

He gave her an odd look. "Thanks."

What was with that look? "Who would have thought you'd meet up after all these years, much less make a love connection? One just never knows how life will turn out," Shereen added flippantly.

"Hmm."

"What does that mean? 'Hmm'?"

He pursed his lips. "Nothing."

She didn't know what to make of this. She didn't know what to make of the fact that her heart was racing so wildly when she shouldn't feel a thing for him.

"Well, you came. You saw me. I'm fine. I'm glad to see you're well." Another deep breath. "But you should . . . you should go back to your fiancée."

He nodded tightly, making her wonder what he'd really wanted. Just as quickly as that thought entered her head, she dismissed it. She didn't care.

He turned and walked to the door. Shereen felt powerful. He was going away just like she'd told him to and her life would go back to normal.

When he was at the door, he stopped. Shereen spoke before he could. "It was nice seeing you again. Tell Yolanda I said hi."

"Yeah," he said, but didn't sound like he meant it. "I'll do that."

"Good." She gave a false smile, hoping it looked like the real thing. Then he disappeared without another word.

And Shereen dropped her head onto her desk, emitting a long, frustrated moan.

"No shit," Ellie said.

"I still can't believe it," Shereen told her. Since Terrence's departure, Shereen hadn't been able to concentrate on work, so she'd called Ellie, the one person she trusted not to open her mouth about this. Jessica might let it slip to Yolanda that Terrence had stopped by to see her, but Ellie wouldn't.

"I wonder what he wanted." Ellie spoke in a singsong voice, almost like she was enjoying the news.

"This isn't funny, Ellie. I have no clue why he came here, and I don't want to know. But I have to tell you, Ellie—" Shereen stopped herself.

"What?" Even over the phone, Shereen could see Ellie's eyes widen with interest.

Shereen fiddled with the phone cord. "I don't know. I guess I just didn't expect to see him again . . . but it's more than that. I thought I was over him. I *am* over him," she corrected. "It's just that, if I'm over him, why did seeing him make me so . . . flustered?"

"Girl, you're still flustered."

"I am, aren't I?"

"Mmm-hmm."

"It's not what you think. It can't be. When Terrence walked out of my life, that was it. It was over. I moved on."

"You didn't expect to see him. It freaked you out."

"Yes." Shereen almost shouted the word. "That's exactly it. God, I knew you'd understand." Her elation fizzled as her stomach sank to her knees. "I don't know what to think. About why he came, that is. I don't know. Maybe my ego is too big, but it almost seemed like . . . like he wanted to see me because he missed me. Does that make sense?"

"Maybe he does."

"But he's engaged to Yolanda! God, he better not try any funky shit, I'm telling you. Yolanda and I already made up over this and I am *not* going to let Terrence come between us again."

"How's Jonathon?"

Jonathon. Shereen sighed. "Jonathon . . . well, I'm not gonna lie. It's not working out. I was interested at first—and don't take this personally—but he told me he still has feelings for his ex-wife. He said he's *trying* to get over her, and I told him that I didn't have time for that."

"Sorry."

"Yeah. Me, too." Shereen's mind drifted back to Terrence. "You don't think Yolanda sent Terrence over deliberately? Remember that woman Jessica interviewed on *The Scoop* a while back? She wrote some book on how you could test your man for faithfulness. There was something in there about leaving your man alone with a girlfriend to see if he'd hit on her. You don't think Yolanda did that to see if I'd hit on him or something?"

"I doubt it," Ellie told her. "But if she did, she's certainly not as secure as she makes herself out to be."

Shereen immediately dismissed the possibility. "No, I don't think she'd do that. So, whatever you do, promise me you won't tell her about Terrence coming over here. If he wants to tell her, fine, but if he doesn't, I don't want her thinking anything."

"There's nothing to think . . . right?"

"Right." Shit, did Ellie think she and Terrence had done something wrong? *"Right."*

"So don't worry about it."

"Thanks, Ellie." Sigh. "I won't keep you."

"All right. I'm going to meet Richard at his office. We're gonna head to Maryland to check out some houses. Maybe I'll give you a call when I get there."

"Oh, no. That's okay. You have fun with your man." Shereen couldn't believe Ellie was actually going to do this with Richard. Maybe he was for real after all, and not just a player. People did get divorced all the time, and maybe Richard truly wasn't happy with his wife.

For Ellie's sake, Shereen prayed that was the case.

"Well, we'll chat later. Keep me posted."

"I will." Though Shereen doubted there'd be anything to keep her posted about.

For whatever reason, Terrence had shown up at her office today. Maybe curiosity. Maybe guilt.

Whatever his reasons, she doubted it would happen again.

"Shaun. Wake up."

Shereen stood over her brother, who lay asleep on the sofa. Either asleep or passed out. Judging by the empty mickey of vodka at the foot of the sofa, he was stone-cold drunk.

"Shaun!" She nudged his shoulder.

He didn't budge.

"Damn, I do *not* need this. Not today."

After she'd given her brother that ultimatum—get a job or get out—he'd actually found a job at a local grocery store as a forklift driver. The pay wasn't bad and Shereen had been thrilled. But last week, when she'd noticed that Shaun wasn't leaving the house anymore, she'd asked why he wasn't going to work.

He told her he'd been fired.

He didn't tell her why, but she suspected he'd been drinking on the job. In recent months, it seemed he couldn't get through the day without vodka.

Since being fired, he didn't do anything. He just stayed home like a couch potato, complaining about how unfair life was.

Days like this, Shereen wished he had a girlfriend—someone else who would deal with him, 'cause the family love thing was wearing thin.

Forget it, she told herself. For one night this week, she'd forget about

Shaun, and Terrence—'cause yes, he was still on her mind—and men in general. Tonight, she was gonna have a good time.

Shereen took a step back and checked out her appearance in the mirror. Then frowned. Reaching for her makeup bag, she found a darker shade of lipstick, applied it over the red, then pressed her lips together to mix the two.

There, that was better.

She added mascara to her lashes, liner to her eyelids, and a hint of gold eye shadow to brighten her eyes.

Just enough makeup to highlight her already pretty features.

She smoothed her hands over her formfitting black dress, satisfied that it looked good. Her hair looked great, with sexy drop curls hanging at her ears and nape, while she'd upswept the rest.

She smiled. She looked perfect.

She was ready.

No, she realized, a frown playing on her lips, she was missing something. A big *L* tattooed on her forehead.

Because she was a loser.

She was all dressed up with no place to go.

Closing her eyes, she groaned. There was a time when it wouldn't have bothered her that it was Saturday night and she didn't have a date. No big deal. She'd spent several Saturday nights home alone, and it certainly hadn't killed her. But tonight, she needed to get out. She wanted to do something.

Fuck it. She didn't need a date to go out. Whatever happened to being adventurous, to meeting new people?

Every day on the radio this week, she'd heard about some new club called Liquid in Adams Morgan. It was supposed to be hot on Saturday nights. And women got in free before twelve.

It was nine-fifteen.

She was gonna go out. She would *not* go crazy sitting at home, thinking about Shaun. Thinking about Terrence.

She supposed she could call Jonathon and see if he wanted to do something. He had called her a couple of times this week, leaving messages to ask if they could get together. But the truth was, she couldn't be bothered with him. She might have issues, but he had a lot more than she did, and she wasn't prepared to stick around and wait while he dealt with them.

Downstairs, Shereen slipped into a light leather jacket, then stylish high-heeled black boots, and exited her house. It was a warm evening in May, the kind of night lovers strolled hand in hand in the park, looking up at the stars.

Just once she'd like to do that this year. Just once. Was that too much to ask?

Yes, it was, because she didn't have a lover, and she wasn't about to take one just to go stargazing and whatnot. While she wanted male companionship, she wasn't that desperate.

Just maybe a little bit horny.

"Forget about it," she told herself as she got into her Audi and slammed the door harder than was necessary. She reminded herself of Aaron and that whole fiasco. That had all happened because she'd been horny.

She put the windows down and headed to the Beltway. She was a driver, and the one thing she enjoyed was a drive on a clear night. Behind the wheel of a car, she felt powerful, in control.

Despite the fact that the rest of her life was a mess.

And it was. She hadn't wanted to accept that fact, but she could no longer deny it. After seeing Terrence in her office last week, she hadn't been able to stop thinking about him. Which was crazy. What woman in her right mind couldn't stop thinking about the man who'd dumped her without so much as the courtesy of an explanation?

God, even now she was thinking of him. How pathetic.

She hit the gas, taking the car beyond the speed limit. She didn't care how fast she drove. With the windows down, the breeze felt wonderful on her skin. Invigorating.

In Washington, she found Liquid easily and pulled in front of the club to check it out. There wasn't much of a crowd—yet. But it was Ladies Night, and the single men would come out for sure, so while she was alone right now, she wouldn't be for long. Shereen circled the block, looking for a place to park.

But even after she lucked out and found a spot, she didn't get out of her car. *What am I doing? This is crazy. God, I'm acting like I'm desperate.*

She pulled out of the spot and took off.

At a gas station, three men in a late-model Lexus—three *young* men—hit on her, telling her how beautiful she was.

"Hey, baby, you're too beautiful to frown like that. Smile."

She flashed a fake smile.

"Oh, that's cold."

The driver blew her a kiss, then sped off, the music so loud she could feel it vibrating in her body.

Shereen climbed back into her car, feeling like a fool. Here she was at a gas station, all dressed up like she had a hot date or something. When on earth had she sunk this low? She wasn't going back to the club, she knew that much. She wasn't going anywhere. Not alone. Why had she even bothered to leave her house?

Ellie was with Richard. Jessica was with Douglas. Yolanda was with Terrence.

And she wasn't even with a friggin' loser.

Yeah, she was pathetic.

On the Beltway back to Maryland, Shereen gunned it. While she had wanted to go out earlier, had needed to go out, now she just wanted to be back at home, Shaun and all.

Just as her speedometer registered close to eighty miles an hour, she saw the flashing lights in her rearview mirror.

"Shit!"

She pulled the car onto the shoulder and had reached into her purse for her license by the time the cop reached her car door.

He lowered his head to her open window. "Do you have any idea how fast you were going, ma'am?"

Hmm. This one was tall, dark, and definitely handsome. She checked his ring finger. No ring.

"I'm sorry, Officer. I wasn't paying attention."

"Rushing to a hot date?" He smiled.

She chuckled mirthlessly. "I wish."

"A pretty woman like you." He clucked his tongue. "I'm surprised."

So am I, Shereen wanted to say, but didn't. She was hardly over the hill, but never in her wildest dreams would she have expected to find herself going on thirty-one without a serious man in her life.

"I tell you what," the trooper continued. "I'll give you a warning. Just promise me you'll slow down."

"Thank you." Grateful, Shereen smiled. He really was extremely handsome. What was it about black men in police uniforms? The state troopers especially. Were they all actually as handsome as they looked, or was it simply the image of power that was a potent aphrodisiac? "I will."

He stood to his full height, over six feet—another plus—then stooped to place his head at the window once more.

Shereen's heart accelerated.

"I know this might sound forward," the cop began, "but do you have a number?"

"Yeah, I got a number."

A smile played on his lips.

"But my mama always told me not to give it to strangers."

By the smile that still lit up his face, it was clear he understood her playful tone. "Well, if I were to give you my number, would you call me?"

"That depends," Shereen replied, being coy. "Are you giving me your number?"

He withdrew a pen and paper and wrote down his phone number, then passed it to her.

"That's my beeper," he told her. "I work so many hours, that's the best way to reach me."

"I see." She placed the number on the seat next to her.

"You're a beautiful lady. I'd love to get to know you."

"I'll call you."

"You do that."

She wiggled her fingers at him with one hand while she pressed the button to wind up the window with the other. Then, as he walked back to the cruiser, she slipped back into traffic.

She might want a man, but she wasn't desperate enough to break another of her rules like she'd done months ago with Aaron. If a guy can't give you his home number, don't give him the time of day. Nine out of ten of them—make that nine-point-nine-nine out of ten of them—had wives or girlfriends at home.

Especially men as fine as him.

Her sorors had dubbed her Sweet Thang. They'd voted her the one most likely to meet a movie star or musician and live a life of luxury, because guys would trip over themselves trying to get her love.

How ironic that she was still the single one—without any prospects for love.

Chapter Fifteen

"OH," YOLANDA SAID, TRYING not to sound disappointed.

"He wasn't signed in any of the draft picks last month, but I've seen him throw a football. The kid's got a lot of potential. If he played at Notre Dame or another high-profile school, he'd probably already be signed. Kent State is smaller, but it's still a Division One school, and the kid's got great stats. Anyway, we've talked before and I think he's now ready to take on an agent. So, I've got to get to him before anyone else does."

High-profile. Division One. Yolanda didn't have a clue what it all meant because she didn't know much about football, so she didn't bother asking Terrence to explain. Instead she asked, "How long will you be gone?"

"Couple days, max."

Yolanda hoped this wasn't the life she was in for, with Terrence calling her from the airport to tell her he wasn't coming home because he had to go see a client.

"I tried to see you earlier, but you were in court."

That was true. And that was sweet of him. She smiled. She could live without him for a few days. "Well, call me when you get to Ohio."

"Of course."

"I—" Yolanda heard a dial tone. Terrence had hung up before she'd had a chance to tell him she loved him.

No sooner had Yolanda replaced the receiver than the phone rang. Instantly, she grabbed it. No doubt Terrence was calling back. "Hey, sweetheart."

"Hello, Yolanda."

It was a good thing Yolanda was sitting down, because her world started to spin out of control at the sound of the male voice she hadn't heard in so long.

"Daddy?"

"Of course it's your daddy."

There was no "of course" about it, the way Yolanda saw it, not when her father had been less regular in her life than her monthly cycle. "How are you, Daddy?"

"I'm all right. I hear you're back in town."

"You spoke to Mama."

"Yeah, she told me."

Yolanda's stomach wouldn't stop fluttering. "Yeah, I'm back. I meant to call . . ."

"That's okay. I know you're busy."

"Mmm-hmm."

Silence.

"I got your letter. I'm glad to hear you've found someone who makes you happy."

"Yeah, me, too."

"Life is short. We all have to grab happiness when we can."

Her father often said things like this, and every time he did, it pissed her off. Because she heard something else underneath his words: "I grabbed happiness with someone else because your mother didn't make me happy." "Yeah, well, what about Mama?" Yolanda always wanted to counter. "If you cared about her happiness, you never would have walked out on her."

"I hear you have a new house. Maybe one day you'll invite me over."

"Yeah, maybe you and Mama." That always shut him up. He didn't like to do anything with her mother, his former wife, the mother of the child he claimed to love so much.

She closed her eyes and drew in a deep breath, willing the anger to subside. Talking to her father, the thought of seeing him, always made her angry. She wanted to forgive him, she really did, but every time she saw her mother, she remembered her father's betrayal and the flames of ire licked at her heart, making forgiveness impossible.

This is why she had as little contact with him as was necessary. Anger had a way of eating you alive. She'd cut James off because she couldn't deal with her anger, and once he was out of her life, she'd felt a lot better. With her father, it was a different story, because she couldn't exactly cut him off. But the less contact she had with him, the better.

Besides, he had a new family, had had them for years. He didn't need her.

And for the life of her, she couldn't understand why her mother always defended him. "Your father is a good man," she would say. Or, "He loves you. Don't let the fact that we're not together anymore stop you from having a relationship with him."

For her mother's sake, Yolanda tried.

"Thanks for checking up on Mama when she fell and broke her hip," Yolanda said. Had it really been that long since she'd talked to her father? Over three months? "She didn't have anyone here, so I appreciate you making the time to be there for her."

Her father sighed loudly.

Well, screw him if he didn't think she was being sincere. He could go back to Gloria, his new wife, and let her lick his wounds.

"Daddy, I've got to jet. I'm doing some research on a sexual harassment case—"

"Yolanda."

She cringed. "Yes, Daddy?"

"My door is open to you anytime. Gloria and I, and the kids—we'd love to see you."

"I'll let you know when I've got time."

"I hope it's soon."

"I'll talk to you later, Daddy."

Another sigh. "All right, baby. You call me when you can."

Yeah, right, Yolanda thought, hanging up. She needed to see her father like she needed a hole in her head.

Throwing her head back on the sofa, she squeezed her eyes shut, but she couldn't shut out the pain in her heart. She wished Terrence were here. He'd help her forget the pain.

Maybe a drink would help. Something bitter, pungent, something that would burn its way down to her stomach.

Yeah, she needed a drink. She had scotch in the pantry.

That would help numb her feelings until the call from her father faded to the dark recesses of her memory.

❖ ❖ ❖

The next day, Yolanda still hadn't put the call out of her mind. At her mother's house, she asked, "Mama, why did you give Daddy my number?"

"He's your father."

Edna sat in her favorite spot, the rocking chair by the window. It was a bright May day, and if it had been anyone else sitting there staring out at the budding leaves, Yolanda wouldn't have given it a second thought. But this was her mama, the woman who seemed content to sit in this rocking chair while life passed her by.

Yolanda had a fleeting memory, the kind she wasn't really sure was a memory. Maybe it was a dream. Whatever it was, she remembered herself as a child, no more than four or five, and she remembered her mother's soft voice as she sang to her while brushing her hair. For some reason, Yolanda remembered the dress she was wearing, some raggedy brown thing, but she hadn't been concerned about her clothes, or all the things she didn't own. She'd cared only about what she did have: her mother.

As her mother sang the soft tune to her—Yolanda wasn't sure what it was—she turned to look at her. And her mother smiled brightly at her, a warm smile, the kind that reaches right into your chest and gives your heart a lift.

And that's where the memory ended. With that smile.

Remembering it broke Yolanda's heart. For it meant her mother *had* been happy for a while. But her father had destroyed that happiness.

"I know he's my father, Mama, but—"

"But nothing." In a rare move, her mother turned and looked her straight in the face. "He gave you life, Yolanda."

And he took yours away.

Edna began rocking again as she turned her attention to outside. "Besides, you have a sister and brother you hardly know."

"*Half* sister and brother," Yolanda stressed.

"They're still your blood. They're as innocent in all this as you are."

That was true, and in the logical part of her brain, Yolanda knew that. Yet she'd never felt close to them. Getting close to them always felt like a betrayal of her mother.

Yes, she sent them birthday cards, and when Christmas came, she sent the obligatory gifts if she couldn't spend time with them. But they were like strangers to her, not like family at all. And not only because they were so many years younger than her.

"You need to spend time with them, Yolanda. Fuss about me less."

"You're all I have." That was the bottom line.

Edna gave her another pointed look. "You heard me."

"Yes, Mama. And I will. When I have some time to socialize." Finally, she and her mother were having more than a yes-and-no conversation, and this is what they were talking about? Yolanda changed the subject. "Terrence and I are talking about a December wedding." Maybe this would make her mother smile. "Nothing big. A civil ceremony, probably . . ."

"That's not going to make you happy."

"What won't make me happy?" A small wedding? A civil ceremony as opposed to a church wedding? At least she wouldn't be eloping this time, and her mother could be part of the wedding, wherever it was held.

Her mother didn't reply, and Yolanda felt they'd just taken one step forward, three steps back.

"Help me up." Edna began to rise, groaning as she did, and Yolanda rushed to her side. Edna gripped her arm. "Thank you, baby."

"Oh, Mama. Have you been to the doctor lately? I don't like this. You broke your hip three months ago, yet you're still in pain."

"Only sometimes."

Yolanda couldn't help it; her eyes filled with tears. "Mama, you've got to take care of yourself. If it's money you need, you tell me. You know I'll do anything for you." *You're all I have,* she added silently.

Edna's eyes held sadness as she stroked her cheek, yet Yolanda felt warmth down to the bottom of her soul. "Sometimes I forget how lucky I am," her mother said.

She meant because of her father. Because even now, the pain of his betrayal ran so deep.

"I love you, baby."

Yolanda's throat grew thick with emotion. Her mother didn't tell her those three little words too often, and hearing them now was strangely bittersweet. Because her mother seemed so sad saying them that Yolanda couldn't help wondering if something was wrong with her mother. Was she sick? Or worse, was she dying?

Yolanda started to cry.

"What is it, baby?" Edna asked.

"It's just that I love you so much, Mama. I hate to see you in pain. I . . . I don't want to lose you."

Edna's lips twitched, at first seeming to form a frown, then lifting into a slight grin. Not a full smile like the one Yolanda remembered in her dream, but still a real one that touched her eyes—and touched Yolanda's heart.

"You're not gonna lose me, baby."

Yolanda helped her mother to the bedroom, praying every step of the way that her mother's words were true. That she wouldn't lose her.

Not yet, Lord. Please, not yet.

Chapter Sixteen

JESSICA'S BODY INSTANTLY FROZE, as if her blood had turned to liquid ice. She felt faint. She felt sick. She wanted to disappear.

"What is this?" Douglas asked, extending the small packet.

He knew what it was, of course. What it meant. Yet he didn't sound angry, which made her feel worse. Douglas never raised his voice, he always wanted to discuss things, but for once in his life she wished he would. It would be so much easier to deal with his wrath than his utter disappointment.

"Where did you get that?"

"What does it matter where I got it?" His voice was quiet, too quiet. "The point is, you lied to me."

Jessica closed her eyes. Swallowed. "Not exactly."

"You can't get pregnant when you're taking the pill," he said matter-of-factly, then tossed the packet onto the bed. He turned and started for the bedroom door, but stopped before he reached it. Slowly, he faced her. Did his lips actually tremble, or was Jessica seeing things? Maybe they did, for he bit his bottom lip before saying, "Why?"

"Oh, Douglas—"

"It's been, what, two months? Two months that you've let me believe you were trying to get pregnant. I even told my parents they might finally become grandparents. Now, I feel like a fool." He paused. "Why would you do this to me?"

Jessica walked toward him. "I'm sorry." She placed a hand on his arm but he shrugged away from her touch. Her insides twisted.

"I don't know what to make of you anymore. You haven't been your-self for quite some time. At first, I thought maybe you were pregnant. Hormones—" He stopped. "What is it, Jessica?"

"Nothing." But she didn't meet his eyes.

"Are you having an affair?"

"What?" She couldn't have been more shocked if Douglas had slapped her. "No. God, no."

His eyes said he believed her. "Then what is it?"

"Nothing. Really."

A muscle flinched in his jaw, the only sign that he was angry. "Even now, you can't be honest."

He did turn then, and started out of the room.

"Wait." Jessica ran to him, placed a hand on his back. His muscles were tense, and it killed her to know she was causing him pain.

"I didn't want to disappoint you," she said when he turned.

"I'm more than disappointed. I'm hurt."

"I know, and I'm sorry. It's just that . . . you wanted a baby so badly, and I thought I did, but when I realized that I didn't, I didn't know how to tell you—"

"You should have told me, Jessica. The truth, I can deal with. It's the lies I can't."

Douglas had been married before, briefly. The experience had left him bitter, and it had taken twelve years for him to marry again. From the beginning of their relationship, he'd told Jessica that he could deal with anything as long as she was honest.

But how many people who said that really meant it? Besides, how do you tell the husband you know craves a child so badly that you're not ready for one?

"You're right, Douglas. And I'm sorry. Please—" She stroked his face. "Please, forgive me."

His broad chest rose and fell with a weary breath. "Don't you want children?"

"Yes," she said emphatically. "I do. Of course I do. It's just that *right now* . . . Honey, you have to understand. I finally have a career I love . . ."

She sensed it rather than saw it. Her answer didn't please him. But what could she do? She was doing what he said, being honest, yet her honesty was clearly not what he wanted to hear.

Still, after a moment, he kissed her forehead. He was good that way, not wanting to end things on a sour note. "Let's talk about this later."

"Okay."

Then he disappeared, and Jessica sought the bed, where she curled into a ball and prayed for sleep.

"Douglas is mad at me," Jessica announced.

She sat on one side of the sofa while Yolanda sat on the other. She was at Yolanda's house, just her this time, not the group.

"You knew he would be."

"I guess I did." She ran a hand through her unruly hair, then sighed.

"He loves you, Jessica. He won't be mad for long."

"I hate disappointing him."

"This is the kind of thing you both have to be ready for. He has to understand that."

"I know . . ."

"But?"

"But . . . I don't know."

"What is it you want, Jessica?"

"I want to give Douglas what he wants."

"That's not what I asked you."

"I don't know what I want."

Yolanda eyed her suspiciously. "There's something else going on with you."

"Maybe there is," Jessica admitted softly.

"You know me, I'm gonna ask you straight. I didn't want to ask before, but does this have anything to do with your first pregnancy?"

Jessica tensed. "Why would you say that?"

"It does."

It had been so long ago and she'd tried so hard to forget that sometimes she actually *did* forget. But the letters were making her remember. "It does, a little. I don't know."

"What I don't get is, why are you thinking about that now? I mean, it's been a long time since . . ."

"I don't know."

"I think about it sometimes," Yolanda said softly. "I remember that night you came back to the dorm all distraught, how I encouraged you to go to the dean. And, yeah, I feel guilty. Jess, none of us knew Andrew would kill himself. . . ."

"I do *not* want to talk about this."

"Maybe you need to get some counseling. It can't hurt."

Jessica waved off the idea. What she needed was to forget about the past the way she had before the letters. She'd received another one, again written in what looked like Andrew's handwriting, and for a moment she'd thought she was going crazy. Literally.

But as she'd done with the others, she'd put it out of her mind. It was the only way she knew how to deal with the situation.

"I think this is just about me not being ready. Because I *do* want to have a child. I do." But the memory of the first time hit her like a ton of bricks. She remembered the pain and the blood. And just like then, her throat started to close and it was suddenly hard to suck in air.

"Jessica? Are you okay?"

"Y-yeah." *Forget Andrew. Forget the baby.* She willed herself to calm down, to force in slow, easy breaths.

"Sweetie, you look—"

"I'm okay." *In. Out. In. Out.* She felt better, but she desperately wanted to change the subject. "H-how's Terrence? He's never around when I come over."

"He's traveling a lot. This is the time of year when free agents are looking for agents, or agents are scouting new talent. It's a busy time of year for him."

"You must get lonely."

"I'm busy. I have a lot to keep me occupied."

"Still . . ."

Yolanda shrugged, and her eyes took on a faraway look. Jessica couldn't help wondering if all was fine in her love life. But Jessica doubted Yolanda would admit that, even to her, if that was the case. Because of Shereen. And because of her pride.

After a moment of silence, Yolanda announced, "My father wants to see me. He's invited me over, but I'm not sure I'm up for a night with the surrogate family."

Jessica didn't say anything. She'd come to understand that the subject of her father was a sore spot with Yolanda and her conciliatory suggestions were never well received. Only Yolanda could deal with this, on her own terms, in her own time. She supposed they all had an issue they weren't willing to share with anyone, not even the group.

"Have you talked to Ellie?" Jessica asked. Ellie had been missing from their last group get-together, another evening at Yolanda's place.

"Yeah. I called her. Apologized. We're cool again. She thinks I'm getting on her case, but it's really Richard's case I'm getting on. That guy is a dog. I don't care what anyone says."

"She's gonna have to figure that out on her own."

"I know. But remember that time in senior year, when that pretty-boy Kappa played her like a baby grand? One of the new ones pledging?"

Jessica nodded. How could she forget? The guy had pretended to like Ellie, but it had all been part of a thoughtless fraternity initiation, to get a sorority sister to write him a love letter he could bring back to his big brothers. Well, instead of just asking a sorority sister to make up a letter—guys did it all the time—this fool took it upon himself to play Ellie. For whatever reason, he'd sensed she'd be easy, and she was. Ellie had fallen hard for him, and after she'd written something personal to him, he'd deeply humiliated her by showing it off to all the guys at his fraternity in the thoughtless way that only guys seem to be true masters of.

"I've never forgotten that, how hurt she was. I wanted to kill the guy, and I think I would have if you all hadn't stopped me." She smiled faintly. "I don't want to see her get hurt like that again. She was crushed, Jessica. Literally devastated. So as much as she pretends she's tough now, I'm afraid for her. No matter what you all think, I love her. I love you all."

"Hey, I know that. No one thinks you have a thing against her." Yolanda was notoriously tough, hard-nosed, and even tunnel-visioned, but none of the group believed she was a self-centered bitch.

"The thing is, I actually understand *why* she's with Richard. She thinks he's safer *because* he's married, that she's got some kind of control in this situation, but she doesn't realize how wrong she is. I just hope she works out all her issues. 'Cause she's gonna get hurt again if she stays with him. And maybe this time, it'll be worse than with the others."

"I hope so, too," Jessica added softly. But she said that as much for herself as she did for Ellie.

It had gone from shocking and confusing to downright terrifying.

And Jessica had no clue what to do.

Every thought, every instinct, told her to run. Get the hell away before this thing got any worse.

As it was, she didn't know what to think. Was it a prank? Was someone trying to get his or her kicks out of scaring her? Or, God forbid, was it worse than that?

This new letter in her hands made her wonder about how far this person would go. She'd read it once, twice, praying it wasn't true, thinking, *Not again, not again* . . .

But it was happening again. This wasn't a nightmare.

She glanced at the letter, though she knew the words. They were burned into her memory.

Once upon a time, not so long ago, on a very cold day in an old Virginia cabin

Jessica could hardly stand to look at this latest letter. Hardly stand to touch it. But destroying it wouldn't make it any less real.

This letter was different from the other ones. Foul, painful. Implicitly threatening.

a nasty whore named Jessica threw herself at Andrew Bell.
You think no one knows, but someone does.
Someone remembers.
Someone knows your secret.

A whimper escaped her as she crushed the letter in her palm. Who? Oh, God, who was doing this to her?

She stuffed the letter into her purse and fled her dressing room, dashed down the studio hall, bumping into Redmond on her way out.

"Hey, baby," he said, concern in his voice as he gripped her shoulders to steady her. "Whassup?"

"Sorry, Red." God help her, was it him? Trembling, she stepped away from him. "I—I've got to . . ."

The walls of the hallway were closing in on her. She needed to get out. Had to get away. She hurried down the hallway, ignoring Redmond as he called after her.

She was almost at the door to the parking lot when she heard, "Ms. Bedford!" Startled, she whirled around.

Denise rushed toward her. Oh, God, was it her? Denise had brought her more than one of the letters, including this one today. "Ms. Bedford, I know you're leaving, but Phillip wants me to go over the notes with you for—"

"For God's sake, not now!"

Denise recoiled as Jessica practically snapped her head off.

"Oh, God . . . I'm sorry," she mumbled, realizing how crazy this all was making her. Turning, she burst through the doors.

Somehow she made it to her Mercedes in one piece. She backed out of the spot and nearly collided with another car. Whoever it was blared the car's horn at her, and she took a moment to rest her head on her steering wheel before continuing.

"Calm down, Jessica," she told herself.

She burned rubber on the way out of the studio parking lot.

About five minutes into her northeast drive home, she spotted the car. It was a dark-colored sedan. Maybe black. Maybe navy. God, she wasn't sure.

But it was following her. That much she did know. When she went to the right lane, it did, too, though not directly behind her. Always a car or two behind.

It stayed behind her all along North Carolina Avenue and followed her through Lincoln Park to Tennessee Avenue.

Breathe, she told herself sternly when her hands began to sweat on the steering wheel. Maybe she was jumping to conclusions. Maybe she was wrong.

Deliberately, she indicated and went to the left lane.

The sedan did the same.

Oh, God!

It *was* following her. What should she do? Should she zip through traffic and try to lose the car? No, that wouldn't work. There was too much traffic for that.

Should she call someone? Douglas? But what would she tell him? Maybe she could call the police.

Her hand trembled as she dragged her purse onto her lap. Her phone, her phone. Where was her friggin' phone?

She glanced in the rearview mirror in time to see the car turn left onto D Street.

She released a shaky breath, then sucked in another so quickly she almost choked.

She hit the brakes, her tires squealing in protest. A red light.

The sedan was nowhere in sight.

Lord, was she going crazy or had that car really been following her? She didn't know what to think anymore!

She looked to her left. And screamed when she saw him.

Andrew!

No, it wasn't Andrew, she realized when she saw the concerned stare on the older black man's face. It was simply someone driving home, like she was, after a day at the office.

Get a grip!

Of course it wasn't Andrew. How could it be him?

The light changed to green and she hit the gas. Cautiously, she glanced around. Andrew was nowhere, yet she could feel him everywhere.

Andrew, who'd been dead for nine years.

Lord help her, was he finally coming back to haunt her?

THE PAST

"NO, ANDREW." JESSICA WIPED her eyes and nose with the back of her arm, unable to stop the tears. "Please, tell me you're lying."

"It's true." His voice was all too calm for the seriousness of what he'd just told her.

"A wife?" It couldn't be true. "You're married?" How could this be true? He'd told her so many times that he loved her and only her. He'd made love to her as if she meant everything to him. How could he do that if he had a wife?

He nodded.

"How long?" When he didn't immediately reply, Jessica's voice grew in pitch. "How long, Andrew?"

Turning, he walked to the window of the cabin and glanced outside. It was a cold January day, but bright, with a light dusting of snow. "Fourteen years."

"Fourteen years?" Her heart plummeted, down to a dark pool of despair she didn't know existed within her. This didn't make sense. "What . . . are you separated?"

"No."

"But you're having problems." She was grasping at straws, but she'd grasp at anything, anything that would help her understand.

He didn't even face her as he shrugged.

"Oh, God." Jessica gripped her stomach, pressing her hand against the life that grew inside. A life she and Andrew had created. Then another horror hit her. "Do you have children? With your wife?"

He did face her then, his handsome face drawn with stress. "Yes, I do. I have a daughter. She's twelve."

"You son of a bitch!" she cried. She wanted to charge at him, punch him, kick him, choke him with her bare hands, but instead she made tight fists, her nails breaking her skin as they dug into her palms.

"I know, and I'm sorry," he said. "I didn't mean for you to find out like this. But things were getting too serious . . ."

"Getting?" God, they already had gotten serious. She was in love with him. She was carrying his child.

"Whatever," he said, then faced the window again. "The point is, now that you know—"

"You face me when you talk to me." Anger had replaced the initial shock, and Jessica's voice was now low and lethal.

He turned. "Now that you know, you understand why you can't have this baby."

She couldn't stop blinking as she looked at him. Who was this man? Certainly not the one who had lain with her several times, whispered words of undying love to her. He was a stranger.

"Of course, I'll pay for the abortion."

"Abortion?"

"Yes. You can't have this baby, Jessica. My wife . . ." His voice trailed off.

No, this wasn't happening. This couldn't be happening. Maybe something else was going on. How could he tell her he loved her if he was really in love with his wife?

"You said you love me, Andrew."

"I don't want this baby." His voice was firm, leaving no room for doubt—and her heart shattered into a million pieces.

She ran to the bathroom, where she threw up. More evidence of the life growing inside her. Or evidence of the fact that she'd made the biggest mistake of her life.

Andrew wasn't waiting for her when she emerged from the cabin's small bathroom. Given what he'd said, she hadn't expected him to be, yet the realization still hurt. In the living room, she found him sitting on the sofa, his elbows resting on his knees, his face buried in his hands. It didn't make sense, but she had the strongest urge to go to him and wrap her arms around him, tell him how much she loved him, that they could work this out.

She was about to do just that when he looked at her over his shoulder. "Will you be okay to get back to Howard?"

The truth, bitter, painful, crept through her body like poison spreading through her veins. For a moment, she wondered if she would indeed drop dead. He didn't love her. He probably never had.

Oh, God.

She sucked in a sharp breath, pressed a hand to her belly. "I'll be okay," she lied.

For she had to be.

"All right then."

So, that was it. "All right then" and that was it. She was supposed to just walk away, leave the man who'd taught her to love, the man whose baby she carried, and go back to her dorm.

And then to an abortion clinic.

She didn't think so.

Yet she managed to keep her dignity and walk to the door without giving in to the overwhelming urge to throw herself at his feet and beg him to change his mind. She needed to get back to the dorm, to her three best friends, whom she knew she could count on to help her get through this.

She even started the car without any tears, only the resolve that her life would be okay even if Andrew didn't want her.

But as she drove down the narrow country road away from the cabin, she had to pull over. Because suddenly the tears began and wouldn't stop.

"Oh, God, Andrew. How could you do this? How?"

Then she felt the hands, Andrew's hands, wrapping around her and comforting her. It was going to be all right.

"Andrew . . ."

"Who's Andrew?"

The firm sound of Douglas's voice awoke Jessica as surely as a glass of cold water being thrown on her while she slept. Her heart raced from fright, until she realized she was in Douglas's arms, not Andrew's arms.

Douglas's arms. *Thank God.* Slowly, her anxiety began to ebb away.

Her arms were wrapped tightly around Douglas's neck, and tears streamed down her cheeks. She didn't dare open her eyes. Instead, she clutched him tighter, thankful to be back from the past.

"Oh, Douglas. Hold me."

He pulled her to him, but still asked, "Who's Andrew?"

"No one," she whispered. "I was having a bad dream. That's all."

He kissed her forehead. "You're safe now."

Yes, she was. Safe.

For now.

She squeezed him hard, needing to know he was real, needing his warmth. This was her life now. Douglas.

Not the letters. Not the past.

Her memories couldn't hurt her. Dreams couldn't hurt her.

But someone could.

The person sending the letters.

What did that person want? What should she do? Part of her wanted to tell Douglas, but she didn't want to worry him. Sometimes he had chest pains, and that scared her, because she didn't know if it was just stress or something more. Douglas always said it was nothing but heartburn, but Jessica didn't want to risk sending him into cardiac arrest with this news.

She could tell her three best friends in the world. Maybe they would know what to do.

No. She couldn't. She'd leaned on the shield once with them—having gotten them to lie to save her butt—and she wouldn't involve them again.

This was her problem.

She would deal with it.

If and when she ever found out if she was dealing with a real threat or with one that had somehow come back from the grave to haunt her.

Chapter Seventeen

"WHAT DO YOU MEAN, she's out of town?" Yolanda asked.

"Just what I said," Shereen replied, though the look on her face said she was as confused about Jessica's disappearance as the rest of them.

"How could she be out of town?" Yolanda continued. The gang was all at her house. Everyone besides Jessica—and she was supposed to be the guest of honor. "You had this arranged, didn't you, Shereen?"

"Of course I did." Shereen ran her fingers along the edge of the lace tablecloth as she sat at the kitchen table across from Yolanda. Ellie, who was smoking, stood near the open back door, taking advantage of the gorgeous late June weather. "We talked about this last weekend. She told me Saturday wasn't a good day because Douglas was taking her to dinner, so it had to be Sunday."

"So she knew we were getting together for her birthday?" Ellie asked.

"Of course she knew. Though I didn't exactly say that. But she had to know. Hell, we *always* get together for her birthday. Even when she was in New York for two years trying to get theater gigs, she still came back for her birthday."

"This isn't like her," Ellie said.

"Not like her? This makes no sense at all. She has never, ever, in all the years that we've known her, taken off to Buffalo for her birthday. And to leave Douglas? No, something definitely ain't right."

"What did Douglas say?" Yolanda asked.

"Just that she said she wanted to go home. She needed a break."

Ellie ground out her cigarette on the ceramic saucer she held, then sat at the table. "This is too weird, I'm telling you. There's been a replacement on the show all week."

"She *did* say she wasn't feeling well," Shereen said. She'd called Jessica earlier in the week when she'd seen the replacement on the show.

"I can understand her feeling sick, or even needing to get away," Yolanda said. "But not to call any of us? That's what doesn't make sense."

"Tell me about it."

"Do any of you know her number in Buffalo?"

"We could ask Douglas."

"Douglas told me not to worry," Shereen explained. "Said Jessica told him she'd get in touch with us when she got back."

"Well, shit." Ellie stood and lit another cigarette.

"I don't know. Maybe we're making more of this than we should."

"I don't think so," Shereen said. "She's been acting strange over the last few months."

"Maybe . . . Do you think . . ." Yolanda eyed Shereen, then Ellie, silently asking for permission to voice what was on her mind. They both looked at her expectantly, so she continued. "Do you think she's having problems with Douglas?" When no one replied, Yolanda continued. "Maybe she is and she doesn't want to tell us because she's embarrassed."

Shereen frowned. "God, I hope not. She adores him."

"You never know," Ellie chimed, blowing smoke through her nose and mouth as she spoke. "Men can have women who adore them, yet still screw around."

"Douglas?" Shereen shook her head, unwilling to contemplate that. "No, I can't see that. He adores her, too."

"I didn't say anything about screwing around." Yolanda gave Ellie a pointed look. "But it could be this whole baby thing."

"You think so?" Shereen asked. "But about having a baby . . . I can't see Douglas pressuring her so much that she'd run away. Honestly, when I see them together, I think of my old pastor and his wife. They were always so gentle, so loving, always holding hands or sharing special looks across a room. I always envied that, and when I saw Douglas and Jessica together the first time, I knew they'd found that rare, special kind of love. No, Douglas and Jessica are the *perfect* couple."

Yolanda said, "Looks can be deceiving."

Yes, that was true, Shereen realized. James and Yolanda had also seemed like a perfect couple. So had she and Terrence. But Douglas and Jessica? Surely they were in different category.

"Girl, if they can have problems," Ellie began, "then no wonder I'm not married."

"If *they* can have problems, then it kinda makes you not want to get married at all." Too late, Shereen realized her words. She quickly glanced at Yolanda. "I mean . . . Well, I don't mean you, I mean me. I'm sure you and Terrence will be fine."

Yolanda smiled. "Thanks."

"What should we do about Jessica?" Shereen asked after a moment.

"What can we do?" Yolanda asked. "We can't go to Buffalo and drag her ass back here. And we can't pry. Whenever she's ready, she'll tell us what's going on."

"I hope so," Ellie said. "Because if there's any one of us who deserves to be happy, it's Jessica. She's been through enough shit."

"Yeah," Shereen agreed. "You can say that again."

"Maybe it's the pressure of being a celebrity," Yolanda suggested. "Because she *is* becoming one. And Jessica has always been painfully shy."

She'd given up a track scholarship because she didn't want to be in the spotlight. Then she'd taken a drama course to boost her self-esteem and get over her shyness. And that had led to the whole fiasco with Andrew Bell.

"You think that's it?" Shereen asked. "A serious case of stage fright?"

Yolanda shrugged. Her idea suddenly didn't seem to make sense, not now, given how far Jessica had come. "I don't know. All we can do is be here for her when she gets back." Though that was the only logical solution, it still pained Yolanda to know that Jessica might be going through something and not sharing it with them. "Jessica's always been a private person, so it won't help to bombard her with questions about what's going on. After all, it may be nothing. We just have to let her know we're here for her. That's it."

"I guess so," Shereen agreed.

"So, here we are, all ready to party, without the birthday girl." Ellie lit another cigarette.

"Should I cancel the stripper?" Shereen asked.

Ellie choked as she inhaled, then sputtered, "Stripper? What stripper?"

"I'm just kidding, you little hoochie-mama Scorpio." She laughed. "I'm saving the stripper for Yolanda's stag."

"No." Yolanda banged a hand on the table. The last thing she needed was some naked man strutting his stuff before her at a raunchy bachelorette party. She'd never understood the thrill of being able to look but not touch. "I don't want no stripper."

"That's a double negative," Ellie told her with a smile. "That means you *do* want one."

"*No.*"

"Oh, cut the prude act," Shereen told her. "You're just as hot-blooded as the rest of us."

"Besides, once we get enough alcohol into you, you'll be begging for those hot bods." Ellie laughed.

"You think so."

"Like it hasn't happened before."

Yolanda made a wry face at Ellie.

"Speaking of strippers, when *is* the wedding?" Ellie asked.

"Yeah, when?" Shereen added, letting Yolanda know it was okay to talk about her upcoming nuptials. Even now, Yolanda hardly mentioned Terrence around her.

"We were thinking of December. We're not sure yet."

"Why isn't he living here?" Ellie asked. "He's in Washington now, isn't he?"

It was something Shereen had wanted to ask a while ago but hadn't dared.

"Yeah, but he's renting a place. Until we get married."

"Girlfriend, who are you trying to fool?" Ellie looked at her with disbelief.

"No, it's not about that. I don't know. Terrence prefers it that way. I think it's kinda romantic."

Kinda romantic? It was kinda strange, Shereen decided. If Terrence was anything like she remembered . . .

"To each his own," Ellie conceded.

"Who wants some cake?" Shereen's stomach was suddenly fluttering, though she didn't know why. Hell, yes, she did. She was wondering about the real reason Terrence wasn't living with Yolanda. And she wondered if it had anything to do with his visit to her office.

"I'd love some cake." Ellie sat down.

"May as well not let it go to waste," Yolanda said, ever practical.

But the cake wasn't as sweet as it should have been, not while Jessica wasn't there and they were all worried if she was okay.

Chapter Eighteen

"MAY I SPEAK WITH RICHARD Duncan, please?" Ellie asked when the receptionist—the one who'd gotten her job after she'd left—answered.

"Who's calling?"

"This is Ms. Grant."

"One moment."

How efficient, Ellie thought, while some soft melody played in her ear.

Seconds later, Richard came onto the line. "Hello?" He sounded gruff, and she wondered if she'd disturbed him.

"Hey, sweetheart. It's Ellie."

"Oh." His voice softened. "Ellie."

"Guess where I am?"

"I don't know. Where are you?"

"My new office." Well, it wasn't really an office. It was a small cubicle, but she had her own phone and a desk and cabinets. It felt like an office.

"You got the job?"

"Yeah." Ellie had applied for a job as a secretary at a local insurance company, but they'd hired her to answer phones instead. Well, that's what they'd said, but when she'd started the job a few days ago, she'd learned that she was really the one who had to make the calls, soliciting business. Either that or file. Or fetch coffee for the boss. Whatever needed to be done.

But she didn't mind. They were paying her twelve bucks an hour—better than her job as a movie extra. Besides, this office was only a seven-minute drive from Richard's office. Yeah, she knew it was hopelessly pathetic, but she'd timed it.

She twirled the phone cord in one hand. "I miss you."

"I miss you, too." But he said it like he didn't mean it. Like he was preoccupied.

"Is this a bad time?"

"Kinda."

She'd heard the same song and dance since last week, and Ellie couldn't help wondering what was going on. He hadn't even called her in the last few days. It had occurred to her that maybe he *was* playing her for a fool, as Yolanda and Shereen had always said, because though he'd told her well over a month ago that he wanted them to move in together, they hadn't even gone looking for a single place. So far, all he had done was show her real estate brochures with photos of different homes. She'd picked out what she liked, and he'd said they would go look at them, but until now, he'd been too busy to actually do so. He'd kept telling her, "It's gonna take some time," but how much time was it actually gonna take?

Perhaps given the recent events—or, rather, nonevents—her voice was a little harsher than she intended when she asked, "When *will* be a good time, Richard?"

"Hey, sweetie, what's with the tone?"

"How come you haven't called me?"

"I had to go out of town. I told you that."

"Yeah, that's what you *said*, but maybe you just don't want to see me."

"Where is this coming from?" He sounded genuinely baffled.

"I'm starting to wonder if you're full of shit, Richard." No, she was wondering that *again*. Every so often, she wondered if he was lying to her, but then he'd do something sweet, like take her to dinner, or send her a dozen roses, or spend the whole night at her place.

Or tell her he was leaving his wife.

Come to think of it, he never told her anything that pertained to the future of their relationship until she threatened to leave him.

God, maybe she was a sorry fool.

But then she remembered his effort to see more of her, the gifts he'd gotten her, his assurance that it wouldn't be too much longer before they could be together. No man could tell you all those things with a straight face and really be lying.

Could he?

Of course not. She wasn't exactly in a desirable position, being the other woman who'd fallen in love with a married man. So, she had to be patient, accept things that she wouldn't normally accept if she were in a normal relationship.

Still, something didn't feel right.

"Sweetie, you know how it is here. I'm just busy, that's all."

Another line flashed on her phone, but she ignored it. "When are we gonna start shopping for houses? Like you promised several weeks ago?"

"I've got people in the office, I'll have to talk to you later."

"Really?"

"Yes, really." He sounded annoyed now.

"Fuck you." She slammed the receiver down, then stared at the phone, her whole body shaking from a surge of adrenaline.

Seconds later, her boss peered in at her. "Everything okay?"

"Yeah," she told him curtly, then picked up the phone to make a cold call. "Just fine."

Everything wasn't fine. Ellie knew it, felt it way down in her soul.

Richard hadn't called her since the day she'd hung up on him. That was four days ago.

Richard *always* called her after an argument or disagreement. Deep down, Ellie knew it was childish, but it had become a game for them. She'd get pissed off, he'd send flowers or call and beg for her to give him another chance. It was the way they communicated.

But this time, nada.

Now, she was really pissed. And, truth be told, scared to death that he didn't love her. But if he *had* been playing her all along, there'd be hell to pay.

At four-thirty, Ellie told her boss that she wasn't feeling well, and he let her leave early. Half an hour was enough time to get to Richard's office before he left for the day. They needed to work things out.

To Ellie's chagrin, he was already gone when she got there.

What now? she wondered as she sat in her Geo Metro, thrumming her fingers on the steering wheel.

She should just go home. But she couldn't. She felt high-strung, ready to do battle. Why?

Maybe it was the fact that Jessica had come back from Buffalo and said that not a damn thing was wrong, yet she was avoiding them all like the plague. Or maybe it was the fact that her relationship with Richard was once again up in the air. Whatever the cause, Ellie was stressed and needed to let off steam.

She needed to confront Richard and find out his true intentions.

Today, she was gonna lay it all down on the line. She wanted a ring. If he was going to be with her, leave his wife, and marry her, then she wanted a tangible promise from him.

So instead of going home, Ellie drove to a nearby restaurant Richard liked to frequent after work, praying he'd be there. The cat-and-mouse game was over. The weird sense of loss she'd felt when she hadn't seen him at the office had made her realize right then and there that she was only punishing herself by staying angry with him. Not hearing from him or seeing him had her going nuts.

"Table for one?" the host asked.

"No, I'm looking for someone." Richard usually sat at the bar. She scoped that area but didn't see him. So she strolled through the restaurant, checking out the tables and booths.

And then she spotted him. He was at a corner booth in the back, his face to her. But he was talking and laughing with someone and didn't notice her as she approached.

Her blood ran cold as she got to the table and saw a gorgeous, *thin,* black woman sitting opposite him.

He was so taken with this woman, he didn't even notice when Ellie stopped at the table and folded her arms across her chest. "Richard."

His smile went flat when he saw her. The woman's eyes widened with fright. "Ellie." Richard scrambled from the booth.

"Is this why you haven't called me?" Ellie asked, fighting the hysteria. God, Richard had always told her he liked her full figure. What was he doing with that anorexic bimbo?

He dragged her to the front of the restaurant before speaking. "What are you doing here?"

"What are *you* doing here, Richard? You haven't called me all week, yet you're out wining and dining—" She stopped abruptly, unable to go on.

"You're the one who didn't want to talk to me," he told her defensively.

"Oh, so now you're with *her*?" She glanced over his shoulder in the direction of the booth.

"Come here." He led her outside.

"You know, Richard, if that's what you want, fine. I don't care." Though she did. Too much. Like the loser that she was. God, he wasn't even hers, and deep down she'd known this day might come, so why was she so upset?

"Tracy is one of my clients."

"I'll bet."

"She is. This isn't the first time I've taken one of my clients to dinner. You know that."

That was true, but she was so . . . beautiful. "Why haven't you called me?"

"I thought you didn't want to talk to me."

"I was only mad."

"Yeah, well, I was mad, too. It's like you don't trust me these days. You don't know what it's like, trying to get out of a bad marriage, then having the woman you love on your back all the time."

Is that how he felt? "I'm sorry, Richard."

"And now you're checking up on me?" He shook his head. "Ellie, I don't know."

Her heart missed a beat. "Don't know what?"

"Maybe we should end things."

No, he couldn't mean that. God, she couldn't lose him. "Richard—"

"Since you obviously don't trust me."

"It's not that I don't trust you," she quickly said, her stomaching doing a somersault.

"I don't know."

He didn't know? God, what did that mean? "Richard, please don't be like this. I *do* trust you. I . . . I'm just stressed. I miss you. And I hate it when we fight."

He gave her a hard stare, then his expression softened. He stroked her face. "I know, baby."

Her world had been on the verge of collapse, but now, with one touch, she was saved. "It's just that I need you so much." She hardly recognized herself, she sounded so pitiful, but she couldn't stop the words.

"I need you, too." He kissed her, and just the touch of his lips against hers recharged her body with strength. When he pulled away, he asked, "What are you doing tonight?"

"Nothing." She shook her head. "Nothing."

"Can I come see you?"

"Of course." She touched his lips, tracing the outline of his faint grin. "You don't have to ask."

His smile grew. "All right. I'll see you later." He gave her a quick peck. "I love you. Remember that."

"I love you, too."

Ellie watched him walk back into the restaurant, forgetting everything she'd said about laying anything on the line. All that mattered was that Richard still loved her.

That truth scared the hell out of her. Because she suddenly realized that she didn't know what she would do if he ever stopped.

Chapter Nineteen

WHEN SHEREEN SAUNTERED INTO the large, brightly lit living room, she found Jessica sitting on the sofa with her legs curled under her and her chin perched on the sofa's back, facing the direction of the bay windows. She was either staring at the beautiful view of Rock Creek Park that bordered her backyard, or she was off in another world. Maybe the latter, for not even the sound of Shereen's sandals clicking on the ceramic floor drew Jessica's attention.

"Hey, girl."

Jessica turned, startled. Smiled. "Shereen." She stood to meet her. "What are you doing here?"

Shereen hugged her. "The mountain had to come to Mohammed."

"What's that supposed to mean? I saw you last weekend. Oh, you still think something is wrong? Well, it's not. I already told you, I'm fine."

Shereen sat, and so did Jessica. "Yes, you've seen us, and yes, you've told us you're fine, but it's what you're not saying that has us scared. Ellie and Yolanda won't say anything—they don't want me to, either—but we're worried about you. You're not acting like yourself."

"Girl, please." Jessica waved off Shereen's concern.

"I'm serious. It's nothing I can really put my finger on, other than the fact that you don't seem like yourself." Pause. "I'd hoped by now you would've shared whatever's bothering you."

"Nothing's bothering me." Jessica was suddenly on her feet. Wrapping her arms around her torso, she walked to one of the huge bay windows.

Shereen followed her. "You can tell me 'nothing' till the cows come home. I know that's not true."

"Hey, can't a girl take a break?"

Jessica attempted a light and jovial tone, but didn't quite succeed. So Shereen didn't back down. "A break is one thing, Jess. But . . . Remember last Saturday, when we were driving to the school? You were convinced someone was following us."

"So I was a little paranoid. In that part of town, who isn't?"

"It's more than that."

"Like what?"

There was no other way to say it than to just say it. "I'm thinking it has to do with Douglas."

"Douglas?"

"Yeah. It crossed our minds that maybe you two are having problems."

Jessica huffed. "Your lives must be pretty dull if all you can do is speculate about mine."

Surprised at her friend's uncharacteristicly sarcastic words, Shereen's jaw dropped, mortified.

"I'm sorry." Jessica sank into the nearby love seat. "God, I didn't mean that."

"It's exactly that kind of attitude that freaks me out. You *never* talk like that."

"The show's just getting to me," Jessica told her.

"Why?"

"I don't know. It just is. Maybe I need a change of pace. That's why I left." She glanced toward the living room entrance, as if looking to see if Douglas was around. He wasn't, but still she lowered her voice. "And yeah, I'm a little stressed over Douglas. He says he understands, but I think he's really disappointed that I'm not ready for a family."

Shereen crouched before Jessica and rubbed her thigh. "I'm sorry, hon."

Jessica shrugged noncommittally. "We'll work it out."

Shereen regarded her friend a moment longer, but Jessica didn't meet her eyes. Sighing, she stood. She hoped that Jessica was telling the truth, that nothing else was going on in her life. But if she wasn't, what could she do? She could only hope that whatever it was would soon pass.

Shereen wandered to a window and glanced outside. A duck and her ducklings were swimming in the backyard's artificial pond. Normally an uplifting sight, but right now Shereen was too troubled to enjoy it. Not only by Jessica's strange behavior, but also by her comment. Though she'd said she hadn't meant the words, maybe she was right. Maybe thinking about Jessica's problems was a way to avoid thinking about her own. Not because her life was dull, as Jessica had suggested, but because it was far from it.

She faced Jessica. "There's something I want to tell you."

"Okay."

"But you have to promise not to tell Yolanda."

"Uh-oh."

"It's nothing bad. Not really." She frowned. "All right, I'll get to the point. It's Terrence. I didn't tell you before, but he came by my office once. And he's called me a couple of times."

"Does this mean what I think it does?"

"I don't know." That was the truth. Terrence had only called to say hi, but Shereen had always gotten the feeling that he wanted to say more. Or maybe that was simply wishful thinking on her part. She faced the window again. "He's not saying anything. Except that he'd like us to be friends again. The problem is, I don't know if he's told Yolanda he's been in touch with me, and if he hasn't, well, I don't know what to do. Should I tell her? And if *I* tell her, what if she gets pissed with me like she did when I told her about Lawrence? But what if I don't tell her and she already knows? She'll think I'm trying to hide this— and that's the last thing I need. I don't want her thinking I'm trying to get with Terrence, because I'm *not*."

"You sure about that?"

Shereen whirled around to face her friend, wondering why she wasn't more surprised—or outraged—by the question. "I told Ellie, and I'm telling you—no. Terrence is my past."

"You've talked to Ellie about this."

"I had to talk to someone."

"Sounds serious." Jessica rested her face in her hands. "Well, for one, I doubt she knows. She probably would have mentioned something to me if she did, and she hasn't said a word. Besides, Terrence has to know how touchy this situation is, so he's probably not telling her for that reason.

"So if I were you, I wouldn't tell her. Yolanda plays like she's strong, but you know how insecure she can be. If you ask me, I still think she's in love with James, but just too afraid he'll break her heart if she gives him another chance."

"You think so?" God, she actually sounded hopeful. How crazy was that?

Jessica's eyes narrowed as she gave Shereen a curious look. "Yeah, I think so," she said after a moment. "But I also think she really wants this marriage to work."

Point taken. "Of course she does. And you're right. I won't say anything. It's better that way."

"You guys didn't have to do this."

"Yes, we did," Yolanda told Jessica in a mock-curt tone. "And lucky for you, we didn't have anything better to do today. So blow out the damn candles, will ya?"

Jessica giggled, feeling touched that her friends cared enough to throw her another birthday party, even if it was a few weeks after the fact.

"Go on," Ellie said. "Make a wish. And make it good."

Jessica looked at the burning candles, opened her mouth to inhale, then closed it. Instead of blowing out the candles, she glanced up at her friends from her seat at Yolanda's kitchen table. It was a funny scene, the three of them standing with their arms crossed, her sitting with her hands in her lap, as if they were her parents and she was the child. Sometimes she felt exactly that way, but always in a good sense.

"What?" Shereen asked.

She shook her head, closed her eyes, then made a wish as she blew out the candles. Everyone cheered.

"And though you are truly the person who has everything—and we couldn't figure out what to get you—we finally figured out what you might like. So . . ." Smiling, Shereen handed her a card.

Simply a card, no present. "Wow, a check for a million dollars," Jessica joked. "Who couldn't use that?"

"Not exactly," Ellie clarified. "But open it and find out."

"Okay." She giggled, giddy, happy to be with her friends again, happy to feel like herself again. She ran her fingers beneath the flap.

But suddenly she remembered the studio, the letters, and her hand paused.

After a full five seconds, Yolanda asked, "What's the matter?"

What indeed? Why couldn't she open this card from her friends? If she trusted anyone in this world, it was the three of them. They had seen her through the darkest hours of her life. Without them, she didn't know where she'd be.

Yet she dropped the card on the table as tears filled her eyes.

Shereen immediately sank into the chair next to her and reached for her hand. "What is it?"

Wiping at her tears, Jessica sniffled. "It's . . . all of you . . . I don't know what I'd do without you."

Ellie knelt beside her. "Hey. That's something you never have to con-
. sider. 'Cause we're here for you. Always."

"Yeah," Yolanda agreed, rubbing her shoulder. "We've got your back."

"I know. That's why I love you so much." Would anyone but these three women have stood beside her the way they had, lied for her to save her butt, all the while knowing that the lie could get them into serious trouble if it was ever revealed? She doubted it. It had been too much to ask, yet they'd been there for her anyway. "Sometimes, I won-der what I ever did to deserve you."

"The feeling's mutual," Shereen said, gently squeezing her hand.

"Go on," Ellie urged. "Open the card."

Smiling through her tears, Jessica did just that. On the front was a picture of a beautiful, serene setting, and it read, "Good Friends Are So Rare." Whatever writing had been printed inside the card had been whited out, and in its place Ellie, Shereen, and Yolanda had written sentimental notes about how much she meant to them. A simple, yet personal gesture that filled Jessica's heart with warmth.

"If you unfold the card—"

"She'll find it," Shereen protested, cutting Yolanda off.

"Find what?" Jessica asked.

"Unfold the card," Yolanda continued, looking sheepishly at the group. "Your gift is in there."

"You know Yolanda," Shereen said, punctuating the statement with a roll of her eyes. "Can't keep her mouth shut."

"Sorry."

Jessica unfolded the card and withdrew a gift certificate of some kind. As she read the details, she saw that it was for a weekend getaway in Fairfax, Virginia.

Virginia. Andrew.

Oh, God.

"Jessica, are you sure you're okay?"

Yolanda's question made Jessica realize that she was squeezing her eyes tightly shut, so she opened them. Took a breath. Forced a smile as she looked at all of them. "I'm just thinking . . . *thanking* God for dear friends. You're all the present I need."

Yolanda's lips lifted in a grin, as did Shereen's. Ellie kissed her cheek.

They all seemed relieved with her answer—like they had expected her to say something else. Did she seem that fragile to them all? Silly question. She should have known that they would sense something was wrong with her, that they wouldn't simply believe everything was okay because she said it was. They were closer to her than any flesh and blood could be.

Which made her wonder why she couldn't share this with them.

As soon as that thought popped into her head, she knew the answer. *Don't get them involved. Not this time. This is your problem.*

And maybe, deep down inside, she was hoping, though she knew it was irrational, that if she didn't tell them about the problem, it would simply disappear.

She looked at the certificate, trying to forget the past that seemed to be rearing its ugly head at every turn.

"It's for you and Douglas," Shereen explained. "For a weekend escape sometime."

"Not that you don't spend enough time together," Ellie qualified. "But, well . . . you can never spend too much time with someone you love." She yelped as Shereen elbowed her in the ribs.

"Thank you." Jessica deliberately ignored the implication behind Ellie's statement. She knew they were all worried about her and Douglas, and she loved them for their concern.

And she appreciated this gift, she really did, but she knew one thing. She wouldn't be using this certificate any time soon. She wouldn't even tell Douglas about it. In fact, when she got home, she'd rip it up.

Her friends wouldn't know the difference.

It was wrong, she knew, but the truth was, she didn't want to be anywhere near Virginia. It held too many memories she wanted to forget.

As far as she was concerned, if she never stepped foot in that state again, it wouldn't be too soon.

Chapter Twenty

"DOUGLAS WOULD KILL ME if he knew."

"Well, you're not gonna tell him," Shereen said bluntly. "And we're certainly not gonna rat you out."

"No, I guess not." Jessica giggled. The thought of what they were about to do already had her embarrassed.

"Guys do it all the time and no one even raises an eyebrow," Ellie said from the backseat.

"True," Jessica agreed. Then erupted in a giggling fit again.

"Getting Janelle to pick her up, that was smart," Shereen told Ellie, glancing over her shoulder at her while she drove. "She'll never figure it out."

It was months before Yolanda's scheduled wedding, and they were having her bachelorette party. Hell, it was really just an excuse to get together and be stupid and relieve stress. The four of them had been pretty stressed lately.

"Who's all going?" Jessica asked.

"Just a handful of our sorors," Ellie answered. "Janelle is picking Yolanda up, Courtney will be there, Charlene. Maybe Lenore."

"That many?"

"Relax," Shereen told Jessica. "They won't rat you out, either." She patted her friend's thigh across the front seat. "You're gonna have a blast."

"I hope so."

Minutes later, they were parked and heading to Fantasies, a male strip club. Jessica couldn't stop smiling. Ellie practically ran from the parking lot across the street to the club's door.

"Hold on, Wild Thang," Shereen called.

Ellie anxiously waved them over from across the street. "I just saw Janelle's car."

"Shit." Grabbing Jessica's arm, Shereen ran with her across the street. They were all supposed to wait in the front of the club for Yolanda and Janelle to arrive, because they didn't trust Yolanda to head inside with only Janelle trying to get her in there. If necessary, they'd all drag her butt upstairs.

"Where's the car?" Jessica asked as they met up with Ellie.

"She just drove past the club, but she'll turn around. Oh, here she comes right now."

The look of stunned disbelief on Yolanda's face was priceless, clearly evident even through the tinted windows of Janelle's Honda. Ellie, Shereen, and Jessica cracked up. Well, Jessica kept laughing—she hadn't stopped since Shereen had picked her up—but this time she really let herself go.

When Yolanda wouldn't step out of the car, Ellie yanked the front door open. "Oh, no," Yolanda was saying over and over while shaking her head.

"Oh, yes." Ellie grabbed her hand, but she held her own, not budging from the car. Ellie turned to Shereen and Jessica. "Give me a hand here."

With one good tug, Shereen and Ellie pulled Yolanda from the car.

"No." But a smile had crept onto Yolanda's face. "I told you guys I didn't want this."

"I don't think you have a say," Janelle commented from inside the car. "Close the door and let me go park."

Ellie closed the door with her hip.

Yolanda stared at Jessica, who continued to laugh hysterically. "I can't believe you got *her* here."

Jessica suppressed her giggling long enough to say, "Shut up and let's go inside."

"Well," Ellie began with a smirk, "even Q.T. is ready to get a little freaky."

"Why not?" Jessica agreed. She'd never been to a strip club before, not even when her sorors would occasionally go in school. Suddenly, the prospect was exciting.

"But my wedding isn't for months. . . ."

"Surprise." Shereen tightly linked arms with Yolanda, and Ellie followed her example.

"Guys . . ."

"Didn't Jessica tell you to shut up?" Shereen asked.

Yolanda chortled. "Y'all are crazy."

"Exactly," Ellie agreed. "Let's go get stupid!"

"Ladies," the emcee shouted, "are you ready for the second half of the show?"

A collective "Yeah!" erupted from the crowd of hot, wild women.

"I said, are you ready for the second half of the show?"

"Yeah!" The women screamed even louder, clapped and whistled.

"That's more like it. Now, for those of you who haven't been here before, you're in for a treat." The emcee, a gorgeous black man, strutted back and forth on the stage. He wore black slacks and a loose-fitting black shirt—unbuttoned to reveal his muscular chest. "Because now, ladies, we do a little addition and subtraction. We add a shower . . . and take away the g-strings!"

There were exuberant cheers all throughout the club.

"You didn't tell me they take it all off here," Jessica said, her eyes bulging as she regarded her sorors. Seven of them—Lenore hadn't come after all—sat at two combined tables along the foot of the stage. Where Jessica was positioned, she had a perfect view of the men as they came from the back room.

"I had no clue," Shereen replied. "But hell, I'm not gonna complain!"

"I don't believe this." Yolanda reached for her beer and downed a huge sip. She'd already had a few and was drunk.

"It's gonna get hot in here." Ellie fanned herself.

". . . so put your hands together for Heartthrob!" the emcee exclaimed, then ran off the stage.

"Oooh, I love him," Yolanda stated.

The lights dimmed, then rose again as Heartthrob, dressed as a fireman, stormed onto the stage. There was a shrill round of applause. Shereen laughed as she stared at Yolanda, who'd claimed she didn't want to be there, yet had her eyes glued to the dancer. Earlier, she'd made it onstage as one of the women celebrating something, in this case, her pending marriage. In a game of musical chairs—complete with the men—Yolanda had emerged victorious, claiming a spot on the last man's lap before her competitor. Her prize was a shooter—an orgasm—which she got to down while draped across Heartthrob's thighs. Since then, he had become her favorite.

"Remember Terrence," Courtney told Yolanda from a few seats over.

"Terrence who?" she scoffed, then reached for her drink.

Then they all watched the show in wonder.

"How do they do that?" Jessica asked when Heartthrob pulled his pants off with one quick jerk.

"There's got to be a science to it," Charlene offered, her eyes never leaving the stripper's incredible body.

"Damn, makes me wish I went into science," Ellie quipped. "I wonder if he's single."

Jessica shushed her.

Heartthrob slowed his dancing routine to place a towel over his penis. The women hollered, and he didn't disappoint. Still holding the towel in place, he unfastened his g-string at the side. The next second, he slipped the g-string off.

"Oh, my God." Ellie's mouth fell open at the hint of his erect penis beneath the white towel.

Jessica erupted in a fit of chuckles. Then, "Oh, Lord!" as Heartthrob took away the towel. "Oh, my God. Douglas . . ."

"He's not quite Douglas, honey," Shereen said, laughing.

Jessica rested her face on a palm. "No . . ."

"Over here!" Ellie called, waving a bill over Yolanda's head.

"Hey—n-no!" Yolanda scrunched down in her seat when Heartthrob approached her wearing nothing but a sexy smile. He gyrated before her specifically, but the entire group had front-row seats as he showed off the goods.

"Lord have mercy," Shereen whispered. Beside her, Jessica dug her nails into Shereen's forearm.

Finishing up with the dance, he kissed Yolanda on the cheek, covered himself with the towel, then accepted the money from Ellie before heading to another table of crazed women.

"I have never seen such a firm ass," Charlene said.

"Who was looking at his ass?" Yolanda asked, then laughed.

"I can't go home. Douglas will know. My face actually hurts; I can't stop smiling."

"I still can't believe Miss I-Don't-Want-No-Naked-Man dancing for me." Shereen laughed. "Look at her."

"Hey, you brought me here. I may as well enjoy myself."

"Damn straight," agreed Courtney.

The scantily clad waiter arrived, and Ellie ordered a round of shots for the entire table. They'd cab it home if necessary.

When the waiter returned with the B-52 shots, someone yelled "Schlo Ho!" then everyone threw their heads back and downed the drinks.

The second stripper did his thing, totally disrobing to the delight of all the females in the club. Then, when the music changed from upbeat to slow, he went to a glass-enclosed shower and moved his body slowly to the soft sound of an R&B beat.

"If you want to help clean Midnight," the emcee announced, "make your way onto the stage."

Jessica was the first to jump from her seat. She climbed onto the stage and was the first one in line.

"We've got an excited one over here," the emcee said as Jessica rushed toward him.

"Wow," Ellie commented, shaking her head slowly as she watched Jessica take the showerhead. "Who would have thought?"

"Who indeed?" Shereen seconded as she craned her neck to watch Jessica hose down Midnight's beautiful body.

"I'm not gonna let her have all the fun." Janelle squeezed out from behind the table and walked the long way around to the stage.

"I'll wait for the one who kinda looks like Richard," Ellie said.

"Richard, Richard." Yolanda shook her head. "Even here, can't you forget Richard?"

"Well . . ." Ellie stretched her neck for a view of the naked man Jessica was still showering. When he turned and she had a full frontal view of him, she let out a low whistle. "Did I say Richard? Richard who?" Tonight, she didn't care about Richard—or any other man, for that matter. She just cared about having fun, being silly. The last time they'd gone to a strip club was during their sophomore year at Howard, an all-girls sorority night event for the pledges who had been on line at the time.

Except for Jessica. Somehow she'd skipped out on them. It had been a group of thirty-four screaming, crazy women.

After a minute, Jessica hopped from the stage back into her seat, grinning from ear to ear.

"I see you're enjoying yourself," Ellie said to her.

"I never did have a bachelorette party before my wedding."

"That's okay. You're allowed to make up for lost time." Shereen snapped her fingers as a funkier tune came on.

"I need another drink," Jessica said. She was really letting loose now. She ordered another round of shooters.

"No more for me," Courtney said when the shooters arrived. "One of us has to be okay to drive."

"Then I'll have yours." Reaching across the table, Jessica snatched it and downed it. "Woo! I'm having a blast."

"Down girl," Shereen said.

"This is great," Jessica continued, eyeing a stripper who'd performed earlier strut by their table. He was soliciting women who wanted a private dance. "I had no idea it'd be so much fun."

Yolanda chuckled. "Neither did I."

"How about a private dance?" Jessica suggested.

Shereen gave her a double take. "Come again?"

"Why not?" The private dances were held in the back area of the club. "Who'll come with me?"

Ellie shot to her feet. "You don't have to ask me twice."

Giggling, Ellie and Jessica headed to that area, scoping out the strippers as they did. Shereen watched as they found Midnight, the stripper Jessica had showered down, and led him to the back.

"Lord help Douglas," Yolanda said. "I think we've created some kind of sexual predator."

"They'll have fun tonight," Janelle said.

"No doubt," Shereen agreed.

The music changed from a slow tune to a funky beat as the next stripper came onto the stage, dressed as a policeman. Shereen didn't know why, but that costume always cracked her up.

Ellie and Jessica returned, Ellie's mouth hanging open, Jessica's face in a permanent smile.

"Someone has got to control Q.T.," Ellie said as they settled into their seats. "Do you believe she complained to the stripper when he said he wouldn't take off his g-string? She told him she'd already seen all he had."

"Damn." Shereen stared at Jessica.

"What?" Jessica asked innocently.

Ellie lit a cigarette.

"It's funny." Everyone looked at Yolanda when she spoke. "I don't think any of us has seen Jessica so out of character since that mess with Andrew Bell."

Immediately, Jessica's smile disappeared. "What did you say?"

Yolanda, though drunk, saw the panic in Jessica's eyes. "What I mean is—"

Jessica's voice raised a notch. "Why did you say that?"

"Jess, I didn't—"

"No, why did you say *that*?" Mortified, she glanced at the other sorors, the ones who didn't know the whole truth about the scandal with Andrew Bell, praying they hadn't heard Yolanda's words. She added in an angry whisper, "Why would you mention Andrew *now*?"

"Andrew Bell, the professor who killed himself?" Courtney asked.

Right there, Jessica wanted to die. God, they'd heard. The music hadn't drowned out Yolanda's comment.

"I'm sorry, Jessica." Yolanda slurred the words.

"What are you guys talking about?" Charlene asked.

"Nothing," Jessica snapped, shooting to her feet. Then, "I don't believe this."

"Where are you going?" Shereen asked her.

"I've got to get out of here."

"But—" Ellie stopped when Jessica hopped onto the stage in favor of scooting past the others at the table for a quicker exit.

"Shit," Shereen said, standing. "I'll get her."

Jessica had passed the table and was rushing to the bathroom when Shereen made it past Courtney and Janelle on her side of the table. She called to Jessica, but Jessica didn't stop.

Instead of heading to the bathroom, Jessica darted toward the club's stairs. Shereen quickly ran after her and met her halfway down the steps.

She grabbed her arm, stopping her. "Where are you going?"

Jessica brushed away tears. "I've got to get out of here."

God, mentioning Andrew was worse than she thought. "How are you gonna get home?"

"I'll take a cab."

"You left your purse up there."

"Damn. Can you get it for me?"

"Not until you tell me why you're acting like this. We all came here to have some fun."

"Who else has Yolanda mentioned this to?" Real fear flashed in Jessica's eyes, and she gripped Shereen's hand. "God, how many people *know*?"

"I . . ." Shereen's voice trailed off. She didn't know what to say.

"It was just supposed to be us. You, me, Ellie, and Yolanda. No one else. If someone else knows . . . Oh, God. No wonder."

"No wonder what?"

"Get my purse."

"I don't know if I'm ready to drive," Shereen admitted.

"Just get my fuckin' purse, will you?"

Shereen, though tipsy, was taken aback by Jessica's harsh words. She rarely swore.

"All right. But I don't think you—"

"I don't care what you think." She buried her face in her hands as two women walked past them up the stairs. "Oh, God."

Angrily, Jessica brushed at her tears, but turned her back when Shereen reached for her. Feeling helpless, Shereen went back up the stairs to the table. She said to Courtney, "Hand me Jessica's purse."

"What's the matter?" Ellie asked.

"Jessica isn't feeling well."

"Damn," Yolanda said. "This is my fault."

Yeah, it was. The mini-crisis had sobered Shereen, and she wondered why Yolanda had blurted out that bit about Andrew. She was sure that Janelle, Charlene, and Courtney knew nothing about it—nothing beside what the official story had been—but now they might have questions.

"I'm gonna talk to her."

"Not now, Yo—"

"I have to." Yolanda made her way out from behind the table. Ellie, Courtney, Charlene, and Janelle all looked at her with confused expressions.

"I'm gonna see you guys," Shereen told them.

"You're not coming back?" Ellie asked.

"Naw. I'm gonna go home with Jessica in a cab."

Yolanda was halfway to the exit before Shereen realized. She ran to catch up with her, but didn't make it to her before Yolanda descended the stairs.

"How *could* you?" Shereen heard as she approached her friends.

"I'm sorry. God, it's the alcohol."

"Who else knows?" Jessica looked at Yolanda with utter panic. "Tell me, Yolanda. I *need* to know."

"Nobody," Yolanda said. "I swear. Jessica, you have to know I'd never tell anyone."

Jessica regarded Yolanda with a mix of horror and disbelief. "You just did."

"I—"

At the sound of Jessica's whimper, Yolanda shut up.

Jessica said, "I don't know anything anymore."

"Oh, Jessica . . ." Yolanda reached for her.

"No. No, don't touch me."

"Oh, God. Don't do this, Jessica."

Jessica turned and ran out the club's doors onto the street. Yolanda moaned and slid her back down the length of the wall until her knees were pressed against her chest.

"I'll talk to her," Shereen said. "Go on back upstairs and enjoy your night."

"As if."

"She doesn't mean what she said. She knows she can trust you." Though for a split second, Shereen wondered if Yolanda might have mentioned anything to anyone else when she'd been drunk. Had Ellie? Did other people know?

This was the one secret they'd sworn on their lives never to reveal.

"I am sorry."

Yolanda looked as upset as Jessica, and Shereen extended a hand to her. Yolanda accepted it, and Shereen pulled her to her feet. Shereen hugged her. "I know you're sorry."

"I didn't mean it."

"I know."

Sniffling, Yolanda stepped back.

"If any of those guys ask what you meant, make something up. Jessica's pretty upset."

Yolanda glanced at Jessica on the street. She paced back and forth with one hand cupping the side of her face, clearly distressed. "I know . . ."

"I'll talk to you tomorrow." Shereen gave her another quick hug, then hurried out onto the Washington street to meet Jessica.

Yes, the whole sordid mess with Andrew had been devastating for Jessica at the time. Yes, she understood her wanting to forget. But Shereen couldn't quite understand why mentioning him now, nine years after the fact, had Jessica so upset.

Especially since Yolanda hadn't blurted out the secret. In fact, Yolanda hadn't said anything that would give the other sorors reason to be suspicious. They might ask a few questions, questions that could be easily answered with a lie or two. Nothing would come of this.

So what was going on?

"Come on," Shereen said to Jessica, wrapping an arm around her shoulder. "Let's get you home."

THE PAST

"OH MY GOD," SHEREEN exclaimed, her eyes bulging with concern when she opened her dorm room door and found Jessica standing in the hallway. "What *happened?*"

Jessica collapsed in her friend's arms. "Oh, Shereen!"

"What's wrong?" Shereen smoothed a hand over Jessica's hair as she cried. "Jess—"

"Shh," Jessica said, shaking her head. Right now, she didn't want to talk, to think. She found a measure of comfort in Shereen's arms, like finding dry land after being lost at sea. And she needed that comfort, even if it couldn't mend her broken heart. She needed to know that someone cared for her after what Andrew had done.

Oh, God. The reality hit her once more that Andrew had lied to her, that he'd never really loved her. "Andrew . . ."

Shereen pulled back and looked Jessica in the eye. "Andrew? Did he hurt you? Jess, what did he do?"

"I don't . . . I can't . . ."

There was a quick knock at the door, then it opened. Jessica turned to see Yolanda and Ellie hurry into the room.

"Madge told us—" Yolanda stopped short when she saw Jessica, her eyes registering shock as she checked her out. Jessica knew she must look horrible; her eyes were no doubt red and swollen from crying. "Jessica, what the hell happened?"

Jessica was glad her three best friends were there. She knew she could tell them anything, but right now she could hardly breathe, much less speak.

Yolanda's eyes darted to Shereen. "Shereen, what's wrong?"

"She mentioned Andrew."

"Andrew?" Ellie asked, confused.

At the mention of his name, Jessica's stomach lurched. She turned toward the large window and hugged her torso.

"Jessica," Yolanda began gently, "what did Andrew do?"

Jessica opened her mouth to speak, but her throat constricted. Only wheezing sounds escaped.

"Oh, God," Shereen said. "You sound awful."

"I'm . . . o . . ." Jessica couldn't get the words out.

"I'll get her some water," Ellie offered. She scooted to the door. When she opened it, several people stood outside. Ellie was immediately bombarded with questions, but Jessica couldn't make out anything specific. She could hardly think. Slowly, she moved to Shereen's bed, then sat on the edge.

A minute later, Ellie was back in Shereen's room. "Geez, you'd think it was Grand Central Station out there."

"Make them go away," Jessica managed in a shaky voice.

Yolanda went to the door, said a few words to the curious crowd, then returned to her friends. "They're gone." Frowning, she stopped before Jessica. "I don't like this, Jess. You have to tell us—"

"Andrew." Jessica swallowed painfully. "He's married."

A full few seconds passed before Yolanda exclaimed, "Son of a *bitch*!"

"What an asshole," Ellie added.

"Married?" Shereen asked. "Oh, sweetie. Are you sure?"

Jessica nodded as new tears fell. Lord help her, her insides literally felt like they were being churned in a blender. When would this pain go away?

Shereen sat beside her and draped an arm across her shoulder. "Jess, I'm so sorry."

"So am I."

"I know this hurts," Shereen continued, "but you'll be okay. Believe me, hon, you'll get over that useless bastard."

How could she get over him when she'd always have a piece of him? Shaking her head, she brushed at her tears. "No, I won't."

"Yes, you will," Ellie told her. "Believe me—"

"I'm pregnant."

The silence was quick and devastating. Horror passed over Ellie's, Yolanda's, and Shereen's faces.

"I'm going to have his baby." A sarcastic chuckle escaped Jessica's lips, but it quickly turned into a sob. "But he's married. He's been married for fourteen years!"

Ellie slumped against Shereen's desk. "Oh. My. God."

"You're sure you're pregnant?" Yolanda asked.

"Yes, I'm sure," Jessica snapped. "God, I'm sorry. Andrew . . . he asked me the same thing." Jessica moaned as she covered her face. "What am I going to do?"

"He needs a good ass-whooping, that's what he needs." Yolanda was pissed.

"Sweetie." Shereen gently rubbed Jessica's back. "How far along are you?"

Jessica's head whipped up, knowing where this question was leading. "I'm not going to have an abortion." Maybe she was crazy, but this baby inside her was the only tangible proof of the love she'd shared with Andrew. She didn't want to lose that.

"Jess, it wouldn't be the worst thing," Yolanda told her, bending before her. "God, how can you have a baby now? Think about your education."

Jessica wanted to think about her education, about all the reasons why she should do the smart thing. But aborting the baby she'd already grown to love would never be the right thing.

"I can't," she whispered.

"You told Andrew about the baby?" Ellie asked. When Jessica whimpered, Ellie added, "He doesn't want it, does he?"

"No. God, I can't believe I was so stupid. I believed all his lies. . . . How was I stupid enough to believe that someone like him could love someone like me?"

"Jessica." Shereen spoke firmly. "Don't talk like that. You're beautiful, smart—"

"I'm average. Boring. And I was always so shy . . . I never even had a boyfriend before I came to Howard."

"And that son of a bitch saw that." Yolanda grimaced. "He saw your vulnerability, Jessica. And he took advantage of it."

"What am I going to do?"

"Whatever you decide, we're here for you." Shereen wiped one of Jessica's tears. "Know that."

"Yeah," Ellie agreed. She sat on Jessica's other side and ran a hand over her hair. "Oh, honey."

"How do I tell my family about the baby? It wouldn't have been so bad if we were going to be together, if he was going to marry me." Jessica whimpered. "God, how do I tell my family that I had an affair with a married man? They'll never forgive me." She lowered her head and softly continued to cry.

After a moment, Yolanda said, "He needs to pay for this."

"Absolutely," Shereen agreed.

Jessica looked up at Yolanda. "What do you mean?"

"What he did, that should be a crime," Yolanda stated. "Taking advantage of a young and vulnerable student."

"We were both adults," Jessica softly said.

"Yeah, but would you have slept with him if you'd known he was married?" Ellie challenged. "God, you slept with him without protection, that's how much you trusted him."

"I wouldn't have even gone to dinner with him if I'd known he was married. God, I feel so . . . *violated.*"

"You *were* violated. And now you're stuck with that asshole's baby." Shereen snorted in disgust.

"You know you can't count on him for a dime of support," Ellie said.

"He wants me to . . . He said he'll pay for an abortion."

"Yeah, so no one will know what the fucker did," Yolanda retorted. "He practically forces himself on you, then expects the problem to just go away."

"Well . . . he didn't really force himself . . ."

Yolanda stared Jessica squarely in the eye. "You said it. You *feel* violated. You wouldn't have gone out with him if he'd told you the truth. He didn't. He deceived you to get you into bed. How different is that from rape?"

There was silence for several seconds, everyone looking at each other as the implication of Yolanda's words hit them.

Ellie said, "I'm with Yolanda. He needs to pay."

"You mean, report him to the dean?" Shereen asked.

Jessica's eyes darted from one of her friends to the next, her chest heaving. Lord help her, the thought of going to the dean was actually appealing. Then she thought better of it. "And say what? That I fell in love with him but now can't deal with the fact that he doesn't love me?"

"It's more than that," Yolanda said. "Damn it, what he did was deceitful and wrong. Now he wants you to just go away. Who knows what he'll do? You need to strike before he comes up with some bullshit story that *you* came on to *him*."

Jessica felt a moment of panic. "You don't think he'd actually do that, do you?"

"Girl, it's not about what you or I think," Yolanda stated. "The bottom line is he's not the person you thought he was, so you have no clue what he'll do in this situation. Do you want to take that chance?"

"Yolanda's right," Shereen said. "I'm telling you, you have to go to the dean."

"He's gonna try and protect his own ass," Ellie commented. "Shouldn't you try to protect yours?"

Jessica looked at each of her friends in turn. "So you think I should go to the dean and say . . ." Her voice trailed off as she contemplated the implied suggestion that had been hanging over them for a few minutes. "Say he *raped* me?"

There was silence, then Yolanda said, "He *did* coerce you into sleeping with him. Maybe not by brute force, but force nonetheless. By deceiving you, that's exactly what he did."

Ellie stood. "I'm with Yolanda."

"Maybe he promised you a starring role in a production, or a better grade in exchange for sex," Shereen offered.

How did they get to this point, concocting a story of revenge because Andrew had hurt her? Jessica didn't know, but she did know that right now she loved Ellie, Shereen, and Yolanda as much as she possibly could. "But he didn't . . ."

"But who's to say what would have happened if you'd rejected him?" Yolanda asked, raising an eyebrow to punctuate her point.

Coercion. *Rape.* God, it sounded so awful. Not at all like what she and Andrew had shared.

But then, what *had* they shared? Something special, beautiful? No, what they'd shared was a lie. Her friends were right. If Andrew had been honest with her, she never would have ended up in his bed.

Instead, he'd lied to her to get what he wanted. Who knew what he'd say about her if she didn't say something first?

Yolanda knelt before Jessica. She placed a hand on her knee. "That son of a bitch has to pay for what he did to you. If he'd done it to anyone else . . . But you, you're the sweetest person I know." There was a chorus of yeahs. "Besides, how many other women has he done this to? And if you don't report him, how many more young, vulnerable women will he victimize?"

It was Yolanda's last line that got Jessica thinking—hard. God, Yolanda was right. Not saying something would be wrong. Andrew would no doubt do what he'd done to her to someone else.

He *had* violated her. So she had to do what she could to spare another girl this kind of pain. How could she not?

Besides, at this moment, she wanted revenge. Revenge because Andrew had lied to her, then broken her heart.

Oh, this would be sweet . . .

Jessica inhaled a shaky breath. "All right. I'll go to the dean tomorrow. Tell him I was raped. And it won't be a lie," she added with conviction. "I didn't have true consent in this situation. Andrew took that away by lying to me." She glanced at each of her friends. "I don't know what the dean will say, but I may need you as witnesses."

"Girl, everyone saw you come in here all distraught. You'll have a dorm full of witnesses if need be."

"I don't want anyone else to know about . . . this."

"Of course not," Shereen said. "But if you ever need anyone else to confirm your state of mind . . ."

Jessica nodded. "Yes, I understand."

"And everything we said," Yolanda began, "it stays right here. Between us. No one but the dean needs to know about it. Then that slimy bastard will get what he deserves."

"This is the right thing to do," Ellie assured Jessica. "And don't worry, hon. We've got your back."

Jessica wasn't crying anymore. She was smiling.

Yeah, she'd known her three best friends would help make everything right. They'd have her back, no matter what.

They always did. They always would.

Chapter Twenty-one

"GOD, I'M GETTING SO FAT," Ellie whined.

"No, you look good," Shereen told her.

"Look at this gut." Standing, she pinched several inches.

"That's easy enough to lose."

"Spoken by the goddess herself." Ellie gave Shereen a sour look.

"No, I'm serious. If you do some sit-ups every day, in no time at all—"

"Jessica isn't coming," Yolanda suddenly said.

The three of them were in Shereen's living room, Yolanda with her legs curled under her on the armchair, Shereen sitting on the sofa, and Ellie standing in the center of the living room like a runway model. None of them had met the Sunday after their outing at the strip club, but a week later, last week, Jessica had also been a no-show at Ellie's cramped apartment in Mount Pleasant. Yolanda had rationalized that Jessica hadn't come because the place wasn't big enough. It was a dumb excuse, but it had gotten Yolanda through the day. But now, two Sundays in a row, it was obvious Jessica was avoiding her, even more obvious because Jessica hadn't shown for the Saturday literacy program at the inner-city school two weeks in a row.

Shereen glanced at the wall clock. "It's early still. She did say she was coming when I spoke to her earlier."

"She hates me."

Ellie sat on the sofa next to Shereen. "No, Yolanda, she doesn't hate you."

"She just doesn't want to see me." Yolanda pinched the bridge of her nose. "Damn." Since the incident at the club two weeks ago, Jessica had retreated into her shell exactly the way she had when she'd learned Andrew Bell was married. Yolanda had called her since then, assuring

her that she had never, ever uttered a word about Andrew and her
secret to anyone except for that one thoughtless blunder at the club,
and while Jessica had told her that she believed her, Yolanda felt way
down in her soul that she didn't.

"I don't think it's that," Shereen said. "I don't know . . . you know
Jessica. She can get weird and just hibernate sometimes. And she was
acting weird before that. Remember?"

"I'm sure you're hearing from her."

Shereen gave a noncommittal shrug, though it was the truth. She'd
spoken with Jessica almost every day since the incident.

Which would only hurt Yolanda if she knew. She and Jessica had
always been the tightest of the group. Not that they all weren't close,
but Shereen and Yolanda had had their problems over the years, and
Ellie had had her spats with both Shereen and Yolanda—usually because of their advice over some man. But no one had ever had a problem with Jessica—nothing serious, anyway—and Jessica had become
the one with whom they'd all shared their quandaries. But when the
fiasco with Andrew Bell happened, Yolanda took charge, taking care of
Jessica in a way that Ellie and Shereen hadn't been able to. They'd
formed an extra special bond after that.

"It's just one of those things," Ellie said. "She freaked. You know how
awful that whole situation was. Who would want to remember that, let
alone fear that others know?"

"But no one knows," Yolanda protested. "And damn, if she thinks I
might have mentioned something, why not the two of you?"

"Because you're the one who made that comment at the club," Shereen replied dryly.

"Not that we think you've told anyone else," Ellie quickly clarified,
eyeing Shereen and Yolanda for any sign of sparks. The last thing they
needed was to get into an argument. "All I can say is that this will pass.
Even if Jessica is angry right now, she won't stay angry for long. It's not
in her nature."

"That's right," Shereen agreed. "She's a Cancer."

Yolanda jumped to her feet. "Oh, stop with that astrological bullshit."

"Maybe we should change the subject," Ellie suggested.

"And talk about the weather?" Yolanda flashed her a dubious look.

Then sighed. "I'm sorry. It's just that I hate it when we fight. Is it me, or does it seem like the Fabulous Four aren't as tight as we were back in the day?" When no one denied what Yolanda was saying, she took that as confirmation that things had indeed gone sour. "And the damn thing is, I don't know what went wrong or how to fix it."

"It'll be all right," Shereen said. If she could forgive Yolanda for dating Terrence, then Jessica would get over this.

"I don't know." Yolanda wandered to the window and stared outside.

"She's really upset," Ellie commented when Yolanda was out of earshot.

"Yeah, I know. She's used to fighting with me—even you—but not Jessica."

"Speaking of that." Ellie's tone was hushed. "What's up on the Terrence front?"

Shereen loved Ellie, she really did, but man she could be clueless at times! With a slight shake of her head and a throw of her eyes toward Yolanda, she told Ellie wordlessly that this was not the time. Not that anything was up with Terrence, but why bring him up now and risk getting Yolanda any more upset?

Ellie got the point, silently mouthing, "Sorry." Then she leaned back on the sofa and announced, "I think we all need a getaway. You know, maybe plan a group trip somewhere. Maybe Vegas. Or an island. Yeah, maybe Jamaica. Some sun, sand, and hot island men."

Yolanda turned to them. "If Jessica doesn't want to see me for one day on the weekend, she won't agree to any getaway."

"You never know."

"You are blowing this way out of proportion. It's been obvious for months that Jessica's clearly under stress. With the show, with Douglas." Shereen shrugged. "It's not personal."

"I hope not." Yolanda sank into the sofa beside her.

"Besides," Shereen continued. "Even if Jessica was pissed, she'd forgive you eventually. Astrological bullshit or not, she's a Cancer, and—"

"Eventually?"

"Forget I said that. I'm trying to say she'll forgive you."

Loud sigh. "I know. I just feel so bad . . . I keep remembering the way she looked at me, almost like she thought I mentioned Andrew on purpose. To deliberately hurt her."

"Look, we've been tight for eleven years," Ellie stated matter-of-factly. "She knows the real deal."

"She does." Shereen spoke with a finality of tone as she squeezed Yolanda's hand for support. Then she changed the subject, because discussing it clearly wasn't making Yolanda feel any better. "Are you guys gonna buy a ticket for the next sorority shindig?" The Theta Phi Kappas were having a dinner and dance to raise funds for some cause. Shereen didn't even remember what this time. Her sorority, true to its social reputation, was always throwing some sort of event.

"Are you kidding?" Ellie guffawed. "I can't go looking like this. I'm too fat."

For as long as Shereen had known her, Ellie had battled with her weight. Over the last year, she'd slimmed down quite a bit, but in the last couple of months the extra pounds had returned. She wished she could help motivate Ellie to keep the weight off permanently, though she loved her just the same.

"Well, I'm not going because I refuse to be dateless." Shereen looked at Yolanda. "But you and Terrence . . ."

"Who knows where he'll be?" Her tone relayed her displeasure. But she quickly added, "It's football season. He's busy."

"Well, I don't have a man, so I won't be going either."

That got Yolanda's attention. She stared at Ellie past Shereen, who sat between them. "I thought you were moving in with Richard."

Ellie shrugged. "I don't know. He's been saying one thing but doing another. I don't know what's going on with him."

In other words, Ellie was getting depressed over her love life. She always overate when depressed about a man.

"I mean, it's been over two months since he said we'd buy a house. At first, he wasn't taking me to look at any houses, and I didn't know what to think. Then we started actually looking, and I felt better, but the truth is, every house I liked, he didn't. Come to think of it, I don't think he liked any of the houses. So, now I really don't know what to think. Maybe his wife is giving him a harder time about the divorce than he anticipated."

Somehow, Shereen stopped herself from rolling her eyes. How many times could she tell Ellie that Richard was a player without going blue in the face? She couldn't make her listen. "Maybe it's a money issue."

"No, it's not money. Richard's loaded. Unless his wife is gonna tie up his money for a while with a nasty alimony suit." Ellie's face lit up at that idea. "Yeah, *that* could be the problem. I just wish he'd talk to me about it."

"Maybe you're right," Yolanda said, and Ellie did a double take as she looked at her. She wore a sad expression, like the fight was gone out of her. No doubt because of the whole mess with Jessica, Yolanda wasn't her characteristic blunt self. "But I hope you don't stick around waiting for him. Ellie, you have too much to offer a man. You deserve someone who respects you."

That was, perhaps, the nicest thing Yolanda had said to her in a long, long time. Ellie reached for Yolanda's hand across Shereen's lap and squeezed it. "Thanks."

"I mean it." Then, sighing, Yolanda released Ellie's hand and stood. "I'm gonna go."

Shereen stood, too. "You are?"

"Yeah. I'm not feeling the greatest."

Because Jessica hadn't shown. Shereen hugged her. "Take care, hon. And try not to worry."

Yolanda managed a weary smile. "I'll try. Later, Ellie."

"See ya."

Shereen followed Yolanda to the door and saw her out. Minutes later, she was back in the living room with Ellie. She sat beside her. "So it's really over with Richard?"

"I didn't say it was *over*."

Now Shereen did roll her eyes. "Oh, no."

"But I'm starting to have serious doubts. Look at me." She gestured to her body as if to say that her weight gain had been a direct result of her problems with Richard.

Which surprised Shereen, because all this time she never knew if Ellie had made the connection.

"Well, I've been wanting to join a gym for a while, so if you want to go with me . . ."

"Oh, that'd be great, Shereen. It's so hard to get motivated without someone to work out with. Yeah, I'd like that."

"Good. Really, hon, Yolanda is right. You've got a lot to offer a man. A decent one. Don't sell yourself short."

Ellie shrugged.

"What's wrong with us—with women? I mean, sometimes we act like the world will stop if we don't have a man. Why do we do that?"

"I don't know."

Shereen laid her head back. "How many men do you know of who sit around pining over the fact that they don't have a woman?"

"Not many, but men are too full of themselves—"

Shereen's head snapped up. "Exactly. If they don't have a woman, they see it as our loss, not theirs."

"True."

"But women are almost ready to take anything that comes along, as long as it's got a working penis. Isn't that crazy?"

"Damn straight."

Shereen laid her head back again, and Ellie followed her example. "So why can't we get past that?"

"Because society tells us that if we're a certain age and don't have a man, we're failures."

"Screw society."

"Easier said than done. Lord knows I've done enough crazy shit for the love of a man."

"Done?" Shereen chuckled. "As in, past tense?"

"I know. I still am. But I'm trying to change."

"I don't know about you, but I'm tired of the double standard. Men don't settle. Why should we? God knows settling is worse than being single."

"No woman's thinking of that when she's lying alone in her bed at night, knowing no man is going to join her."

Shereen made a face as she rolled her head in Ellie's direction. She hadn't felt that way when lying in her bed. Not until recently, anyway. She'd always been satisfied with her life, even if she was thirty with no prospects for marriage.

Ellie angled her head to face Shereen. "Speaking of men, now that Yolanda's gone, tell me—what's the deal with Terrence?"

"There is no deal," Shereen whispered. The mention of his name always made her a little uncomfortable, like she thought Yolanda might be a fly on the wall hearing every bit of the conversation. Or in this case, standing outside her front door. Though she wasn't doing anything wrong, so she never understood the feeling. "He hasn't called. I haven't seen him."

"That's good." Pause. "Right?"

"Of course it's good." While Shereen and Jessica were close, Shereen preferred to talk to Ellie about Terrence, because if somehow she let anything slip—not that she would—but if she did, and she got stupid and emotional or something over Terrence, Ellie would understand that more than Jessica. Sometimes, though, Shereen regretted that she'd ever mentioned anything to Ellie about Terrence. Because while Ellie wouldn't say it, Shereen could read in Ellie's eyes that she thought Shereen still had a thing for him.

Which she didn't.

"Mind if I light up?"

Shereen nodded, and Ellie reached for her purse. Seconds later, she was taking a deep drag off her cigarette and sighing in satisfaction, like the true addict that she was.

"If you ask me, I don't think that relationship's gonna last."

"Why not?" Shereen asked, suddenly curious. She reached for the plate from beneath the poinsettia on the nearby end table. The poinsettia was still thriving since the past Christmas. She placed the plate on the coffee table for Ellie to use as an ashtray.

This was the first time Ellie had commented on Yolanda and Terrence's relationship, other than in the beginning, when she'd said she thought Yolanda's dating Terrence was reprehensible.

"I *never* see him around. I know he's not living with her, but there's not even a sign that he goes to visit. No oversized T-shirt lying around. No extra coat on the coat tree. Nothing."

Shereen had assumed that she didn't see Terrence with Yolanda because Yolanda was somehow making sure they didn't run into each other. Insecurity reasons. It hadn't dawned on her that Ellie, and probably Jessica, hadn't seen much of him, either.

And Ellie was right on the money about no signs of Terrence at Yolanda's place. What was up with that?

"Hell, I hear more about Terrence from you than I do from Yolanda."

"No one buys someone a rock that big and then doesn't stick

around." And it was a big rock. The kind that immediately said money.
Exactly the kind of ring she knew Yolanda would pick out herself. "He's
a busy guy."

"Maybe. But I don't know. It's just a feeling."

Shereen had had the same feeling, but always felt bad when she did.
It was like a perverse sense of hope she couldn't understand.

"God, Ellie. This is awful of us. We shouldn't be sitting here talking
about Yolanda like this. This isn't right."

"Like y'all don't talk about me behind my back." Ellie raised an eyebrow as she stared at Shereen, daring her to deny that.

"That's different. None of us dated Richard."

"What does that have to do with anything?"

"Nothing, I guess. Okay, I hear you. You're saying we talk about you
because we care about you. We don't want to see you hurt."

"Exactly. And it's the same with us talking about Yolanda. Or when
we talk about Jessica. It's not betrayal. If we didn't talk about each other,
we wouldn't care."

"True." Shereen held on to that. Ellie was right. How different was it
for her to talk about Terrence and Yolanda than for her to talk about
Jessica and Douglas? Or Ellie and Richard?

Not at all.

Then why did she feel so guilty?

"Don't you think it's strange," Ellie continued, "that she never men-
tions anything about the wedding? Whenever we ask her what's going
on, she gives a quick answer, then changes the subject."

Shereen had noticed that as well, but hadn't dared to mention it.
"Yes, but I just figure Terrence is busy. This is a hectic time of year for
him, representing all those superstars."

"Amazing, isn't it?" Ellie dipped her ashes onto the plate. "In that
way, he's perfect for Yolanda. She's always wanted security—that is,
money. With a guy like Terrence, she'll have that and a whole lot more."

And that, Shereen suddenly realized, was what had bothered her all
along: the thought that maybe Yolanda didn't actually love Terrence, but
loved the fact that he'd be a good partner because of his job. Yolanda
had always been a fighter, no doubt because she'd been raised in the
projects. She'd fought her way through school with her brain, securing

an academic scholarship because her family didn't have the money to send her to university.

And while she was a lawyer who would certainly have a successful career, being with Terrence would definitely mean security for her unlike what she was used to.

Was that what their relationship was about?

Hadn't Jessica recently said that she thought Yolanda was still in love with James but just afraid he'd break her heart again?

What if Jessica was right? If she was, then that meant Yolanda wasn't really in love with Terrence.

And if she wasn't in love with Terrence . . .

And nothing. What did it matter to her?

"What are you thinking?" Ellie asked.

"Huh?" Her friend's voice startled her out of her thoughts.

"You've got a weird look on your face. What are you thinking?"

"Just about what you said, that's all."

Ellie flashed her a wry grin. "Mmm-hmm."

"Mmm-hmm nothing." But Ellie continued to grin. "Oh, Ellie, don't make something out of nothing."

"If you say so." Then Ellie chuckled and took another drag off her cigarette.

Chapter Twenty-two

"I CAN'T BELIEVE YOU, MAMA." Yolanda stared at her mother with a baffled expression.

"You should go."

Yolanda paced back and forth before her mother, who sat on the old, tattered sofa instead of in her usual spot by the window. "Why would you tell Daddy I'd be there?"

"Because you need to be there."

"Need?"

"You *should*," Edna corrected.

Yolanda didn't understand. "That was my decision to make. Not yours."

"Maybe. But if I didn't make it, you'd probably never agree to do it. And it is your father's birthday. He'll be so happy to see you."

Why should you care? Yolanda asked silently. After all this time, her mother still cared about what would please her father, while he didn't give a damn about her.

"Since you insist on me going, why don't you come, too?" If her mother accompanied her, maybe she could stomach this evening.

"Oh, no." Edna shook her head. "I'm sure Gloria wouldn't want me there."

"Who—" Yolanda stopped herself before she said "cares." Clearly, though Yolanda would never understand why, her mother did care. And for that reason, she didn't want to offend her.

Instead she said, "Are you sure, Mama? They've been married so long, Gloria can't consider you a threat."

Edna waved off Yolanda's suggestion. "That's not the point. Your father's ex-wife has no place there. You, on the other hand, will always be his daughter. You should be there."

Yolanda wanted to protest that while she might be his daughter, she felt as much an outsider to his new family as any stranger, but she kept her mouth shut.

"All right." For whatever reason, this was important to her mother. "For you, Mama."

A smile warmed Edna's face, a real, full smile, which made Yolanda's acquiescence to see her father completely worth it. She'd do anything to see her mother smile.

As Edna eased off the sofa and approached Yolanda, Yolanda smiled, too. Because while her mother walked slowly, she no longer had that awful limp. At least she was regaining strength in her hip.

She wrapped Yolanda in a hearty hug, a hug she felt way down in the depths of her soul. Her mother was in better spirits today, and that gave Yolanda hope. Maybe one day, she'd reach out and recapture life.

Edna ended the hug and placed a gentle hand on Yolanda's back. "Go on. You have to get ready."

Yolanda took a few steps toward the door, then stopped. She turned. "Mama, I know I've asked before, but I have to ask again. Are you sure you don't want to come live with me? I've got a big backyard and you can plant a garden there, or sit on the porch swing and watch the sun set . . ."

"Don't be silly. You're about to be married. I don't think your husband will want his mother-in-law hanging around."

"Trust me. Terrence won't mind." It would be months before they got married. And even if Terrence did complain, Yolanda wouldn't care. The last person in the world she would abandon was her mother, the person who'd given her life.

"I'm fine, sweetheart, but I love you for worrying."

"All right, Mama. I love you."

"I love you, too. Now go on."

Yes, her mother was definitely in better spirits today, Yolanda reflected as she left the apartment and headed for her car. That was a definite plus.

And one less thing for her to worry about.

Because, truth be told, she was worrying about a lot these days.

About Terrence, though she'd never tell her friends that. Until recently, she would have told Jessica, but after the incident at the strip club, their relationship suddenly wasn't the same. And while part of her knew it was crazy not to share this with even Shereen, another part of her didn't quite trust that her friend didn't still want her man. If she told Shereen that she suspected Terrence's feelings were cooling off, maybe Shereen would be glad.

Yolanda settled into her Range Rover. Maybe that was stupid. Hadn't they agreed not to let a man come between them? Shereen had seemed sincere.

So what was the problem?

The problem was that ever since Terrence had seen Shereen that night in February, Yolanda had sensed his withdrawal. Not in overt ways, but subtle ones. Little by little, like blood slowly draining from your body until you're dead.

Like that business about not wanting to move in with her yet. What was that about? She hadn't questioned him at the time because she'd sensed he hadn't wanted to talk about it. But why the hell had he bothered to move to Washington now if he wasn't going to move in with her? It's not like she was seeing more of him; he was on the road all the time.

The whole thing made her wonder about Terrence's motives.

Which made her think of James. And her father. She rarely thought of James, and she tried to think about her father as little as possible. Because thinking about them hurt. Now, thinking of the men in her life and how they'd betrayed her had her wondering if she was just plain stupid for trusting another man at all.

She bit her bottom lip as she drove. No, that wasn't fair. Even if it was hard, she would not judge Terrence by James's actions, nor by her father's. She hadn't begged Terrence to propose to her.

Still, she wondered.

Before he'd seen Shereen that night, he'd had much more time for her. They'd done more together, like go out to dinner, or rent movies and chill out on the couch all night. Terrence had seemed genuinely excited about the wedding, discussing it often, asking what she wanted and didn't want.

But now, as their wedding date got closer, Terrence seemed less and less excited. These days, he never had time to talk about their wedding, much less help plan it. And regarding the date, he said he couldn't commit to one. Not until after football season was over. When Yolanda had suggested Valentine's Day—which would be after football season and surely not a conflict—he'd simply said maybe, that he'd have to discuss it when he had more time.

Maybe it was nothing. She certainly hoped that all these negative thoughts stemmed from the situation with Jessica, that her discomfort over that issue had her overreacting. That and the prospect of having a lovely dinner with her father. *Yeah, right,* she thought sarcastically. *As if a nice dinner at that house will be possible.*

Oh, well. She was already en route there. She might as well decide to have a good time.

Collin Burke's face broke out in a huge smile when he saw Yolanda standing on his doorstep. "Sweetheart, you came."

Yolanda walked into his embrace, but only halfheartedly. Why was it that even now, when she saw her father, goose bumps popped out on her skin?

"Your mother told me you might show up, but I didn't know if you would." He released her, stepping back to let his eyes roam over her. "It's good to see you."

"Happy birthday, Daddy."

"Thank you."

"I didn't bring a present. I didn't know what to get."

"Don't you worry about that. You being here is all the present I need."

Her father truly seemed happy to see her, and Yolanda couldn't help but feel a measure of guilt at having put off this reunion for so long.

"Well, come in." He stood back and spread his arms, gesturing to the house's entrance.

Yolanda took one tentative step into the single-family dwelling. It was nicer than she'd expected, but why was she surprised? She'd known that Gloria's family had money. Part of her—hell, more than part—had wondered if Gloria's money was the reason her father had left her

mother. But on the few occasions she'd seen her father and Gloria together, they'd seemed genuinely in love with each other.

Still, the sight of them together was one she could barely stomach.
It was a vivid reminder of her father's betrayal, and made her remember
the painful year her mother had spent in a severe depression.

"Hello, Yolanda." Gloria stepped into the foyer, smiling brightly. She
wore an apron over a conservative blue dress, a clear sign that she'd
been in the kitchen. Yolanda kissed the shorter woman's cheek. That
was another thing she never understood about her father's betrayal.
Gloria had nothing on her mother when it came to looks.

Forget it, she told herself. *It's ancient history.*

"It's nice to see you, Gloria."

"Shanika and Jaleel are in the living room."

"Yes," Collin said, placing a hand around her waist. "Let's go see
them."

"Are you sure you don't need any help in the kitchen?" Yolanda asked
Gloria. That would be preferable to spending time with two children
she barely knew.

"No, I've got everything under control. You go ahead."

Whatever Gloria was cooking smelled scrumptious, and Yolanda's
belly grumbled. Maybe this evening wouldn't be too bad. It was, after
all, only one day. After this, she wouldn't have to show her face here
for another long while.

In the living room, Shanika and Jaleel lay on their stomachs, both
involved with some video game on the television.

"Hello, you two," Yolanda said.

"Hi."

"Hey."

They barely acknowledged her.

"Jaleel and Shanika." Her father spoke brusquely. "You come greet
your sister properly."

Both stood and went into her arms, but the greeting felt forced—on
all sides. Yolanda didn't hold it against them. She hadn't seen them in
well over a year.

But she did notice a change. They were both wearing glasses now.
"Wow, you both have glasses. What happened?"

"Too much time at the computer and in front of the TV." Collin shook his head ruefully.

Yolanda sat on the leather recliner. "How old are you now?" She was embarrassed to ask that question, but there was such an age difference between her and them that she forgot.

"I'm thirteen," Shanika answered.

"And I'm fourteen," Jaleel said.

"You should talk to them about school." Collin placed his hands on his hips. "I tell them all the time how well you did—without computers and the Internet and all that extra stuff. They're not doing as well as I know they can."

Yolanda forced a smile. She was sure Shanika and Jaleel didn't appreciate their father's speeches about a big sister who for all intents and purposes might as well be a phantom.

"Tell them," her father urged, "how to become a lawyer, it took hard work and discipline." He was suddenly talking to Shanika and Jaleel, not her. "She had to get good marks, or she never would have been able to go to Howard. She got a scholarship."

Jaleel rolled his eyes as if he had heard this story a thousand times. For his sake, Yolanda was glad her father hadn't noticed.

"I did get good marks," Yolanda concurred, albeit halfheartedly. What else was she supposed to say? When it came to the role of big sister, she really sucked. She knew that.

"I'm trying." Shanika approached the recliner and rested her upper body on the armrest. "But math is hard. So is English. And science."

All subjects Yolanda had excelled in. She couldn't relate. "You just have to try. If you don't understand, tell your teacher."

"I do," Shanika whined.

"Then maybe you and few friends should get together a few days a week after school. You help them with the subjects they don't understand, and they can help you with the ones you don't understand."

"What a great idea," Collin said.

Jaleel was back on his stomach, reaching for the video game controls. "My friends don't get it, either."

How ironic, Yolanda suddenly realized, that she could sit down one-on-one with a stranger's child and help him or her learn the complex calculations of algebra, yet she hadn't been there to do the same for her half brother and sister. Sure, she'd been in Philadelphia for several years, but on the rare occasions when she saw her siblings, she counted the minutes until the visit was over rather than considered ways she could positively impact their lives.

She didn't want to form an attachment. Maybe it was irrational, but any closeness to her father's new family felt like a betrayal to her mother—and her mother had been betrayed enough for one lifetime.

As she watched Jaleel play with skill and determination, Yolanda couldn't help wondering why, if he could figure out a complex video game, he couldn't understand math. Perhaps he simply wasn't trying hard enough, because working on homework took time away from fun things like video games. Oh, well. She didn't know what else to say. One day, they would have to learn. She hoped they wouldn't have to learn the hard way.

When she was a child, she hadn't had the distractions of video games and computers to prevent her from doing her schoolwork. And even if those things had been popular, her parents wouldn't have been able to afford them.

For that matter, every time her mother prepared a meal, Yolanda was by her side in the kitchen, helping out however she could. Not sitting in the living room watching television.

My, how times have changed.

"All right, everyone," Gloria called from the dining room. "Dinner is ready."

Shanika and Jaleel scrambled off down the hallway. Yolanda started after them.

Collin fell into step beside her. "That's one thing I always respected about your mother. She made sure you had a sense of responsibility. Gloria . . ." He blew out a frazzled breath. "She has a different idea of how to raise children. But then, it's a different time."

"Hmm," was all Yolanda said. But she was wondering, why on earth did her father have to mention that now? He must have read her thoughts. Was he trying to appease her in some way for the fact that he'd left her mother? If he had respected Edna so much, why did he do that?

All these questions swirled within her mind as she and her father strolled into the dining room.

◆ ◆ ◆

She was having an out-of-body experience.

From somewhere above the dining room table, she could see herself seated, Jaleel and Shanika across from her, her father at the table's head, Gloria to his immediate right. Everyone was talking and laughing— everyone but her. Because while her body was among them, her mind and spirit were not.

She looked distant, like a stranger. Like she didn't belong.

Her father's sudden boisterous laughter brought Yolanda's detached spirit crashing back into her body. She felt woozy, almost like she'd awoken from a dream. But this dream was real. She was actually at the dinner table with her father and his family. Instantly, she found herself wishing that she could truly disappear.

Why couldn't she simply enjoy the evening? Eating dinner with a stepfamily was hardly an abnormal phenomenon. Rationally, she knew that, yet the experience was extremely discomfiting.

It was Gloria and her father. She could deal with Shanika and Jaleel, even though they didn't feel like her siblings, but watching her father and Gloria exchange smiles, listening to her father praise his new wife's cooking, hearing their loving terms of endearment . . . Try as she might, Yolanda couldn't stop thinking that he should be saying these sweet things, acting this wonderful way, toward her mother.

She felt like a spoiled child, one who couldn't get over the fact that her mommy and daddy were no longer together. It was completely pathetic, yet she still couldn't stop the feelings.

"Love, will you pass me the potato salad?" Collin asked. "I don't know what you put in it this time, but this is the best potato salad I've ever tasted."

Gloria blushed as she handed him the bowl.

For goodness sake, it was only potato salad, not caviar.

"Thank you, love. Now, if you could pass me another piece of that roast. It's so tender, it melts in your mouth. Mmm-mmm-mmm."

"Here you are, darling." Gloria lifted two slices of the precut meat onto his plate.

Yolanda darted her eyes to her food when she saw her father glance her way. She hoped her troubled emotions didn't show on her face.

"Yolanda, why aren't you eating?" Her father's voice held concern.

She wasn't eating because she felt queasy. Her nerves were doing an anxious jitterbug all along her skin and inside her body. Try as she might, she couldn't stomach any more of this "happy family" union.

She bolted to her feet. "I . . . I've got to go."

"What?" Her father shot her a stunned look.

She glanced around the table. "I'm sorry, Daddy. Gloria. I—I'm not feeling well."

"Can I get you something?" Gloria asked.

"No, no. I just have to . . . excuse me."

She fled the table and hurried to the foyer. Behind her, she heard hushed voices and knew they were all wondering what was wrong. Let them wonder. She had to get out of there.

But by the time she was slipping into her shoes, her father appeared.

"Why are you doing this?" His tone was a mix of confusion and anger.

So he knew she wasn't actually sick, merely trying to escape. Good enough. "I came here for Mama, but—"

"Can't you even enjoy one dinner with us, with me?" Gone was the confusion, leaving only the anger. "For God's sake, I'm your father."

Without thinking, Yolanda blurted out, "Oh, spare me."

"*Excuse* me?"

She hadn't meant to disrespect him like that, but now that she had, she wouldn't apologize. Not to the man who offered no apologizes for ruining her life. "You heard me."

"You know, for years you've had this bitter attitude toward me, but I had hoped you'd grow out of it. Finally *grow up*."

She couldn't stop her own anger from flaring. "Don't you dare talk to me about growing up."

Her father glanced nervously over his shoulder as Yolanda raised her voice. With his eyes off her, she quickly opened the door and stormed onto the front porch. To her chagrin, he followed her.

"What's your problem?" he asked.

"Forget it." She just wanted to get out of there. "I was out of line."

"No, I won't forget it. I want to know, finally, so *maybe* we can work on getting past whatever it is that's bothering you."

Her chuckle dripped with sarcasm. "Oh, that's good."

"Dammit, Yolanda, I'm trying to be serious."

He had no idea what serious was. But if he wanted serious, he'd get it.

"My *problem*," she began, emphasizing the word, "is that I have a father I'm ashamed of." At the surprised look on his face, she forged ahead, before she lost her courage. "Yes, ashamed of. I mean, here you are with your new family, and it's like you totally don't remember that you had a family before."

"That's not true."

"Isn't it?" she challenged. "I have to beg you to check on Mama, and dammit, you know you ruined her life. All because you got tired of what you had at home and had to go and get yourself a *sweeter* pie. That is so pathetic. So shallow. As far as I'm concerned, a real man doesn't leave his family for another one.

"But you did, and what can I say? You wanted something new—now you have it, so you should be happy with it. But you certainly shouldn't expect me to want to be any part of it. God, Mama put her whole life in your hands, and you stomped all over it, just because you wanted something different. So if I seem angry, you're damn right I am. I can't stand men who think with their penises, not their brains. Okay? Maybe you've changed now, and for Gloria's sake I hope you have, but you still hurt Mama. You still hurt *me*, so don't expect me to feel comfortable watching you get all kissy-face with your new wife and family."

"Are you finished?"

"Oh, yeah, I definitely am."

She whirled on her heel and was down the first couple steps when her father spoke. "I understand that you're angry with me, and I realize that right now, no matter what I say, you probably won't be ready to hear it. But I want to tell you that things aren't always what they seem. Maybe you're too young to understand that . . ."

"What does that mean?"

He shook his head ruefully. "Exactly what I said. Sometimes, there's more to a story than those who aren't directly involved know about."

"I *was* involved."

"I'm talking about me and your mother."

"What?"

"Ask her."

"That's what I thought," Yolanda replied sourly.

Collin calmly said, "Your mother should be the one to tell you.

Besides, I'm sure you won't believe a word I say." He sighed. "I do love you, Yolanda. No matter what you think."

"Just not Mama." Why did it still hurt so much?

"I said what I had to say. If you want to come back inside, I'll be happy to have you. But if not, that's your choice."

She hadn't expected this response, wasn't prepared for it. "I'm not hungry."

"Very well."

" 'Bye, Daddy."

He didn't respond; instead he walked quietly back into the house. And to her surprise, Yolanda's heart felt like someone had just cut it in two.

She drove home like a woman possessed, her father's words echoing in her mind. Anger replaced the earlier melancholy, the sudden fear that maybe she *hadn't* known everything. Her father was playing some kind of game, trying to trick her into feeling guilty. She'd been there. She'd seen what had happened to her mother when he'd walked out on them. Edna had been depressed for months, her life slowly ebbing out of her as surely as if she was dying from some disease. She'd never been the same since.

God, she hated this. She hated that he was trying to justify his actions. Why couldn't he finally be a man and admit that he'd done wrong?

Perhaps that was all she truly wanted. An apology so she could finally forgive him. But the more he gave her bullshit excuses, the more she clung to her anger.

Still, later that night as she tried to sleep, she thought of her father's cryptic words. She wished she could forget them, but the truth was, they haunted her.

Because she couldn't help wondering if they were true.

She couldn't help wondering if there was something she didn't know.

THE PAST

WHEN YOLANDA, JESSICA, SHEREEN, and Ellie stormed into Dean Robert Pascal's office bright and early Monday morning, the older black man with salt-and-pepper hair immediately looked at them with concern.

"Dean Pascal," Yolanda said, walking straight to his desk, "we need to talk to you."

He sat upright in his chair and looked at each of them in turn. "This sounds urgent."

"It is," Yolanda agreed. Glancing over her shoulder, she looked at Jessica. Jessica met her eyes with a tentative gaze. Yolanda knew this was hard for her; it was hard for them all. But when she gave her friend an encouraging nod, Jessica stepped forward.

"I can have more chairs brought in," the dean announced.

"That's okay," Yolanda said. "I'd rather stand."

"Me, too," Jessica replied, taking a place at Yolanda's side.

Ellie and Shereen sat in the two chairs opposite Dean Pascal's desk, while Yolanda and Jessica stayed on their feet.

"All right," the dean said. "I'm listening."

Jessica opened her mouth, but as much as she tried to say something, she couldn't voice a single word. She wanted to do this, she really did, but her courage had died the moment she'd stepped into this office and realized the severity of what they were about to do.

She felt Yolanda's gaze on her, and glanced her way. Nervous, Jessica couldn't meet her eyes.

"Something's happened," Yolanda said, quickly taking over. "Something involving one of the professors."

Dean Pascal's eyebrows shot up. "How bad is this?"

"Very," Ellie said from behind Yolanda.

"Which professor?"

Yolanda replied, "Professor Andrew Bell."

The dean nodded, his lips set in a tight line. "What happened?"

"Jessica," Yolanda said softly, making eye contact with her friend. Jessica looked terrified. "Jessica, honey. You should be the one to tell him."

The dean's gaze went from Yolanda to Jessica. "I promise, no matter what you say, I will be fair and unbiased."

"Andrew . . ." Jessica finally said, then heaved a weary sigh. "He . . . well, I was in his drama class, and we've been spending some time together . . . and . . ." Jessica's voice trailed off, unable to say anymore.

Shereen squeezed Jessica's hand. "It's okay, hon. You can do this."

Jessica whimpered softly. All eyes were on her, waiting for her to speak. But this was harder than she'd thought possible, because she still loved Andrew and didn't want to see him hurt. That's why she'd called him last night and left a message saying she needed to speak with him immediately, but he hadn't gotten back to her.

Even now, she was a fool. He didn't care about her. Why should she care about him?

"We had a relationship," Jessica blurted out.

The dean eyed her curiously, then said, "What kind of relationship are we talking about here?"

"Sexual," Shereen chimed.

"I see." Dean Pascal pushed his chair back and stood, then began to pace the area behind his desk.

"Tell him the rest," Ellie whispered when Jessica faced her and Shereen.

"You can do it," Shereen added quietly.

"He's married," the dean said, his words floating on a sad sigh. "But, I guess that's never stopped men from cheating before. You say you're in his drama class?"

"Yes," Jessica replied. "And . . . I want to make this clear. I never would have spent any time alone with him if I'd known he was married."

"I understand."

Hearing Jessica's words, Yolanda feared she would say the wrong thing. This wasn't about Jessica justifying her behavior. It was about Andrew getting what was coming to him. So she interjected, "This wasn't a consensual relationship."

Dean Pascal's eyes bulged in shock, and for a good several seconds everyone could hear the sound of falling snow outside, that's how quiet the room was. He stared at Yolanda for a long while, then turned his gaze to Jessica. "What exactly are you saying?"

Jessica looked down at the floor, then back at the dean. She had to do this. That's why she was here. "He made me . . . he said if I didn't have sex with him . . ."

Shereen jumped up. "He forced her to have sex with him in exchange for a passing grade."

"Oh, good Lord." The dean threw his head back and looked up at the ceiling. Then he faced them all, his expression hard and serious. "Do you understand what you're saying?"

"Yes," Yolanda replied. "Professor Andrew Bell raped Jessica."

Again, silence filled the room. Yolanda, Jessica, Shereen, and Ellie waited to hear the dean's response to their bombshell.

"Rape. That's a *very* serious charge."

"We know," Yolanda said. "And that's why we're here."

"Jessica," the dean said, then gritted his teeth. "What's your last name?"

"Bedford," Jessica told him.

The dean's gaze went to Yolanda, then to Shereen, then to Ellie. He folded his arms over his chest. "What's your part in this?"

"We're her best friends," Ellie told him.

"She came to us right after it happened," Shereen added.

"So this happened once?" the dean asked, looking at Jessica for verification.

"Um," Jessica hedged. "Well, not exactly."

"How many times?"

"A . . . few."

"That sounds like an affair," the dean commented frankly.

"She was afraid," Yolanda piped in. "We know how this may look, but Professor Bell lied to her, manipulated her, and ultimately violated her. Jessica's been interested in a drama career forever. She thought that if she didn't sleep with him, he'd fail her. And she couldn't afford to fail."

"Where did this happen?" the dean asked.

"In his cabin," Jessica answered.

"So, you went to his cabin with him, knowing full well he wanted sex from you?"

"Yes, but I didn't know what else to do," Jessica replied. "I thought if I didn't go, he would fail me. And I didn't want to fail."

"If you knew the type of person Jessica is," Shereen began, "you'd understand. She's very shy, very trusting. She felt she had no other way out than to do what he wanted."

The dean turned and peered outside the window at the snow-covered earth. "God, I can't believe this." He faced Jessica again. "Why didn't you come forward after the first time?"

"Because I was afraid," she said simply. "I didn't think anyone would believe me."

"So why are you coming forward now?"

Silence once again filled the room as the four friends looked at each other, then at the dean. Jessica faced Yolanda with a questioning expression. Yolanda understood her silent question, and nodded in response.

She would never be able to do this without her three best friends. They gave her strength. So, riding on that strength, she said, "Because I'm pregnant."

"Oh, good Lord." Dean Pascal groaned his disgust.

"I told him about the baby, but he wants me to get rid of it."

"Even now, he won't do the right thing," Yolanda said. "That's why we're here. Because Professor Bell has destroyed her life and doesn't even care."

Yes, Jessica thought, thankful for Yolanda's summation, that was exactly why they were here. Andrew had used her and didn't care about the aftermath. He'd betrayed her, lied to her, and he deserved to pay. . . .

"This is very serious indeed," the dean said, settling into his swivel chair. "It cannot go unpunished." He shook his head ruefully as he reached for a pad of paper and a pen. "I'll need your names."

"Jessica Bedford."

"Yolanda Burke."

"Shereen Anderson."

"Eleanor Grant."

Chapter Twenty-three

GOOD THINGS HAPPEN TO GOOD people.

Good things come to those who wait.

What a load of bull. While Shereen didn't consider herself a saint, she did think she was a good person. She'd taken her brother in out of the goodness of her heart. She'd been patient in waiting for him to smarten up.

But hadn't she waited long enough? Was she to be a martyr for his cause? Surely that's what she'd be if things didn't change. Because Shaun Jerome Anderson was going to send her to an early grave!

Shaun had promised her he'd go and look for work. But clearly he hadn't, because his car hadn't moved since she'd left for the office this morning. She knew because she'd placed two twigs by his rear tires and they were in the exact same position as they'd been hours earlier.

So, the sight of him lazing around on the sofa couldn't have enraged Shereen more as she entered her Maryland home, especially after another tough day at work. Enough was enough.

She kicked off her pumps, wriggled her toes when they were finally free, then marched into the living room. She didn't say a word to her brother, simply snatched the remote from his fingers and zapped the television off.

"Hey," he said, the laugh over the show dying on his lips.

"Hey, yourself."

He sat up. "Can I have the remote back, *please*?"

She ignored his request, instead tucking the remote beneath her bosom as she crossed her arms over her chest. "You told me you were going to look for a job today. Remember that conversation?" It had been a good two months since he'd been fired from the job at the grocery store, and he hadn't worked since.

"I . . . did."

God, she could smell booze on his breath. "Where'd you go?"

"To that place down the street."

"What place?" Lord, she felt as frustrated as any parent, and she hadn't even given birth to a child!

"You know. The corner store."

"The corner store? Damn, Shaun, can't you come up with something better than that? Mr. Chin isn't gonna hire you for his family-run operation."

He shrugged.

"Sitting around here all day is not going to get you work. And don't bother lying; I know you didn't go anywhere. Your car's in the same damn spot it was when I left this morning."

"Can I have the remote now?"

So he was deaf, too, not just lazy. She took the remote with her to the kitchen, where she would tackle the real problem. Opening the cupboards, she searched for signs of liquor. She didn't know where Shaun got money for booze since he didn't pay a dime of rent and never had any money to help with the bills.

In the living room, she heard the television come to life.

Whatever.

She found no liquor in the kitchen, except for a couple of bottles of wine, which were hers. They had to be somewhere. She marched out of the kitchen and up the stairs to Shaun's bedroom. Screw his privacy. If he was going to act like a six-year-old, she'd treat him like one.

She opened his closet. Lord, what a mess. She didn't see anything there. But when she dropped to her knees and looked under his bed, she saw at least a dozen bottles lying side by side.

Vodka. Hard stuff. He'd become an alcoholic right beneath her nose.

She grabbed as many as she could hold, then went to the bathroom and began dumping their contents. When she was on the third bottle, Shaun appeared.

"Yo, what the hell are you doing!"

"You need to find a job. And you need to quit drinking. Dammit, didn't you learn your lesson?"

It had been a night of drinking that ended his basketball career before it had even begun.

"I'm twenty-six years old, man. You can't treat me like this."

"When you start acting like a twenty-six-year-old, we can talk then."

"Fuck you." He stormed into his bedroom and slammed the door.

Shereen leaned her butt against the bathroom counter and closed her eyes. She hated this. She was losing control in her own house. What was she going to do? The longer her brother stayed, the harder it was to get rid of him, and the crazier she'd get. Because she could tell him until she was blue in the face to get a job, and he simply wouldn't listen. For whatever reason, he acted like she owed him. Like the whole family did.

He didn't think she'd kick him out.

And truthfully, though she should, she didn't know if she could.

All she knew was that this whole situation was making her insane.

She was emptying the fourth and last bottle she'd been able to snag when the doorbell rang. At this hour, it was probably some kid out canvassing for money. Hell, she already had a twenty-four–seven charity case. Shereen wasn't in the mood.

But when the doorbell rang again—two quick, urgent blasts this time—and when Shaun didn't exit his room to answer it, she made her way downstairs.

And got the shock of her life when she saw who stood on her front step.

"Terrence." His name escaped on a breathless whisper.

His eyes lit up as he looked at her, his lips curling in a lopsided grin. "Hey, Shereen."

"W-what are you d-doing? Here?" And how did he know where she lived?

He rested his tall frame against the doorjamb, his grin evening out. "What do you think?"

"How should I know?" Her heart was suddenly beating harder than was normal. "I'm not a mind reader."

He continued to smile.

"Where's Yolanda?" She glanced over his shoulder, though she knew damn well Yolanda wouldn't be there.

He followed her gaze, then met her eyes once more. "Why would I bring Yolanda here?"

"Why wouldn't you?"

He didn't say anything, just gave her an intense look, one that unnerved her at the same time that it made her warm.

"I don't like this, Terrence. You coming here like this."

"Aren't you going to invite me inside?"

Lord, was he deaf, too? Maybe it was a testosterone thing, she thought, remembering her brother.

Yet she stood back to let him pass.

"I hope you don't expect anything fancy." Not that she owed him any apologies. She hadn't invited him here. "This is a simple house."

"I didn't come for the house."

Shereen's eyes flew to his, but what she saw there scared the shit out of her. She spun around and headed for the living room.

"It's good to see you."

She turned to find him right on her tail. Entirely too close. "How did you find this place?"

"You're listed."

Damn.

He took a step toward her, getting even closer. She sucked in a much-needed breath. "Terrence, why are you here?"

"Because I needed to see you."

Her throat was suddenly dry, and she swallowed. "What, you need my help or something?"

"Kinda."

"Just tell me what you want." She sounded weary, but she was tired of this game. They'd been playing it ever since the first time he walked into her office. Now, it had to end.

"I'm not sure you want to hear it."

"No more games, Terrence."

"All right. I came because I miss you."

Nervous giggle. "Yeah, right."

"And I think you miss me, too."

Her eyes bulged. "You're crazy."

"Maybe I am. For letting you go."

•

Was the room spinning, or was her head going to explode? She took a step backward. "Terrence, this is . . . I don't get it."

He took another step toward her. "Then let me explain. The reason I'm here, the reason I moved to Washington, is because of you. For you. Not for Yolanda."

"But you're getting married to her!"

"Not anymore. I told her we were moving too fast and should slow things down." At her baffled look, he added, "If you don't believe me, ask her."

Terrence had called off the wedding? He'd come to Washington for *her*? God, she couldn't think. She found the sofa and sank into its softness.

As Terrence stood over her, he looked larger than life. Just as he always had. Was it that quality that drew her to him even now, so many years after he'd broken her heart? Or was it the memory of the very special love they'd once shared?

"If you tell me this is all too sudden, I'll understand. But the truth is, I never stopped loving you. Never forgot about you. Yolanda and me—I thought it would work. But that's because you weren't in the picture. Shereen, when I saw you at that party . . . I knew then that I couldn't marry Yolanda. Not when I still have feelings for you."

Shereen could hardly believe what she was hearing. "You called off the wedding?"

"Yes."

"When?"

"Over a week ago."

Why hadn't Yolanda told her? Told any of them?

Terrence sat beside her, and the smell of his musky cologne enveloped her. His essence enveloped her, trapping her like a deer caught in headlights.

"I didn't plan this. It's nobody's fault." He softly stroked her cheek, let his fingers linger there. "But you know, Sweet Thang, I was always crazy about you."

Shereen wanted to swat his hand away, but all she could do was think about what he'd said. That he'd called off the wedding, yet Yolanda hadn't told her. She didn't understand.

Before she knew what was happening, he framed her face and tilted it upward, then covered her lips with his. It was wrong, she knew, but she was helpless to stop it.

And the truth was, she didn't want to stop it. She didn't want to think; she wanted only to feel. Because this felt so good. God, she'd missed this. Missed him.

But when his hands circled her waist and he pulled her close, Shereen's brain started working again. She remembered Yolanda. She remembered that Terrence had dumped her for no reason. Slipping her hands between them, she heaved him away.

"Go," she managed. Barely.

He drew in a deep breath, exhaled it audibly, and for a moment, she thought he would say something. But he didn't. She couldn't decide if that bothered her or pleased her.

After a moment, he stood and strolled toward the front door. Slowly, Shereen rose, watching the strong muscles in his back move with each step, captivated by this man who had once broken her heart. But she didn't follow him. She almost let out a sigh of relief when he opened the front door, but instead she sighed in frustration when he turned and hurried back to her.

There was a question in his eyes, something she couldn't quite read, something that made her suddenly wary.

"There's something I have to know . . . then I'll leave." He placed both hands on his hips as he looked her straight in the eyes. "Were you dating Brad behind my back in college?"

Brad? Who was Brad? Oh, shit. *Brad.* The guy who wouldn't stop sweating her even though she'd been involved with Terrence.

She looked at him like he was crazy, because the question *was* crazy. "No. Where would you get an idea like that from?"

"Damn."

"Did someone tell you that?"

He gritted his teeth. "All this time, I thought it was true. That you were seeing Brad—cheating on me—God, I can't believe I was so stupid."

"You're not giving me any answers, Simms." So easily she'd slipped into calling him by his last name, the way she had when they were dating.

"I've gotta go."

"Wait a minute." She placed a hand on his arm to stop him from leaving. Mistake. She pulled it away. "You tell me this and you're just gonna walk out of here?"

"It's not you." He stroked her chin, then dropped his hand to his side. "I'm mad at myself. I should have known better. I never should have broken up with you."

"Terrence . . ."

He turned and walked out of her house.

Stunned speechless, Shereen watched him go. Only when she heard his car start and drive off did she finally return to the sofa.

For the life of her, she had no clue what had just happened.

By the next day, Shereen had figured it out. It had taken her a whole night of reliving Terrence's visit, his kiss, his question about Brad, for her to realize the truth.

Someone must have told Terrence that she'd been seeing Brad behind his back. That was why he'd broken up with her. Finally, after all these years, she had her answer.

Of course, she hadn't been seeing Brad. Shereen didn't give her heart easily, but when she did, she gave it completely. Terrence should have known that—in fact, he had, but he'd also had an issue with trust. So whoever had told him the lie about Brad had known how much that kind of betrayal would hurt him.

Before going to Howard, Terrence had been seriously involved with a girl from his high school in Cincinnati. After graduation, they'd promised not to see anyone else. He'd been planning to marry her and had even given her a promise ring. But only months after being away at school, he'd learned that she had cheated on him with one of his best friends.

When Shereen had met Terrence in her junior year, the attraction had been mutual, immediate, and strong. But because of what had happened with his ex-girlfriend, trust had been a major issue in the beginning of their relationship. Shereen had understood; she'd understood everything about him. His deep sense of loyalty. His desire for comfort in stability. He was a Taurus, a fellow earth sign—and the perfect match for a Capricorn. So she hadn't given up on him, and he'd soon realized that her love for him was sincere. After that, they were as tight as two lovers could be. As far as she'd been concerned, he was the best thing that had ever happened to her, and she was sure he'd felt the same way. That was why she'd been not only devastated but completely perplexed when he'd up and dumped her in senior year without even so much as a formal good-bye.

Shereen blew out a frazzled breath. A mountain of work sat before her, but try as she might, she simply couldn't concentrate on work. Not when Terrence's words still weighed heavily on her mind.

There's something I have to know . . . Were you dating Brad behind my back in college?

She didn't want to consider this, that one of her friends could have told him that lie, but Yolanda, Jessica, and Ellie had known the story about his ex-girlfriend, had known about his issues with trust. How easy it would be to hurt her by telling Terrence such a lie, because given his issues, he'd likely believe it.

And he'd break up with her. Break her heart.

Jessica wouldn't do it. She was too sweet and genuinely caring to do something like that. Ellie simply wasn't underhanded that way. Besides, she had no motive to hurt her.

But Yolanda. Yolanda had the perfect motive.

Lawrence.

And this was the perfect payback. Breaking up Shereen and Terrence. The icing on the cake was getting engaged to him years later so that she could flaunt Shereen's failure in her face.

"Ms. Anderson." Rudy's voice sounded on the speakerphone. "There's a call on line one for you."

Shereen ignored her. She couldn't deal with any company business right now. Her mind was still reeling from everything she'd learned.

Yolanda had assured her that she hadn't gotten involved with Terrence to hurt her. Shereen had been dumb enough to believe her.

Yolanda was full of shit.

Though they'd been friends, Yolanda had always, always been jealous of her. Shereen was prettier, Shereen had had it easier, Shereen was lighter-skinned—all that crap. Shereen had tried—and she'd thought she'd succeeded—to prove to Yolanda that she didn't think she was any better than Yolanda just because Shereen's father had owned a successful business while Yolanda had come from the ghetto. And Lord knew, Yolanda was a beautiful woman, so Shereen certainly hadn't understood her jealousy on that front.

It was clear now that she didn't understand her at all.

And that thought hurt her more than anything. The fact that she had tried her hardest to be a friend to someone who had given her a tough time right from the beginning—and she'd thought she'd bridged the gap. Yes, she'd suspected that Yolanda hadn't gotten over all her jealousy issues in college, but Shereen had figured that the eight years since graduation would have given them all time to mature.

Instead, Yolanda was still the old Yolanda, insecure and vindictive, the type who could blurt out Jessica's personal business without batting an eye, probably the same way she'd told Terrence the lie about Shereen and Brad.

Shereen didn't want anything more to do with her.

She was tired of the games. She was tired of Yolanda's jealousy. She was tired of their one-sided friendship.

So now, as much as it hurt, she had to cut Yolanda out of her life. Because for deliberately hurting her the way she had with Terrence, Shereen could never forgive her.

"Get out," Ellie said.

"It's the truth."

"Damn, girl. I can't believe it. Yolanda told Terrence that you were seeing Brad?" Ellie repeated what Shereen had told her in wonder.

Shereen was at Ellie's small apartment, sitting on a well-worn sofa. Today of all days, she didn't feel like going home to deal with Shaun.

"You know, I should have known. Suspected something. Yolanda acted different for a long while after Terrence dumped me, but I chalked that up to some sort of morbid pleasure she got out of seeing me in pain—because of the whole Lawrence issue. Never in my wildest dreams would I have thought she'd want to hurt me like that."

"You think she liked him back in the day?"

"This has nothing to do with her liking Terrence. This has to do with her not liking me."

Ellie pouted. "You really think that's the case?"

"What else can it be?" That question had plagued Shereen all night. "I always knew she was insecure where I was concerned, but we were friends. Weren't we? God, maybe even that was a lie."

"For what it's worth, I don't think she meant to hurt you. Now, I mean."

Shereen gave Ellie a doubtful look. "Yeah, right."

"It just doesn't make sense. Lawrence—that was so long ago. I can't see anyone in their right mind holding a grudge for nearly ten years."

"Yeah, well, Yolanda's an Aries. They can hold grudges forever."

"Have you told Jessica?"

"No." Shereen spoke softly. "She's already dealing with enough."

"You did that for Yolanda." Ellie's voice held a hopeful note. "Because you didn't want to give Jessica more reason to be angry with her. Oh, Shereen. You still care about her."

"That was never the issue." A sudden pain stabbed through her heart. "Why would she want to hurt me like this? That's what I want to know, Ellie. Why?"

"I don't know, hon. Like you said, so much has changed, gotten better, since our days at Howard. There was a time you two would fight like cats and dogs, but deep down, we knew you loved each other." Ellie reached for her pack of cigarettes. "Maybe you two just need to talk this through."

"I talked to her about this already, remember? She had every chance to come clean then, tell me about this Brad bullshit. And you know what? So much time had passed, I would have forgiven her. But now . . ."

Ellie's mouth formed an *O* as she blew out a ring of smoke. "I don't know what to say."

What could anyone say? Nothing would justify what Yolanda had done.

Ellie and Shereen could gloss over the truth all they wanted, but they couldn't change the facts. Yolanda had done this to hurt her. And there could only be one reason why.

For whatever reason, and though she might not even know it, deep in her heart, Yolanda hated Shereen.

Chapter Twenty-four

"I'M GONNA HAVE TO CALL you back."

"Uh . . ." Yolanda frowned. "Okay."

The dial tone blared before she could even say good-bye.

Damn. That was weird. What was wrong with Shereen? That was the third time this week she'd been short with her. And she hadn't called back once, though she'd promised that she would.

Yolanda dialed Shereen's home number and left her a message: "Shereen, I know you're busy, but I wanted to let you know that I'm having a get-together at my place. An end-of-summer bash. Jessica has agreed to go . . . So, I'm hoping you'll be there. Call me. Please."

Ellie opened the driver's-side door and stared down at Shereen. "God, girlfriend, you have got to try and smile."

Shereen moved her lips, but she wasn't sure if she formed a smile or a frown.

"Damn, is that the best you can do?"

Shereen grumbled. "I don't want to be here."

"I know that, but maybe Yolanda is trying to make amends."

"She doesn't even know I'm angry with her. She doesn't even know I know anything."

Ellie shrugged. "You gonna come out?"

Shereen had seriously debated dropping Ellie off, then turning around and going home. Ellie's new-used car was in the shop once again, but Shereen was sure Jessica would give her a ride home. However, now that she was here, after finally speaking with Yolanda and telling her that yes, she'd be here, she couldn't figure out a decent excuse not to go inside. Besides, she wanted to see how much Yolanda would tell her, considering that for the past few weeks she'd known that Yolanda and Terrence were no longer an item.

So she had to go inside. To continue playing this game Yolanda had started. But she hoped it would end today.

Shereen got out of the car.

"There we go." Ellie smiled her approval.

"Let's do this."

Ellie led the way to the front door. Shereen lagged behind. When she reached the porch, Yolanda was opening the door.

"Hey!" Yolanda's face lit up when she saw them.

Ellie hugged her, but Shereen merely flashed Yolanda a smile and stepped past her into the house. She found Jessica sitting cross-legged on the sofa.

"Hey, sweetie." Shereen bent to kiss Jessica's cheek. "Long time no see."

"Busy, busy."

"I know." In the last month, Jessica had been doing the nightly entertainment segment on the news as well as hosting *The Scoop*. "Things are looking up for you."

"I guess so."

Ellie greeted Jessica, and Shereen quickly sat in the armchair when she saw Yolanda coming her way.

Yolanda flashed her a puzzled look. "What's up?"

"Nothing." God, it was going to be hard to be here and pretend everything was cool. "You tell me."

Yolanda shrugged. "I don't know. I just get the feeling you're mad at me or something."

"You didn't do anything for me to be mad at you," Shereen replied sweetly, wishing instead she could blurt out what was on her mind. But she wouldn't do that, not until she gave Yolanda the chance to come clean on her own.

"You got anything to munch on?" Ellie craned her neck toward the kitchen. "I'm starved."

"Chips and dip. Hamburgers for the barbecue."

And you know Ellie is trying to lose weight, Shereen thought.

"I brought a salad," Jessica told them.

Shereen gazed Jessica's way to find her staring at her. Clearly, she'd read her mind. Her lips lifted in a small smile. "Great. You always make the best salads."

"Why don't we sit outside?" Jessica suggested. "It's such a gorgeous day." In the mid-seventies with a comfortable breeze, it was picture-perfect.

"May as well start up the barbecue," Yolanda added.

They all made their way through the kitchen to the back door, but Shereen hung back. So did Jessica.

"What's *up*?" Jessica asked her.

"Nothing."

"You sure?"

Shereen nodded. "It's been one of those weeks at work, ya know?" Jessica linked arms with hers. "I hear you."

Shereen whispered, "I see you and Yolanda are tight again."

"Mmm-hmm." She'd had time to get over the incident at the club and now felt better about it. She knew Yolanda hadn't mentioned Andrew on purpose. Besides, Yolanda hadn't said anything that could really hurt her. And she also felt better because no letters had come in the last six weeks. "You were right. I overreacted. Yolanda didn't mean to hurt me."

Shereen made a face, but Jessica didn't see.

"Hey, what are you two whispering about?" Yolanda asked.

"Oh, Jessica was just telling me about a hot rendezvous with Douglas." Shereen giggled when Jessica looked mortified.

"Well, don't keep that shit to yourself." Ellie had a cigarette lit and was standing in one corner of the deck, leaning against the railing. "Some of us haven't had any in a while."

Shereen glanced at Yolanda, but Yolanda didn't meet her eyes. Instead, Yolanda looked at Ellie and replied, "Like we're supposed to believe you haven't been giving Richard any."

Ellie shrugged, but a smile played on her lips.

Jessica said, "I thought you and Richard were through."

"What can I say? When it comes to sex, he knows what I need."

"What you need is your head examined." But Shereen smiled as she said the words, and Ellie smiled back at her. Ellie had confided in her that while she'd told Richard she wanted to cool things off, he was spending more time at her place again. When she was hot, he was cold, and vice versa. They were never on the same wavelength.

"You're just a nympho." Yolanda laughed.

"Shut up and get that barbecue going," Ellie countered.

Yolanda opened the barbecue. "And you need to stop smoking. That habit will kill you."

"Hey, something's gotta curb my other craving."

There were chuckles all around.

"You hear that?" Yolanda glanced at Shereen and Jessica. "She's a nympho, I'm telling you."

"At least I'm not an ax murderer."

"That's right," Yolanda jibed, "compare apples and oranges."

"I thought we were talking about bananas," Jessica commented, then laughed again.

"Damn." Ellie threw her a surprised glance. "Douglas really must be giving you some good sex."

Jessica smiled, remembering a recent hot night. "Actually, he is."

"Stop," Shereen said. "I'm the only one here who ain't gettin' any, so all this talk ain't fair." She eyed Yolanda, but Yolanda was busy putting hamburger patties on the grill.

"I made some fresh lemonade. Someone want to grab it?"

"Sure." Shereen opened the back door and went into the kitchen. She took the pitcher of lemonade from the fridge. When she turned, she saw Ellie behind her, and was so startled she nearly dropped the pitcher. "Damn, Ellie. You scared me."

"Sorry. I just came to grab the chips and dip. I can't wait for a burger. I'm hungry now." She lifted both bowls from the table. "Hey, so far things are cool."

"Yeah, so far." Shereen headed back outside, not allowing Ellie to continue the conversation. Jessica and Yolanda, now both standing at the barbecue, were giggling about something.

The sight shouldn't have bothered her, it was something she'd seen millions of times over the years, but she remembered that Yolanda had laughed with her that way, and all she could think was, *Were you sincere when you laughed with me that way, Yolanda? Or was everything a lie?*

Placing the lemonade on the wooden picnic table, Shereen realized that she forgot the cups, so she went to retrieve some. Seconds later, she was back outside.

"Thanks," Yolanda said to her.

"No problem."

Shereen sat and watched Yolanda flip the burgers. She thought of all the other times they had gotten together, tried to remember the positive things about them, but all she could think of was Terrence's visit. Of what he'd told her and what she'd later figured out.

"So." Shereen folded her hands onto the table. "How are you and Terrence?"

"Oh, we're fine," Yolanda answered.

It was her standard answer, the one she'd been giving for months, and right now, it pissed Shereen off. She was lying.

"Have you set a firm date for the wedding?" *Please come clean. Don't lie. Not about this.*

"The wedding?" Yolanda repeated, buying time. "I told you. February."

Shereen unfolded and refolded her hands. "The fourteenth?"

Was that a nervous flicker in Yolanda's eyes? "Yeah."

"Ah." Beneath the picnic table, Shereen had one leg crossed over the other and was shaking the top leg nonstop. "A Valentine's wedding. How romantic." Then, "You don't care that it'll be mid-week?"

Yolanda seemed caught off-guard by the comment. "Uh, well . . . we still have to finalize the day."

"Hmm."

No one else spoke. They didn't dare.

"What's with the sudden interest in my wedding?" Yolanda smiled, but it didn't reach her eyes.

Shereen raised an eyebrow. "Why don't you want to talk about it?"

"Who said I don't want to talk about it?"

"It's just that you never do."

"That's not true."

"Well, *rarely.*"

"So?"

Shereen unfolded her hands and drummed her fingers on the table-top. "I figured you'd have asked us about being bridesmaids—or something—by now."

"I did. I asked Jessica to be my matron of honor."

Shereen's eyes flew to Jessica. She didn't know why, but it felt like a betrayal to learn this. Why hadn't Jessica told her?

Damn if she wasn't overreacting. There wasn't a conspiracy going on. She had to get a grip.

Still, she couldn't stop her voice from sounding strained when she asked, "When?"

"A couple of weeks ago."

A couple of weeks ago, Terrence had already called off the wedding. *Why are you doing this, Yolanda? Why are you lying?*

"I meant to ask you and Ellie about being bridesmaids. I just hadn't gotten around to it. But I figured you'd know that was a given."

Ellie watched as the emotion on Shereen's face changed from disbelief to sadness to something darker. Sensing her friend was about to explode, she quickly spoke. "You wanna know something funny? There's this guy at work, this *Chinese* guy, and I think he's interested in me. Do you believe it?"

"Why's that so hard to believe?" Shereen asked. Some things were harder to believe, yet they had come to pass.

"Because he seems so conservative. This short thing with dorky glasses, who always wears a tie even on dress-down Fridays. The last guy I'd expect to like a black woman. But he's been asking me to lunch almost every day. I keep telling him no."

"Because of Richard." Yolanda shook her head.

"Because I'm not ready for anyone else." Ellie had finally gotten the courage to tell Richard their relationship wouldn't work, but her words had fallen on deaf ears. Because once again, the more she pushed him away, the more time he spent with her, the more promises he made, the more sex he gave her—and damn if her weakness wasn't sex. It seemed she'd never be rid of him.

"Look at her." Shereen clapped her hands together. "She's blushing."

"I am not." But she covered her cheeks with both palms. "Besides, I'm sure it's the boobs. I swear, some men think I'm a pinup or something."

"If he's nice, I say go for it." Jessica reached for the bag of buns and opened them. "Lord knows there aren't enough decent guys around these days."

"They're all players," Shereen added.

"Dogs," Ellie contributed.

"Or unavailable," Yolanda said.

Shereen's eyes shot to Yolanda's at that comment. Was that meant for her?

Yolanda's eyes met hers, held, and for a moment, Shereen thought she would say something about Terrence. But she didn't.

It was just as well.

Yolanda glanced down at the sizzling burgers. Fleetingly, she thought the heat there was nothing compared to the simmering anger she saw in Shereen's eyes.

What was up? From not returning her calls to these glaring looks, something was definitely wrong.

For a moment, she wondered if Shereen knew. She could almost read it in her eyes. *You're a liar.*

She wasn't *really* lying. She just hadn't found the perfect time to tell her friends that things between her and Terrence had cooled off. Besides, Terrence hadn't told her they'd never get married, only that he thought they were moving too fast.

She supposed she should tell her friends that, but something stopped her. Pride, maybe. No, it was definitely her pride. It was a hard thing to let go, especially in this situation. If Terrence had been involved with anyone but Shereen . . .

But did Shereen sense she was holding back the truth? Was that why she seemed so miffed with her?

"Pardon me?" Yolanda said when she realized Ellie was speaking to her.

"Don't make mine well-done. Haven't you heard the latest? Well-done meat isn't good for you. The rarer the better, at least in terms of fighting breast cancer."

"Where'd you hear that?" Yolanda challenged.

"Believe it or not, I *do* leave the bedroom on occasion to come up for air—and to watch the news. You should try it sometime."

Yolanda threw half a bun at Ellie. It hit her across the side of the head.

"Hey!" Giggling, Ellie grabbed the bun and whipped it back at

Yolanda, who dodged the piece of flying bread before it could hit her shoulder.

Before they knew it, there was an all-out, silly food fight.

Yolanda pretended not to notice that all Shereen's shots were aimed specifically at her.

THE PAST

EVEN BEFORE JESSICA STEPPED into her dormitory, she knew something was wrong.

She sensed it in the eerie quiet that surrounded the building, saw it in the gray clouds that hung in the sky.

Her boots crunching in the snow, she hurried up the dorm's concrete steps. The door opened before she reached it, and Hanna and Margery, two of her dorm mates, stepped outside. Startled, they both paused, then looked at her with glum expressions before silently scrambling down the steps.

Weird, Jessica thought, glancing over her shoulder at them as she opened the door. They didn't look back.

Inside, a group of girls stood off to the right. They were huddled together, a couple softly crying, others holding each other. Wondering what was going on, Jessica stared at them, but no one looked her way.

The feeling that something was seriously wrong stayed with her as she went past the group and headed up the stairs. Keisha, a fellow student in her drama class, descended as she ascended.

"Hey, Keisha."

"Hey," Keisha replied in a tear-filled voice, then continued past her.

Goose bumps popping out on her skin, Jessica quickened her pace, taking the remaining steps two at a time. On the second floor, she immediately went to Shereen's room. She knocked the door, and Ellie opened it an instant later. One look at Ellie's distressed expression and Jessica's stomach dropped.

"Jessica," Ellie said softly. "You heard."

Jessica stepped into the room. Shereen sat cross-legged on her bed, her eyes downcast, while Yolanda stood near the window gnawing on a fingernail. "Heard what?"

Shereen's eyes flew to Jessica's. "Oh, sweetie."

Jessica dropped her purse and tote bag to the floor. She had a very sick feeling in her gut, one she couldn't explain. "What?" When Yolanda and Shereen exchanged concerned glances, Jessica anxiously repeated, *"What?"*

Ellie was suddenly beside her, placing an arm around her waist. "Oh, Jess."

Jessica shrugged her off. "What's going on?"

Yolanda strolled toward her, a somber look marring her attractive face. "I don't know how to tell you this."

"Just tell me."

"Andrew," Yolanda said on a sigh. "He's . . . dead."

Tiny prickles of ice pierced Jessica's skin across the back of her neck, then quickly spread down her spine. "Dead?" Frantically, she looked at her friends. "What do you mean, dead?"

"He killed himself." Ellie whispered the words.

"How could he have killed himself?" Jessica asked, as if the idea was preposterous. "He wouldn't. He *couldn't.*"

"It's true." Rising, Shereen slowly walked toward Jessica. "He left a note. Everyone's been talking. I can't believe you didn't hear already . . ."

"Just tell me what the note said." Jessica spoke angrily, though she wasn't angry with her friends. But anger was oh so much more preferable than despair.

"Apparently," Ellie began, "the investigation got to him."

God, no. Ellie couldn't mean . . . Jessica felt the room begin to spin. "What are you saying?"

Yolanda replied, "Jess, we don't know for sure, but some of the big sisters are saying that he left a suicide note for his wife. In it, he apologized for what he'd done. Said he couldn't live with himself because he'd disgraced her and Howard . . ."

"Oh, God." Jessica faltered, and Yolanda caught her.

"Oh, Jess," Yolanda said ruefully. "I know."

"He did this because of me?" The realization too horrible to accept, Jessica stepped away from Yolanda. Her body began to shake as the room spun faster.

"Because of us," Ellie said, stressing the last word.

"Because I said he raped me. Because I lied." Jessica clutched her stomach as she crumbled to the ground. "Oh, God."

Yolanda sank to her knees beside her. "Jessica, don't—"

"I killed him."

"No, hon." Shereen wiped at a tear. "You didn't. How were we to know—"

"How?" Jessica quickly said, suddenly realizing that she needed to know. "How did he die?"

Yolanda paused before answering. "He drove into an eighteen-wheeler."

"Oh, my God." How desperate he must have been to do that, all because of her. "God forgive me."

"Sweetie." Yolanda gently rubbed Jessica's arm. "This isn't your fault."

"I never should have gone to the dean."

"You can't blame yourself because you reported him."

Jessica swatted Yolanda's hand away and bolted to her feet. "Maybe I couldn't blame myself if I'd told the truth. But I lied. Dammit, I wanted him as much as he wanted me—maybe even more—but I couldn't deal with his rejection and now . . . now he's dead."

Jessica stifled a sob with both hands as the devastating reality crashed down on her shoulders once more. She took two steps to the right, stopped, turned and faced her friends, then doubled over in pain. "Oh, God. Andrew . . ."

"Jessica, don't do this to yourself." Ellie's voice cracked as she spoke. "I hate to see you like this."

"I *killed* a man."

"He killed himself," Yolanda retorted. But her voice was heavy with guilt.

"I killed him—as surely as if I'd put a gun to his head."

Ellie moaned, then dropped onto Shereen's bed. "Believe me, Jessica, we all feel like shit."

"If we could do it over . . ." Yolanda's voice trailed off.

"We didn't know," Shereen said. "How could we have known?"

A million thoughts were spinning in Jessica's head, but a thick haze surrounded them and she could hardly grasp one. This all seemed like a bad dream.

But it wasn't. Andrew was dead. Because of her.

Her hands trembled, and she wrung them together harshly. "I should go to the dean, clear his name. It's the least I can do."

"Jessica, listen to me," Yolanda said. "I'd be the first one to say you should—*if* it would make a difference." She brushed away tears. "But what good will it do to go to the dean now? It won't bring Andrew back. And who knows how you might be reprimanded."

Jessica buried her face in her hands and began to wail. Andrew was really dead. How could she go on?

She pressed a hand to her belly, feeling her one reason to go on.

Her baby.

Their baby.

It was the last piece she had of Andrew, and she would cherish it.

Forever.

Chapter Twenty-five

IT WAS DARK WHEN JESSICA returned to her dressing room, well past business hours when her segment on the evening news was done. So the sight of the pink envelope on the floor when she opened the door immediately gave her pause.

It had been weeks since she'd received a letter about Andrew, and she'd started to feel she could put the disturbing incidents behind her. But the modicum of peace she'd found in these past weeks was instantly shattered. Because she didn't have to open this envelope to know what it contained.

Another letter.

The fear returned, fluttering like a trapped butterfly inside her stomach.

The letter wasn't going to go away. She couldn't ignore it. Tossing the clipboard she held onto the nearby sofa, she bent to retrieve the envelope.

Her fingers shook so badly that at first she couldn't grasp it. Whimpering, she finally lifted the envelope and held it with both hands.

There was one word on the envelope: her name written in neat, block letters. She lifted the flap and withdrew the card. It wasn't your typical Hallmark card; this one had been generated on a computer and printed on one of those inkjet printers.

It's Never Easy to Lose a Child.

"No, no, no, no, no!" Jessica slammed a hand to her forehead as she fell into a heap on the floor. It wasn't the actual anniversary of when she lost the baby, but whoever was sending her these damn cards didn't care about that. He or she simply wanted to make a point—the point that someone knew.

A tear trickled down her cheek as she opened the homemade card.

But the bastard's now in a better place. I wonder what your viewers would say if they knew of your filthy past? That you cried rape when you never were, that your lie sent a man to his death? Hmm. What an interesting show that would be.

"No, please, no." Jessica lay her head on the cold floor, curling her body into the fetal position. She clutched the card to her stomach as tears poured out of her eyes.

Oh, my God. You're bleeding.
Oh, shit. Jessica!
It hurts . . .
Call 9-1-1!

The pain was as fresh as the night she'd lost the baby.

And the guilt. Guilt because she'd sent her lover to his death with a lie. Guilt because she'd lost their baby.

Someone knew. Someone knew everything.

"Oh, God. No. Nooo . . ."

Hours later, Jessica had somehow made it home. She'd stopped at a downtown restaurant first, where she'd sat at a table and ordered a half carafe of wine. But she barely drank even half a glass. Not only could she not keep anything down, she knew that getting sloshed would not solve her problems.

But surprisingly, sitting in a crowded restaurant on a Friday night, even though she was alone, gave her a measure of comfort. There, surrounded by strangers, she felt safe.

There, she was just an average person from Washington, not a person someone wanted to hurt.

So, she'd sat and thought about who could be doing this to her. The last three letters had simply arrived at the studio, not by courier and not by mail. Meaning it had to be someone nearby, someone who had been brazen enough to drop the letters off personally.

There went the theory about Elizabeth Vodden. Last Jessica had heard, she'd moved to Louisiana with her husband.

Who else could it be? Frustrated, she realized it could be anyone. While she believed Yolanda hadn't meant to hurt her, it was entirely plausible that if she could carelessly mention her affair with Andrew at the club, then she could have mentioned it another time. In the past, Lord knew, maybe even Shereen or Ellie had opened her mouth about it. Secrets had a way of getting out.

This, she knew the hard way.

Still, for her friends to tell that painful secret, the one they'd sworn to never tell a soul . . . the very thought was so agonizing it was almost too hard to bear.

The reality was, her involvement with Andrew hadn't been secret. When she'd gone to the dean with her accusation of rape, other sorors had found out. Indeed, they'd empathized with her plight. How dare a professor coerce her into giving him sex in exchange for a passing grade?

But no one had ever blamed her, because they hadn't known she was lying. Lying because she'd been left pregnant and alone and scared to tell her family the truth—that she'd willingly gotten involved with a man twice her age, a man she believed had loved her but had lied to her simply to get her in his bed. The truth had been too devastating to admit.

And when Andrew Bell killed himself, people had still sympathized with her. How selfish of him to commit suicide and leave her feeling guilty for doing the right thing—exposing his indiscretion!

Most people hadn't known about the baby, but those who had, just a few sorority sisters on her dorm room floor, had once again comforted her when she'd miscarried.

All around, she'd had sympathy and support.

So, when she'd received the first letter at the studio, she'd been truly confused. Who would do this to her? And why? No one had ever blamed her in all this.

She'd passed the first letter off as a bizarre coincidence at best, and at worse, a thoughtless prank from a classmate who was jealous of her success. But the next letter made it clear that someone close to her—or close to Andrew—was responsible. Who else would know about the cabin in Virginia, or the type of things Andrew would say to her, and she to him? Only her three best friends.

And anyone they might have inadvertently told.

Or Andrew's wife.

Jessica had initially considered her a suspect, then dismissed that thought. If she'd wanted to hurt Jessica, she could have done so years ago, when all this was fresh. Why, years later, put herself in the situation of having to remember all the pain and public humiliation she'd gone through?

Still, one never knew. Maybe her career in the spotlight, proving that she had not only survived the past but succeeded, enraged Mrs. Bell. Who knew what lies Andrew had told his wife about her?

All the thoughts about who and why and what this person wanted had given Jessica a headache, and she'd finally left the bar, a new plan taking shape in her mind.

Now at home, as she stepped out of her car and made her way to the front door, she knew exactly what she had to do.

She found Douglas in the study, his head buried in notes for the show. Working in television was hectic and meant long hours, and almost everyone took work home with them.

That fact solidified her decision, made the excuse she was going to give him more plausible.

Quietly, she walked across the hardwood floor. When she was almost directly behind him, he sensed her and turned. His face lit up with a smile.

It was a simple thing, but tonight it made her want to cry. She would do anything to spare him any pain and humiliation.

"Hello, sweetheart." He stood and wrapped his arms around her, then covered her lips with his.

"Hi."

"You feel tense." He moved his hands to her neck and began to gently massage.

He always knew when something was wrong. It was one of the very special things about him. What she was about to do would kill her, but for Douglas, she'd do anything.

"I am tense."

"What's the matter?"

She stepped away from him. Following her, he placed his hands on her shoulders. She lifted her own hands to cover his.

When she didn't respond, he kissed the back of her head.

"It's work," she told him on a weary sigh.

"You're doing too much."

If only that were it. This wouldn't hurt so much if she didn't love her job. "Yes. And it's starting to get to me."

"They can find someone to replace you on the evening news."

Jessica whirled around in Douglas's arms and pressed her face against his broad chest. She inhaled deeply, inhaling his scent, confirming for herself all that was important.

"You're really upset about this."

"Yes." Her voice was a mere whisper, and she was surprised to find tears streaming down her cheeks.

"If you're worried that—"

"I'm quitting."

Pulling back, he framed her face as he stared at her. "What?"

She couldn't look at him, for fear he'd see the lie in her eyes. She turned away.

"Jessica, I thought you loved your job."

"I do. I did. But . . ."

"Come here." He enveloped her in his arms once again. After a moment, he looked down at her. "You sure everything's okay?"

She glanced at the floor. Nodded.

"Then why quit both? Just a few months ago you told me how much your career meant to you."

"I want to start a family." She blurted that out because she didn't know what else to say, and the pleasantly surprised expression she saw on his face made her feel much, much better. "I don't want to be a working mother." She pressed her hands against his chest. "I want to stay at home, raise my children properly. So many of the children I see on the weekends don't get that kind of attention because they only have one parent, and . . . that's not what I want for my children. Our children."

Cupping her chin, Douglas stared at her for a long moment, like he wasn't sure he could believe her. "Are you sure?"

"Yes." Her voice cracked a little, but she continued. "I know you've been ready for a while, and now . . . I'm ready, too."

"Oh, baby." He scooped her in his arms and whirled her around.

This is the right thing to do. Douglas is so happy. He's all I need.

When he released her, she said, "So I'm not crying because I'm sad sad, but happy sad. In a way this is bittersweet . . ."

"You don't have to do this."

She palmed his face. "Yes. I do. This is what I want." She smiled, Douglas's happiness making her happy. "I guess I'm more like my sister than I thought." Camille had graduated from Howard nine years before Jessica, but she'd gone there solely for an education as her life goal had been to get married and raise a family. Now, she was married to a successful surgeon, living in Buffalo, and raising four children.

"God, I love you." Douglas enveloped her in his arms.

She savored his strength, his love, his warmth. "I love you, too, sweetheart."

She would be all right. She was doing the right thing.

She'd do anything to spare Douglas pain. Anything to bury the past, once and for all.

Chapter Twenty-six

"GREAT JOB, YOLANDA. YOU SAVED the case."

"Thanks." Yolanda smiled at the senior partner as he peered into her office before continuing down the hall.

"Congratulations."

Yolanda looked up to see the receptionist give her two thumbs-up. She smiled her thanks, then lowered her eyes to the brief on her desk.

"Way to go, Yolanda." A junior partner flashed her a bright smile as she walked by.

It had been like this since she'd returned from court an hour ago, with compliments coming from practically everyone at the firm. This was her first case with her new firm, a sexual harassment one—always difficult to prove. Indeed, the case had almost been lost when the victim, Sharon Byfield, suddenly announced that she didn't want to testify against her boss. She'd been hoping for a judge only, but the defendant had requested a jury, and Sharon hadn't wanted to testify before a crowd of strangers. Where the firm's other lawyers had failed, Yolanda had been able to convince Sharon that she could testify, that she *should*— and not let her boss win. In the end, Sharon's calm, rational, consistent testimony had sealed the defendant's fate. Yolanda had no doubt that the jury would find him guilty by a preponderance of the evidence.

Yolanda picked up the receiver and dialed Terrence. On days like this, after a victory, she liked to celebrate. The official celebration with her colleagues would come with the announcement of damages after the jury rendered its verdict. But since Yolanda was confident of the trial's outcome, she wanted to share her joy with the man she loved.

"Hello?"

Yolanda's eyebrows bunched together at the sound of the deep, un-familiar voice. "Hello?"

"Yolanda?"

Oh, God. *James.* Somehow, she'd called her ex-husband, not her fi-ancé. Not knowing what to say, she hung up.

God, how stupid. He knew it was her. Now he was going to wonder why she'd called. How had she made such a blunder?

Her elbows propped on her desk, Yolanda dropped her face into her palms. Deep in her heart, she knew the answer to that. Also a lawyer, James had been the one she shared her legal successes with. He was the one she would call after a victory like today's. But they'd been divorced for over a year, so why on earth call him now?

Habit. Albeit a bad one.

She reached for the phone again and this time dialed Terrence's cell. It was the best way to reach him these days.

He answered almost immediately. "Hello?"

"Hey there."

Pause. "Yolanda?"

"Yeah, it's me, baby." Nervous, she fiddled with the phone cord. "How are you?"

"I'm fine. But busy."

"All right, I won't keep you. I was wondering what you're doing this evening."

Another pause. "My schedule's really tight."

"Can't even spare an hour?"

He sighed. "I don't think that's a good idea."

Why was she letting him do this to her? This wasn't like her. Never in her life had she begged a man for anything.

Maybe because she was waiting to see if he'd admit to her what in her heart she already knew. He'd seen Shereen. She didn't know if the two had gotten involved, but the way Shereen was acting, consistently giving her the cold shoulder, she knew it was all about Terrence. It couldn't be anything else.

"How's Shereen?" she asked before she could stop herself.

"This has nothing to do with Shereen. I already told you, we're rush-ing things. We need more time to get to know each other."

"Right." Somehow the word escaped around the lump lodged in her throat. "And how're we gonna get to know each other when you don't have any time for me?"

"We'll have to talk later."

Yolanda chuckled soundlessly. Lord, she was a fool for hanging on. She hadn't even held on to James like this.

"Go to hell, Terrence. It's over. Stay out of my life."

She slammed down the receiver. That was more like it. Taking control instead of begging some man who didn't want her to work things out.

He wanted Shereen.

It made sense. He'd been head-over-heels in love with her years ago, but still, the reality hurt.

Men! Who needed them?

She shot to her feet and marched to the door, closed it, then sat atop the oak desk as she picked up the receiver.

"Shereen Anderson," Yolanda said when the receptionist answered.

"Ms. Anderson isn't taking calls right now. Would you like her voice mail?"

"Tell her it's Jessica. She'll take the call."

Yolanda felt a moment of satisfaction when, seconds later, Shereen's extension rang. Shereen answered, her voice saccharine-sweet. "Hey, Jessica."

Yolanda hesitated for a second. What was she doing? This was dumb, childish. Yet she couldn't stop herself from saying, "You won, Shereen. He's yours."

Silence. Then, "Yolanda?"

"Yeah, it's me."

There was another pause before Shereen said, "This isn't about winning or losing."

So she wasn't even gonna play like she had no clue what Yolanda was talking about. Damn, she *had* been in touch with Terrence. "Like hell it isn't."

"Yolanda, I don't want to talk about this."

"You said you were over him, but all this time you still wanted him."

"Don't put this on me. I have nothing to do with your problems."

"So you *have* talked to him. What else have you two done?"

"Yolanda—"

"Why couldn't you just be happy for me?" Yolanda didn't know why she was pushing for a fight. If Terrence didn't want her, he didn't want her.

But arguing with Shereen was better than them not talking at all.

"God, you're so . . . Forget it. I don't have time for this. You know, I always knew we had our issues, but despite them, I thought we were friends. But the truth is, you've always had a problem with me, deep down. I can't fight that anymore."

Shereen's comment struck a chord with Yolanda, for it held a ring of truth, but still she said, "Why is it always me who's got the problem?"

"I'm not the one who showed up here with *your* former man."

"So you *did* pursue Terrence."

Exasperated, Shereen blew out a ragged breath. "No, I didn't. And this isn't about Terrence. This is bigger than that. Look, I've got to go."

"Yeah, you do that. You call him."

"I am not going to call him."

"But you want to."

Shereen grumbled in response. "You don't get it." After a moment, she added, "We made a promise to each other, to never let a man come between us again. As much as it hurt me that you were engaged to my ex, the only man I ever loved, I kept that promise. *You* didn't. You never had any intention of keeping it."

"You're admitting that you want him."

"Oh, grow up!" Shereen shouted. "God, I don't want to have this conversation. I can't deal with you."

"You can't deal with anyone, can you? Not if you can't have everything your way. Sweet Thang, who's always used to getting what she wants."

There was dead air for a long while, and Yolanda wondered if Shereen had hung up. But finally she spoke. "You told me once that Terrence didn't tell you why he broke up with me in college. Is that true?"

Yolanda heard a desperateness in her voice, and her heart suddenly ached to tell her friend the truth, but she couldn't give her what she wanted. If she told the truth now, Shereen would never understand.

So instead she said, "God, your ego amazes me."

"Forget it. Good-*bye*." Shereen hung up.

Yolanda held the receiver to her ear for several seconds, her mind swirling with a million thoughts. She'd wanted a fight, and she'd gotten it, but this one wasn't like the ones they'd had in their Howard dorm.

This time, she wondered if she'd gone too far.

Blown it.

But Lord help her, she was too stubborn to call Shereen back and set things right.

Shereen slammed the receiver down and emitted a loud cry. She'd had enough of Yolanda, enough of her jealousy, enough of her lies.

Still, it hurt like hell. She had loved her as a sister, had wanted to give her the benefit of the doubt.

You told me once that Terrence didn't tell you why he broke up with me in college. Is that true?

Shereen had practically begged her, in that moment, to tell her the truth. *Please tell me the truth,* she'd almost added, but hadn't. Yolanda knew how much the truth meant to her, and the fact that she didn't come clean proved one thing. Yolanda had wanted to hurt her. She couldn't mistake Yolanda's response for sincerity by any stretch of the imagination.

Why? That's all Shereen wanted to know. Didn't Yolanda realize that she was much more important to her than Terrence? Terrence hadn't even given her a chance to defend herself when he'd heard she was cheating on him. That, as much as she wished she could blame it on Yolanda, was his own fault. If they'd talked back then and straightened things out, their relationship could have been saved. But he hadn't given her the chance.

He was hardly worth their friendship.

But this really wasn't about Terrence. He had merely become a pawn in this game of Yolanda versus Shereen, and for the life of her, Shereen didn't know how she'd gotten caught up in it.

At times like this, she didn't even know how she and Yolanda had become friends.

Pain stabbed at her heart, at her soul, when she remembered how they'd become friends. Despite Yolanda's sharp tongue, Shereen had grown to love her, because she'd easily recognized that Yolanda's feistiness was actually a cover for a heart of gold. More than any of the Fabulous Four, Yolanda had been there for her when her brother had gotten into that devastating accident that had almost cost him his life. Jessica and Ellie had been too emotional to deal with her pain, but Yolanda had been strong, taking her to the hospital when she hadn't been able to drive. Yolanda had also gone to all her professors and gotten her assignments when all Shereen had been able to do was cry.

Shereen squeezed her eyes tightly shut. Why did that memory hurt so much?

She knew why. How could someone do all that for you, be there for you when you needed her the most, yet deep in her heart truly resent you?

Much later, Yolanda lay in her bed, the covers pulled up to her neck in the air-conditioned room. For over an hour, she had lain very still, staring into the darkness, asking herself a million questions.

Tonight more than any other, she missed the presence of a man in her bed. She was alone. And she was lonely.

But it wasn't so much a man she wanted as she wanted something to erase the ache in her heart.

It didn't matter how self-sufficient she acted, how together she pretended to be. When push came to shove, she knew that she wasn't.

She'd had a lot of time to think since her argument with Shereen. They'd argued about Terrence, but he wasn't really the issue. Yolanda knew that, deep in her heart. He was merely a way for her to test Shereen's friendship, her loyalty.

Yet that made no sense, because the reality was, Shereen had every reason to be pissed with *her* for getting involved with Terrence. Yolanda had always claimed that she hadn't done it to hurt Shereen, and consciously she hadn't. But subconsciously? She had to wonder. The answer was locked in a dark, cold place in her heart, a place she rarely opened because it held feelings she didn't truly understand.

But like Shereen had said, this whole thing wasn't about Terrence. Hell, Yolanda wasn't even upset about their breakup. Which she should be—if she really, truly was in love with him. Instead, she felt an odd sense of relief.

Nor were her problems with Shereen about Lawrence, that horny little fool whom no woman in her right mind would pine over. No, it was about testing the limits of their friendship because Yolanda had always been afraid to trust it, to believe that Shereen, a girl who'd come from the right side of the tracks, who'd had everything growing up while Yolanda had had nothing, could really, deep down in her heart, love and accept her unconditionally.

Finally, a tear streamed down the side of her cheek, past the top of her ear, and into her hair.

God, she was pathetic. A loser. She needed a shrink.

She'd pushed James away with her tough-as-nails attitude. She'd pushed Terrence away.

And now, she was pushing Shereen away. Yolanda seemed hell-bent on making her deepest fears a reality. Yet knowing this didn't give her power. It made her feel helpless.

Why push away the very ones who loved you the most? It didn't make sense.

To protect your heart.

Her mind wandered to her parents, to their failed relationship. Was that where her problems had started? With her father? Was it as simple—and as complicated—as that?

She remembered her father's words at his house. He'd more or less said that something else had happened in her parents' relationship, something she knew nothing about. Instead of listening, she'd completely ruled out the possibility. Because if there *had* been another reason for the divorce, something she hadn't known, it would mean that all this time, all these years, she might not have been fair to her father. And that thought, that possibility, scared her to death.

For it would mean she was wrong.

Still, wrong or not, she suddenly realized that she had to know. She couldn't go on until she did.

Saturday was two days away. In two days, she would see her mother.

And she would learn the truth, once and for all.

Chapter Twenty-seven

THE TRUTH WAS THERE, surrounding her, but like a haze of smoke, she couldn't grasp it.

Pieces of memories—or questions, maybe—came to her in dreams the last two nights, and each morning she had awoken with the feeling that there was something she should know, something significant she had missed concerning her parents.

If her mother didn't work nights, Yolanda would have seen her before the weekend. Because all she'd been able to think about was the truth that kept eluding her, not her work at the firm.

Her mother lay on the sofa, her eyes closed, her body still, when Yolanda entered the apartment. Panic, quick and devastating, winded her.

Yolanda rushed to her mother's side. "Mama!"

At the sound of Yolanda's voice, Edna stirred. A wave of relief washed over Yolanda. God, she'd thought the worst without any reason. It was a pattern that summed up her life.

Contentment filled Edna's eyes. "Yolanda."

"Are you okay, Mama?" Yolanda still needed to be sure.

"Mmm-hmm. Just tired."

Normally, Yolanda would let her mother rest and come back another time, but today she couldn't. She needed answers, and while she could get them from her father, she needed to hear the truth from her mother.

"I thought you were busy with some big case."

"I was. I am."

"But you still came by to check on me."

"Not really, Mama," Yolanda said. There was no point beating around the bush. "Mama, I have to ask you something."

Edna sat up and dropped her feet to the floor, her joints cracking as she moved. Once again, Yolanda thought of how much her mother had aged in the last sixteen years.

"Your father told me you might want to talk."

"Daddy spoke to you?"

"Mmm-hmm."

If her mother had just told her that she'd had an affair with the Pope, Yolanda couldn't have been more surprised. Until this moment, she'd held on to the hope that her father had been lying about there being some other reason for the split, but the fact that he'd called her mother meant there was definite truth to his claim.

"It's time," Edna continued, "that you know the truth. I had hoped that as the years passed you would get over your anger toward your father, mostly because I was a coward." She stroked Yolanda's cheek, gave her a rare smile. "But you're so protective of me."

"Of course I am, Mama." Someone had to look out for her.

"And I love you for that, I really do." She sighed, a weary sound, full of burdens. "And I know, on some level, I encouraged your anger toward your father. Not directly, but because I never did the right thing to stop it."

Yolanda was confused. "Mama, what are you talking about?"

"The truth. The fact that I hid it from you all these years. Because it was easier that way. And you were all I had." Edna's voice cracked, and the sound broke Yolanda's heart. "I didn't want to lose you. . . ."

Yolanda wrapped an arm around her mother's shoulder and pulled her close. "Mama, you would never lose me."

"Look at how you turned against your father."

"That's because he hurt you—"

"No, that's what I'm trying to tell you. Your father didn't hurt me. I hurt him. And I hurt myself."

"That doesn't make sense."

Her mother wept softly. "Even now, it still hurts. I know it shouldn't, but it does."

"What, Mama?" Had her mother committed some crime? Yolanda couldn't imagine her mother doing anything so horrible for which she felt deeply ashamed. For it was shame Yolanda heard in her sobs, saw in her eyes. "Whatever it is, I'll always love you. You have to know that."

Edna wiped away her tears and inhaled a sharp breath. "I will tell you this once, then I never want to talk about it again."

"Sure." God, what could it be?

"Sixteen years ago, I told your father I wanted a divorce."

"Why? Was he cheating on you?"

Edna dismissed that idea with the wave of a hand and a huff, as if the idea were completely ludicrous. "I was never in love with him. Sixteen years ago, I told him I never would love him, and I wanted to end our marriage. He begged me to change my mind, but I wouldn't. It had been pointless, almost from the beginning. Except for you."

Her mother wasn't making any sense. "Did Daddy tell you to say this? Are you saying this so I won't be mad at him anymore?"

"You're not listening. Or maybe I'm just not explaining myself. No, I guess I'm not. Yolanda, I was in love with someone else."

"That's crazy." How could that be? Yolanda would have known.

"It's the truth. We were supposed to get married, but he got someone else pregnant and married her instead."

This wasn't her mother. This was someone else. Someone or something had possessed her mother's body.

"In those days, he really had no choice. I understood that. But I always held on to the hope that one day he'd come back to me. Then I got pregnant and had you, and I was all right. For a while. But I met Arthur by chance when you were about thirteen, and we started talking again. I realized I was still in love with him."

"You had an affair?" Yolanda almost choked on the words.

"No, not physically, but mentally, yes. Emotionally, all I could think of was Arthur. Divorces had become more common, and he told me that he'd never been happy with his wife because he still loved me. He told me he was going to leave her. I was elated. My life was finally coming together."

"Daddy knew this?"

"He knew something was wrong. When he married me, he knew that I'd been in love with someone else, but for whatever reason, he loved me despite that. We all grew up in the same area, and when he learned that Arthur was marrying someone else, he figured he had his chance with me.

"When I married your father, I wanted things to work. I prayed about it every night. For a while, I thought I'd learned to love him, until I met Arthur again."

"You were going to leave Daddy," Yolanda said, but she was like a robot, merely repeating the words without any feeling. "What happened?"

A soft sob escaped Edna's lips, as though the pain was raw, fresh. But it was, Yolanda realized. Her mother had never gotten over it.

"Your father kept asking me what was wrong. So I told him that I was leaving him for Arthur. Never, as long as I live, will I forget the look of pain in his eyes. It was the first time I saw him cry."

"Daddy?" Again, Yolanda couldn't believe what she was hearing. She'd never seen her father shed a tear in all the years she'd known him.

"Yes. He didn't want to lose me. But I'd made up my mind. I was going to take you and leave."

"Why didn't you?" Glancing down, Yolanda saw that her mother was wringing her fingers painfully. Yolanda placed a hand on them to stop her.

Edna's hands stilled. "I met Arthur at a coffee shop one day, prepared to discuss our future." Edna paused. "He told me that he couldn't leave Carol. She was pregnant again.

"I know it was irrational, she was his wife, but I'd stopped sleeping with your father, and I'd assumed he'd stopped sleeping with her. So this was . . . devastating. He said he still loved me, would always love me, but with two children, he didn't think it was right to leave.

"And your father, bless his heart, when he found me in a heap on the bedroom floor, bawling like I was going to die from the pain, he actually comforted me, even though he knew I was crying over another man."

Yolanda wanted to say something, but her mother's story had her mesmerized, both horrified and fascinated at the same time.

"I didn't have to tell him. He knew. And despite all that, he told me he still loved me and we could work things out." The tears fell freely down her face now, and Yolanda reached for a Kleenex off the coffee

table and wiped her mother's tears away. "I told him no. I couldn't go
on living a lie anymore."

"But what about Gloria? He married her only months after your divorce was final." Yolanda had always assumed he'd been sleeping with
her while married to her mother.

"I don't remember where he met Gloria, but she was the best thing
that happened to him. She saved him, I think, because for a while he
thought he couldn't live without me, the way I thought I couldn't live
without Arthur. The difference was, I couldn't. I was a mess for months.
I couldn't take care of you, much less myself."

"So that's why Daddy had me for four months?" After Yolanda had
taken care of her mother for a few months, her father had come to
remove her from the apartment. At the time, Yolanda had thought her
father had taken her in some crazy custody battle. And she'd resented
him for it, because her mother had been so depressed and needed her;
without Yolanda, she'd have no one to take care of her. Why was it
only now that she could see the sense in it, that her father had been
looking out for her because her mother had been emotionally crippled?
Instead, she'd used the separation from her mother as more reason to
be angry with her father.

"Yes. But when he told me how angry you'd become, how unhappy
you were, I realized I had to snap out of my depression. For you. But
I never forgot about Arthur. Never stopped loving him."

"Even now?" It seemed impossible. But, good God, it made sense.
Like a puzzle with missing pieces, it was all fitting together.

"Yes. Even now, though he's dead and gone. He died of a heart attack
four years ago."

Four years ago. That was exactly when her mother had inexplicably
retreated into an impenetrable shell. Her mother had stopped calling,
stopped visiting, stopped answering her phone. The times Yolanda had
called and actually reached her, Edna barely uttered two words. And
the few times she'd seen her on her trips from Philadelphia, Edna was
distant and desolate. Yolanda had concluded that her mother didn't like
James.

"A part of me died all those years ago when Arthur ended our relationship, but when he passed on . . . I wanted to die, too."

Yolanda didn't understand this. Her mother's feelings for Arthur were more like obsession than love.

"So you see, your father did his best, given the circumstances. Oh, Yolanda, I should have told you before . . ."

"It's okay, Mama." Though the truth was, it wasn't okay. God, all this time she'd been angry with her father, almost to the point where love had turned to hate, and it had all been based on a lie. So much could have been avoided if her mother had told her the truth years ago.

Which made her think of her father. He'd had opportunity after opportunity to tell her the truth—and justifiably so—to help douse the flames of her ire. But he hadn't. He'd chosen instead to protect her mother.

Like a man who still loved her.

"Oh, God," Yolanda blurted out, emotion overwhelming her, threatening to suffocate her.

"I'm sorry." Edna took Yolanda in her arms. And Yolanda held on to her, like a lifeline, no longer the tough girl she'd always tried so hard to be. For right now she didn't have to be that girl, she just had to be herself, the girl who'd had so many questions and no real answers. The girl who'd been afraid to trust, afraid she'd always lose the ones she dared to love. So she allowed her mother to hold her, to sway her, to comfort her, while the child in her and the woman she'd become finally, after all these years, had a good, long cry.

Chapter Twenty-eight

"WHEN WILL I SEE YOU again?"

"I'm not sure, baby."

Ellie frowned while she watched Richard dress, but more out of habit than because she was actually upset. It was weird—and she knew she was screwed up—but having gone full circle with Richard, from being his once-in-a-while lover to a more serious partner back to his once-in-a-while lover was somewhat comforting. And at least she felt a sense of control.

The moment of panic she'd suffered a while back when he'd told her that maybe they should end things was one of the worst moments of her life. So now, while she didn't see him as often as she wanted to, and while they weren't looking for houses and she didn't have a ring, she wasn't worried. She knew Richard wasn't going anywhere.

He was almost as pathetic as she. He couldn't last long without her body any more than she could last long without his.

Yeah, they were both a pathetic pair. But Ellie would do anything to avoid that feeling again, where her whole body had broken out in a cold sweat and she'd felt sick enough to throw up. He didn't like pressure, so she wouldn't pressure him.

Richard's marriage would be over soon enough; even if his wife didn't know about her, she knew he was spending several nights with another woman. Who knew if she still wanted him despite his infidelity, but Ellie had no doubt she'd get over that. Sooner or later, she'd kick his ass to the curb.

The same way Ellie should kick his ass to the curb. Yet she couldn't. How had she let this man get under her skin?

She ignored that thought as Richard gave her a chaste kiss good-bye.

When he was gone, Ellie brushed her teeth, stripped out of her negligee, and ran the water for a shower. She was just about to step into it when the phone rang.

A grin broke out on her face. She wondered if Richard had forgotten something or if he was simply calling to tell her that he loved her. Probably the latter. He'd been doing that more these days since she'd stopped pressuring him about their future.

Go figure.

She didn't even bother with her bedroom voice, she felt that much in control. "Hello?"

Then, seconds later, "Oh, my God. Oh, my God!"

She was in a tunnel, long and dark and filled with haze, with no glimmer of light. She whirled around and around, reaching for something solid, something to hold on to, to help her find a way out.

"Ellie."

"Huh?" She glanced to her left. Found Shereen staring at her.

"We're here."

Slowly, Ellie looked around. They were at the departure terminal at BWI airport in Baltimore, outside of American Airlines, but for the life of her, Ellie didn't remember a moment of the drive from Washington.

"Your flight leaves in forty minutes. You have to check in."

Ellie managed a nod.

"God, hon. You look so . . ."

Ellie closed her eyes, fought the tears. She had to be strong, or she'd never make it to San Antonio. "I'm okay."

"You're all set. You just have to give your name at the counter and you'll get your boarding pass."

Ellie squeezed Shereen's hand, but it was as much for her own comfort as it was to express her thanks. "I don't know what I'd do without you. I'll pay you back."

Shereen arched one perfect eyebrow as a crooked grin played on her lips. It wasn't a doubtful look, but rather a look that said when it came to their friendship, there was nothing Shereen wouldn't do for her.

Shereen reached into her purse and extracted her wallet. Pulling out several bills, she stuffed them in Ellie's hand.

"No, Shereen. You've done enough."

"Take it. God knows you need it."

Ellie didn't argue; she did need the money. "Thank you."

"You have a credit card?"

"Yeah."

"Then I'll call and make a car rental reservation for you. My company gets an excellent rate with Dollar."

Though Shereen was right beside her as she called from her cell phone, Ellie didn't hear a word she said. She stared out the window, watching the other passengers exiting cabs and cars, hugging loved ones good-bye.

Were any of them rushing to see a mother who was suddenly on her deathbed?

"Are you sure you're okay to go there by yourself?"

Shereen's voice pulled Ellie from her thoughts. "I have to be."

"Because if you're not, and you need me to go—"

"No, Shereen. I know you're busy." Though the offer alone was like a ray of sunshine on the bleakest of days, and Ellie loved her for it. Her only wish was that her father could pick her up from the airport, but she hadn't been able to reach him. No doubt he was by her mother's side, encouraging her to hang on with words of love.

"Call me when you get there. Let me know how your mom's doing."

Ellie still couldn't believe the call she'd received, that her mother had been in a head-on collision and was now in serious condition. She prayed she'd make it. Ellie couldn't lose her—at least not without having the chance to say good-bye.

"I should have gone home ages ago." Guilt, like a snake, wrapped around Ellie's heart. "Why did I wait so long?"

"Oh, sweetie. Don't do this to yourself."

"You're right. It won't change things." She had avoided going home because she'd always felt like a failure. Both her parents were doctors. She was a thirty-year-old college graduate with no clue where her life was going. She could never answer her parents' questions: *Why don't you have a job? What are you doing with your life?*

"Thanks for taking me to the airport."

"Girl, please."

"No, I know you had an important meeting this morning." It was at least a forty-five-minute trip to BWI from Shereen's office, even longer during rush hour. Shereen wouldn't make it back to work until the afternoon. "I tried to reach Jessica, but she wasn't home."

"I still can't believe she quit her job."

"Neither can I."

Opening the door, Shereen stepped out onto the pavement. She reached for Ellie's small travel bag in the backseat.

Ellie exited the passenger side and rounded the car to Shereen. She took the bag from her. "Thanks."

Shereen gave her a quick hug. "You'd better go. Call me. Or call Jessica."

Shereen never mentioned Yolanda these days, but right now, Ellie was too concerned about her mother to ask what had happened. So, instead she said, "I'll call you."

"Love you, sweetie."

"Love you, too."

At the San Antonio International Airport, Ellie didn't bother with the rental car. Instead, she took a cab to St. Luke's Baptist Hospital. Her body was so cold and numb, she hadn't stopped shivering on the plane. With her nerves all jumbled, she knew there was no way she could drive.

The meter read twenty-two dollars as the cab pulled into the hospital's driveway. Ellie handed the driver forty bucks and was out of the car almost before it came to a complete stop.

"Your change," she heard him say, but she simply shook her head and hustled to the emergency ward doors.

Ellie was about to walk through the automatic doors when the sound of anxious voices startled her. She whirled around to see paramedics rushing toward her with a gurney. She jumped to the side and let them whiz by. A person lay on the gurney, very quiet, very still. She didn't know if it was a man or a woman, because all she could see was a bloodied face. The sight of the body brought reality crashing down on her shoulders. God, her mother was really somewhere in this place, fighting for her life.

She had to get to her.

Everywhere there were people, some crouched on their haunches, their faces buried in their hands. Some huddled together, softly crying. Some leaning over loved ones who lay on gurneys, holding their hands, whispering words of comfort. Others still sat in the large waiting area, sick or injured and waiting to be seen.

Oh, God.

It was the smell that always got to her. The smell of sickness and death, not at all camouflaged by the sterile hospital scents.

She made her way to the information desk, asked the woman who sat there where Cynthia Grant was. And learned that her mother had been in emergency surgery.

Emergency surgery. Oh, God.

The woman directed her to the ward where her mother was now resting in a private room. No, she didn't know how the surgery had gone, but Ellie could ask the doctor if he was available.

Ellie was back in the tunnel, surrounded by darkness. Only when she heard good news would the light return.

Cynthia Grant, the poised and elegant woman Ellie had always known, was barely recognizable as she lay on a hospital bed with bandages wrapped around her head and tubes coming out of her face and arms.

Her condition, thank the Lord, had improved dramatically and she'd been upgraded from serious to stable condition. Ellie had been by her side for hours. At times she had stirred as the anesthetic wore off, but she hadn't fully awakened.

Ellie had prayed for the best while trying to mentally prepare herself for the worst. What she wasn't prepared for was the fact that her father was nowhere to be found.

He worked at Methodist Hospital as a surgeon, and while she'd first thought it likely that he could be in surgery, she now had to wonder why he wasn't by her mother's side. Even delicate surgery couldn't last this long, could it? She didn't know; she'd never gone to medical school as her parents had hoped and she had no clue about medical matters.

But that didn't ease Ellie's mind. It was late evening; if her father had been working at the time of the accident, surely he would be finished by now. So where was he? Out of town? Yes, that made sense. Maybe he was at some medical conference and couldn't be reached.

Which meant there was nothing she could do to find him. For now. But at least she was here for her mother.

And as soon as her mother woke up, she would tell her where her father was. Then Ellie would call him and he would come home.

Swirls of light penetrated the darkness, like two arms reaching for her, wrapping around her, lifting her up.

Ellie's eyes popped open. She glanced to her left. Sunlight spilled through the large window, bathing her in light.

She remembered where she was at the exact moment she realized that she'd actually gotten some sleep. Her head whipped to the right.

Cynthia smiled at her.

The smile was pure sunshine, and it embraced Ellie, filled her with warmth. Immediately, she was at her mother's side. "Ma."

Cynthia moved a hand across the bed, but she was too weak to lift it. "Baby."

Ellie lifted the hand, pressed it to her cheek. Her mother wiggled a couple of her fingers. Barely, but it was enough to let Ellie know she was alive and kicking.

Fighting.

"How're you feeling?"

"Oh, I've been better." Her voice was a whisper, but it didn't waver. Another good sign.

Ellie was so happy she wanted to cry. But suddenly she remembered her father. "Ma, do you know where Dad is? No one's been able to reach him."

Cynthia looked away as something—discomfort, sadness maybe— flashed across her face.

"What's the matter, Ma? You don't know where he is?"

She moved her head, only barely, but it looked like a nod.

"Ma, I don't understand."

A moan escaped Cynthia's lips as her eyes fluttered shut.

Ellie stared down at her. Even with her eyes closed, her expression was still pained.

The effort to speak had exhausted her. Ellie would let her sleep. Later, when Cynthia woke up again, Ellie would deal with finding her father.

When Cynthia woke up hours later, she immediately asked for food. Such a simple, ordinary thing to ask for food, but for Ellie, it was proof that her mother would be okay. If Cynthia Grant had her appetite back, then she was well on the road to being her normal self.

While she was no longer groggy from the anesthetic, Cynthia still suffered discomfort. But the nap had done her a world of good and she was in much better spirits.

Which is why Ellie found it strange that her mother hadn't asked for her father. As Cynthia had eaten her meal, Ellie had waited for her to mention him. She hadn't. Then, she'd figured her mother would ask about him after the doctor finished examining her. Still, she hadn't.

Was it possible her mother wasn't concerned because she thought her father was at work? Ellie didn't know, but she knew it was high time she located her father.

"Ma?"

"Yes, darling?"

"I brought this up before but you were too out of it to talk. No one has been able to find Dad." Before she even finished her statement, her mother made a face. Ellie studied her a moment, then frowned. What was going on? "Is he at a conference or something? That's all I can think of, because I've left messages for him at home, but he hasn't shown up and he hasn't called. Do you know where to reach him?"

"Don't bother."

Ellie was taken aback by her mother's blunt response. "What do you mean, don't bother?"

"Your father is out of town."

Was Ellie mistaken, or was there a hint of bitterness in her mother's tone? No, that didn't make sense. Maybe her father was at an important conference and Cynthia didn't want to bother him. Still, he should know his wife had been in a serious accident. "He needs to know what happened to you."

Cynthia rolled her eyes.

Ellie could no longer ignore the negative vibes her mother was sending out. Something serious was going on. Something Ellie didn't understand. Her mother was raising all kinds of questions but giving no answers. "I've got to tell you, Ma, I'm completely confused."

"I'm sure you are." Cynthia didn't meet her eyes.

"Ma?" Ellie spoke almost desperately. Cynthia finally looked at her. Her eyes were serious, intense. Almost grave. An eerie feeling passed over Ellie, leaving a chill in its wake. She reached for her mother's hand, found it as cold as she suddenly felt. "My God, Ma. What is it?"

"I'm leaving your father."

Ellie couldn't have been more stunned if her mother had announced she was gay. Harvey and Cynthia Grant, the perfect society couple, were getting a divorce? No, this couldn't be true. The doctor had said her mother hadn't suffered any brain injuries, but perhaps he was wrong. Her mother's bizarre statement must be related to the accident.

"I know what you're thinking." Cynthia's lips twisted in a crooked grin. "That I hit my head and went crazy. I assure you I didn't."

Ellie was only mildly relieved. Because if her mother was in control of her faculties, that left her more confused than ever. "I don't understand."

"Even if I wanted you to contact your father, I couldn't tell you where to find him. All I know is that he's somewhere in the Virgin Islands."

"You and Dad are having problems?"

"That's an understatement."

Ellie suddenly felt like a prodigal daughter, or worse, a stranger. She didn't know her parents anymore. Harvey and Cynthia had always been a loving, happy couple—at least that's the appearance they'd projected to the world. And to her. Had she been blind all these years?

"So, you and Dad are having problems, and he's in the Virgin Islands for what, some R and R? To give you both some space—"

"He's there with his little slut."

Cynthia's words were like a slap in the face, that's how much they stung Ellie. She opened her mouth, but try as she might, she couldn't find a voice for the thousands of questions tumbling in her mind.

"He has a *girlfriend*." Cynthia said the word with distaste. "Some twenty-four-year-old volunteer at the hospital."

"He—Dad told you that?"

"She's not his first."

Oh God, oh God, oh God. "No."

"It's true. I lived with it for years, out of shame. I didn't want anyone to know. But this accident . . . Life is too short. I can't accept his infidelity anymore."

Her father was vacationing with his girlfriend, a woman younger than his own daughter. Dr. Harvey Grant? It didn't seem possible, let alone plausible.

But the bitter look on her mother's face told her that it was indeed true.

Ellie remembered phone calls with her mother over the past months, how she'd sounded like something was bothering her but wouldn't say what. Lord help her, it all made sense now.

Anything but this, God. Anything but this. Ellie's eyes went heavenward. In that instant, she was hit with the glaring parallel too obvious to ignore.

She whimpered.

"I know it's a shock," her mother said. "And you're probably wondering why I put up with it. I certainly didn't need him for money. I don't know what to say other than I believed in my marriage vows and always prayed he would change. But when he didn't, I slowly started to fall out of love. Now I'm ready to move on."

"Oh, Ma."

The always stoic Cynthia put on a brave smile, even as her eyes brimmed with tears.

If this was divine intervention, Ellie had certainly gotten the point.

Rebirth.

It's a beautiful thing.

Like a caterpillar emerging from a cocoon, perhaps confused at first, but finding it has an exquisite set of wings. Wings that will make it a better being, because now it can do more than simply crawl; it can fly.

Rise.

Thousands claimed they were reborn after traumatic or near-death experiences, and now Ellie knew that such claims were true.

Her mother had been reborn. In the days since she'd been released from the hospital, not only was she doing much better than her doctors had expected, she had also reclaimed her life in a way that Ellie could only admire. She was flying, rising above her old life and the burdens that had weighed her down. Soaring. Ellie hardly recognized her mother.

Ellie had helped her move from her posh Elm Creek home and into an apartment one quarter the size. While Ellie had advised her to speak with a lawyer first, Cynthia had assured her that she didn't care about Harvey's money; she didn't need it. She didn't need anything from him in order to go on with her life. She needed only herself and her pride. She had both.

But it wasn't only her mother who had been reborn. It might not have been life-threatening, but her mother's admission that her father had been unfaithful for most of their marriage had affected Ellie as profoundly as if she'd been zapped by a lightning bolt. She'd known at that moment, right there in the hospital room, that she had to change her life.

James had cheated on Yolanda, and Ellie had known it was wrong, but that betrayal had not affected her as acutely as learning of her father's infidelity. Perhaps because Yolanda had always presented a strong, tough, impenetrable facade, Ellie had ignored the deeper level of devastation such a betrayal in marriage can cause.

Maybe it was seeing her mother, a woman who had always been elegant and composed, on the verge of tears. That and the fact that her father's betrayal was so hard to accept. These were her parents. They were supposed to love each other forever. Her father wasn't supposed to cheat on her mother once, let alone several times. He was supposed to love her as wholeheartedly as Ellie did.

The fact that he didn't had left Ellie shaken.

So, she had been reborn that day when she heard the news, and now that she'd returned to Washington, she knew it was time. Finally, once and for all, she was going to put Richard behind her.

And to do that, she had to see his wife.

She needed to be shocked into reality, much the same way she'd been shocked by her mother's news, by putting a face to Richard's wife. It was the best way she could figure to finally set him free.

Though she'd never been to his house, she knew where Richard lived. She'd looked him up in the white pages. Sometimes when she'd been home alone and missing him, she'd been tempted to drive by his place. Just to see what it was like. What his family was like. Did he play outside with his children? Did his wife sit on the porch in the evenings? Did she plant a garden in her spare time? In the end, Ellie had been too much of a coward.

Besides, it had been easier to pretend that his wife didn't really exist. If Ellie didn't know whom she was hurting, how could she be doing anything wrong?

It was mid-afternoon when Ellie pulled in front of Richard's posh town house in Georgetown. Her stomach fluttered with a burst of nervous energy. Now that she was there, she wasn't exactly sure what she was going to do. She hadn't come to tell Richard's wife about their affair. Just to see her, to know she was real.

She stared at the house, waiting for some type of sign, until she realized how ridiculous that was. If she was going to do this, then she should just do it. Before she could chicken out and drive off, Ellie pulled the keys from the ignition and hopped out of the car.

She didn't stop moving until she reached the front porch. She rang the doorbell.

Waited.

Richard's wife was a homemaker, that much she knew, so unless she was at some appointment or out with the children, she should be home.

As Ellie reached for the doorbell again, she heard the sound of footsteps. She quickly dropped her hand to her side. The door opened slowly, and Ellie held her breath.

Richard's wife was a beautiful woman, shorter than Ellie by a good few inches. Her coloring and the angle of her eyes said she had Asian blood somewhere in her background. Ellie had hoped to hate her on sight, but the woman's face lit up with such a genuine smile that it was impossible for Ellie to feel anything but an immediate and profound sense of guilt.

Why would Richard cheat on her? She seemed beautiful both inside and out.

"Hello," the woman almost sang, and Ellie's stomach sank to her knees. All right—she'd come, she'd seen, she knew the woman was real. Yet she couldn't leave. Not yet.

"Hello, Miss . . . ?"

"Mrs."

Ellie forced a smile. "Oh."

"Can I help you?"

"Uh . . ." She scrambled to come up with a reasonable explanation for being at this woman's door. She hadn't thought of what she would say, only of what she wouldn't say. "Do . . ." *Think, Ellie, think!* "Do you . . . believe in Jesus?"

"Yes." Richard's wife nodded and opened the door wider to step onto the porch. "Yes, I do."

"Good. That's good. Well . . . I'm here to . . . I'm a Jehovah's Witness, and I just wanted to come by and spread the word." *Lame, lame, lame!*

Richard's wife didn't find her lame, however, because she said, "Oh, that's wonderful. I'm a Baptist. But I believe there's only one God, so no matter what your faith, we're all brothers and sisters."

"Yes." Ellie crossed her arms over her chest, feeling like a big fraud. *Though shalt not commit adultery,* came into her mind.

"Would you like to come in?"

"Oh . . . No, that's okay. Since you're a believer."

"I've just made some cinnamon rolls. Fresh out of the oven."

Food, her one weakness besides sex. And damn if she didn't need some sugar badly right now. "Well, all right then."

"I'm Katy," Richard's wife said as Ellie followed her into the house.

God, she even looked like a Katy.

Katy faced her. "You are?"

"E-uh, Cindy." Nervous giggle. "Cynthia really, but my friends call me Cindy."

"I'm a Katy. Not to be confused with Kate."

While Katy headed into the kitchen, Ellie surveyed the walls in the hallway. If she'd wanted to deny it before, she couldn't any longer. Richard and Katy were everywhere: in their huge wedding picture and numerous family portraits.

"Come on back," Katy called.

What am I doing? This is nuts. Yet she did as Katy told her, walking on wobbly legs to the back of the house and the kitchen.

It was exactly the kind of house she would have liked, each room with its own distinct character. The kitchen was painted a pale pink, with a wallpapered border filled with colorful fruits. It had a center island with a sink, exactly the type she would have liked if she and Richard had gotten a house together.

She'd wanted Richard, but he belonged to someone else.

"Sit, please."

Ellie sat at the small wooden table near the back door, while Katy placed cinnamon rolls on a plate.

"One? Two?"

"Huh?"

"Cinnamon rolls?"

"Oh." God, here she was sitting in the woman's kitchen, as if they were friends. The bad thing was, she liked Katy. Which made the fact that she'd been screwing her husband for almost a year especially difficult. "Two."

"Coffee? I know it's late, but it's fresh. I like a cup in the afternoon."

She was nothing like this woman, Ellie realized. Katy was a small thing, skinny as hell, flat-chested. As a person, wholesome. Sweet. Way too trusting. Who in their right mind let strangers into their houses in this day and age?

Ellie couldn't help wondering if Richard been attracted to her because she was everything his wife was not. She wasn't wholesome, far from it. She'd had her share of men, always hoping that one of them would be Mr. Right. Katy had probably dated only Richard. Hell, she'd probably been a virgin on her wedding night. Did Ellie satisfy Richard's wilder, kinkier side?

That sudden thought bothered her, because it made her wonder if all men would want only one thing from her.

He's there with his little slut. Ellie heard her mother's words once more, but she heard them with Katy's voice, as if *Katy* was calling her a slut.

"Cindy?"

"Hmm?"

"Coffee or juice?"

"No, I'll have juice." She *was* trying to eat a healthier diet.

"Orange okay?"

"That's fine."

Seconds later, Katy placed the plate and glass of juice on the table, then settled into the seat next to her. Ellie didn't want to get stuck answering questions she couldn't—namely questions about the Jehovah's Witness faith—so she said, "That's your husband in the pictures?"

Katy beamed. "Yes."

Ellie grabbed a cinnamon roll. "How long have you been married?"

"Ten years."

"You seem . . . happy." Ellie devoured half the roll in one bite.

"Yes. Very. We went to Hawaii for our anniversary last month."

So that's where Richard had gone when he'd disappeared. He'd told her he had to go away on business.

Ellie polished off the roll, but it stuck in her throat, just above where her heart was lodged. She washed the roll down with the juice, but she couldn't wash away the lump of emotion.

"I take it you don't work outside the home."

"Nope. I'm a mom and a wife." She giggled, and Ellie forced a laugh as well, though nothing about this situation was funny "My family is my world."

"That's wonderful. These days, it's rare to meet someone with a firm sense of family values." *Hypocrite.*

"You are so right. I tell you, the world is a mess. Children don't get enough attention and love at home." Her petite shoulders rose and fell. "I'm blessed to have a husband who can provide for us so that I can stay home and do the best to properly raise our children."

"Amen to that." A pain shot through Ellie's chest, and she reached for the second cinnamon roll. "So, you and your husband—you're happy?"

"Oh, yes. I thank God every day for our wonderful marriage. What about you? Are you married?"

"Me? Naw." Pause. "But I was involved with someone recently. It didn't work out."

"I'm sorry," Katy said, sounding truly sincere. "From everything I hear, dating isn't easy these days, but hang in there. You'll find Mr. Right."

Ellie shot to her feet, taking the cinnamon roll with her. She couldn't stay here and listen to advice from Richard's cute, virtuous wife, who had no clue how much of a slimeball her husband was. "I, uh, I have to go."

"Oh." Katy sounded genuinely disappointed.

"Yeah. I have to go. You know, spread the word."

"Of course."

"It was nice talking to you. Enlightening."

"Really?" Katy smiled. "Well, if you're ever in the area again, please do drop by."

Ellie reached for her hand to shake it, but Katy surprised her with a hug. She'd been sleeping with the woman's husband, and here she was, hugging her.

She stepped out of Katy's embrace.

"Would you like another cinnamon roll? Maybe a couple for the road?"

"Yes," Ellie replied without hesitation.

She was going to need them.

Chapter Twenty-nine

HE WOULDN'T GO AWAY.

Shereen had avoided Terrence for weeks. Rudy was under strict instructions not to forward his calls. So was Shaun. She hadn't responded to his numerous messages, and on the two occasions he'd reached her at home, she had quickly ended the conversation. She had hoped that he would get the picture and simply disappear. Yet he kept calling. Kept leaving messages saying he needed to see her.

Just because Terrence was no longer with Yolanda didn't mean he could pick things up where he'd left off with Shereen. In fact, *because* he had been involved with her friend, and because for some reason Shereen still felt bound by their pact even though Yolanda hadn't honored it, she had told herself that if she never saw Terrence Simms again it would be too soon.

If only her heart would agree with her brain.

After weeks of pressure, she'd finally buckled yesterday when he'd called her at work. Rudy had said, "Talk to him, Shereen. If for no other reason than to tell him to stop calling." So she'd spoken to him, and much to her chagrin, she'd realized how much she missed him.

That's how she found herself in the lounge area of the Willard this evening, waiting for him to join her for dinner.

She was on her second glass of wine when she saw him approach. Her reaction was always the same at the sight of him; her heart did a little dance and her breathing got shallow. She wished she didn't have any reaction to him, much less a sexual one, but Lord help her, he was fine. Even across a crowded room, she could feel his sexual energy.

Shereen didn't rise when he reached her. Instead, she sat coolly at the bar, one leg crossed over the other, ample skin revealed through the skirt's side slit.

There was nothing cool about Terrence's reaction. Shereen could see the fire in his eyes as he drank in the sight of her. "Wow. You look beautiful, baby."

"Terrence, don't call me that. I'm not your baby." Yet her heart went into overdrive.

A smile played on his lips as he stared at her, as though he didn't know whether or not to take her seriously. But when she continued to act as cool as a cucumber, his smile faded. "I thought you wanted to see me."

"*You* wanted to see *me*." Though the truth was, she wanted to see him, too, even if she hadn't been able to admit that to herself until now.

"Shereen, don't be like that."

Shereen glanced at the bald pianist. Not because she was enjoying the romantic tune he was playing but because she needed to break eye contact with Terrence. The pianist smiled at her.

She turned back to Terrence. "Ever since you came back into my life, it's been a mess. Yolanda and I aren't talking."

"And you blame me?"

"Yes," she said quickly, then, "No. No, I don't." She'd love to blame her problems with Yolanda on one tangible thing, but she couldn't.

"Then what's the problem?"

"How many years has it been since we were an item? Do you really expect me to believe you've still got a thing for me?"

"Is that the problem?" He stepped closer and leaned an elbow on the bar. "You don't believe me?"

"You walked away, Terrence. Because you chose to believe a lie rather than my love for you."

"I was young, stupid."

"You didn't trust me."

"I was young, stupid."

"I don't see how a few years changes anything."

"It's been more than a few years. Trust me. I've changed."

Her eyes met his in a silent challenge, and when he didn't back down, a jolt of electricity shot through her. She reached for her wine, stared at the rose-colored liquid. "Why now?"

"Because I'm still in love with you."

Damn. Shereen sipped her wine, slowly, hoping it would calm the erratic beating of her heart.

"I made reservations in the Willard Room for dinner, but I think I'd prefer we go upstairs."

She should feel offended at his presumptuousness, yet all she could feel was excitement. "You got us a room?"

"I'm living here. For now."

"You . . . you are?"

"Until I find a place." He shrugged. "Or until I decide whether or not I'll stay."

"I see."

"Do you?"

She did. He would stay in town if she wanted him to stay. It was up to her.

"We can order room service. It's very good."

"It should be," Shereen replied flippantly. "Do you know how much this glass of wine cost?"

He ignored her attempt at humor and stood tall, giving her a serious look. The look unnerved her, and she downed the dregs of her wine.

He extended her an arm. "So, are you coming?"

It's the wine, she told herself when she stood and accepted his arm, steadfastly refusing to acknowledge the voice that whispered to her, *Stop fighting it. You know you want him.*

Later, Shereen was no longer blaming the wine.

And she wasn't at all surprised that before she and Terrence had had a chance to order any food, they'd fallen into bed. The sparks between them were as hot as they were undeniable, even after all this time.

Making love with Terrence again had made their time apart seem like days, not years—that's how right it felt. And the sex had been fabulous, better than with any of the lovers she'd had over the years since their breakup.

You're still in love with him, she'd realized as they'd climaxed together. Oh, she wished she could block out that voice. It would be so much easier if she felt nothing for Terrence. But how could she continue lying to herself?

Now, she lay in the crook of his arm, staring at the ceiling in the dimly lit suite. Though she wanted to, she didn't regret what had happened.

But that didn't mean she wasn't confused.

Terrence stirred, planted a kiss on her temple. It was a comforting kiss, much like the ones he'd given her years ago, and as much as she wanted to savor it, she instead felt a mix of conflicting emotions. She had loved this man so much once. But times had changed, and so had they.

"What are you thinking?" he asked.

She was silent for a long moment, so long he had to ask the question again.

"About us."

"What about us?"

She didn't lie. "I don't know about this."

He shifted so he could face her. "What's not to know? We still connect. There's no doubt about that."

"There's more to life than sex." Even spectacular, toe-tingling sex.

"I'm not talking about sex."

She eyed him warily, but even in the darkness she saw the truth on his face. He really did still love her. "This isn't an easy situation."

"It seems simple to me. You want me or you don't."

"And what about Yolanda?" Shereen hadn't planned to mention her, but now that she had, she realized how much she wanted to know about their relationship.

Terrence had been trailing his fingers up and down her spine, but at her question, his hand stilled. "What about her?"

"You were going to marry her."

"That was the plan," he said softly. "I really can't tell you how we got to that stage, because when I think about it, I know we rushed things. I guess it's because we had a lot in common. We got along."

"You thought you could build a marriage on that?" It hurt to hear about their relationship, more than she'd anticipated, but she couldn't stop the questions.

"I didn't really think past the fact that we got along well. We could talk. She's ambitious; so am I. She told me about her ex, how he'd cheated on her . . ." His voice trailed off.

"Did you ever discuss me?"

"Yes, but only briefly."

Shereen said, "She's the one who told you about Brad."

"Yes."

God, as much as she'd known it had to be Yolanda, hearing the truth from Terrence hurt. A lot.

"Yolanda and I talked about this when we met again. Just once, but she had the chance to tell me that she was mistaken. Instead, she let me continue to believe that lie."

"Maybe she figured it wouldn't make a difference now."

"I think she knew that it would."

Yeah, Shereen could see that. The insecure Yolanda who wasn't sure Terrence would still love her if she told him the truth.

But Terrence's statement was about more than Yolanda's insecurity. And Shereen's head was spinning so hard, she didn't know what to think. He was saying all the right things. Or, at least the things she wanted to hear. "So, you both got along well and you asked her to marry you."

"She asked me."

Shereen actually smiled at the thought that Yolanda had proposed to him. "God, she's always gotta be in control."

"One day she said that we'd make a good team. I hadn't been seriously involved with anyone since Howard, and I wanted to settle down, so I figured why not? But when I saw you again, I knew I hadn't gotten over you."

Shereen wanted to ask if he thought Yolanda had pursued him to hurt her, but that would be unfair. Besides, as she'd told herself over and over, her problems with Yolanda weren't really about Terrence.

"Were you in love with her?"

"I never stopped loving you."

It was the answer she'd prayed she'd hear. Needed to hear. If he had been in love with Yolanda, that would change everything. But what would Yolanda say if Shereen and Terrence got involved again?

Given everything that Yolanda had done, why did she care?

"I need some time to think," Shereen announced.

"I understand." He tightened his arm around her waist, and her body flooded with heat. "But right now, can we spend the night not talking?" He kissed her nose. "Or thinking?"

"Just doing?" Shereen giggled. It was amazing how comfortable she felt in his arms, even after all this time.

"Yeah, something like that."

Terrence pulled her close and covered her lips with his.

Chapter Thirty

FALL IS SUCH A MAGICAL time.

Magical in the way the leaves change color, from vibrant green to brilliant orange and magnificent red. Magical in the way the atmosphere seems calmer, more peaceful than the hectic summer.

A magical time to fall in love.

Jessica stood on the back porch, looking out at the maples and oaks, listening to the lulling rhythm of their leaves rustling in the wind. There was a chill in the air today, but she found it both refreshing and invigorating.

Since she'd worked her last day at the studio over a month ago, Jessica had stood here like this many times. Staring at nature, at its majesty, gave her hope. Made her forget that she'd given up the job she loved because somebody wanted to hurt her.

The studio executives didn't understand her decision. They had offered her more money, which she'd turned down, but that had only left them more confused. The ratings had skyrocketed with her, people loved her, wasn't she happy? She'd assured them it wasn't the network. They'd begged her to rethink her decision. She'd finally agreed to a leave of absence.

But she had no plans to go back. Because while she missed her job, she hadn't received a single letter from her stalker since she'd left. Her mail had been forwarded from the studio, and all of it had been from fans who missed her.

Wrapping her arms around her torso, Jessica made her way down the back porch onto the grass. She looked up at the magnificent array of golds, oranges, and reds sprinkled through the leaves of the maples and oaks in her vast backyard. And as often happened when she came out here for solace, her mind drifted. Drifted to the past and her secret. Drifted to a place she didn't want to go because someone wouldn't let her forget.

It had been an early October day so many years ago, much like this one, when she'd fallen in love with Andrew Bell.

Andrew.

She closed her eyes, willing the memory away. What good would come of remembering how they'd fallen in love? That love had been wrong and it had led to her greatest pain. She only hoped that his ghost would stop haunting her now that she'd given up the job she so loved.

She wanted, finally, to reclaim her sense of security.

She hated that it had been taken away from her. Her utmost wish was to go back to the time when she didn't think of Andrew every day. She didn't want to find him in everything that was good in her life, like watching ducks swim in her backyard pond, or feeling Douglas's arms creep around her in the middle of the night. She wanted her life back. Yes, she regretted what had happened with Andrew. She always had. Always would. But the past was the past, she couldn't change it, and she wanted finally to move on.

Inhaling the scent of fall, Jessica turned and headed for the front of the house. She'd check the mail, then go inside and start dinner.

A scream rose in her throat when she saw her car, but it got trapped there, and for a full three seconds she couldn't breathe. Her knees gave out and she stumbled, falling onto the concrete.

No! Oh God, no!

She had to get up. Had to get away. Adrenaline shot through her veins, giving her a surge of strength. She heaved herself off the ground and scrambled to her feet.

Then she turned and ran into the house, not daring to look back.

The flash of light made her scream. Then terror gripped her as her eyes flew open and she saw the blur of a shape. The shape of someone rushing toward her.

"Jessica! Oh, my God!"

A familiar voice, not a stranger's. *Douglas.* Sweet, sweet Douglas.

Douglas rushing toward her. Douglas dropping to the floor. Douglas gathering her in his arms, wrapping her in safety.

At last.

"Baby, what happened?"

Jessica fought the fear that held her captive. Relieved, she broke down and cried.

"Jessica, look at me." He framed her face. "What is it?"

How long had she been here? How many hours had it been since she'd closed every blind, drawn every shade, locked every door? She didn't know. All she knew was how afraid she'd been, how confused about where to go and what to do. So she'd run to the dining room and huddled in a dark corner. And that's where Douglas found her— in a quivering mass on the dining room floor.

"D-did y-y-you—" She was so cold from fear, her teeth were clattering.

"Baby." He held her tight. Gave her his warmth.

"Y-you saw it?" she finally managed. It had been years since she'd felt such paralyzing, numbing fear. She'd had just one other severe panic attack in her life.

The night she had sent her lover to his death.

"Yes, I saw it. Did you call the police?"

"N-no."

"I'll call them now."

"No." She gripped his jacket. "D-don't leave m-me."

"Someone hurt you?" Douglas's voice was full of pain.

"Just stay. With me."

Douglas lifted her to her feet, helped her to stand. His strength absorbed her fear. When she stopped shivering, he said, "Sweetheart, I know you're frightened, but I have to call the police."

This was her worst nightmare coming true. All this time, she'd wanted to protect him. But how could she protect him if the stalker knew where she lived?

"Sit here." Douglas pulled out a chair. "I'm going to the kitchen to use the phone."

He wasn't supposed to find out. Oh God, not like this. "Douglas, wait."

"It's okay now, Jessica." He helped her into the chair.

The memory of the mangled blood and fur, the corpse of some animal splattered on the hood of her car, made a shiver trickle down her spine. Had Douglas seen that, or had he only seen the word *whore* spray-painted all over her Mercedes?

"Wh-what was it?"

"I'm not sure," Douglas said, indicating he'd seen the animal. "When I saw the car . . . I just ran inside to check on you."

To make sure she was okay. He loved her so much, which made what she had to do all the more painful.

"I won't be long." Douglas took a tentative step away from her, as if making sure she wouldn't fall apart. When she didn't, he turned and hustled toward the kitchen. Her mind racing, wondering what to do, Jessica jumped up and followed him. She had to tell him before he called the police. It was time. She reached the kitchen's entrance just as Douglas picked up the wall phone. She blurted, "Don't."

He stared at her, baffled. "Don't call the police?"

"No."

"There's a dead animal on your car—"

"I—" Deep breath. "I have to tell you something."

That got Douglas's interest, and his forehead dimpled as he gave her an odd look. Slowly, he replaced the receiver, then made his way over to her.

She had to do this. There was no avoiding it. Deep down, she had feared he would find out sooner or later, and now she couldn't put it off. Not now that the threat had come to their house.

"What is it?"

"Can we sit down?"

"Sure." But he sounded confused.

Wringing her hands, Jessica led the way to the living room. Once there, she flicked on the lights, then eased onto the sofa. Douglas sat beside her.

"This is serious."

"Yes, Douglas, it is." Pause. "I've kept something from you, and I don't know what you'll think of me once I tell you."

He covered her linked hands with one of his. "Just tell me."

So she did. About Andrew and what had happened at Howard. How someone had started sending her letters at the studio months ago. How she'd quit to escape it, to protect him, but she'd failed. Someone wanted to make her pay for her past.

"The first letter came months ago?" he asked when she finished.

That he didn't first ask about Andrew surprised her. "Yes."

"And you're just telling me now?"

"Y-yes."

Douglas abruptly stood. "You didn't trust me."

Oh, God. He didn't understand. Jessica flew to her feet beside him. "I was afraid, Douglas. Afraid of what you'd think of me because of what I'd done."

"You made a mistake nearly ten years ago. Did you really think I'd hold that against you?"

"I-I didn't know what to think. Douglas, a man is *dead* because of me. How could I tell you that?"

"The one thing I asked of you was honesty. But all you've done is lie to me for months."

"I know, and I'm sorry. Believe me, I just wanted to protect you."

"Protect me?" His tone said he didn't believe her.

"Yes. Oh, Douglas, you know how much I love you. I'd do anything for you."

"Except tell me the truth."

Jessica inhaled a shaky breath. "I'm telling you now."

Douglas sighed. Such a sad sound. "Oh, Jessica."

He didn't believe her. "Douglas . . ."

He steeled his jaw. "I'm gonna call the police."

"No, wait, Douglas. Please, I know you're upset, but let's talk about this."

"This isn't the time to talk."

Her heart was breaking. "I'm sorry. I don't know what else to say."

Douglas didn't respond. Instead, he turned and walked away from her. And then he was gone.

Jessica felt forces pulling at her, dragging her into a pit of darkness. She couldn't fight them. Not now. So she curled into a ball on the sofa and prayed for her body to go numb. She didn't want to feel anymore.

◆　◆　◆

Jessica awoke abruptly, panting, her body wet with sweat. It was morning and sunlight poured into the room. She was in her bed. But she was alone.

On Douglas's pillow she saw a slip of paper.

A note. Frantically, she reached for it. Started to read.

Jessica,

I have always told you that I could deal with anything, as long as you were honest with me. To learn that you don't trust me hurts me deeply, and I don't know what to think of our marriage anymore. You have lied to me so much in this past year that I hardly recognize you. I'm going away for the weekend, but don't worry, the police will patrol the house every half hour to make sure you're safe. I left Detective Lopez's card downstairs. Please call him. I'm sorry. I know you need me, but I need to be alone right now.

Douglas

It was as she'd always feared. The worst had come to pass.

Douglas couldn't forgive her. He wanted nothing to do with her.

And the worst part was, in her heart, in her soul, Jessica couldn't blame him.

Chapter Thirty-one

JESSICA DIDN'T WANT TO alarm her friends, so when she called and asked that they meet at her place for dinner on Sunday evening, she tried to sound as upbeat as possible. "We hardly meet here," she told Shereen's answering machine. "I figure it's about time."

She left the same message for Ellie and Yolanda, as none of her friends were home. That was yesterday. Now, it was almost noon on Sunday and none of them had called her back. She couldn't help wondering what was going on.

She needed them now, just as she had needed them so many years ago.

She dialed Shereen's number.

"Hi, Jessica. I'm sorry. I meant to call you. About tonight, Yolanda's gonna be there, right?"

"Yeah."

"I hate to do this, but I'm gonna skip this one."

While Jessica had been dealing with her own problems in the last month, she hadn't communicated much with her friends. Now she realized she had no clue how everyone was faring. "You won't come because Yolanda will be there?"

"I'm not gonna lie to you. We're not talking."

"What?"

"Look, I don't want to get into it right now."

"You have to come," she said desperately. "I won't take no for an answer."

"Jessica, is something wrong?"

"Yes. And it's serious. That's all I'll say over the phone."

"What time?"

"As soon as you can get here."

"See you in a bit."

Next, Jessica called Ellie and Yolanda, who gave her similar protests about not being able to make it. Ellie said she wasn't feeling up to a get-together. Yolanda asked if Shereen would be there.

"I'm leaning on the shield, Yolanda. Please. I need you."

"Sweetie, are you okay?

"Not really."

"Oh, my God. What is it?"

"I'll tell you when you get here."

"You don't think she's sick, do you?" Ellie gave Shereen a worried look.

The two were in Shereen's car, en route to Jessica's house. Only minutes after Jessica's call, Ellie had called Shereen. "I'm too scared to drive," she'd told her. "Can you pick me up?"

Shereen had immediately headed to Ellie's place.

They'd both been speculating about what could be wrong. But Ellie's question made Shereen's body go cold with fear. "Sick? You mean like, really sick?"

"She's been acting weird for months. All this time, maybe she's been fighting some disease."

"Don't say it. God, Ellie. Don't even think it."

"I don't know what to think. She told me it was a matter of life and death."

"She said that?"

Ellie nodded.

"Shit." Shereen hit the gas, hoping no cops were around as she sped toward Jessica's house.

THE PAST

Jessica knew she should stay away, that she didn't have a right to be there, but she couldn't make herself turn around and leave. How could she be anywhere else when she had to say good-bye to Andrew?

Staring into the sanctuary from the back of the church, Jessica could hardly believe that Andrew's cold, lifeless body lay in the pine casket at the front.

"Oh, Andrew. Why did you do it?"

Swallowing a sob, she opened the back door and crept inside.

The church was packed, a testament to just how much Professor Andrew Bell was loved. Quietly, she slipped into the back row, the only place she saw a space. To her immediate left a burly white man was softly crying. It was a disturbing sight, seeing such a big man cry, and Jessica couldn't help staring at him.

Suddenly she recognized him. He was the truck driver whose rig Andrew had driven into. She'd seen him on the news.

Jessica looked away, his grief too much for her to deal with. Her eyes went to the floral-covered coffin and immediately filled with tears. It wasn't just her guilt that made her sad. Even now, she loved him. There was a hole in her heart she couldn't imagine ever being filled now that Andrew was gone. If only she could make herself believe that he'd gotten what he deserved for lying to her, maybe she could get through this, but she couldn't. Not when she'd spent the best moments of her life with him.

Jessica barely heard a word the minister said, and was surprised when the pallbearers stood and lifted the coffin. As the choir began a heart-wrenching rendition of *Amazing Grace*, the pallbearers slowly walked down the church's aisle.

Somehow, Jessica didn't fall apart.

The truck driver bawled louder when the casket passed, and his uncontrollable sobbing was Jessica's undoing. She broke down and wept, her whole body feeling the pain of her grief. She'd told Shereen, Ellie, and Yolanda not to come with her today, that she needed to be alone to say good-bye to Andrew, but she needed them now. She needed them to hold her up, because she was falling, falling into a pit of despair.

Brushing her tears, she looked up to see a woman in black walking up the aisle behind the coffin. Her arms were wrapped around the shoulders of a young girl, and the girl's arms were wrapped around the woman's waist. Both seemed inconsolable.

Andrew's wife. And his daughter. The family he hadn't told her about, until it was too late.

There they were, real. Two lives devastated, because of her. Seeing them made Jessica's pain worse.

As Andrew's widow neared her, her blood-red eyes went to Jessica. As Jessica met the woman's anguished stare, Jessica's body numbed. And then she felt a stab of cold in her heart as the woman's eyes locked on hers, narrowed.

She knows, Jessica thought. *She knows who I am.* Jessica wanted to look away, break the spell, but couldn't.

Then the daughter was staring at her, glaring at her, as if she were the very devil. . . .

Later, when Jessica returned to the dorm, she went straight to Shereen's room, where she found Yolanda, Shereen, and Ellie. They were all on their feet close to the door, as if they'd expected her to enter at that moment.

Shereen stepped forward, and Jessica collapsed into her arms.

"It's over," Jessica sobbed. "Andrew's body is in the ground."

Shereen ran a hand over her hair. "It's gonna be okay, hon. From now on, everything will be okay."

Jessica pulled back from Shereen, looking at her with disillusion. "No, it's not okay. And it's never going to be okay again. I have to live with myself, with what I've done. I'm not sure I can do that."

"Jess." Yolanda released a weary breath as she moved toward her. "Oh, sweetie. I'm so sorry. I wish we could turn back the clock."

"So do I," Shereen said.

"We all do," Ellie added. "We're all gonna live with this."

Jessica wiped at her tears and glanced around the room. It looked different, even though she'd seen it thousands of times. Nothing seemed the same anymore, not with Andrew dead.

"I wish this was a nightmare," Jessica said, wandering farther into the room. "That I'd wake up and this would be a nightmare."

"Why don't you sit?" Shereen suggested. "You've had a rough day."

"I don't want to sit."

"We can order food," Ellie suggested. "Maybe a pizza. With anchovies."

Whirling around, Jessica shot Ellie a mortified look. "Pizza? I just came from the funeral of a man I *killed,* and you want to order a pizza?"

"I . . . I . . ." Ellie stammered. "I just meant, you have to eat."

"I think that's a good idea," Yolanda said.

Jessica looked at all of them in turn, feeling as if she suddenly didn't know them. They didn't get it. They'd never get it, because they hadn't loved Andrew the way she had.

"Tell us what you need," Shereen said softly, a tear running down her face.

"I need . . ." A sob escaped Jessica's lips. "I need Andrew."

Guilt overwhelmed her, and Jessica turned and hugged her torso. She walked toward the window and stared out at the sky. It was gray and bleak, just like how she felt.

Forcing in a slow breath, she rested her head on the cold window-pane. She wanted to slink into a dark hole until she was all right again.

But that wasn't going to happen. She knew she would feel horrible forever, and knew she deserved to feel this way.

"We want to help you," Yolanda said. "What do you need?"

"No one can help me," Jessica replied softly.

She felt a stab of pain in her belly then, an all-too-real reminder of the piece of Andrew she still carried.

His child alive inside her while he was dead.

God help her.

"Maybe you should see a doctor," Ellie suggested. "Get something to help you sleep."

"Yeah," Shereen agreed. Then she moaned. "I still can't believe this."

Jessica didn't say a word, and for several moments everyone was silent, absorbed in their own grief and guilt.

Suddenly Ellie said, "Jessica."

Jessica started to turn and face her friends, but she felt another sharp cramp and rested the side of her head against the window. The pain . . . Jessica tried to force in steady breaths, but couldn't.

"Jessica." Ellie's voice held a note of concern. "Oh, hon, you don't look so good."

Jessica cried out as another sharp pain burst inside her abdomen.

Yolanda hurried to her. "Jessica, what is it?" Then, "Oh, my God. You're bleeding."

Shereen ran toward her. "Oh, shit. Jessica!"

"It hurts," Jessica managed as she gripped her stomach, fighting the blinding pain.

"Call 9-1-1!" Yolanda yelled.

"My baby . . ." Jessica wailed. "Oh, please, no . . ."

But her cries were useless. The life inside her was dying, the only piece of Andrew she had left.

And right now, Jessica wanted to die, too. . . .

The phone rang, jarring Jessica back from the past to the present. Her heart raced frantically from the memory of Andrew's funeral and her miscarriage, and she was thankful to find herself in the familiar surroundings of her home.

The phone rang again.

"Douglas." Jessica jumped up from the chaise and ran to the phone on the other side of the living room. She hoped, prayed, it was him.

"Hello," she said, breathless from her sprint. She waited, no answer. "Hello?"

The dial tone sounded in her ear.

Jessica frowned. How many times had the phone rung while she was sleeping? Had the person calling hung up, thinking she wasn't home?

Or . . .

A chill passed through her as Jessica replaced the receiver. She hurried to the front door and peered out the window beside it. A cruiser was parked in front of her house.

She rested her forehead against the cool window, feeling a modicum of relief that she was safe, even as her heart ached over missing Douglas.

"Girl, you've got me worried out of my mind," Yolanda said, pacing the living room floor in front of Jessica, who sat on a sofa. "Can't you tell me now?"

"Not until Shereen and Ellie get here. I only want to say this once."

"That bad?"

Jessica gave a slight nod. Though already, she felt better with Yolanda there. She'd feel even better when her other friends arrived.

After she'd read Douglas's note, she'd had a good, short cry, then realized that she had to take action. If not for herself, then for him. To protect him before this situation got any worse.

All last night, as she'd slept alone, she'd thought about everything that had happened in the past several months. And she'd realized that only one person could be doing this.

The doorbell rang, pulling Jessica from her thoughts. "Can you get it?" she asked Yolanda.

Yolanda flashed her a look that said she was expecting a lot, but she trudged out of the living room nonetheless.

The doorbell sounded a second time before Yolanda could open the door. When she did, Shereen's eyes immediately met hers, and a moment of discomfort passed between them.

"Hi," Shereen said tightly.

"Hey, you two."

"Please tell me Jessica isn't dying," Ellie said, stepping into the house.

Yolanda's eyes widened in horror at the thought. "God, I don't know. She hasn't said anything. She wanted us all to be here."

"Oh, no." Ellie whimpered.

Yolanda led the way to the living room, and Shereen followed behind her and Ellie. Shereen wouldn't be anywhere else—not when Jessica needed her—but it was weird to be there with Yolanda for the first time since their fight. Two enemies coming together for a mutual friend.

"Where's Shereen?" Jessica asked the question just as Shereen rounded the corner to the living room. She smiled when she saw her. "Oh, good. You're here."

"Of course." Shereen gave Jessica a warm hug.

Everyone watched Jessica stroll to the bay window and peer outside. Everyone waited, watched, and when Jessica didn't speak, Ellie asked in a frightened whisper, "Jessica, are you dying?"

Jessica whirled around, faced them. "No. No, of course I'm not dying."

"Then what's going on?" Shereen asked.

"This . . . this is about Andrew."

"Andrew?" Shereen, Ellie, and Yolanda spoke at once.

"Andrew Bell?" Yolanda asked for clarification.

Jessica nodded.

Yolanda looked confused. "How can this be about Andrew?"

Jessica walked from the window toward the sofa and love seat where her friends sat. "Someone knows everything. About our affair, that I was pregnant. That I cried rape."

"What?" Shereen stared at her in horror.

"Several months ago, I got a letter," Jessica began, then told them the whole story about the letters and implied threats, and finally about the animal on her car Friday night. It had really been a toy, a mutilated stuffed cat mixed with ground beef and ketchup, but Jessica hadn't known that when she'd seen the mess on her car.

When she finished her story, she was crying softly. "I finally had to tell Douglas the truth. How could I keep it from him any longer? But he left me yesterday. He thinks I don't trust him, and the truth is, I didn't. You can't have a marriage without trust, can you?" Jessica released a shaky breath, trying to maintain control. "I don't know what to do."

"He'll be back," Shereen assured her. "He loves you."

"He's hurt. Trust has always been a big issue for Douglas—that's why his first marriage failed. I honestly don't know if we can work this out."

"Douglas is no fool," Ellie said. "He knows you're the best thing that ever happened to him."

"I hope so," Jessica said, but her voice said she doubted it. "God, I'm so afraid. I thought this would all end when I quit. But whoever's doing this is serious. He or she came to my house, knows where I *live*. The animal wasn't real, but I know it was a warning. What if the next time this person hurts me? Or Douglas?"

"What did the police say?" Shereen brought a hand to her neck. The thought that there was a real threat to Jessica's life was too horrifying to contemplate.

"They think it was a prank, but just in case it's some obsessed fan, they're patrolling the house on a regular basis."

"Sweetie, why didn't you tell us about this before?" Yolanda asked.

Jessica looked at each of her friends in turn. Swallowed, but the painful lump in her throat wouldn't go away. "It took me years to forgive myself for sending that man to his death. Years to forgive myself for involving you all in the lie. I didn't want to involve you again. But now . . . I need you. Douglas thinks I don't trust him, but I was trying to protect him. Maybe you'll all be mad at me, too."

"We wish you would have told us," Shereen quickly replied, standing. "But we're not mad at you."

"Yeah," Yolanda seconded. She stood, too, followed by Ellie. "We should have been there for you. We're your girls."

Jessica's arms trembled as she extended her hands, reached for her friends. They were there for her, had always been. They were her safety net. Every time she fell, they caught her.

Shereen took one extended hand, Yolanda took the other. Ellie pressed a hand over both Shereen's and Yolanda's.

United.

For her.

"I know we've all been caught up with our own lives lately, our own problems." Shereen glanced at Yolanda, met her eyes, then looked at Jessica again. "But we're here for you. We're gonna see you through this."

"Yeah." Ellie offered her a comforting smile. "As long as you're not dying or anything, we can deal with it."

"And first things first, we've gotta find out who's doing this to you," Yolanda said.

"Remember how upset I got at the strip club?" Jessica's eyes wandered to Yolanda's. "When you mentioned Andrew, I panicked. Because if you'd said something to someone else, let the truth slip to one of our sorors, it could have been *anyone* sending the letters."

"I swear I never said anything to anybody."

Jessica considered her words. "If none of you said anything, then only one thing makes sense. It has to be Andrew's widow." She paused. "But somehow, that doesn't seem right. She's got to be in her late forties, early fifties. I can't imagine her coming here and spray-painting my car, much less doing that whole thing with the stuffed cat."

"After all this time?" Shereen frowned. "I can't see that either."

"You never know," Ellie chimed. "A woman scorned . . ."

"Why now?" Yolanda placed her hands on her hips. "She hasn't done anything in years."

"I never even heard from her when all this happened," Jessica said. "And that's when she would have been angry."

"You never know what a woman can do when she's been hurt. Who knows? Maybe it took her all these years to finally snap."

"Ellie could be right," Yolanda agreed. "I've seen cases like this."

Jessica had to be sure. "I know I asked you all this before, but please, think hard. And this isn't about laying blame. It's about trying to find out the truth. Did you tell anyone, *anyone,* even a lover, about what I did?"

"What *we* did," Yolanda stressed. "We all went to the dean with the story that you'd been raped."

"Yolanda's right," Shereen agreed. "Hell, we all practically coerced you into saying that's what happened."

Ellie added, "We're all in this up to our ears."

At that moment, Jessica's heart couldn't have been filled with any more love. Her friends refused to let her take all the blame, even though she'd gotten them into the whole mess by turning to them for support. They'd done what they could to protect her, because they loved her, never knowing the devastation her lie would bring.

Yolanda made a face. "You said the letters sounded like stuff you'd written to Andrew, or what he'd written to you?"

"Yes."

"Then it's someone who was close to him."

"Maybe another professor," Shereen offered. "Oh, God. What if he was seeing someone else?"

"I never thought about that."

Ellie shrugged. "It's possible. With men, you never know."

"It's Mrs. Bell," Yolanda insisted. "It's gotta be. If Jessica wrote Andrew letters, she probably found them after his death. Where would a lover find them? No, it's Andrew's widow."

Jessica had come to the same conclusion. Mrs. Bell had lost the most and could still be bitter, even after all this time.

But what if they were wrong?

"So." Jessica swallowed. "What next?"

"I'll find her," Yolanda announced. "Then we'll pay her a visit. Put an end to this crap once and for all."

There were agreements all around, and as Jessica watched and listened to her friends, a smile twitched at her lips. After a moment, it fully exploded.

She wasn't alone.

She never would be, not while her three best friends in the world still had breath.

Chapter Thirty-two

THE MEETING AT JESSICA'S had been awkward to a degree, but at least Yolanda had come out of it with a purpose. A purpose was what she had needed for a while, something to concentrate on beside her own problems. Because her own problems had been weighing her down, and she hadn't yet figured out how to deal with them.

James had called her. A few times. Despite the fact that she'd hung up the time she'd mistakenly dialed his number, he had known it was her. And that had been all the initiative he'd needed to get in touch with her and try to resume a friendship.

Much to her own surprise, Yolanda found she actually wanted to talk to him. She'd thought her feelings for James had died long ago, but hearing his voice, chatting casually with him, had proven to her that she was wrong.

Then, there was her father. It was hard to undo years of bitterness overnight, but at least they were talking. They had a long way to go, and while it was difficult, Yolanda was taking steps in the right direction to salvage their relationship.

Difficult steps, both with her father and with James.

And then there was Shereen. Seeing her again, Yolanda had realized how much she missed her. She wanted their friendship back. She'd be a better friend this time, a wiser one. One who didn't let her own fears and insecurities destroy their relationship. But Yolanda wasn't sure Shereen wanted anything to do with her.

So absorbing herself in Jessica's problem was exactly what she needed right now.

Yolanda had been in court most of the day, assisting a senior partner with an attempted murder trial, but she'd asked a clerk to track down

Doris Bell, which, in the end, had been easy; she was listed. She lived in Anacostia, in the southeastern part of D.C. It was one of the city's poorer neighborhoods. Maybe that explained her sudden bitterness toward Jessica—she had run out of resources while Jessica was rising to fame. Anxious to tell Jessica her news, Yolanda called her the moment she returned from court.

"I found her," Yolanda said when Jessica answered the phone.

"God, you did?"

"Mmm-hmm. She's in Anacostia."

"The southeast."

"Mmm-hmm. Not the best of neighborhoods. Which may explain her motives."

Jessica blew out a frazzled breath. "I can't believe it."

"I told you I would find her." Yolanda smiled, happy that she was able to help her friend. "I say we go there today."

"Today?"

"The sooner the better."

"Yes, that makes sense." Pause. "Oh, Yolanda. What if she truly is crazy?"

"Sweetie, I guarantee you, she won't be crazy enough to mess with me."

"No." Yolanda could hear a smile in Jessica's voice. "I don't think so."

"Let's do this. All of us." The thought of seeing Shereen again had Yolanda nervous, but she'd deal with anything to help Jessica. "We're all in this together. Will you call Ellie and Shereen?"

"Sure. It's probably best that we all meet at my place. Everyone can park here, then we can head to Mrs. Bell's place in one car."

"Good idea," Yolanda agreed.

"All right. I'll see you after work."

"Okay."

"And Yolanda."

"Hmm?"

"Thanks."

"Girl, don't even mention it."

"Hey," Yolanda said when Jessica opened the door for her. She'd gone to Jessica's place straight from work, and it was now a few minutes after six.

"Hey." Jessica smiled as she hugged her.

Yolanda looked beyond Jessica's shoulder as the two separated. "Everyone here?"

"Ellie's here. I couldn't reach Shereen, but I did leave her messages at the office and at home."

"Did you try her cell?"

"Yeah, but it wasn't on."

"I'm sure she'll be here," Yolanda said. She and Jessica started toward the living room. For a brief moment, Yolanda wondered if Shereen would be a no-show because of her. Just as quickly, she dismissed that thought.

Shereen would be there. For Jessica.

About thirty minutes later, the doorbell sang. Jessica jumped up from the love seat. "That's gotta be Shereen."

She hurried out the living room and to the front door. Nerves tickled her stomach at the thought of confronting Mrs. Bell, but it was something that had to be done.

The smile on Jessica's lips flattened when she swung open the door and didn't see Shereen. "Denise." She looked at her with surprise. "What are you doing here?"

Denise gave Jessica a hundred-watt smile. "Hi."

Denise had never come to her house before. This must be serious. Jessica immediately thought of Douglas. "Denise, is something wrong?"

"Wrong? Oh, no. Well, nothing out of the ordinary." Denise fidgeted from one foot to the next. "Uh, Douglas forgot some papers and Phillip wanted me to bring them over." She looked past Jessica into the foyer. "Is he here?"

"No," Jessica answered, once again feeling a void in her heart. At least Denise hadn't come to bear bad news.

"Maybe I should come in. Show you what Phillip needs so you can explain it to Douglas."

Jessica opened her mouth to protest, but Denise was already stepping into the house. Denise glanced around the large entranceway. "Wow. Nice place."

"Thank you. About these papers—"

"It'll only take a minute." Denise reached into the large tote bag she carried. "They're right here."

Denise passed a large manila envelope to Jessica, but she let it go before Jessica fully grasped it. It fell to the floor.

"Sorry," Denise said.

Jessica bent to retrieve it. "No problem. Look, if these papers are really impor—" Jessica's words died in her throat as she stood. A tremor passed through her entire body, rendering her cold.

Denise had a gun on her!

"Denise—"

"Shut up," Denise snapped.

The nervous, klutzy girl was gone, replaced by someone Jessica had never seen before—someone full of anger and hate.

Jessica held up a hand cautiously and repeated, "Denise."

"Shut the fuck up!"

Jessica was almost too baffled to be scared. What the hell was going on?

"Open it." Denise gestured to the envelope with her semiautomatic handgun. "Go on."

"Hey, Jess. What's taking you—" Ellie stopped short as she saw Denise. Screamed when she saw the gun.

Denise's eyes darted frantically from Jessica to Ellie. "Who are *you*?"

Yolanda came running into the foyer. "Is everything—" She stopped. "Oh, shit."

"Shut up. All of you!" Denise glared at Jessica, her nostrils flaring. "Are you having a fuckin' cocktail party?"

"N-no," Jessica stammered.

"How many more people are here?"

"No one." Jessica stared at Denise, confused. "Denise, I don't understand."

"Everyone into the dining room." No one moved, and Denise angrily barked, "Now!"

No one said a word as they filed into the nearby dining room. Jessica turned to glance at Yolanda, and when she did, Denise shoved her harshly. Jessica fell forward, as did the envelope.

Yolanda reached for Jessica and caught her before she hit the floor. Then she turned to Denise. "You psychotic bitch—"

Denise extended her arm and firmly held the gun on Yolanda. Her finger went to the trigger. "What did you say?"

"Denise, no!" Jessica stood tall and sheltered Yolanda's body with hers.

Denise's lips twitched, her eyes narrowing, her expression hardening. "It isn't smart to call someone with a gun psychotic, now, is it?"

"Please," Jessica begged.

Denise's expression softened a little, and exhaling deeply, she lowered the gun. "Tell your friends to shut up. This doesn't have to be hard—if everyone cooperates." Then she gestured to the envelope. "Pick it up."

Jessica did as she was told.

"Now open it. And read it."

Her hands trembling, Jessica opened the envelope and extracted the pile of papers. She looked down at the top sheet.

Today you pay the price for your sins.

Jessica's head whipped up to Denise. She stared at the younger woman, into her dark brown eyes. *"You?"*

Denise raised the gun on her, but her hand shook. "Don't look at me like that."

Yolanda glanced at Ellie, who was quiet and looked scared. Then she turned to Denise. She said softly, "Will you please tell us what's going on?"

"You're the one who sent me the letters," Jessica stated in a bewildered tone.

"What?" Denise chuckled sardonically. "Stupid little Denise couldn't possibly outsmart you, right? Well, I did. And today is your judgment day." She looked at Ellie and Yolanda. "I didn't plan on killing anyone else, but I can't very well leave any witnesses, now, can I?" Her eyes went back to Jessica. "More innocent lives lost because of you."

"Look," Ellie began gently, "I don't know what's going on—"

"That's right, fatso, you *don't.*" Denise leveled the gun on her. "So shut up!"

"This is about Andrew." Jessica spoke calmly, as though she wasn't scared to death. She looked at her friends, whose faces said they were as confused and scared as she felt. Once again, she looked at Denise. "Why?"

"Take a good look at me. Do I remind you of anyone?"

It was the way Denise spoke, and perhaps a familiar timbre in her voice, a voice Jessica hadn't heard in years, that made a chill creep up Jessica's spine.

Oh, God. It wasn't Mrs. Bell who was harassing her. It was Andrew's daughter.

"You're . . ." Jessica's voice faltered. "Andrew was your father."

"Bingo."

Funny, the few times Jessica remembered that Andrew had a daughter, she thought of her as a young girl. But naturally, that young girl had grown up over the years.

"My name is Denise Audrey Bell," Denise said, filling in the blanks. "Ten years ago, you killed my father. That's why I'm going to kill you."

Chapter Thirty-three

"YOU'RE ANDREW'S DAUGHTER?" ELLIE'S voice trembled as she spoke.

"My father was a good and decent man." Denise ignored Ellie and spoke directly to Jessica. Her voice broke. "He didn't deserve what you did."

"This is crazy," Yolanda muttered.

The gun flew to her. "You. *Shut* up. This is between me and Jessica."

"You've involved all of us now," Yolanda countered.

"Yolanda, please." Jessica extended a hand to her and squeezed it. "Denise is right. This is between me and her." She looked at Denise. "So please, let them go . . ."

"No." Denise almost sounded apologetic. "I can't."

Jessica's hands started sweating and her heart rate accelerated as her breathing came in quick spurts. She felt the beginnings of a panic attack, but she fought it. For Douglas, for her friends, she had to be strong.

"Denise, I—I'm sorry."

Denise cackled. "Oh, that's good. Now that I have a gun to your head—"

The phone rang.

Jessica jumped. So did Denise.

After a moment, Denise recovered. She looked at Jessica, who looked at her.

"I should get that," Jessica said. "It's probably Douglas on his way home—"

"Liar! I know Douglas isn't coming home. I heard him and Phillip talking. I know he left you. Thank God he figured out that you're really an evil bitch."

Jessica was rendered speechless. God, if Denise knew that she and

Douglas were having problems . . . No wonder she'd come here tonight.

"It could still be him," Jessica added. "Calling to see if I'm okay. If I don't answer the phone . . ."

"You still think I'm stupid, just like you thought I was stupid years ago."

Jessica's forehead scrunched as she regarded Denise. The woman truly was crazy. "I didn't know you years ago."

"You didn't think anyone would question your story," Denise went on, "but I knew my father would never have raped you. He was a good man, and you took him away from me." Her face contorted in pain as she held the gun with both hands. "Say it. Say he didn't rape you."

Jessica's eyes filled with tears. "No, he didn't rape—"

"But he lied to her," Yolanda quickly interjected. "If he hadn't—"

"I told you to shut up!"

"If you're going to bring up the past, then you deserve to know the truth," Yolanda continued, unfazed. "Believe me, I know what it feels like to believe something all your life, only to find out things aren't what you thought they were. Your father never told Jessica that he had a wife, a family. If he had—"

"Stop it. *She's* the whore. *She* seduced my father." Her gaze went to Jessica. "I saw all the letters you'd written my father in a box at the cottage. There were some notes he'd written to you but never sent, and I realized he never sent them because he felt guilty for getting involved with you. For being weak when you seduced him. But you continued to seduce him away from us."

"You're wrong," Ellie said, and Jessica's heart filled with warmth. She loved Ellie and Yolanda for defending her. "Jessica was a virgin before she met your father. She only got involved with him because he lied to her. He told her he was single, that he was in love with her."

Denise covered her ears. "Stop it."

"I'm sorry, Denise." Jessica's voice was raspy. "I never meant to hurt you."

"Too late," Denise replied, once again angry. "You need to be punished."

"Fine. Punish me. Not my friends."

"We're not going to leave you," Ellie said, her voice never wavering. Jessica gave her a thankful look.

"That's right," Denise said. "You're not going to leave. Because no one's going anywhere."

"Come on, buddy." Shereen gave the horn a quick blast when the driver before her paused too long at the light. "Move."

She'd missed Jessica's calls; she'd been in a meeting that lasted most of the afternoon and had ended late. Now, she was en route to Jessica's house. She hoped the gang hadn't headed off to Mrs. Bell's place without her.

She reached for her cell and punched in Jessica's number again. Again, it rang until the answering machine picked up.

"Why aren't you answering?"

Frowning, Shereen hung up and continued to drive. They had to be there. They wouldn't do this without her.

"I really ought to get that," Jessica said when the phone rang again.

"Leave it."

"Please. It could be Douglas." Jessica whispered a silent prayer that Denise would acquiesce. If it was Douglas, she could alert him to the fact that everything wasn't fine. At least if she could get to the front door on her way to the phone, she could see if a cruiser was outside. If there was one, she could try to get the cop's attention. "He'll be concerned if I don't answer."

Denise bit her bottom lip as she considered Jessica's request. After a moment, she shook her head. "No. If the phone was in this room . . ." The ringing stopped. "There. No need to worry now."

Jessica whimpered.

"Oh, are you sad?" Denise taunted her. "Don't worry. It'll all be over soon." Denise's gaze went to Ellie and Yolanda. "First, you need to tie up your friends. You have any rope?"

Jessica felt a sinking feeling in her gut. The seriousness of the situation hit her with renewed vigor. If she tied up her friends, how would they ever get out of this?

She threw a worried glance at Yolanda and Ellie. Yolanda gave her a tight nod. Jessica answered, "There's rope in the garage."

"No," Denise said immediately. "We'd all have to go . . . and that's too risky. You must have panty hose."

Jessica nodded. "Upstairs."

"Let's go." Denise jerked the gun from Jessica to Yolanda to Ellie. "Put your hands behind your heads and walk in front of me. You drop your hands, you get shot."

Ellie led the way up the stairs, followed by Yolanda, behind whom walked Jessica. Jessica's heart raced as they silently climbed the stairs. Should she turn around and shove Denise down the stairs? That was a possibility. It could work. But what if when she turned, Denise shot her?

Jessica angled her head slightly to the left, enough to see that Denise held the gun mere inches from her back.

The woman was clearly unstable, and as much as Jessica wanted to, she couldn't take the chance of trying to overpower her.

Not yet.

When Shereen pulled into Jessica's driveway, she frowned. Jessica's car was there. So was Ellie's. And Yolanda's.

If the gang was all here, why had no one answered the phone?

There was a chill in the air as Shereen got out of the car, and she huddled into her leather jacket.

But as she climbed the steps, she wasn't sure if the cold came from the night air or from within her heart. She definitely felt a weird sensation, one she couldn't explain. Like something was wrong but she didn't know what.

Shereen rang the doorbell. And waited.

Nightfall had descended on the city by the time Jessica finished tying up Yolanda and Ellie. Now, she sat at the dining room table, a pen in hand, a paper before her, and Denise standing over her shoulder.

"This is what you're going to write," Denise said. "Dear Douglas, I know that you probably won't understand my actions, but I hope you can forgive me. Ten years ago, I lied and told the world I was raped, and I've been living with the guilt ever since. This lie drove a man to commit suicide, a good and decent man who didn't deserve to have his life devastated by my selfish motives. I'm not good enough for you, and now that you've left me, I can no longer go on." Denise paused. "Why aren't you writing?"

"Uh, you're talking too fast."

Denise jabbed a finger into Jessica's hair. "Start writing."

Jessica gave Denise a sideways glance. "I have to do this in my own words, so it will sound like me."

Denise frowned. After a moment, she said, "Fine. We can do it again if it isn't right. Make sure you say that the pressure made you snap. Yeah, that's good. You snapped and that's why you killed your friends."

"No one will believe that."

"Write it, or I'll kill your friends right now. Oh," Denise mocked when she saw a tear roll down Ellie's face. "It's not fair, right? Well, this is her fault." She pointed to Jessica. "If she'd only told the truth years ago . . ." Denise's voice cracked. "I miss my father so much . . ."

The doorbell rang.

Jessica's eyes flew to Denise's.

Angrily, Denise brushed away her tears. "Who the fuck is that?"

"I—I don't know." Jessica's heart pounded with excitement. Maybe it was a police officer coming to check on her. She glanced at Yolanda and Ellie, whose eyes held the hope she now felt. They were both tied securely to dining room chairs, and they were gagged. Jessica felt horrible for that. She'd wanted to tie their hands and feet loosely, but Denise had watched her, making sure she didn't.

"Whoever it is will go away," Denise said, but for the first time tonight, she sounded really worried.

"It could be a cop," Jessica explained, hoping to keep the excitement from her voice. "They've been patrolling the house ever since you vandalized my car."

Fear flashed in Denise's eyes. "Start writing the letter."

Slowly, Jessica pushed back her chair. This was her one chance. If Denise shot her, so be it, but if she didn't go for it now, she might not have another opportunity.

"What are you doing?" Denise asked.

Jessica jumped up and ran.

◆ ◆ ◆

Shereen frowned when no one answered the door. All the cars were there; the lights were on. Someone *had* to be home.

She tried the handle. The door was unlocked, so she pushed it open.

Instantly, she saw Jessica running toward her. Her brain registered that something was wrong, but couldn't grasp anything beyond bewilderment.

"Shereen! Get out!"

Shereen barely had time to notice the woman behind Jessica before a shot rang out. It whizzed past her ear and lodged in the wall near the door.

Jessica's eyes bulged and she spun around and lunged at the other woman. Her head plowed into the younger woman's stomach, knocking her onto her back.

The gun went flying.

A surge of adrenaline drove Shereen into action, and she charged ahead, running toward the gun as it slid on the ceramic floor. But the crazy woman escaped Jessica and scurried on all fours for the gun as well.

She reached it a split second before Shereen did, wrapped her fingers around the handle . . .

Shereen kicked the woman's hand, sending the gun sliding several feet away. The woman screeched out in frustration.

Jessica growled from deep in her belly, the sound resembling a warrior's cry, as she jumped on Denise's back, forcing her face down on the floor. Denise squirmed, rolled over. Jessica's wrist hit the ceramic tile hard, but instead of pain, she felt a burst of power. As Denise tried to pin her body on top of Jessica's, Jessica kneed her in the gut.

Denise groaned in pain and collapsed onto her back. Instantly, Jessica was on top of her, wrapping her hands around her neck.

Squeezing . . .

"You want to kill me," Denise managed with difficulty, "just like you killed my father."

Jessica squeezed harder, and Denise wheezed as she struggled to suck in air. Jessica's heart beat so loudly in her ears, she thought her head might explode.

For threatening her for months, for nearly taking her life and the lives of her friends, Jessica *could* kill her.

The thought was so violent, it shocked Jessica. Her hands trembling, she loosened her tight grip on Denise's neck.

Denise coughed, started crying.

Oh, God. She could have killed her. Bringing her hands to her face, Jessica started crying, too. Crying because her lie had led to so much pain, not just for her but for the family she hadn't known Andrew had had, and also for her friends. Crying because she could no longer see an evil, demented person in Denise, but the sad little girl she'd been on the day of her father's funeral.

Crying because it was over.

She looked down at Denise, listened to her sob. Through her tears, Denise looked up and met her eyes.

For several seconds, neither Jessica nor Denise said a word. Then Jessica whispered softly, "I miss him, too."

Denise sniffled, wiped her eyes.

"I'm sorry," Jessica added. "So very, very sorry."

Jessica was startled to feel Shereen's hand on her arm then, having been so absorbed in her fight with Denise that she forgot her friend was in the room. Shereen lifted her up, and Jessica rushed into her friend's arms, hugging her tightly as relieved tears fell from her eyes.

Chapter Thirty-four

MUCH LATER, AFTER JESSICA, Ellie, Yolanda, and Shereen had completed their reports at the police station and were ready to leave, Jessica noticed Mrs. Bell exiting from a back room in the police station. Her thin face was drawn, and she was clearly distressed.

"That's Mrs. Bell," Jessica said, pausing.

Shereen put a hand on her shoulder. "Let's go."

"No." Jessica shrugged away from Shereen's touch. "I need to talk to her." Jessica was already walking down the hallway.

Jessica was aware that her friends were protesting, but she continued to walk toward the older woman.

"Mrs. Bell." Hearing her name, she looked up and met Jessica's eyes, startled. "You may not know me, but I'm—"

"I know who you are."

"Yes, of course." How could the woman forget her? "I don't mean to bother you, but if you'd give me a moment of your time . . ."

Mrs. Bell exhaled a weary sigh.

"Please."

"Go ahead."

The pain etched in the lines of the woman's face made it hard for Jessica to look at her. It was her fault that she no longer had a husband. Her fault that her daughter had been driven to commit a horrible crime.

"Mrs. Bell, I'm sorry for everything that happened ten years ago. About having an affair with your husband." Jessica's throat clogged with emotion, but she went on. "But most of all, I'm sorry for the lie I told that caused so much devastation." Jessica took a deep breath. "Your husband didn't rape me. I was angry with him when I learned he was married, and that's why I said that. But I swear, I never meant to hurt you, Mrs. Bell. I had no clue Andrew was married. If I had . . ."

"I realized that," Mrs. Bell quickly said. "In the beginning, I was disillusioned, angry. I never believed he raped you. I hated you for saying that, and yes, I did blame you for Andy's death. And maybe a part of me even wanted some kind of vengeance. But in Andy's letter to me before he killed himself, he admitted to the affair. And he admitted that he'd gotten you pregnant." Doris glanced away, then back at Jessica. "So as much as I was angry, I knew he wasn't blameless. You were so young, practically a child. No doubt scared to find yourself pregnant by a married man. I couldn't let the anger consume me. I had to go on. For my daughter." Her voice trailed off, ending on a sniffle. "I'm so sorry about what she did. If I'd only known . . . She's manic-depressive and sometimes goes through serious bouts of depression."

"Because of Andrew."

Doris nodded grimly. "Yes. That's when her problems started. She became severely depressed after his death, despondent. She just couldn't accept that he'd left us. She had to go on medication and had been taking it for years. In the last couple of years, however, she started to show great improvement. When she got a job at WGRZ nine months ago, I thought she was fine. She'd even stopped seeing her therapist since the beginning of the year, with his blessing—and she stopped taking her medication. She was hoping to live drug-free, and I supported that decision. I guess I wanted to believe she was getting better so badly that I didn't notice she was getting worse."

"I hope she gets help."

"So do I."

"If you need anything," Jessica began, reaching into her purse, "anything at all, please let me know." She retrieved a pen and paper and wrote down her number. She handed the paper to Mrs. Bell.

Mrs. Bell nodded as she accepted the slip of paper.

"Anything," Jessica repeated. "I mean that."

"Thank you."

Jessica smiled softly, then turned to walk away.

"Jessica."

She halted. Turned.

Tears were streaming down Mrs. Bell's face. "Thank you."

A warm feeling flooded Jessica and a smile lifted her lips. For with those two words, she'd finally been forgiven.

In Yolanda's car, Jessica laid her head back and sighed. "God, what a day."

"Tell me about it."

"I'm just glad it's all over."

Yolanda squeezed Jessica's forearm. "Yeah, me, too."

"I always knew this would come back to haunt me. I'm just sorry the rest of you were involved. Then and now."

"I wouldn't have been anywhere else."

Facing Yolanda, Jessica smiled. "I love you for that."

"Honestly, if we hadn't been there . . . I don't even want to think about what could have happened."

"Neither do I. Let's talk about something else. What's up with you and Shereen?"

Yolanda sighed. "We're not talking."

"I can't believe it," Jessica replied, her tone saying the whole situation pained her. "After everything we've been through, all these years we've been friends, you two are gonna stop talking now."

"I tried to talk to her," Yolanda protested, but at Jessica's skeptical look, she confessed, "All right, maybe I came on a bit strong."

"Oh, Yo."

"I wanted us to be communicating. I thought a fight was better than not talking at all."

"I say we all get together tonight. To celebrate."

"I don't think so."

"Yes. For what it's worth, Shereen's torn up over the whole thing."

"She is?"

"Of course she is. You're the one, need I remind you, who came back to town with Terrence."

"I know. But honestly, I didn't do that to hurt her."

"Then why don't you tell her that? Do you know how good I feel now, having actually apologized to Doris and Denise?"

"That's because you've always been so sweet and loving. Even when you should have been angry."

"Oh, your tough exterior never fooled me. Nor any of us, for that matter. I guarantee you, Shereen will be happy to hear from you."

"I guess I should try to talk to her." But the thought was scary. After their last argument, she'd wondered if she and Shereen would ever bridge the gap between them.

"Tonight."

"It's so late. Maybe tomorrow."

"Hasn't this whole ordeal taught you anything? Tomorrow may be too late."

"God, Jessica, I don't know."

"Tonight," Jessica repeated, forcefully this time.

Then she dug in her purse and retrieved her phone.

Chapter Thirty-five

"LET'S POP OPEN SOME CHAMPAGNE!" Ellie exclaimed. "This calls for a celebration!"

"I've got wine," Yolanda said. "Go ahead and grab it."

Ellie hopped up from the sofa. As she passed Shereen, who sat in the armchair by the window, she poked her fingers into her cheeks, telling her to smile.

"I still can't believe everything that happened," Shereen said. Jessica was the reason she was here at Yolanda's home tonight, especially this late. None of them wanted to go back to Jessica's house after what had happened. "I don't want to think of what might have happened if I hadn't shown up when I did."

"Thank God you did," Jessica commented.

"Thank God that psycho's off the streets," Shereen added emphatically.

"At least she'll get the help she needs."

"I hope they lock her up and throw away the key," Yolanda said from her corner in the living room.

Shereen's eyes wandered to Yolanda, but Yolanda didn't look at her. Sighing, she glanced outside through the lace curtains, not really seeing anything as she gazed into the darkness.

"Wine, everyone." Ellie skillfully carried a bottle of red wine and four glasses into the living room. She passed Yolanda and Jessica glasses, but when she extended one to Shereen, Shereen waved it off.

"None for me, thanks."

Ellie shrugged, then opened the bottle and filled the three glasses. "To Jessica." Ellie raised her glass. "To her getting her life back. And to us."

The three of them clinked glasses and drank, but it was a hollow victory with Shereen sitting in the corner, observing it all like an outsider.

Shereen must have realized that, too, for she suddenly stood. "I'm sorry, everyone. I have to go. It's late."

Ellie's shoulders drooped. "Shereen."

"I'll talk to you later." She barely faced them as she hurried to the door.

"I'm sorry," Jessica told Yolanda.

"It's not your fault."

"Go after her," Ellie said.

"I don't know."

"Yes," Jessica agreed, her voice filled with hope. "You know Shereen. She's a Capricorn, girl. Sensitive as hell."

Yolanda's eyes misted. Jessica never talked about all that astrological stuff. That was Shereen's passion.

"You think so?"

"Quick," Ellie said. "Before she drives away."

"You're right." Yolanda jumped up. "You're right."

Opening the door, Yolanda was taken aback to find Shereen standing on the front porch. Her back was to the door, her head hanging forward, and as Yolanda quietly closed the door behind her, Shereen didn't turn around. Pain shot through her heart. How had they let things get this bad between them?

"Shereen." Yolanda spoke her name very softly, but was certain Shereen heard her, even though she didn't respond. Yolanda took another step. "Is this what it's come to between us? You don't even want to look at me?"

Shereen turned then, faced her.

"I hate this," Yolanda continued, before Shereen could say anything. "You and me fighting like this."

Shereen chuckled mirthlessly. "You're blaming me again."

"No." Yolanda shook her head as she walked toward her. "You have every right to be angry with me. I know that."

"You're damn right I do."

"Oh, Shereen. How did we get to this point?"

Shereen's gaze fell to the ground. "I don't know."

"Shereen, I'm sorry. I really, truly am. I never meant to hurt you."

In response, Shereen blew out a heavy breath.

"All right, maybe part of me did. It was stupid, childish. I don't know. You always seemed to have everything—men, money, beauty."

"We were supposed to be tight. I loved you like the sister I never had."

"And I had to grow up to realize that. Look, a lot of things have happened in my life recently, stuff that has totally pulled the rug out from under me."

"You're talking about Terrence?"

"No, stuff with my family. Let's just say it's made me look at things differently. Realize that I've always been quick to judge, slow to forgive."

Silence fell between them. Then Shereen asked, "Was it all a lie? Our friendship?"

"No. Shereen, how can you even ask that?" Shereen shrugged in reply, then Yolanda said, "No, you're right to ask. But I never stopped thinking of you as one of my best friends. This was a test. A big test, but if we can get past this, we can get past anything."

Not if Yolanda didn't tell her the truth. Of her own free will. "And what about Terrence?"

"I have to tell you something, Shereen. And I only hope you can find it in your heart to forgive me." She released a shaky breath. "You asked me once if I knew why Terrence broke up with you. I told you no."

Shereen's heart rate doubled.

"That wasn't true. I knew. God, I'm sorry. I don't know how it happened, only that it did. We were at some frat party, and you were dancing with Brad. I was having a lousy night. I could barely get any guy's attention, and there you were with two guys who wanted you. I was drinking, or I probably never would have said anything, but when Terrence came to talk to me, I did something that I regret. I pointed out how close you and Brad seemed to be getting. I made some offhanded remark, something about how could he trust you when so many guys were always after you. Something like that. But I swear, I *swear*, I never thought he'd break up with you."

At last Yolanda had come clean. Shereen wanted to smile. Instead, her eyes misted.

"What?" Yolanda asked when she saw that Shereen was staring at her with a peculiar expression.

"That's what you said?"

"Yeah. And I'm sorry."

"And he thought that meant I was having an affair with Brad?"

"Like I said, I never thought he'd take me seriously. But I guess because he knew we were friends, he thought I was trying to warn him."

"What an idiot."

Yolanda gaped at her. "Pardon me?"

"Terrence." She shook her head ruefully. "What an idiot."

Yolanda had expected Shereen to be angry with her—not with Terrence. That she wasn't made her heart jump with hope. "Shereen, I was so jealous of you, I didn't know if I was coming or going. But it wasn't really you. I know that now. It was me I wasn't satisfied with."

Yolanda couldn't have been more surprised when Shereen threw her arms around her and squeezed the life out of her. "You're not mad?"

"Girl, that was nine years ago. All I wanted was for you to tell me. I needed to hear the truth from you. To know that you were sorry."

"I am."

"I believe you. And I forgive you."

Yolanda tried to fight it, but she couldn't stop her eyes from filling with tears. It had been that easy, while at the same time being that hard. "I want us to be close again. I know I have a weird way of showing it, but I love you, girl. I've always loved you— even if you are too perfect for your own good."

"I'll forgive you for that because you're an Aries, and I know Aries have a hard time expressing what they really feel." But Shereen was smiling, her whole body was smiling, now that a burden had been lifted.

"I hope you and Terrence work things out," Yolanda said. "And that I *do* mean, from the bottom of my heart."

"Forget Terrence. I want to talk about you and me."

"I'm serious. I was infatuated with him, with his job more likely, but that's over. And if he makes you happy, I want to see you happy."

Shereen's voice broke. "Knowing that you've still got my back, that you're still one of my best friends in the world, *that* will make me happy."

"I've got your back, girl." Yolanda wrapped her in the warmest of hugs, a healing hug that said nothing could come between them, not anymore. The past was over, buried, and they had tomorrow to look forward to. "I always will."

Despite the chill in the fall air, Shereen felt warmth around them, like a force erasing all the anger and the pain. For the first time since she'd met Yolanda, Shereen finally felt that they were truly at peace. They'd put all the ugliness behind them and now could get on with the business of being friends.

There was a knock on the door, and Yolanda and Shereen turned. Ellie peered her head outside. "You two worked your shit out?"

Yolanda looked at Shereen, and Shereen looked back at her.

"Yeah," they both said in unison.

"It's about time!" Ellie scurried onto the porch and took them both by the hand. "Then get your butts back in here so we can finally toast Jessica's good news right."

Yolanda and Shereen exchanged smiles as Ellie pulled them inside.

They had a whole lot more to toast than Jessica's good news.

Ellie was right. It was about time.

EPILOGUE

"YES, MY PLACE," ELLIE SAID when Yolanda complained that her apartment was too small. "We never meet at my place, and this time we're gonna. Pack an overnight bag and bring your pledge shirt."

"*Tonight?*"

"Yeah, you got a problem with that?"

"I could have used more notice."

"Like you have some hot date. Get your ass over here."

"I don't know what kind of crazy shit you have planned," Yolanda said.

"You'll find out."

When she hung up, Ellie called Shereen. She gave her the same spiel she gave Yolanda, telling her to pack an overnight bag and bring the T-shirt she'd worn when she'd crossed over to Theta Phi Kappa sisterhood.

"A sleepover?" Shereen asked. "Tonight?"

"Yeah. Like we used to do back in the day."

"If this is a Saturday night and you want to spend it with your girls, times must be tough."

"Just be here, okay?"

Shereen chuckled. "Okay. I'll be there."

Next, Ellie tackled Jessica. "Now, I know how much of a homebody you are, but we're all getting together at my place for a sleepover, and you're coming."

"I am?"

"*Yes.*"

"Tonight? Why such short notice?"

"You got something better to do?"

"Well . . ."

"Well, forget it. You're gonna be here, even if I have to collect your ass myself."

"All right."

"And don't bring a salad. Junk food only allowed."

Jessica giggled. "A couple of hours?"

"Mmm-hmm."

"I'll be there."

Shereen lay on a comforter on the floor between the coffee table and sofa, staring at the ceiling, a hand placed under her head because she didn't have a pillow. Yolanda sat cross-legged near her feet. Jessica lay stretched out on her side on the sofa, while Ellie sat on a beanbag chair, her back resting against the wall.

"What do you want to talk about next?" Shereen asked.

They'd spent the last two hours catching up on all they'd missed in each other's lives. Ellie's discovery of her father's infidelity and her once and for all breakup with Richard; Jessica's decision not to go back to work, despite the fact that the threat was over; Yolanda's startling discovery about her mother's secret love, her realization that her father wasn't the bad guy, and her attempt to repair their relationship; Shereen's pleasure over the fact that Shaun had held down a job for two months straight and was getting help to deal with his drinking problem.

"Men," Ellie said in response to Shereen's question.

"Oh, Ellie." Shereen sat up. "Don't you ever have anything else to talk about?"

"What else is there?" Ellie objected.

"She's right," Jessica said from the sofa. When everyone threw surprised glances her way, she added, "Douglas has totally forgiven me. He said our marriage had always been so perfect that something *had* to come along and test it sooner or later, but that we got past the dark hours. I think he's right. Maybe we *did* need this, to see how well we could handle adversity."

"Judging by that hundred-watt smile, I'd say you handled it very well." Shereen patted Jessica's leg. "I knew you would."

Jessica said, "Only brighter days to look forward to, as they say."

"Well, *I* met someone." Ellie reached for the wine bottle and dumped the remaining dregs into her glass. "Anyone want more wine?"

"No way are you gonna leave us hanging," Yolanda told her. "You met someone new?"

A contented sigh fell from Ellie's lips. "Yeah."

"Well, don't go off into la-la land now," Shereen told her. "Tell us the details. Where'd you meet him? At a club?"

"No." Ellie stuck her tongue out at her. "I met him at a gas station."

"God, let me guess," Jessica began, "he offered to pump you . . . I mean, your gas."

Everyone chuckled.

"Ha ha. Very funny. Not! I filled my own car with gas, thank you very much. But just as I was replacing the pump, I heard someone tell me that my tire was low."

"There had to be some type of *pumping* in this story." Yolanda clapped her hands together as she laughed.

"Anyway." Ellie eyed them all through narrow eyes, but she was smiling, too. "I looked to see who was talking to me, and it was like *whoa*! I swear, when I saw him, it was like . . . time actually stopped. The world stood still. I know, corny clichés, but it's true. I have never, ever had such a strong and instant reaction to any man in my life."

"Wow." Jessica sat up. "This sounds serious."

"I think it is. But you want to know what's truly weird?" That got everyone's attention, and she waited a full few seconds before dropping her bomb. "He's white."

"Get out," Shereen said.

"I'm serious. White, blondish brown hair. Tall—you know that's a must—and *damn* fine."

Yolanda's eyebrows shot up. "You, who always said you had to have a dark-skinned man, are attracted to a white man?"

"I know." Ellie's voice was almost a whisper. "This is so weird for me, because I never thought I'd go for a white guy, but this isn't about color. I swear it was love at first sight."

"He could be purple for all I care, as long as he's single," Yolanda told the group.

"Amen to that," Jessica said. "Just tell me his name isn't Richard."

"Uh-uh, girl. If I never meet another Richard as long as I live, it will be too soon. His name is Allan."

Ellie's eyes got all dreamy, and Jessica couldn't help smiling. It was nice to see her friend happy. Which made her think of what Yolanda had recently told her. "Speaking of men, don't you have something you want to share with us, Yolanda?"

"Oh." She paused, folded then unfolded her hands. "James and I are *talking.*"

"No shit!" Ellie exclaimed.

"Like I said, we're *talking*. Taking things slowly."

"Code for 'I'm still madly in love with him,' " Jessica added, smirking at her friend.

"Ain't that the truth?" Ellie said. "You may have kicked his ass to the curb, but we all knew you were still in love with him."

Yolanda shrugged, but didn't deny Ellie's statement.

"I hope things work out for you both," Shereen said. Yolanda wore a happy expression, making it obvious to everyone that she still loved him. She'd never stopped.

Yolanda said quietly, "Thanks, Shereen."

"You're welcome. And since we *are* discussing men, I may as well let you know . . . Terrence and I are talking, too."

"Talking, ha!" Ellie rolled her eyes playfully. "For a woman who's been in a sexual drought so long, don't even try to play like you haven't quenched your thirst."

"Ellie!" Shereen protested. Ellie shot her a look that challenged her to deny it. And when she saw that even Yolanda was giving her the 'Yeah, right' expression, she said, "All right, we're seeing each other, but I don't know where it will lead."

"I hope you two finally settle down," Yolanda said. By the look on her face, she meant it. It was almost amazing how drastically their relationship had improved since their heart-to-heart a month ago. "I don't know of anyone who's taken a longer route back to each other than the two of you."

Shereen shrugged while Ellie said, "Now, you know that's true."

"I'm ready for more wine," Shereen announced.

"Deny it all you want . . ." Ellie practically sang as Shereen hopped up and made her way to the kitchen. Her red pledge T-shirt boasted the number fourteen on the back, indicating her place in the line from shortest to tallest—she was the fourteenth tallest. As she returned with another bottle of wine, her sorority name, SWEET THANG, written in gold, was evident on the front of her shirt.

"None for me, thanks," Jessica said.

"Still?" Shereen asked her. "You haven't had any since we got here."

"I'll have some." Yolanda held up her glass.

Shereen was filling Ellie's glass when Jessica suddenly spoke.

"Oh, I can't keep this from you any longer."

There were collective whats? and all gazes shot to her.

Jessica chuckled at their concerned looks. They'd probably never stop worrying about her. "It's nothing serious. Well, it *is* serious, but in a good way. Though I'm having quite the dilemma."

"Anyone else lost?" Yolanda asked.

Jessica looked up at Shereen, who was standing, at Yolanda, who still sat cross-legged, then at Ellie, who was standing across the coffee table from Shereen.

"Well?" Shereen prompted.

Jessica put on a mock frown. "I can't figure out which one of you will be the godmother."

One tension-filled second of silence passed, then two, as Jessica's news fully registered. Then delighted squeals erupted all through the room.

"Oooh!" Shereen's voice bubbled with excitement. "You're pregnant!"

"Oh, my God."

"It's about time."

Then her three friends were on their feet, screaming and jumping around as if this living room were a college dorm. For tonight, it was.

Jessica stood as they all crowded around her. "I'm about three months along."

Yolanda gaped at her. "And you're just telling us now?"

"I wanted to make sure everything was okay."

Shereen threw her arms around Jessica, squeezing the hell out of her, then instantly backed off, as though she thought she might have hurt her. "Oh, sweetie, this is the *best* news!"

"The absolute best." Yolanda hugged her.

"I'm thrilled. Aunt Ellie." Ellie wrapped Jessica in a hug when Yolanda released her.

There were delighted screams again, and this time, Jessica joined them. She couldn't help it. Their excitement on her behalf was contagious.

"Maybe we're making too much noise," Jessica said when they settled down.

"Puh-lease," was Ellie's protest. Then her face softened, took on the look that so many women acquired when looking at a cooing little baby. "A baby. Oh, I'm gonna cry."

Shereen placed an arm around Ellie's shoulder and pulled her close. She felt like crying, too. This was fabulous news.

"Wait a second," Yolanda suddenly said. "You said something about not knowing which one of us will be its godmother?" Her hands went to her hips in a firm motherlike stance. "You know we're all gonna be godmothers, girl, ain't no ifs, ands, or buts about it."

"I was considering that," Jessica said, liking the idea.

"There's nothing to consider. It's a done deal."

"I guess I don't have a choice."

"You know it."

"Damn straight."

"There's only one choice."

They were all grouped together now, arms extended left and right over each other's shoulders, much like football players in a huddle.

"It better be a little girl," Ellie told her.

"Yeah." Shereen smiled. "A little Theta Phi Kappa."

"If it's a she," Jessica said slowly, "she's gonna be able to choose whatever sorority she wants."

"Hell, no." At Yolanda's proclamation, they all stared at her. "Look, I know other sororities are great, I'm not saying that. But if it weren't for the Theta Phi Kappa sorority, we never would have met. And even if we'd met on campus somewhere, if it weren't for our sorority, we never would have become such great friends."

"She's got a point," Ellie said.

"See, even Ellie agrees with me."

"And so do I," Shereen said. "If it's a girl, she's gotta be a Theta Phi Kappa."

"I'm gonna start buying red-and-gold dresses from now on," Ellie said.

Jessica giggled again. "You all are nuts. We don't even know if it'll be a girl."

"Of course it's a girl." They all spoke at once, not a hint of doubt in their voices.

And then Jessica knew it, too.

Yeah, a little girl. A little Theta Phi Kappa.

She liked the sound of that.